Adjusting to the near-darkness, her gaze wandered around the edges of the pool. Judith could hear the wind wailing through the trees. She hugged the raincoat closer and shivered in spite of herself.

Then she saw it. Huddled in the corner was another pile of clothes. It was like a flashback to the scene at the bottom of the staircase.

Oh God, she thought, *not another body*. Judith swayed slightly, then forced herself to approach. She got within two feet before she recognized the form of a young woman. Sucking in her breath, Judith reached out a trembling hand to feel for a pulse.

The young woman's arms flailed and her legs kicked. Then she let out a blood-curdling scream that was almost swallowed by the next gust of wind.

One of the flying feet caught Judith off-guard, and she tumbled backward. Losing her balance, she fell into the swimming pool, where the wet tangle of raincoat and night-gown weighed her down.

At least, Judith thought as her head struck the hard tiles at the pool's side, *this one's still alive. But am I?*

Bed-and-Breakfast Mysteries by
Mary Daheim
from Avon Books

MARY DAHEIM

CREEPS
SUZETTE

A BED-AND-BREAKFAST MYSTERY

AVON BOOKS
An Imprint of HarperCollinsPublishers

AVON BOOKS
An Imprint of HarperCollins*Publishers*
10 East 53rd Street
New York, New York 10022-5299

Copyright © 2000 by Mary Daheim
Excerpt from *Estate of Mind* copyright © 1999 by Tamar Myers
Excerpt from *Creeps Suzette* copyright © 2000 by Mary Daheim
Excerpt from *Death on the River Walk* copyright © 1999 by Carolyn Hart
Excerpt from *Liberty Falling* copyright © 1999 by Nevada Barr
Excerpt from *A Simple Shaker Murder* copyright © 2000 by Deborah Woodworth
Excerpt from *In the Still of the Night* copyright © 2000 by The Janice Young Brooks Trust
Excerpt from *Murder Shoots the Bull* copyright © 1999 by Anne George
Inside cover author photo by Tim Schlecht
Library of Congress Catalog Card Number: 99-94991
ISBN: 0-380-80079-9
www.avonbooks.com

First Avon Twilight printing: January 2000

Avon Trademark Reg. U.S. Pat. Off. and in Other Countries, Marca Registrada, Hecho en U.S.A.
HarperCollins® is a trademark of HarperCollins Publishers Inc.

Printed in the U.S.A.

10 9 8 7 6

CREEPS
SUZETTE

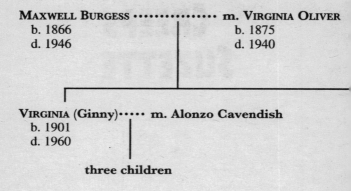

MAXWELL BURGESS •••••••••••••• **m. VIRGINIA OLIVER**
b. 1866   b. 1875
d. 1946   d. 1940

VIRGINIA (Ginny)••••• **m. Alonzo Cavendish**
b. 1901
d. 1960

three children

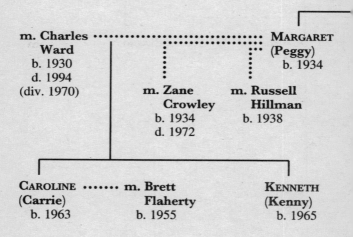

m. Charles ••••••••••••••••••••••••••• **MARGARET**
Ward   **(Peggy)**
b. 1930   b. 1934
d. 1994
(div. 1970)   **m. Zane**   **m. Russell**
                     Crowley   **Hillman**
                     b. 1934   b. 1938
                     d. 1972

CAROLINE ••••••• **m. Brett**   **KENNETH**
(Carrie)   **Flaherty**   **(Kenny)**
b. 1963   b. 1955   b. 1965

Burgess Family Tree

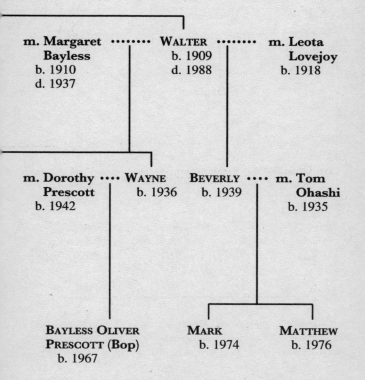

m. Margaret ········· **WALTER** ········· **m. Leota**
    Bayless   b. 1909   **Lovejoy**
    b. 1910   d. 1988   b. 1918
    d. 1937

m. Dorothy ···· **WAYNE**   **BEVERLY** ···· **m. Tom**
    Prescott   b. 1936   b. 1939   **Ohashi**
    b. 1942   b. 1935

BAYLESS OLIVER   **MARK**   **MATTHEW**
 PRESCOTT (Bop)   b. 1974   b. 1976
     b. 1967

ONE

JUDITH McMONIGLE FLYNN grabbed the fire extinguisher from the kitchen wall, aimed it at her mother's feet, and squeezed the lever hard. A thick cloud of white spray all but enveloped Judith and obscured the rest of the kitchen.

"Hey!" Gertrude yelled, dancing as much as her arthritic legs would permit. "Cut that out! I'm not on fire!"

"Then move," Judith yelled back. "You're standing right by the flames."

Gertrude coughed. "Nasty," she gasped. "I can't . . . breathe."

"Good," Judith said as the flames died out. "You're the one who set the dishtowel on fire. It serves you right. I think you did it on purpose." She opened a drawer, got out some rags, and began to mop up the foamy residue left by the extinguisher.

The white stuff must have looked like whipped cream to Sweetums, who appeared from behind Gertrude's walker and put out an experimental paw. Judith lunged for the cat, slipped on the wet floor, and fell flat on her face.

It wasn't turning out to be a good day.

To Judith's dismay, Gertrude was chortling. "I love a good belly flop," she said, stopping to catch her breath.

"You're not bad, kiddo. But you better get up. The cat's lapping up that funny-looking foam like it's dessert."

"He wouldn't!" Judith clambered to her knees and grabbed Sweetums. "That stuff's poison. I wonder if I can make him throw up, just in case."

Gertrude tipped her head to one side as she gazed at the squirming orange, yellow, and gray mass of fur. "He does that all by himself. Hairballs. Gruesome."

"I know that, Mother," Judith retorted, finally getting to her feet and carrying Sweetums to the sink. "Now if I can put my finger down his throat . . . Oww! He bit me!"

"Can't say as I blame him," Gertrude remarked, turning on her walker. "What's for lunch?"

"Mother . . ." Judith eyed the tooth marks on her index and middle fingers, then decided she might as well give it another try.

Sweetums, however, had other ideas. With a sharp twist of his head and a terrible growl, he wrenched himself from Judith's grasp and streaked for the back door.

"Damn!" Judith cried. "He's gone. Now he'll probably go off into the shrubbery where we can't find him and he'll die."

"I've thought about doing that myself," Gertrude said. "The trouble is, I can't get down on my knees. I'm too stiff. It doesn't seem right to hide yourself standing up. On the other hand . . ." She stopped, and her small, wrinkled face went blank. "Did you say pickled beets?"

"What?" Judith's gaze was still fixed on the cat's door where Sweetums had beat his hasty retreat.

"For lunch. Pickled beets. They sound mighty tasty."

"Pickled beets?" The response came not from Judith, but from her husband, Joe Flynn, who had just come down the back stairs and into the narrow hallway that led to the kitchen. "I hate pickled beets, Jude-girl. You know that."

Judith whirled on Joe. "Then I quit for the day. You get dinner."

"Dinner?" Gertrude echoed. "I thought it was lunch."

"I can't," Joe said, his green eyes looking startled. "I'm going golfing with Bill."

"Golfing?" Judith was aghast. "You don't like golf. Neither does Bill."

"I didn't say we were going to play golf," Joe said. "We just go over to the lake and wander around the pitch-and-putt course."

Fists on hips, Judith glared at Joe. "Does Renie know what you and Bill do in your so-called retirement?" she asked, referring to her cousin Serena and her husband, Bill Jones.

"Sure," Joe replied. "It's exercise. Sometimes we walk around the lake. It's over a mile."

"Then why do you call it golfing?" Judith demanded.

"Because we always meet at the pitch-and-putt course," Joe said reasonably. "Say, did you know your hand is bleeding?"

"Oh!" Judith had forgotten about the cat bite. "I'd better get some antiseptic," she said, racing for the back stairs and the third-floor family quarters.

"What about lunch?" Gertrude called after her. "What about pickled beets?"

Judith didn't respond.

After cleansing the tiny wounds and applying a couple of Band-Aids, Judith went in search of Sweetums. She got as far as the small patio when Joe called to her from the back porch.

"Where're you going, Jude-girl?" he asked, hands in pockets and a vaguely wistful expression on his round face.

"I'm looking for Sweetums," Judith replied. "He may have eaten some of that fire extinguisher foam."

"I hope he didn't eat all of it," Joe remarked. "I wanted to save some for your mother."

"Joe . . ." There was a tired note in Judith's voice. The Flynns had been married almost eight years. Joe and his mother-in-law had declared a cease-fire, but had never negotiated a truce. Which, Judith thought fleetingly as she glanced at her mother's small apartment just beyond the patio, was why Gertrude preferred living in the converted toolshed instead of under the same roof as her daughter's second husband.

"I'll help you look for Sweetums," Joe volunteered.

It was an offer that Judith didn't want to refuse, yet she was becoming increasingly annoyed at having her husband follow her around like a lost pup. It had been only two months since Joe had retired from the police force January first, and he hadn't seemed to be able to adjust. Judith loved her husband deeply, but he was getting on her nerves.

Joe searched the area along the east side of the old Edwardian-era house, including the mammoth laurel hedge that belonged to their neighbors, Carl and Arlene Rankers. Judith concentrated on the flower beds in the backyard, but had no luck. She moved to the west side of the house, peering under the azaleas, camellias, and rhododendrons. There were rose bushes, too, but they had been pruned in the fall and provided nowhere to hide.

At last, the Flynns met at the front of the house. The huge forsythia bush that threatened to take over the porch was in full bloom, a glorious, golden promise of spring. The deep red camellia was in bud, and some of the bulbs were a good three inches above ground.

But there was no sign of Sweetums.

"Do you think he might have gone off to the Rankers yard or over to the Dooleys?" Judith asked, rubbing her cold hands together. The early flora might show signs of spring, but the damp air was still redolent of winter.

"Should we look?" Joe asked without much enthusiasm.

Judith was hoping her husband would volunteer to go by himself.

"I'll call first," she said, heading back inside. "Why don't you start the appetizer tray for the B&B guests?"

"Isn't it kind of early?" Joe inquired, glancing at the old schoolhouse clock in the kitchen.

"It depends on what you fix," Judith said, and then let out a little yip.

Sweetums was in the hallway by the pantry, wrestling with a rather large bird.

"How about braised starling?" Joe asked, giving the cat a disgusted look.

"Damn." Judith marched over to Sweetums, who glared at her with little yellow eyes. "Surrender your prey," she ordered.

Sweetums tossed the dead bird around like a dishrag. "Joe," Judith pleaded, "can you take care of this? I have to get Mother's lunch." Judith's head swiveled in every direction. "Where *is* Mother?"

"Maybe," Joe said in equable tones, "the cat ate her first."

"Good grief." Judith started back outside.

"I'll come with you," Joe called after her, "but I won't go inside."

"Then don't bother," Judith snapped. "Get rid of that damned bird."

Looking glum, Gertrude was sitting at her cluttered card table in the toolshed's small living room. "Where's lunch?"

Relieved to find her mother in one piece, Judith managed a thin smile. "I'm going to fix it now. I'll be right back."

She met Joe at the porch steps. "I put the bird in the garbage," he said, exuding unnatural pride. "What can we do next?"

Judith ground her teeth. "Pay bills," she said. "Why don't you take over that job?"

Joe made a face. "I had to do that when I was married to Herself," he said, referring to the woman who had whisked him away from Judith some thirty years earlier. "I swore I'd never do it again."

"Well, don't break a sacred oath on my behalf," Judith retorted, stomping into the house. "I had to keep track of everything when I was married to Dan. The only thing he could count was the number of Twinkies in the economy-sized box."

"He sure couldn't count calories," Joe remarked.

Judith couldn't argue. Her first husband, Dan Mc-

Monigle, had weighed over four hundred pounds when he had eaten himself into a fatal fit at the age of forty-nine.

"Look, Joe," Judith said, regaining her usual patience, "if you don't want to handle the checkbook, I'd still appreciate it if you'd go through this month's bills. January was fine— we had plenty of business during the holidays. But this month is really tight, which is why I haven't paid everybody yet. Except for St. Valentine's Day, which luckily fell on a weekend, the B&B hasn't been full since after New Year's. Plus, you got a regular paycheck in January, but this month, it's your pension. I was thinking that maybe you could work out a budget for us, at least during the lean months, the leanest being February and March."

Joe, who was leaning against the refrigerator, frowned at Judith. "Are you saying we can't make it on my retirement?"

Mixing tuna salad, Judith tried to smile. "No. That's not true. Originally, you were going to wait until you were sixty-two to retire so you could collect Social Security. But that's a year and a half away."

"I decided I'd go out at sixty," he said, on the defensive, "because the benefits are good, and after thirty-five years on the force, I'd had it."

"I know," Judith said, spreading the tuna mixture on buttered white bread. "It was your call. But couldn't you go over our accounts and see what we can do to manage our money better?"

Joe's frown deepened. "I suppose. Hell, Jude-girl, before we got married, you used to get along here at Hillside Manor without any help from me."

Puzzlement crossed Judith's face. "I know. I can't imagine how I did it. Maybe I used mirrors." She piled potato chips next to the sandwich, added some apple slices, and started for the back door. "Here," she said, using her hip to nudge the counter where she kept her computer. "I have separate programs for us and for the B&B."

Joe grimaced. "I hate computers."

"You used them at work."

"Only when I had to."

"Try it. Please?" Her black eyes were pleading.

"Later, maybe," Joe said. "What are we doing after lunch?"

The February sun shone through the windows of Moonbeam's Coffee House, though a fire crackled in the grate. Judith, however, felt glum as she stirred her latte and listened to cousin Renie talk about how well Bill Jones had adjusted to retirement.

"He still sees a few of his nut-case patients and serves as a consultant to the university's family therapy department," Renie reminded Judith. "Granted, that doesn't take up much of his time, but I don't think I've ever seen Bill so busy. He actually gripes about it."

Judith gave Renie a mordant look. "Very funny. Do you know I had to sneak out of the house to meet you here? Joe traipses after me like a little kid."

"Not good," Renie said with a shake of her head. "Bill and I've been lucky. Our transition has been almost painless."

Judith knew how smoothly Bill Jones had eased into retirement a year and a half earlier, and couldn't help but resent it. He'd never taught summer quarter, so his wife was used to having him home. Bill was a morning person; Renie slept in. As her cousin had pointed out, Bill was still involved in consulting and private practice. Renie, meanwhile, had her graphic design business, which she ran out of the Jones basement.

"The truth is," Renie admitted, "we don't see all that much of each other during the day. Joe needs to find something to occupy his time. A hobby, volunteer work, whatever. He's at loose ends."

"I'm at wits' ends," Judith asserted, tugging at her short salt-and-pepper hair. "For Christmas, I bought him a big stamp album, a new fishing rod, some oil paints, and Shelby Foote's complete history of the Civil War. He's been indifferent to all of it, except the fishing rod, but he doesn't go winter steelheading, and everything else is closed until spring. Joe prefers watching me make tuna salad and wrestle with the cat."

"Don't you have chores for him?" Renie inquired, polishing off her mocha.

"Of course. He ignores them." Judith grimaced. "I started making a list two years ago."

"You need to get away," Renie declared, after a brief silence during which the cousins had waved and nodded to three of their fellow Our Lady, Star of the Sea parishioners. "Take a break. From the B&B. From Joe."

"Hunh." Judith rested her chin on her hand. "How do I do that? I can't go anywhere without him, and even if I could, we're quasi-broke."

Renie's brown eyes sparkled with mischief. "What about free room and board at a secluded palatial mansion with servants to attend to your every whim?"

Judith gave Renie a scornful look. "What about a teepee next to the Rankers' hedge with Sweetums sitting on my head?"

"I'm not kidding," Renie insisted. "Do you remember Beverly Burgess?"

Judith's high forehead wrinkled as she searched her memory bank. "The name's familiar, but I can't place her. Did we go to high school with her?"

Renie shook her head, which was currently adorned with a very unflattering pixie cut. "Bev went to that exclusive private high school, Forest Glen. I met her at the U. We had several classes together until we both branched off into our respective majors. Although she married—her name's Ohashi now—and moved away, we kept in touch with letters, and I've had lunch with her a few times when she's come home."

Judith nodded slowly. "Yes, I did meet her once or twice, but it was a long, long time ago. On the small side—like you—only blond."

"That's Bev." Renie stopped as the cousins greeted Mr. Holiday from the pharmacy across the street. "Bev's husband, Tom, is an archaeologist. Bev majored in anthropology, which is how they met. They're in Egypt right now on some major dig. Bev works as Tom's assistant, and they won't be able to come home until this summer. Whatever pots and pans they're digging up are a big find, and would cap off Tom's career."

"Sounds fascinating," Judith remarked. "But what has some hole in the desert got to do with my harried state of mind?"

"Bev called me last night," Renie said. "Actually, it was today in Egypt. Anyway, she's been getting letters from her mother saying that someone's trying to kill the old girl. She wanted to know if there was any way I could stay at the house for a few days to see if her mother's nuts or if she really is in danger."

Judith sat up very straight. "That's awful. Is it true?"

"I've no idea," Renie replied. "Neither does Bev, but it certainly worries her. She feels utterly helpless, being so far away."

Judith gave Renie a puzzled look. "Why you? What about relatives or other friends? What about a private detective?"

Renie wadded up her napkin and tossed it on the low table between the matching armchairs. "A private detective is out. Bev already suggested it, but this is an old, wealthy family that doesn't care for strangers in their midst. At least that's the way Leota Burgess feels about it. I met Bev's mother a couple of times, so I'm considered a friend. And it seems I'm the only chum from around here that Bev's kept up with. You know how it is—most people aren't letter writers."

"What about family?" Despite herself, Judith felt a twinge of interest.

"That's the problem," Renie said with a sly smile. "Bev's mother thinks that one of them may be the aspiring killer."

"Wow." The intrigue level rose in Judith's brain. "How old is Mrs. . . . Burgess, is it?"

"Right. Leota Burgess is almost eighty, but Bev says

she's still mentally sharp. Physically, she's got all the usual ailments of the elderly—arthritis, neuralgia, and so forth." Renie sat back in the armchair, watching her cousin closely.

"It's hard to believe that there's no one Bev—or Mrs. Burgess—can trust within the family circle," Judith said.

"It's a sticky situation," Renie replied. "For one thing, Bev never got along with her sister and brother. She was the child of a second marriage, and they resented her. Which brings up another reason why I feel I should help her out. When we were in college, there were times when Bev felt she should get away from her sorority house, but didn't want to go home. Her half-brother and half-sister tended to make her life miserable. So Bev would stay with us. She was at Grandma and Grandpa Grover's one year for Thanksgiving. That's probably one of the times you met her."

"Yes, I vaguely recall that," Judith said. "Wasn't that the year that Uncle Al put a frog in the gravy?"

"You mean the frog that was wearing suede pants?" Renie shook her head. "No, that was the time that Auntie Vance knocked out Uncle Corky with a drumstick. Bev thought it was all pretty funny."

"Her relatives must have been more restrained," Judith said.

"Most other people's are," Renie replied. "But the point is, I've always felt a special bond with Bev. To me, she was always The Little Rich Girl Who Had Everything Except What She Needed. She might have found our family a trifle eccentric, but she sensed there was a lot of love. I guess I feel sorry for her and want to help."

"Does Bev have kids?" Judith inquired.

"Two," Renie replied, glaring at a young couple who clearly wanted to take over the chairs that the cousins were occupying in front of the fireplace. "They're boys, Mark and Matt, who've just finished their degrees—Mark got an MBA and Matt completed his undergraduate work in marine biology. They're celebrating by taking a road trip across the United States and Canada," Renie explained. "They left this morning."

"That seems hardhearted," Judith remarked. "Couldn't they have stayed around for a while to make sure their grandmother was safe?"

Renie gave Judith an ironic look. "They did, for about a month, but they think Granny's batty. Of course young people think all old people are batty. We know better, don't we, coz?"

"But my mother *is* batty," Judith remarked.

"Mine isn't," Renie countered. "Yet."

"She will be." Judith paused, sorting through what she was already calling The Burgess Problem. "Of course Bev's mother isn't as old as our mothers."

"That's right." Renie continued to study Judith while the young couple indignantly took their beverages outside to sit in the brumal February sun. "Well?"

Judith grimaced. "I'd feel like a third wheel. I barely know Bev."

Renie poked Judith's arm. "I didn't really know that old high school chum of yours who owned the B&B up on Chavez Island. But I went with you to house-sit the place and damned near ended up being accused of murder."

There was no disputing Renie's statement. She'd gone beyond the call of duty. Inside her head, Judith felt as if a wrestling match was going on between Responsibility and Adventure. Or Good and Evil. Or maybe just between whether or not she could leave Joe and her mother and the B&B without serious repercussions.

"The Rankerses are back from their annual sun break," Judith said more to herself than to Renie. "Unless she's stuck with her grandchildren, Arlene probably wouldn't mind taking over at Hillside Manor. She's done it before, and seems to enjoy it."

"It's a huge house, out in Sunset Cliffs," Renie said in an undertone. "A gated community. Very exclusive."

"As long as Arlene and Carl are around, Mother never misses me that much," Judith murmured. "They spoil her."

"A full complement of servants—maid, cook, butler, housekeeper. You won't have to lift anything heavier than a Waterford glass filled with Glenmorangie Scotch."

"I wish Herself wasn't still in Florida." It never ceased to amaze Judith that Joe's first wife, Vivian, had been able to make friends with Gertrude Grover. "Of course, she's due back any day."

"The house was the first one built in Sunset Cliffs," Renie said, her eyes roaming around the interior of Moonbeam's. "In fact, old Maxwell Burgess, the timber baron, once owned the entire area, including where the golf course is now. He was Mrs. Burgess's father-in-law. Her husband, Walter, died about ten years ago, leaving her enormously wealthy."

Judith burst out laughing. "Coz, the way you describe all this, it sounds like a perfect setup for murder. Maybe Mrs. Burgess isn't crazy."

Renie avoided Judith's gaze. "I'm only stating facts. You can make of them what you will."

"So I can." Judith's laughter subsided.

"I can always go without you," Renie said, still not looking at her cousin. "After all, you and Bev have no ties."

"Joe would be very upset." Judith pursed her lips. "He'd feel abandoned. I'd be sending him the wrong message about his retirement."

"Architecturally, it's a Richardson-inspired house," Renie said, staring up at the ceiling. "Very Romanesque, built just at the end of the nineteenth century."

"On the other hand, my absence might force him to find something to do," Judith said.

"It's called Creepers," said Renie in her natural voice.

Judith gave a little start. "What? Creepers?"

Renie locked gazes with Judith. "The house. Where we'll be staying. In Sunset Cliffs."

"Creepers?" Judith made a face. "I don't know . . ."

"Today's Friday. I'll tell Mrs. Burgess to expect us Monday morning, around ten-thirty. Okay?"

Virtue, goodness, responsibility, and perhaps common sense fell to the canvas and couldn't get up.

"Okay," said Judith, then cocked her head at Renie. "Did you really say Creepers?"

Renie nodded.

"Oh," Judith replied, getting up from the armchair. "I wonder why."

"We'll soon find out," said Renie.

TWO

"I CAN'T GO," Judith said into the cordless phone an hour later. "Joe's feelings are hurt and Mother thinks she's coming down with a cold. Mike called, and he and Kristin and baby Mac might be stopping by next week for dinner. Mike has a couple of days off from the ranger station up at the pass."

"That's tough," Renie retorted. "I already called Bev to tell her we'd do it, and I woke her up because I didn't realize it was the middle of the night in Mugwump, Egypt, or wherever the hell they are."

"Can't you do it alone?" Judith asked, a pleading note in her voice. "I haven't seen my son and his family since before St. Valentine's Day." Little Mac was now almost eight months old, and crawling around with a frenzy. Judith felt that he changed every day, and never wanted more than a couple of weeks to go by without catching up on her first grandchild.

"Of course I could do it alone," Renie said in a testy manner, "but we work pretty well as a team, in case you haven't noticed. Plus, you're better than I am when it comes to dealing with batty old ladies. My mother isn't nearly as goofy as yours."

Judith sank onto a stool by the kitchen counter. "I'm really, really sorry. I just can't. Besides, what do you expect to find out? That Mrs. Burgess is nuts or that she's about to get herself killed? If it's the latter, will you sit by her bed at night with a gun in your hand?"

"I thought we'd play it by ear," Renie said, sounding snide. "Your instincts about these things are better than mine. Since when did you quit sleuthing?"

"Ooh . . ." Judith twitched on the stool. "I'm not a real sleuth. I just keep getting into situations that sometimes require—"

"Bull," Renie interrupted. "You are a one-woman murder magnet. I don't know how, I don't know why, but you seem to attract homicidal maniacs."

"I've told you before, part of it is because I run a business where I meet a lot of different people," Judith said. "Part of it is because Joe was a homicide detective before he retired. And the rest is . . . well, just coincidence. Besides," she added rapidly, "if I'm the Grim Reaper, I'd think that somebody like Mrs. Burgess wouldn't want me around."

"She doesn't have to know how grim you really are," Renie snapped. Then her voice suddenly softened. "Where's Joe?"

"Uhh . . ." Judith glanced at the hallway, then the dining room. "I'm not sure. He must be up in the family quarters."

The front doorbell rang, indicating that guests were arriving. The back door was reserved for family and friends.

"I've got to go," Judith began, carrying the phone with her as she turned around and crashed into Joe. "Yikes!" she cried, dropping the phone. "Where did you come from?"

"The dining room," Joe replied, looking alarmed. "Are you okay? I think somebody's at the door."

As the doorbell rang again, Judith scooped up the phone. "Coz? I'll call you back later." As she headed through the dining room to the entry hall, she called to Joe over her shoulder: "Stop hovering. You scared me half to death."

"I'll help greet the guests," Joe offered, trailing along behind her.

Judith ignored him. A middle-aged couple was standing

on the doorstep, luggage in hand. "Welcome to Hillside Manor," Judith said, forcing a bright smile. "Do come in. You must be the—"

The phone rang. Reining in her patience, Judith shoved the receiver at Joe. "You answer," she said under her breath.

As Judith asked the guests to register, Joe clicked the phone on. "It's for me," he said with a surprised expression. "It's Renie."

Judith gave her husband a curious glance, then led the visitors upstairs. They were named Drabeck, and had come from across the state for a family reunion that was to be held downtown at the Cascadia Hotel. Judith put on her best innkeeper's face as the Drabecks explained how they didn't want to pay the high room charges at the Cascadia, and had heard that Hillside Manor was highly recommended. After ushering them into Room Three, the largest of the second-floor bedrooms, she hurried back downstairs.

Joe had just hung up the phone. "I didn't realize Renie wasn't well," he said with a worried expression.

"What?" Judith thought she hadn't heard right.

"This palsy thing," he said, frowning. "When did that start? She doesn't seem to shake very much."

"Palsy?" Judith suddenly understood. Renie was playing upon a case of Bell's palsy she'd had years earlier after developing adult chicken pox. "Well. It's a recurring problem." That much was true, Judith thought, though Renie had never really gotten the disease again. "Stress aggravates it." That might not be true, but it sounded good. "She needs to get away. But of course she's not at all steady on her feet." Renie was never too steady, though probably "clumsy" would have been a more apt description. "I hated to turn her down, but as we discussed, you and Mother and the guests need me here."

"Poor Renie." Joe passed a hand over what was left of his graying red hair. "Bill's never mentioned her medical problems."

"You know how Bill is," Judith said, placing crackers

on a pewter tray. "He's very tight-lipped about some things. But I'm sure Renie will be okay as long as she goes into the hospital every day for her electric shock treatments. I'm not sure if she can drive, but maybe they'll have somebody at her friend's home who can give her a lift. Of course," she went on, "it's embarrassing. One side of her face gets absolutely frozen and her eye droops. She probably has to patch it, but she insisted before that it doesn't totally impair her vision, except for depth perception."

"My God!" Joe exclaimed. "I'd no idea."

"You were married to Vivian at the time," Judith said, taking a bowl of liver paté from the refrigerator. "How could you know? You and I were out of touch for over twenty years."

"Don't remind me." Joe came up behind Judith and put one arm around her shoulders and the other around her waist. "I've been kind of a pain lately, haven't I?"

Judith juggled the tray and the paté. "Well . . . I think it's taking a while for you to settle into retirement. You did go out a year early."

"I know," Joe said, nuzzling Judith's ear. "I'm like one of those college players who turns pro before their senior year. Maybe I needed more seasoning."

Judith leaned against Joe. "But not more spice."

"It's only four-thirty," Joe said, glancing at the school-house clock. "How about spicing up an otherwise humdrum afternoon?"

Judith started to protest, then managed to set the tray and the paté on the counter. "Why not? If you've got the spice, I've got the thyme."

While the four guests were drinking sherry and eating appetizers in the living room, Judith and Joe sat in the front parlor, sipping Scotch. A mellow feeling filled the room as Joe convinced Judith that she should go with Renie to help take care of her friend's mother.

"The old lady's sick, right?" said Joe as they warmed

themselves by the small stone fireplace. "How much can Renie help if she's sick, too?"

Judging from what Joe had said so far, Judith gathered that Renie hadn't mentioned Mrs. Burgess's fears for her life. "I still don't feel right about leaving you and Mother."

Joe grinned, and the magic gold flecks were back in his green eyes. "Are you afraid I'll whack her?"

Judith smiled back at her husband. "No, you've managed before when I've had to leave. Carl and Arlene are excellent buffers. If," she added on a dubious note, "they agree to help out with the B&B."

"I'll help out. And they'll pitch in." Joe was still grinning. "I called them while you were serving the guests."

"Oh." Judith bit her lip. "Of course I'll only be half an hour from Heraldsgate Hill. But I feel guilty, even if it's only for a couple of days."

Guilty, Judith thought, *because the premise is a big, fat lie.* It wasn't like Renie to tell such a tall tale. On the other hand, her cousin must really want Judith to come along. But for whose sake? Her own—or Renie's? In fact, they both should be more concerned for Leota Burgess. Even if she was imagining things, she was still a weak, and no doubt frightened, old lady.

Judith lifted her glass and gave Joe a warm smile. "To a most sympathetic husband." *And a gullible one, too.*

The gold flecks were still shining in Joe's eyes. "To a pleasant stay at Sunset Cliffs. You and Renie will probably have a wonderful time."

Judith's smile froze. "Yes. I'm sure we will."

The weekend turned out much busier than Judith expected. A tour bus from California had run into mechanical troubles, and some of the travelers had been put up at Hillside Manor Saturday night, filling all six rooms. On Sunday, a group headed for a big family reunion discovered there had been a mix-up in their reservations at two other local B&Bs. Ingrid Heffelman from the state association had called to see if Judith could take in at least five people.

She could, which not only filled the rooms for the second straight night, but made Judith's February profit and loss statement look less dismal.

Meanwhile, Judith and Renie had exchanged phone messages regarding their departure plans for Monday, March second. The last message came from Renie at ten o'clock Sunday night while Judith was next door, making final arrangements with Carl and Arlene. Renie asked if Judith could drive, and if so, not to bother calling back. Unlike the Flynns, the Joneses owned only one car. Bill would drop Renie off on his way to the chiropractor.

By ten the following morning, Judith was ushering some of her guests out through the entry hall. Four more remained upstairs, and since checkout time wasn't until eleven, she didn't feel right about hustling them along.

"I'll handle it," Joe said. "Finish packing, and forget about your duties here. As of now, you're on vacation."

Giving her husband a grateful smile, Judith hurried up to the third floor to add a few last-minute items to her suitcase. She was back in the kitchen ten minutes later, ready to go.

"I must say good-bye to Mother," she told Joe as she headed out the back door. "I suppose she'll be cranky."

The day was mild, with only a few clouds moving slowly across the blue sky. *False spring,* Judith thought as she passed the patio and the statue of St. Francis, then noticed that the pussy willows had burst into full bloom almost overnight. She wished she had time to pick a bouquet for the entry hall. Maybe Arlene would do it.

A piercing shriek emanated from the toolshed where the door stood ajar. Judith froze, then saw her mother struggling on the threshold with her walker.

"Help!" Gertrude yelled. "I'm being attacked! By pirates!"

"Mother!" Judith hurried to steady the old woman who was teetering dangerously on the walker. "What is it? Something on TV?"

Frenziedly, Gertrude shook her head. "It's real. It's here. It's hideous."

Judith peered over the top of her mother's head. Renie stood by Gertrude's card table. She was attired in a beige wool cape, matching slacks, and knee-high black boots. A patch covered her left eye.

Judith burst out laughing. "It's Serena, Mother, your niece. She's playing a little joke on you."

Warily, Gertrude turned around. "Serena?" She peered through her trifocals. "What are you doing in that get-up?"

"It's a long story," Renie replied. "First of all, you're not used to seeing me dressed up."

"Dressed up?" Gertrude had hauled the walker back inside. "You look like some Halloween freak. And what's wrong with your eye?"

"That's the long part of the story," Renie said, sounding a little impatient. "I just wanted to see you before we took off for a couple of days. I stopped at my mother's first. And yes, she, too, had a fit."

"Deb," Gertrude said scornfully. "My sister-in-law is always having a fit. What now, did her stupid phone break?"

Aunt Deb was as enamored of the telephone as Gertrude was hostile to it. And though they constantly wrangled and criticized each other, they were basically devoted.

"Mom's not used to seeing me dressed up, either," Renie went on. "And when I'm not wearing my ratty everyday outfits, she insists I paid too much for the good stuff. I can't win."

"You could win the booby prize in that rig," Gertrude rasped, then turned a puzzled face to Judith. "You're going away? Where? How come?"

"I told you, Mother," Judith said quietly. "We're going to help out an old friend. I'll be in Sunset Cliffs, just ten miles away."

"Sunset Cliffs," Gertrude muttered. "That's where all the swells live. You two won't fit in unless you've been hired as scullery maids."

Renie let out a big sigh. "On that vote of confidence,

we're off. Bye, Aunt Gertrude." She kissed the old woman's wrinkled cheek.

Judith embraced her mother. "I'll call," she promised.

"Don't," Gertrude snapped. "I won't answer."

They left the toolshed. Collecting her suitcase and handbag from the house, Judith bade Joe a fond farewell. Renie gave him a hug.

Joe regarded his wife's cousin with concern. "Are you sure you can do this? You look kind of frail."

"I'll be fine," Renie assured Joe. "Your wife will be my eyes, not to mention my chauffeur. Thanks for lending her to me."

Three minutes later, the cousins were pulling out of the driveway in Judith's Subaru. "You went to a lot of trouble to convince Joe you had Bell's palsy again," Judith remarked, turning the car around in the cul-de-sac.

"What?" Renie was lighting a cigarette.

"Coz," Judith said in disgust, "do you have to smoke in the car?"

"Definitely," Renie replied. "Mrs. Burgess probably doesn't allow smoking in her mansion. Thus, I'm going to inhale as much tar and nicotine as possible between here and there."

Judith sighed. "Okay, but open your window. It already smells terrible in here." She waited for Renie to comply, then continued speaking: "And Joe's right. You *do* look terrible. I don't mean the outfit—it's very sharp. But somehow you've managed to grow pale and drawn, and it's almost as if one side of your face *is* paralyzed."

"It is," Renie said as they reached the crest of Heraldsgate Hill. "Still, it's a light case this time."

Judith's head swiveled as they drove along the avenue, which was flanked by commercial enterprises, churches, apartments, and an occasional residential holdout. "What are you talking about? You don't have to convince me you're sick."

"I *am* sick, dopey," Renie asserted, purposely blowing smoke in Judith's direction. "I don't tell big whoppers even

in a good cause like you do. The palsy started in right after
I left you at Moonbeam's Friday afternoon. I was going to
tell you about it, but you hung up on me. I went to the
doctor Saturday, but they said it should go away in a few
days without additional treatment. I hope Mrs. Burgess
doesn't scare as easily as our mothers."

"Goodness." Judith felt upset as they began to descend
the other side of the hill and were once again in a residential
area. "You should have told me."

"I didn't get a chance," Renie said. "We kept playing
phone tag. We haven't really talked since Friday."

"Goodness," Judith repeated, and went silent until they
reached the turn-off from Heraldsgate Hill to the bridge that
led over the ship canal. "To think I wasn't really lying to
Joe. Except that you *did* tell him Mrs. Burgess was sick,
right?"

"She is," Renie responded, throwing her cigarette butt
out the window. "That is, she has all sorts of ailments, not
to mention being sick at heart because she thinks somebody
is trying to put out her lights."

"Good point," Judith agreed, as the six-lane thoroughfare
took them past the city zoo. "By the way, you better fill
me in on the family background and whatever else you
know about them."

Renie shrugged, then lighted another cigarette. "I don't
know that much, and some of it's just general stuff I've
picked up from reading about the history of the area. Did
you ever hear of Maxwell Burgess?"

Judith tried to ignore the cloud of cigarette smoke drifting her way. "He was some kind of timber baron way back,
wasn't he?"

"Right, before the turn of the century," Renie said. "The
Evergreen Timber Company. It's still around. Anyway, old
Maxwell has been dead for many years, as has his wife.
But in the 1880s, one of the timber parcels he bought was
what became Sunset Cliffs, overlooking the sound and the
mountains. Great setting, way beyond the city limits then,
and even though they've changed the boundaries at least

twice, it's still part of an unincorporated area just north of the dividing line."

"I know where it is," Judith said. "I've seen the entrance over the years."

"Right," said Renie. "Anyway, Maxwell clear-cut the whole parcel by the mid-1890s, then got the idea of building a house. As legend goes, he was overcome with a fit of remorse, and reforested the place. But later, when some kind of panic came along and Evergreen Timber was having financial troubles, he started selling off lots. Big ones, for big houses for people with big bank accounts. That's how Sunset Cliffs became an exclusive gated community some time around World War One."

"Have you ever been inside?" Judith asked, finding the patch on Renie's left eye disconcerting. "I haven't."

Renie shook her head. "While Bev and I were friends in college, I was never invited. I never figured out if I was too shabby to present to her family, or if she was embarrassed by her wealth. Mainly, we socialized on campus and just off-campus. The coffee house and foreign film era, as you may recall."

"I do. You and I once went to a Fellini film, and the projector broke down. We thought it was part of the movie, and couldn't figure out why everybody else was stomping their feet and jeering."

"Right. We thought it was one of Fellini's cinematic innovations," Renie recalled. "Where was I? Oh, the family. Maxwell had a daughter, Virginia, and a son, Walter. Walter's first wife died young, leaving him with two very small children, a boy and a girl. He married Leota a short time later, and, as I mentioned, they had Bev, their only child together. Her half-brother, Wayne, runs the timber company, and her half-sister, Peggy, has had a checkered marital career. I think the current husband is number three."

"Are these the suspects?" Judith asked with a frown.

"I suppose, at least in Mrs. Burgess's mind. Wayne and his wife—I think her name's Dorothy—live nearby in Sunset Cliffs. Peggy is now married to the pro at the golf

course where they have a house on the fifth green, or something like that."

"So they're all close at hand," Judith remarked, as traffic
began to get bogged down along the gaudy commercial
thoroughfare that led ever northward.

"Yes," Renie agreed. "Peggy has two kids, boy and girl,
and Wayne and his wife have a son called Bop."

"Bop?" Judith wrinkled her nose.

"That's right. It stands for something, but I don't know
what."

"So nobody lives in the big old mansion except Mrs.
Burgess?"

"Just the servants," Renie answered vaguely. "I don't
know much about the present setup. Bev wasn't entirely
clear about it."

If the Yellow Brick Road had led to Oz among exotic
forests and colorful poppy fields, the highway to Sunset
Cliffs was crowded with motels, used-car lots, and fast-food
restaurants. When the cousins finally made a left at the city
limits, the north side of the street boasted card rooms, taverns, pull tabs, and other minor vices that were legal in the
unincorporated neighborhoods. Five minutes later, they
were out of the low-life section and into a high-rent residential neighborhood.

Then they arrived at the arched entrance to Sunset Cliffs.
Shafts of sunlight filtered through the tall evergreens that
shaded the impeccably groomed golf course on their left.
Beyond the gatehouse and on their right, they could see
nothing but dense shrubbery and more trees. Judith and
Renie were five minutes from the hurly-burly of the highway, but in that short span, they had entered a different
world.

The cheerful uniformed young man in the gatehouse
asked their names and destination. He never missed a beat
when Renie turned to him head-on and displayed her eye
patch.

"Jones and Flynn to see Mrs. Walter Burgess at Creepers," Renie announced.

The guard checked his clipboard. "You're right on time. I've got you down for eleven o'clock."

"Where *is* Creepers?" Renie asked. "We've never been here before, and I don't have an exact address."

The cheerful smile remained in place. "There are no addresses in Sunset Cliffs," the young man replied. "Only house names." Carefully giving complicated directions, he lifted the barrier arm and waved them through. "You can't miss Creepers," he called after them. "It's the last house on Evergreen Drive."

Judith drove at the decorous posted speed of fifteen miles an hour. "You have to make an appointment to get in?" she asked Renie.

Renie nodded. "Security is very tight. Which, now that I think of it, would automatically limit the number of suspects on Mrs. Burgess's hit parade."

"To people who are known to the guards," Judith mused as they drove among tall stands of evergreens and thick bushes of salal, Oregon grape, and huckleberry. "To familiar faces." She grimaced as they came to the first fork in the road. "To family."

"To family," Renie agreed. "Let's hope we can avoid meeting the rest of them. Otherwise, we could end up on their hit list, too."

Judith glanced at Renie to see if she was joking. But the eye patch and the limited mobility on the left side of her cousin's face made it impossible to tell.

Judith suddenly felt an ominous tingle in her spine. Maybe she shouldn't have come. The rest that Judith had in mind wasn't of the eternal kind.

THREE

THE DEEPER THEY drove into Sunset Cliffs, the more curious Judith became. This was a far cry from the neighboring palatial estates with their manicured lawns, swimming pools, and tennis courts. There wasn't a house in sight. The cousins were surrounded by second-growth forest with tall, spare evergreens that almost blotted out the sky. Uphill and down they drove, winding on the serpentine road until they finally spotted a large if undistinguished house through a heavy stand of rhododendron bushes and lush ferns.

"I was beginning to think nobody lived here," Judith remarked.

"There's a white brick house over here on the right," Renie pointed out. "The sign says 'Wind Rest.' It's got a mailbox. How quaint."

They reached the second fork where the road dipped down, then abruptly rose again. Beyond the evergreens and a stand of madrona trees, they could see the sound below them and the mountains to the west. Then they were back in the deep woods where more houses began to appear at discreet distances.

"They all look empty," Renie said. "Maybe most of the owners winter somewhere else."

"I'd hate to drive these roads in snow and ice," Judith

said as they passed under a small arched bridge with globe lights and scrollwork carved into the sturdy concrete. "I wouldn't even want to drive here at night."

"Look," Renie said, pointing through the windshield. "It's the chapel the guard mentioned. Goodness, it's beautiful."

Judith agreed. The small, perfect church could have been set in an English village. The gray stone building was Perpendicular in style, with delicate tracery around the windows and a handsome bell tower. The chapel looked as if it had always been there, and intended to remain.

Along Evergreen Drive, however, almost every architectural form had been used. There were sprawling Italian villas, small Moorish palaces, English Tudor, French chateaux, Dutch Colonials, and variations on contemporary Americana. Some of the homes dated back to the early twenties; at least two`others were still under construction.

"Are we lost yet?" Renie asked as the road seemed to wind on forever.

"I don't think so," Judith replied, gesturing to her left. "That house is called Evergreen. I'll bet it's the one that belongs to Bev's half-brother, Wayne."

"Probably," Renie replied, craning her neck. "Damn, I can't see with this stupid patch. What does it look like?"

"All one floor, mansard roof, tall arched windows and doorway," Judith said, almost veering off the road. "Circa 1960, I'd guess."

"That's about right," Renie responded. "Wayne must be in his mid-sixties. He and—what did I say?—Dorothy probably got married about then."

The road seemed to narrow, and there were no more houses, even at a distance. A gentle hill rose before them and at the top, there were two large iron gateposts crowned with lions. The small, tasteful sign read "Creepers."

"We made it," Judith cried, reaching the crest of the hill and a circular driveway. "Oh, my God!"

"Hmm," murmured Renie. "That's the ugliest house I've ever seen."

"I thought you knew what it looked like," Judith said. "You described it."

"I know I did," Renie responded. "I was parroting Bev's description. 'Richardsonian, Romanesque.' Whatever the hell that means."

"It means ghastly," Judith retorted. "It looks like a home for mental patients."

Going well under the fifteen-mile-an-hour speed limit, the cousins continued up the drive. The house was huge, five stories of dark stone relieved only by an occasional decorative beige band. There was a tower on the near side with dormer windows and a tall chimney. Another tower, not so tall, but bigger all around, stood on the other side of the house. Most of the windows were almost floor-length and rather narrow. The large front porch with its arched openings and stout pillars presented a formidable aspect. Above it was a balcony, with more arches and pillars topped by a roof that jutted out from the front of the house. Up close, Judith and Renie could see that the basement windows were barred.

"Maybe it *is* a home for mental patients," Renie said. "I'd go nuts if I lived there."

"Had I but known . . ." Judith whispered. "Gosh, coz, I was sort of thinking stately homes of England. You know, like the mansion we stayed at in Wiltshire."

"Don't remind me," Renie snapped. "In case you've forgotten, the mistress of the house was murdered during our brief visit. I prefer not to have history repeat itself."

"Very late Victorian," Judith remarked, pulling up in front of the house, which seemed to loom over them. "Ugly period. There's not much like it anywhere else around here."

"A good thing," Renie replied, then pointed out the passenger window. "I think I know how it got its name. Much of the lower floors are covered by what looks like Virginia creeper."

"Covered like a tombstone," Judith said. "That's what it looks like—one big tombstone. With windows."

"They're probably buried inside, like a mausoleum. They've got windows so the rich can still look down their noses at everybody else after they've passed on," Renie remarked. "It figures."

As the cousins got out of the car, Judith noticed movement behind one of the lace curtains that covered the glass in the big double doors. "We've been spotted," she whispered. "Maybe we should have gone to the tradesmen's entrance."

Renie glanced over her right shoulder. "I'm wondering if Creepers will be even uglier when I have the use of both eyes. Doesn't this house remind you of Pittsburgh or Savannah or Buffalo?"

"We've never been to any of those places," Judith answered, opening the trunk and removing the two suitcases. "How would I know?"

"I've seen pictures," Renie said. "Huge old stone houses actually look okay in context. Impressive, as well as imposing. But this one is definitely not a Pacific Northwest style."

Judith handed Renie her suitcase just as a stooped, white-haired man in a butler's uniform opened the front door. "Mrs. Jones?" he inquired, squinting far beyond the cousins. "Mrs. Flynn?"

"Over here, Mr. Magoo," Renie muttered, trying to keep her good eye on the butler and the walkway. "Yes, we've arrived," she went on, raising her voice. "Where should we put the car?"

"I'll take it to the garage out back," the butler replied, moving forward and bumping into a thick pillar. "Later, if you will. Where is it now?"

"Holy Mother," Judith said in an undertone. "I don't want a blind man driving my Subaru."

"Maybe he's some kind of jokester," Renie said, stumbling over an old-fashioned hitching post that depicted a liveried black footman. "I mean, he must have seen us drive up. Oops!" Renie made another misstep, squashing a couple of promising primroses.

"Watch it," Judith said out of the side of her mouth. "You've already uprooted a hitching post and stomped on the flowers. Maybe it's a good thing Mr. Magoo can't see."

Guiding Renie by the elbow, Judith ascended the stone steps to the wide porch. Empty planters awaited their spring finery, and an ancient swing with a striped awning was covered with clear plastic.

"I'm Kenyon, at your service," the butler said, making a very stiff bow. "Welcome to Creepers. Mrs. Burgess is waiting for you in the library."

"Okay," Renie said as they entered the house, then whispered to Judith: "Do you suppose she looks like a gargoyle? As I recall, she used to be nice-looking."

"Shh," Judith urged. "Kenyon may be blind, but it doesn't mean he's deaf."

But Kenyon was either too deaf or too polite to react. He offered to take the luggage to the visitors' quarters as soon as he led the way into the library.

Judith was still goggling at the huge entry hall, complete with fireplace. The hearth was flanked by what looked like choir stalls, and a refectory table was cluttered with knick-knacks, empty vases, and what appeared to be antique music boxes.

The library was down a side hall and off to the left, behind another room where the double doors were tightly closed. Kenyon rapped softly on the heavy oak. A woman's voice called out rather loudly; the cousins guessed that Kenyon was indeed both deaf *and* polite.

With effort, he opened the heavy door. "Mrs. Jones and Mrs. Flynn," Kenyon said deferentially. "Or is it Mrs. Flynn and Mrs. Jones?"

"Never mind," said Mrs. Burgess, not unkindly. "You may go, Kenyon."

The door closed slowly behind the cousins, who were left alone with their hostess. Judith and Renie couldn't help but stare: Wearing a chic navy pantsuit, Leota Burgess was seated at an oval table. She had a trim figure, and her white hair was swept back in a smart, expensive cut. Her skin was remarkably unlined, her makeup discreet. The bone structure was delicate, the eyes a riveting blue. She looked closer to sixty than eighty, and retained a timeless beauty. It was only her hands, with the swollen joints and liver spots, that betrayed her.

"Poor Kenyon." Mrs. Burgess sighed. "He's getting very feeble. Do sit down, girls. You must be Serena Grover," she said, nodding at Renie. "You really haven't changed that much."

Flattered, Renie put a hand to her breast. "That's awfully kind of you to say. I'm Serena Jones now, and this is Judith Grover Flynn."

Mrs. Burgess gave Judith a royal nod. "Please sit. I'm delighted to have both of you here. I understand your need for a companion, Serena. What happened to your eye?"

"It's a long story," Renie replied, sinking into one of two leather wingback chairs. "I don't want to bore you."

"You won't," their hostess replied. "I'll send for tea, and we can get better acquainted."

To Judith's surprise, Mrs. Burgess turned to an old-fashioned speaking tube. "Tea for three, Edna. And some of Ada's delightful finger sandwiches."

As they waited for their tea, the cousins allowed themselves to be subjected to Mrs. Burgess's well-bred probing. "My, my," the older woman said to Judith after a small gray-haired maid had delivered a trolley to the library. "Your first husband must have been quite stout. Did he find exercise difficult?"

"Dan found moving difficult," Judith blurted. "He . . . ah . . . wasn't terribly ambitious."

"What a shame," Mrs. Burgess said, though the comment was merely polite. Gesturing at the three tall windows behind them, she turned to Renie. "I was going to have Edna open the drapes, but thought perhaps the light might strain your good eye. Shall I keep them closed?"

"Either way is fine," Renie said. "You have quite a book collection in here."

Mrs. Burgess glanced with indifference at the glassed-in

floor-to-ceiling bookcases. "Collectors' items, mostly. The kind of books no one ever actually reads, except perhaps my grandson Kenneth. My father-in-law, Maxwell Burgess, was very keen on rare first editions. Personally, I prefer romance novels. They always have a happy ending." The blue eyes suddenly lost focus. "Life isn't like that, is it?"

Judith, who had just finished a delicious salmon finger sandwich, smiled sadly. "No, it's not. I gather that lately you've had cause to be unhappy."

Leota Burgess sat up very straight, as if she were calling on some inner reserve of strength. "Yes. People—even people we know and love—have cancerous emotions buried inside that make them commit the unthinkable."

"Like attempted murder?" Judith asked softly.

Mrs. Burgess's face paled. "Yes. Like that."

"Do you want to tell us about it?" Renie asked, sounding genuinely sympathetic.

Leota Burgess hesitated as various emotions flitted across her face. "Not just yet," she finally said. "You'll want to get settled into your quarters. We'll lunch in my room, at one." She smiled as she gave the cousins a single nod. Apparently, they were dismissed.

Kenyon was outside, propped up against a large sepia-toned photograph that might have been Sunset Cliffs before it was clear-cut. The trunks on the evergreens were huge, indicating that some of the trees had been four or five hundred years old.

"This way," the butler said, leading Judith and Renie back down the side hall, into the entryway, and through an open arch that led to a massive central staircase. Judith could see the second floor through the mahogany railing. Wheezing a bit, Kenyon stopped halfway up. Then, with a unanimous deep breath, they reached the final step before Kenyon passed out.

Photographs and oil portraits lined the walls. One was identifiable, Leota Burgess some fifty years earlier in a Balenciaga ball gown. On their left, the butler pointed to a closed door.

"The mistress's suite," he said, and continued down the dimly lighted hallway. The room reserved for the visitors was two doors down. "I hope this will be satisfactory," Kenyon murmured as he slowly opened the door. "Please let me know of any inadequacy."

The first inadequacy that struck Judith was the lack of a bed. She turned to say something, but the butler had already slipped away. Renie, however, was opening another door.

"Wow," she breathed, bumping into a velvet-covered settee, "this isn't a room, it's another suite. Look, two beds, chairs, tables, gophers."

"Gophers?" Judith stared at the large, overly decorated bedroom. "Those are ceramic cats. Very Victorian."

"With only one eye, they look like gophers to me," Renie replied. "Which bed do you want, coz?"

"It doesn't matter," Judith said, gazing at the two brass single beds and dull ruby velvet coverings that matched the settee and the draperies. "They're both the same. I'll take the one by the window."

Further exploration revealed a large bathroom with old-fashioned hexagon tiles on the floor and a deep tub with a mahogany surround. Renie guessed that the toilet seat was also mahogany.

Unpacking their limited wardrobe and toilet articles, Judith hung most of the clothes in an antique armoire that featured a full-length mirror. "Who's Kenneth?" she inquired.

"A grandson," Renie responded, placing a couple of cashmere sweaters in the drawer of a massive bureau. "Isn't that what Mrs. Burgess said? If Bop is Wayne and Dorothy's kid, and Matt and Mark belong to Bev and her husband, then Kenneth must be Peggy's boy. I think there's a daughter, too."

"Do they all live around here?" Judith asked as she closed the empty suitcases and stored them inside the armoire.

Kicking off her shoes, Renie sat down on the bed nearer to the bathroom. "Mark and Matt are on their road trip, but

I gathered from Bev that when they weren't away at school, they sometimes stayed here. Of course they were raised abroad, in the vicinity of whichever dig their parents were working at the time. I'm not sure about Bop, though I think Bev mentioned that he'd opened a pizza place over on the highway."

Judith snapped her fingers. "I saw it, on the left, just before we turned off to head for Sunset Cliffs. Bop's Pizza Palace. He probably lives around here somewhere."

Renie shrugged. "Maybe he still lives with Wayne and Dorothy. As for Kenneth and his sister, I don't know much about them, including the girl's name." Renie paused, then went on. "I seem to recall that the last time I saw Bev, she and Tom had come home to attend their niece's wedding. That would have been about four years ago."

Returning to the sitting room, Judith studied the collection of silver dishes, cloisonné vases, and what looked like a mustache cup made of real gold. "I wonder why Mrs. Burgess is putting off talking to us? Could it be that she isn't used to confiding in people, especially virtual strangers?"

"That'd be my guess," Renie said, fingering one of the ceramic cats that she'd mistaken for a gopher. "I suppose the motive is money. What else could it be?"

Judith turned away from the antique objects and looked at Renie. "You sound as if you think her fears are well-founded."

Renie shrugged. "It's hard to say. Maybe she's lonely, maybe she's bored. Frankly, if I stayed holed up in this place for very long, I'd get some funny ideas, too."

"You're right, it's very oppressive," Judith agreed, then glanced at her watch. "It's not quite noon. Want to explore? I'll lead you by the hand."

"Sure," Renie replied, slipping back into her shoes. "Inside or outside?"

"Outside first, since it's such a nice day," Judith said, throwing her tan corduroy jacket over her wide shoulders. "Do you suppose they dress for dinner?"

"You mean, as opposed to eating in the nude?" Renie grinned at her cousin. "I hope not. I left all my formal wear in the glove compartment of our car."

In the entry hall, the cousins saw the maid who had brought their tea into the library. She was now rolling the trolley back toward what Judith assumed was the kitchen.

"Edna?" Judith called in a warm voice.

The little gray-haired maid gave a start, then turned around. "Yes? May I help you?"

Judith and Renie approached the servant. "I'm Mrs. Flynn," Judith said, introducing herself, "and this is Mrs. Jones. You must tell the cook that those sandwiches were delicious."

Edna's cheeks grew pink. She was at least seventy, and the black uniform and white apron hung on her as if she had lost weight or it had been handed down by a larger woman.

"I'll tell Ada," she said in a breathy voice. "Ada is our cook. Ada Dietz. She's a fine cook."

"She certainly is," Judith agreed, exuding amiability. "Tell me, how many servants are employed at Creepers?"

Briefly, Edna looked stumped by the question. Then, with clawlike fingers, she began to count. "There's Ada, the cook. Kenyon, the butler and chauffeur. Ms. Kenyon, the housekeeper. And myself. That makes . . . four." The maid looked rather pleased with herself.

"Have you all been in service here a long time?" Judith inquired.

"Oh, my yes," Edna replied with a quivery little smile. "Most of us have been with the family for over fifty years."

"Wow," Renie said. "That's quite a record for one household, isn't it?"

Edna nodded, the white lace cap slipping a bit. "Indeed. But the master and mistress have always been excellent employers. You couldn't ask for better."

"Amazing," Judith remarked. "You all must have joined the family while their children were young."

"Yes," Edna replied. "They were. Teenagers. Indeed,

Miss Beverly was only eight when I came here."

A heavyset woman dressed all in white appeared from around a corner at the end of the hall. "Edna," she began in a sharp voice, then stopped as she saw the cousins. "Excuse me. I was looking for that trolley. We'll need it to serve lunch."

"Mrs. Dietz?" Judith said, again wearing her friendliest smile. "I'm Mrs. Flynn and this is Mrs. Jones. We already know you're a wonderful cook."

Ada Dietz came forward, walking as if her feet hurt. "Ah. Our guests. Welcome to Creepers." The smile she gave Judith and Renie seemed forced.

Thinking she might be committing a breach of etiquette, Judith put out a hand anyway. "How do you do? We were just visiting with Edna about your length of service and devotion to the Burgess family."

Ada shook both the cousins' hands with a firm grip, but shot Edna a dark look. "You have, have you? Now, Edna, you're not telling tales out of school, are you?"

Edna shook her head; the lace cap slipped further back on her head. "Oh, no. I'd never do that."

"Of course you wouldn't," Ada said, and while she was smiling, her brown eyes were hard. "Now let's move along, Edna."

Huddled over the trolley, Edna started down the hall. "She's not used to guests," Ada said, following the maid's progress. "We live very quietly here at Creepers. Except for family, of course. Excuse me, ladies, I must get back to work."

Judith and Renie were left staring at each other. "What was that all about?" Judith remarked.

"Maybe," Renie ventured as they headed back down the hall, "nothing more than the servants protecting their masters. The rich, especially the kind who live in Sunset Cliffs, don't like gossip."

"Possibly," Judith responded, but she wasn't entirely convinced. "I'm curious about the servants in general. It's hard enough to get somebody to prune a tree these days, let alone keep regular hired help. What does Mrs. Burgess do, pay them each a six-figure salary?"

"Where's an application?" Renie grinned as they went outside. "I'm really good at running a dishwasher."

To Judith's dismay, the Subaru was no longer parked in the drive. "Oh, dear," she fretted, "do you suppose Kenyon drove it into a tree?"

"I hope not," Renie said. "Maybe they've got a gardener or somebody who can drive."

"But Edna told us that Kenyon was also the chauffeur," Judith said with a shudder. "Can you imagine him on the freeway?"

"Yes," Renie replied, "and it's a fearsome thought. I hate it when drivers signal with their white canes."

"Let's find the garage," Judith said, still worried. "It must be at the rear of the house."

Renie stumbled on the last porch step, and had to snatch at Judith's arm to steady herself. "It's the lack of depth perception that bothers me most."

Judith was about to say something sympathetic when a black Lincoln Town Car entered the circular drive. "Let's see if Kenyon's driving this one," Judith said, still hanging on to Renie.

"He can't be," Renie replied. "He hasn't run over us yet."

It wasn't Kenyon who emerged from behind the wheel, but a dapper old gentleman wearing a long black cape and a hat that looked as if it should belong to Zorro.

"I'll trade the eye patch for the hat," Renie murmured as the new arrival came toward them with a sprightly step.

"Mrs. Jones and Mrs. Flynn, I presume," the man said, putting out a hand. "I'm glad you're here. I'm Dr. Moss."

"Oh," Judith said, not entirely sure how Dr. Moss fit into the scheme of things. She was, however, impressed by his friendly manner and the fluffy white mutton chops that matched his fluffy white hair.

"I'm the family physician," Dr. Moss said as he shook hands. "I'm just dropping by to see Mrs. Burgess."

Assuming that since Dr. Moss knew of the cousins' arrival, he also knew why they'd been summoned, Judith posed a candid question: "Do you think Mrs. Burgess has any cause for alarm?"

Dr. Moss sighed and looked beyond the cousins to the tall tower with the even taller chimney. "Well, now. You certainly come to the point."

"That's why we're here," Renie put in. "Mrs. Burgess hasn't confided any details yet."

"Then I shall leave it up to her," Dr. Moss responded. "Leota Burgess is a very intelligent woman. And yes, she has all her faculties intact."

"Even smart people operating with a full deck can be paranoid," Renie noted.

The doctor shot Renie a sharp glance. "My patient is not a fanciful woman, Mrs. Jones. May I ask how your Bell's palsy is coming along?"

Surprised, Renie put a hand to the patch. "You can tell?"

The doctor gave Renie a kindly smile. "I've been in practice for many years, my dear. It's not a serious disease, but it is a nuisance."

Looking off toward the front entrance, Judith noticed that Kenyon was hovering behind the lace curtains. "How long have you been with the family, Doctor?"

"Since I started my practice. A very long time." The smile grew grim. "Too long." With a sigh, he excused himself and headed for the front porch.

"Jeez," Renie said as they turned the corner on the north side of the house, "is everybody around here older than dirt?"

"Our mothers are older than dirt," Judith responded, gazing up at the second, shorter and stouter tower. The whole house seemed to glower down on the cousins, and Judith suddenly felt as if they were being watched. To prove she wasn't being fanciful, a drapery moved at a first-floor window. "Creepers is giving me the creeps," she said.

"It's pretty weird," Renie agreed. "What did Dr. Moss mean by 'too long'?"

Judith shook her head. "Who knows? Maybe he wants

to retire and the family won't let him. Maybe he knows all the family secrets, and they don't rest easy on his aging shoulders." She paused in mid-step. "Good grief, there's a whole bunch of buildings this way. It looks like a small village."

From the southwest end of Creepers, Judith and Renie could see a four-car garage, somewhat newer than the house, or perhaps it had originally been a stable. Another one-story building sat further away, and to their right were some smaller outbuildings. Yet they all seemed isolated in the vast garden that stretched as far as the eye could see.

"This must be gorgeous in the spring and summer," Judith said, proceeding toward the garage. "Did you see the terrace at the rear of the house?"

Renie nodded. "It must have a view of the mountains and the sound. There are tennis courts just beyond that one-story building. I wonder if it's a pool house."

"One of the smaller places looks like a cottage," Judith said, surveying the first of the garage doors. "Damn," she breathed, "there aren't any levers. The doors must be automatic."

They were about to give up when a tall woman in a navy raincoat came out from the terrace. "May I help you?" she inquired in a polite if impersonal voice.

"Yes," Judith replied. "We're visiting Mrs. Burgess and our car has been moved. We wondered if it was in the garage."

"The Subaru?" The woman offered a thin smile. "Yes, I put it there myself. Do you wish to take it out?"

"No, no," Judith responded. "I was just . . . checking."

The woman, who appeared to be about the same age as the cousins and was handsome in a severe sort of way, chuckled grimly. "Perhaps you were afraid that Kenyon drove it."

"Well . . ." Judith shifted her weight from one foot to the other.

The woman waved a hand. "No need to explain. I'm Sarah Kenyon, the housekeeper. Excuse me, I must do the weekly grocery shopping. It takes at least two hours."

"Well." Judith gazed after the woman who had opened the third door by remote control. "Ms. Kenyon is certainly a lot younger than Mr. Kenyon."

"A May-December romance?" Judith murmured. "Why do I have trouble picturing Kenyon sweeping a young woman off her feet?"

"I have trouble picturing Kenyon sweeping," Renie said. "I don't think he's strong enough to hold a broom."

Strolling through the gardens, Judith and Renie passed a folly, a wishing well, three fishponds, and a rose arbor. At the edge of the gardens, almost in the forest, was a large greenhouse. They continued walking toward the western edge of the property, enjoying the gray waters of the sound and the clear view of the mountains. A freighter was moving north, heading out to the ocean. As they drew closer to the cliff's edge, they could see a half-dozen sailboats, taking advantage of the good weather.

The cliff itself, which ran as far as the eye could see in both directions, was about a hundred yards of almost sheer rocky earth. Ferns and other small plants clung to the dark soil. A two-foot wall made of the same stone as the house apparently delineated the property line. There was a single gated opening and, next to it, what looked like a tiny house.

Judith peered through the window. "It's some kind of tram," she said. "Look, you can see the track going all the way down to the beach."

"That must be the only way to get there," Renie remarked, lighting a cigarette. "I suppose some of the other cliff-side houses have them, too." She gazed downward and pointed to the base of the cliff. "See, there are the railroad tracks for the north- and east-bound trains out of the city."

Judith was jiggling the door to the tram. "It's locked, of course."

Renie moved away from the cliff's edge. "I'd say this would be a good place to shove Mrs. Burgess into the next world. It's very isolated. The whole setup is isolated. I'd rather be in prison."

"It's not unlike that," Judith said as they walked back through the gardens. "These people have locked themselves away from the rest of the world. Their money has, in a way, imprisoned them. I think it's sad."

"You would," Renie retorted, exhaling smoke and glancing around as if she were a teenager on the lookout for spying teachers. "You have such a soft heart. I think they're a bunch of snobs who can't deal with reality. If you haven't cleaned your toilet lately, how can you be part of the human race?"

"Still . . ." Judith began, then glanced at her watch. "Oops. It's almost one. We better not be late for lunch."

The cousins hurried to the house, wondering if they should go in the back way, through the terrace. Renie extinguished her cigarette in an empty planter as they proceeded to the rear entrance. Since Sarah Kenyon had come out that way, they thought the door might be unlocked.

It wasn't. After they pushed the bell twice, Ada Dietz appeared, looking harassed. "Come in, come in," she said impatiently. "You should have gone to the front. I just gave Edna the trolley to take upstairs. You'd better hurry. Mrs. Burgess doesn't like to be kept waiting."

They were standing in an entryway where they could see the kitchen off to their right. Ahead of them was a door and what looked like an elevator.

"Can we get up this way?" Judith inquired.

"No," Mrs. Dietz responded. "Go down the hall and to the main staircase. The back stairs and service elevator are strictly for staff use."

Judith and Renie obeyed, and three minutes later, Mrs. Burgess gave permission for them to enter her spacious suite. Their hostess was seated at a linen-draped table by the fireplace. The furnishings were probably oak, old and heavy, but would fetch eye-popping prices in an antique shop. Green and gold damask covered the walls and matched the draperies. The fireplace mantel was crowded with framed photographs, some very old, others quite recent.

"Do sit," Mrs. Burgess said with that air of regal command. "I thought you'd gotten lost."

"We were admiring your gardens," Judith said, appreciatively eyeing the dishes on the trolley.

"Try the crepes à la reine," Mrs. Burgess said. "Dietz has a way with pastry, and the filling is quite good. There's a choice of salad dressing, but I always prefer a vinaigrette."

"Did Mrs. Dietz make the rolls, too?" Renie asked, scooping food onto her plate.

Mrs. Burgess nodded. "They're soft. I don't care for a hard roll. They can injure the mouth."

Tasting the crepe, which was as delicious as Mrs. Burgess had claimed, Judith searched her brain for a way to get their hostess to confide in them about the alleged attempts on her life.

"You've certainly had your staff a long time," she finally said. "They must be very loyal."

Mrs. Burgess's blue eyes shrewdly regarded Judith. "They are. I hope." She patted her mouth with a linen napkin, then sat up very straight, again apparently drawing on her inner reserves. "This is quite difficult for me," she said through stiff lips. "I'm unaccustomed to confiding in people I don't know well. Indeed, I've never been one to discuss my private feelings." Leota Burgess paused again and cleared her throat. "What you really want to know is why I think someone is trying to kill me. Shall we start with the fire?"

FOUR

"THE FIRE WAS the first attempt," Mrs. Burgess said with what Judith interpreted as forced calm. "At the time, I thought it was nothing but carelessness. It was toward the end of October, the twenty-eighth, I believe. I had a bit of a cold and was staying in bed. My granddaughter, Caroline, had brought me a candle which she insisted would help. Aromatherapy, she called it. I nodded off, and apparently the candle fell from the night table into the wastebasket where there were several used tissues. I woke up to find the wastebasket on fire and the room filled with smoke. Fortunately, I was able to call Sarah—Ms. Kenyon—and she came at once. Meanwhile, I had thrown a glass of water into the wastebasket. Luckily, Edna had just refilled it for me before I drifted off to sleep."

"That doesn't sound terribly serious," Renie remarked.

Mrs. Burgess shot Renie a reproachful look. "It would have been if I hadn't awakened."

"How did Sarah get in?" Judith asked, hoping to stave off a sharp retort from her ever-prickly cousin.

"Until recently," Mrs. Burgess said a bit grimly, "I haven't locked my doors. That's different now. At night, I keep both sitting room and bedroom doors locked."

"That's wise," Judith said. "The main thing, though, is that you weren't hurt."

Mrs. Burgess nodded. "Yes, though I had quite a severe coughing spell. The damage, of course, was minimal. Naturally, we didn't put in an insurance claim, nor did we have to call the fire department. Imagine how disruptive it would have been to have all those firefighters stomping around the house." Mrs. Burgess shuddered at the thought.

"What came next?" Judith queried.

Their hostess leaned back in her chair and sighed. "A most disagreeable accident the Monday before Christmas. I was out on the front porch, waiting for Sarah to bring the car around. Kenyon, you see, doesn't drive anymore. I don't know what kept Sarah, but just as I started to go down the steps to see if she was coming from the garage, a large terra cotta planter crashed an inch or two behind me. Even though it missed, I was so frightened that I fell and sprained my ankle."

Judith envisioned the balcony that loomed over the front steps. Vaguely, she recalled the planters, which, like the ones on the porch itself, were currently empty of flowers.

"Did Sarah—Ms. Kenyon—arrive immediately after that?" Judith asked.

A troubled expression passed over Leota Burgess's face. "I believe I fainted, if only for a moment. When I came to, Sarah was there, out of breath and terribly alarmed. She and Kenyon helped me inside, and Dr. Moss was called. I must have been in a state of shock, because I'd forgotten about the planter. But he and Sarah had seen it, and they were very concerned. Yes," she continued, her jaw set, "it could have been an accident. There's no wall in that part of the balcony, and the planters directly above the steps could have been moved by the wind. You may recall we had quite a storm last December. The wind blows very hard around here because we're so close to the sound. Several trees were toppled, and two of the homes were damaged."

Judith recalled the storm. It had blown down two Japanese maples in the Dooleys' yard and sent Sweetums fleeing for safety in the downstairs bathroom where he'd scared the wits out of a maid of honor at a wedding reception Judith was hosting for a friend of Mike and Kristin's. In her panic to get out of the bathroom, the poor girl had accidentally dropped the bridal bouquet in the toilet.

"Then," Mrs. Burgess continued, carefully folding her napkin and placing it next to the Wedgwood luncheon plate, "in late January I had a severe case of gastritis. Mind you, I've always had a very strong digestive system. Dr. Moss had the cheek to inform me that at my age, I could develop such problems. But it recurred a week ago, and I hadn't eaten anything unusual. I chided Dr. Moss, and he merely laughed. Then when I reminded him of the other incidents—which he certainly knew of firsthand—he stopped chuckling. I told him someone was trying to kill me."

Renie was leaning forward in her chair. "What did he say?"

Mrs. Burgess made a fretful gesture. "Oh, he listened, but I think he thought I was just a fanciful old lady. Old! Why, the man's at least ten years my senior. I was very annoyed with him, and insisted that if it happened again, he must have my stomach pumped and analyze the contents." Again, Mrs. Burgess shuddered, no doubt at the imagined indignity. "When I said that, he took me more seriously."

"And nothing's happened since?" Renie inquired.

"No," Mrs. Burgess replied. "I'm making certain that no one except Dietz and Edna have access to my food. But it was after this last episode that I telephoned Beverly to relay my suspicions. I don't think she believed me at first, but after the fourth call, she finally allowed that perhaps I wasn't fantasizing. I suppose that was when she contacted you, Serena."

"Yes," Renie replied slowly. "I'm sure it was. In fact, she called me three times. Which is why I'm here." Renie gave Mrs. Burgess a reassuring smile.

"Who," Judith asked, "was here when you had the stomach problems? Family? Friends?"

"Friends?" Mrs. Burgess echoed with a sad shake of her head. "No, so few are left in my circle. Those who remain head for the sun or a cruise ship as soon as the temperature drops below fifty degrees. The younger ones also go away in the winter, usually to ski in Europe."

"And family?" Renie prodded.

"Family members are always in and out," Mrs. Burgess replied, toying with a diamond-studded watch on her left wrist. "As I recall, several of them had stopped by—my stepson, Wayne and his wife, Dorothy, who live just down the road. Their son, Bayless—they call him Bop because his full name is Bayless Oliver Prescott Burgess—stops by all the time, too, which is fine, except that he drives that ridiculous pizza truck. It looks so out of place at Creepers."

"Was anyone else here that day?" Judith inquired.

"Peggy and Russell," Mrs. Burgess answered. "Peggy—her real name is Margaret because she was named after her mother—is my stepdaughter. Her husband, Russell Hillman, manages the golf course. They have a house called The Willows on the links. Then there's Caroline, Peggy's daughter by her first marriage. I think I mentioned her. She lives some seventy miles north of here, in an artists' community, but she visits often. She was spending the night. I believe the child is lonely. She's separated from her husband, Brett, who moved to a beach town on the ocean about a hundred and fifty miles away. I haven't seen him since they broke up, which happened last spring."

"That's it?" Renie asked.

Mrs. Burgess lowered her eyes. "No. There's Kenneth. He's Caroline's brother, Peggy's son by her first husband, Charles. Kenneth has an apartment in town, but he's been living here off and on. He'd come to stay at Creepers through the holidays. I'm afraid he's a rather unsettled young man."

"What happened to Peggy's first husband, Charles?" Judith asked, finishing a second roll.

"Peggy divorced him years ago," Leota Burgess replied, tight-lipped. "Naturally, Walter and I disapproved of divorce in general, but Charles Ward really wasn't a suitable husband for Peggy. He was later killed in a car accident not far from here."

"Then Peggy married . . . Russell?" Judith was trying not to drown in a complicated sea of relationships. She made up her mind to put together a family tree when she and Renie went back to their suite.

"No." Mrs. Burgess was still looking taut around the mouth. "Her second husband, Zane Crowley, was a photojournalist who was killed while on assignment in Vietnam in 1972. Peggy remained single for many years. Then she met Russell Hillman, who had come to work at the golf course. They were married a year later."

Peggy and Russell, with Caroline and Kenneth; Wayne and Dorothy, Bop's parents; Bev and Tom, whose sons thought Granny was one base short of an infield. Or maybe just off-base. Judith tucked the names into a pocket of her brain and wondered if someone among them was a would-be killer.

"When did Matt and Mark arrive at Creepers?" she asked.

"The first of February," Mrs. Burgess said. "They were here when I had the second gastritis attack, and had the nerve to tease me, as if I were senile."

"They weren't here around the holidays?" Renie asked.

"No. I hadn't seen Beverly's boys for over a year. They've been raised primarily abroad, and have acquired some peculiar foreign ideas. But," Mrs. Burgess continued with that same tight-lipped expression, "what can you expect with a Japanese for a father?"

"Tom Ohashi's not Japanese," Renie retorted. "His grandparents were born here, in the city. His father was still teaching at the university when my husband joined the faculty. Tom's thoroughly American."

Leota Burgess gave Renie a pitying look. "By citizenship, yes. But he's still a Japanese. Now don't mistake me," she went on, wagging a finger. "I'm as broadminded as the next. Perhaps you recall, Serena, that when Beverly's sorority was divided about accepting that Italian girl, I spoke out on her behalf."

"I was never in a sorority," Renie shot back. "And I don't recall."

Swiftly, Judith intervened before Renie and their hostess could get into an argument. "All this background is informative, but what can we do to help you?"

Mrs. Burgess's face turned bleak. "I don't know. This was Beverly's idea. I suppose she felt I needed protection. Perhaps she was salving her conscience since she can't seem to leave that husband of hers and his silly ceramic fragments. She may have thought that fresh eyes and ears would be useful. If you engage the household and family members in conversation, you might get them to reveal something—suspicions, observations, unusual behavior on the part of someone. I know that trying to elicit information from people is very difficult. Do you think you could try?"

Judith's dark eyes sparkled. Her openness, her genuine interest in others, and her sympathetic manner never failed to pump the unsuspecting. "Oh, yes," she responded. "I—we—can certainly try."

Out in the hall, Renie almost fell over Edna, the maid. "Sorry," Renie said, propping the little woman up.

Edna was very pink. "Oh . . . please! It's my fault. I was in the way. I came to . . . collect the luncheon things. The mistress doesn't usually linger over her meals."

"We were chatting," Judith said with a smile. "She was giving us some of the family history."

The little maid shrank back, as if Judith had struck her. "Oh! Dear me." Her faded brown eyes darted from Judith to Renie and back again. "Did the mistress . . . Did she mention Suzette?"

"Suzette?" Judith turned to Renie, who gave a faint shake of her head. "No. Who's Suzette?"

Edna put both hands over her mouth and her eyes grew

wide. "No one," she finally said, removing her hands, which had begun to tremble. "I made that up. I do, sometimes. I make up stories. Ada says I'm daft." With surprising agility, Edna ducked around Judith and went into Mrs. Burgess's suite.

"Well?" Judith said.

"Not made up," Renie replied.

"Maybe not," Judith said, moving down the corridor. "Was Edna listening at the door?"

"Probably," Renie said. "She may not be deaf, like Kenyon."

Cocktails were at five, dinner at six, which seemed rather early to the cousins, given the one o'clock luncheon time. Judith and Renie spent half an hour putting together a Burgess family tree. Relying on her graphic design skills, Renie did the actual work, while Judith tried to figure out birth and death dates, along with marriages. When they had finished, they decided to walk down the road to Evergreen, the home of Wayne and Dorothy Burgess. Judith reasoned that if they were supposed to elicit information from the other family members, they might as well start now.

The tall, curved arches of the newer home echoed the earlier architecture of Creepers. But Evergreen was a much smaller residence, and its aspect seemed friendly by comparison. The sprawling one-story house could have been found on Heraldsgate Hill or in almost any other neighborhood around the city. There was no formal gate, only the sign that identified the property, a mailbox, and another sign that read "Service."

"Dare we?" Judith asked as they teetered at the edge of the paved driveway.

"Why not? We're Mrs. Burgess's guests, and we're supposed to talk to people. We can't do that through the mailbox."

Judith hesitated, then started up the drive. Three cars— a dark green Volvo, a brown Mercedes-Benz, and a red Toyota SUV—were parked outside the triple garage. "Are we on a fool's errand?" she asked.

"It wouldn't be the first time," Renie responded. "Look, you said on the walk over here that you were inclined to believe Mrs. Burgess. Have you changed your mind in the last fifty feet?"

"You're the one who seemed skeptical," Judith pointed out. "She's certainly not senile, but she might be fanciful. If she's right, then I'd hate to see it proved on our watch."

"We can't stay at Creepers forever," Renie said as Judith poked the doorbell. "Three—four days, that's all I can offer. It's lucky I've finished my annual report designs, but I have some new projects coming up."

"I thought you said only a couple of—" Judith was cut short by the appearance of a young Asian houseboy, dressed in a white jacket and dark pants. "Hello," Judith said cheerily. "We're here to call on Mrs. Burgess. Mrs. Wayne Burgess. Dorothy Burgess." She spoke slowly and carefully, lest the young man's English was inadequate.

"Mrs. B.?" the houseboy replied. "Cool. I'll let her know. How about some names?" He grinned in an engaging manner.

Startled, Judith grinned back. "We're Mrs. Flynn and Mrs. Jones, staying with her mother-in-law at Creepers."

"I wondered," the young man said. "I didn't see a car out here and that dude from the gatehouse hasn't called us. Hang loose, I'll be right back."

"He's not going to be here for fifty years," Renie murmured after the houseboy had left them standing in the slate-covered entrance hall. "I'll bet he goes to the community college up the road."

The cousins had just taken in a glimpse of the sunken living room with its tiger- and leopard-skin accessories, when a too-thin middle-aged woman with graying red hair appeared from a side door.

As Judith and Renie introduced themselves, Dorothy Burgess barely masked her suspicion. "Come into the solarium," she said in a tone that sounded as if she'd prefer inviting the cousins into a dungeon.

The solarium was off the formal dining room and faced

west. Enough trees had been cut to allow a narrow view of the sound and mountains. With an indifferent gesture, Dorothy indicated that her guests should sit in one of a half-dozen cushioned wrought-iron chairs.

"So you're Bev's spies," she said, brushing her long pageboy off her forehead. "What have you learned so far?"

Judith could see from the set of Renie's short chin that she was annoyed by the question. "Most of the family secrets," Renie responded. "Your mother-in-law is very garrulous."

"No, she's not," Dorothy retorted, picking up a gold cigarette case and matching lighter. "She's very reserved. You've come to Creepers for nothing."

"Then the attempts on Leota's life don't worry you?" Renie shot back.

Dorothy laughed, then took a deep drag on her cigarette. "No," she said, flicking at an overflowing ashtray. "Leota watches too much TV. Soap operas at noon, police and detective shows at night. She's living out one of those dramas, with herself as the heroine in jeopardy. I humor her—we all do. I'm sure she's enjoying this immensely."

Judith glanced at Renie. The one o'clock lunchtime and the early dinner hour were explained by Mrs. Burgess's TV schedule.

"Has Leota ever done this before?" Judith asked. "Fantasizing, I mean."

"Not that I noticed," Dorothy replied. "But good grief, the woman will be eighty this coming June. Isn't she entitled to be a bit gaga?"

She was, in Judith's opinion. Gertrude had been very sharp until the last few years, and she was older than Leota. "You have a point," Judith admitted. "I also suppose she gets bored."

"Of course," Dorothy said, frowning at Renie, who had also lighted up. "Who doesn't? Most of my friends are still alive, and I still get bored. How much fun do you think it is watching Derek water these damned plants?" She gestured at the masses of flora in the solarium, which included some beautiful orchids.

"Derek?" Judith said.

"The houseboy." A mischievous expression crossed Dorothy's face. "He's lazy, he's flippant, he's unreliable. I keep him on just to annoy my husband, Wayne. Besides, the kid needs the money to finish his associate arts degree at the community college."

Judith softened a bit toward Dorothy Burgess. "Your husband runs Evergreen Timber, doesn't he?"

Dorothy's face shut down. "Yes." She stubbed out her cigarette and immediately lighted another. Judith wondered why the plants didn't die from all the carbon monoxide.

The sudden silence prodded Renie. "I did a project for Evergreen Timber five, six years ago. They were trying to rev up their corporate image. Reforestation, animal preserves, all that sort of thing to make the company look like good guys instead of robber barons. Do you remember that campaign?"

"No." Dorothy shot Renie a withering glance.

Renie was neither withered nor blighted. "It's coming back to me now. Evergreen had gotten a bad rep for some big trade-off with the National Park Service. Old-growth timber that the environmentalists got up in arms about. It wasn't the first time, either. I don't think I met your husband then, I worked with his PR people. I haven't paid much attention since, but it seems to me that the tarnish still hasn't worn off."

"I don't meddle in my husband's business affairs," Dorothy said with a forbidding expression. "Look, have you two got anything interesting to say or is this it?"

"This," Renie said, standing up and extinguishing her cigarette, "is it. Thanks, Dorothy. To quote Groucho Marx, 'I've had a good time, but this wasn't one of them'." Renie stomped out of the solarium, bumping into a large pineapple plant en route.

"I guess we're going," Judith murmured. "By the way, who's Suzette?"

Dorothy's face fell. "Suzette?" she echoed stupidly. "Oh. Suzette. I don't know. That was before my time."

Their hostess didn't bother to see the cousins to the door.

Judith and Renie argued all the way back to Creepers. Judith didn't see why Renie had been rude to Dorothy Burgess. Renie didn't see why Judith gave a rat's ass about Dorothy. They were still arguing as they changed for cocktails and dinner.

"Dorothy is one of those bored corporate wives," Renie asserted. "You learned about that type when we were up at Mountain Goat Lodge with the phone company execs."

"Don't remind me," Judith shuddered. "They all kept dying on us."

"That's beside the point," Renie countered. "Dorothy's a parasite. And why do we have to be nice to everyone? I didn't agree to come here to make friends. What else did you want to find out?"

Judith, who had slipped into a dark green jersey dress, struggled with the zipper. "I don't know. She might even be right about Mrs. Burgess's fantasizing." Stepping in front of the mirror on the armoire, she made a face. "I look fat in this. Tell me I'm fat."

"You're not fat," Renie declared. "You're big-boned. Statuesque is the proper term, I believe."

"That's what I'd like to think, but I'm also fat. I put on six pounds over the holidays that I never lost." Judith frowned at her image. At five-nine, she could afford the extra weight, but she tended to believe the scales and not her own eyes. "I look like a blimp."

"No, you don't. You'll lose the weight. You always do. Let's go," Renie said. "I could use a drink."

The drawing room was long and narrow, jammed with heavy, dark furnishings. A grand piano stood at one end, covered with a black and red Spanish shawl and several framed photographs. Tiffany lamps, lamps with fringed shades, lamps supported by half-draped goddesses rested on the floor and atop a half-dozen tables. There were cameo glass vases, sterling silver pitchers and dishes, Russian enamel jars, mother-of-pearl loving cups, Lalique figurines, and mirrors framed by elaborate scrollwork. A pair of fierce fire dogs sat on the inlaid hearth, looking as if they'd bite anyone who had the temerity to come too close.

"We're being suffocated by several million dollars' worth of antiques," Renie complained. "I'd give my eye-teeth for just one of those lamps, but all shoved into one space, I want to run like a deer."

Kenyon shuffled into the room and took up his post behind a counter ornamented with a glass front and a pattern of entwined ivy. Renie leaned on her elbows and ordered a bourbon and water; Judith followed with a request for Scotch-rocks.

"So now what?" Renie asked as they wandered back to the fireplace. "When does the revelry begin? Or does Kenyon put on one of those fringed lampshades and that's it?"

It was. Except that Kenyon didn't go for the lampshade. After twenty minutes, the cousins requested a refill. Judith lingered at the bar.

"Does the name Suzette mean anything to you?" she asked the butler.

Kenyon blinked several times. "I know the name," he replied.

"Who is she?" Judith persevered.

"I believe you should ask the mistress that question," he said, fumbling with a couple of shot glasses. "I'm not at liberty to say."

The mistress arrived five minutes later. Without being asked, Kenyon presented Mrs. Burgess with a vodka martini.

"Well?" she said, bestowing a regal smile on the cousins. "Have you accomplished anything this afternoon?"

Renie reported that they'd called on Dorothy Burgess. "She doesn't seem like a very happy person."

"Dorothy claims she's frustrated," Mrs. Burgess replied. "She once had dreams of her own career. That wasn't possible, of course. By marrying Wayne, she had to dedicate herself to his career with Evergreen Timber. He worked his way up through the ranks. My husband didn't think his son should be handed everything on a silver platter."

"You've got about five of them right here," Renie remarked.

Mrs. Burgess frowned. "Is that supposed to be amusing, Serena?"

"No," Renie replied quite seriously. "But suddenly I feel sorry for Dorothy. What did she want to do?"

Carefully arranging the long skirt of her blue cocktail dress, Mrs. Burgess took a sip from her drink before answering. "When Wayne met her, she was studying to become a physical therapist. But when they became engaged, naturally we felt that she should quit school and be a proper wife. Wayne had already finished his education, and was working for my husband. Dorothy needed to learn how to entertain, to run a household, to be there for Wayne when he had problems at work. I won't say that Dorothy was happy about that, but she came from a good family background—her father was Joshua Cole Prescott, the judge— and she knew where her duty lay. We built their house as a wedding present. Then Bayless—Bop—came along a few years later and she had her hands full. Bop has always been sort of an unruly child."

"Bop's the pizza guy, right?" Renie asked.

"Yes." Mrs. Burgess grimaced. "So undignified, and I tried to discourage him. But he took the money my husband left him in trust and bought a property out on the highway. I don't believe he has much business sense, but what can you expect?"

A middle-aged woman in a tight black pantsuit breezed through the door. "Am I too late for a cocktail?" she asked, coming over to Mrs. Burgess and kissing the older woman on the cheek.

"Not at all, Peggy," Mrs. Burgess replied. "Kenyon will mix your favorite Scotch and soda at once."

Peggy gave the cousins the once-over. "You must be Bev's buddies," she said, reaching out a hand. "I'm Peggy Hillman. Which of you is Serena?"

"I am," Renie replied. "This is my cousin, Judith Flynn."

"Hi, Judith." Peggy shook hands with a firm grip. She had tastefully tinted blond hair and a ruddy heart-shaped face. While she carried some extra weight, her figure looked firm, even voluptuous. Judith felt even more blimp-like by comparison.

"What did you do to your eye, Serena?" Peggy asked. Her voice was husky, but not unpleasant. "Poke it with a sharp stick?"

Renie went through the explanation one more time.

"That's rough," Peggy said, almost sounding sympathetic. "Say, *Maman*," she continued, turning to Mrs. Burgess, "I'm staying to dinner. Russ has to give a lesson at the club tonight. I don't feel like eating alone. Again."

"That's fine, dear," Mrs. Burgess replied. "I'm sure that Dietz has prepared plenty of food."

The conversation was taken over by Peggy, who recounted her day, though not without amusement. A visit to the manicurist, a shopping spree at Nordquist's, lunch with friends at the clubhouse, a search of antique shops for a certain kind of decanter she wanted to give Russ for his upcoming birthday.

Dinner was served in the formal dining room, beginning with lobster bisque and followed by a savory pork loin, garlic mashed potatoes, herbed vegetables, and more of Ada's wonderful rolls. Dessert was a wonderful strawberry pie, served with coffee. At precisely five minutes to seven, Mrs. Burgess adjourned to her suite.

"So what do you think?" Peggy asked after her stepmother had gone upstairs. "Is she nuts or what?"

"What do you think?" Judith asked.

Peggy, who had brought a second Scotch and soda to the table, turned thoughtful. "She's not nuts. She may be a little paranoid. God, she's sitting on almost a billion bucks. Papa has been gone for nearly ten years. I suppose having all that money can weigh on you, make you think that someone wants it before you're ready to go on your own."

"But," Judith noted, "the family seems quite well-off."

"We are," Peggy admitted. "Papa made sure we'd be all right. He left all of us a tidy sum, including the grandkids. But of course," she added a trifle wistfully, "that was ten years ago."

"Is anyone hurting by now?" Judith asked.

Peggy finished her drink and set the blue Venetian cocktail glass aside. "I honestly don't know. Bev and Tom have never been interested in money. Wayne and Dorothy—" She stopped and gave the cousins a wry look. "You must be surprised that I'm blabbing all this. But even if we're not quite sure that *Maman* is really being threatened, we have to keep our options open. Who? Why? And money's a terrific motive."

Judith nodded. "What about Wayne and Dorothy?"

Peggy leaned back in her chair, her bust nearly bursting through the single-breasted jacket. "Wayne should be retiring this year. He's sixty-two. But he's afraid to leave Evergreen Timber the way things stand. The company has its financial problems, you see. My brother doesn't want it to go out of the family's control."

"But surely," Renie pointed out, "the family is the major stockholder."

"Yes," Peggy agreed. "It is. Or rather, *Maman* is. I don't think she's aware of how bad things are with Evergreen. Wayne wouldn't want to worry her. But the CEO's job would pass to someone outside of the family. Wayne's son, Bop, is unsuited for the role, and our Kenny—Kenneth, as *Maman* calls him—has no head for business, either. Wayne feels he should stay until he's sixty-five or even seventy. If he retains a hands-on approach, he may be able to pull Evergreen out of the Dumpster."

"That bad, huh?" Renie remarked. "Are you saying that Wayne wants to dip into your stepmother's capital to rescue the company?"

"Ask Wayne," Peggy responded. "I honestly don't know. One thing he has done is cut back his own salary along with some of the other top executives. I might add that's not been a popular move."

"Do either your son or daughter work?" Judith inquired as Kenyon entered the room to pour more coffee.

Peggy shook her head. "Not really. Caroline fancies herself a poet, and Kenny is active in animal rights." She paused to put a hand over her cup. "No more for me, Kenyon. I've got to get going." Peggy stood up. "It's nice to see some new faces around here. I'll probably drop by tomorrow." With a smile, she started from the room, telling Kenyon there was no need to see her out. "After sixty years, more or less, I know my way around. G'night all."

"Human," Renie remarked after both Peggy and the butler were out of earshot. "She's almost like a real person."

"Marrying a golf pro might do that to you," Judith said, sipping her coffee. "I gather Mrs. Burgess doesn't really approve of the match."

"I don't think she thought much of Peggy's first two husbands," Renie said.

"Being divorced and then widowed while raising two kids can't be easy even if you're rich," Judith said. "I had enough trouble raising one."

Renie nodded. "And you were not rich. Didn't Mrs. Burgess say that Peggy's first husband was killed in a car wreck? Even after all those years apart, that must have been rough. He was the father of her children."

"True," Judith agreed, then grew silent. "What now? Have we seen the last of our hostess for the evening?"

"Who knows?" Renie stood up. "Let's go into the library. I should call Bill. And Mom. By the time I'm through with her, it'll be bedtime."

The cousins proceeded to the library. Typically, Renie's conversation with her husband lasted less than two minutes. Like Gertrude, Bill abhorred the telephone.

"He's fine," Renie announced. "All three kids are gone for the evening, and Clarence likes his new bed jacket."

"Clarence," Judith said, narrowing her eyes at Renie, "is a rabbit. Rabbits don't wear bed jackets."

"No? We would have gotten him a smoking jacket, but Clarence doesn't smoke." Renie handed the receiver to Judith. "Here, call Joe. I have to fortify myself before I call Mom. I wonder if there's any brandy in here?"

As she dialed the number at Hillside Manor, Judith ignored Renie's rummaging around the bookcases and in the desk and various cupboards. Joe was unusually excited to hear his wife's voice.

"It seems like you've been gone for days," he said. "You're okay? It's a nice house? How's the food?"

After assuring Joe that all was well, Judith asked how things were going at the B&B.

"Smooth," Joe replied. "The guests are all squared away, and Carl and Arlene are out in the toolshed playing three-handed pinochle with your mother. When will you be home?"

Judith hemmed and hawed a bit. "Honestly," she concluded, "we're not sure. But it won't be long. Renie has to get started on some projects."

"Good, good. Look, Jude-girl, if you're lonesome I could drive out there tomorrow and we could have breakfast someplace close by. How about it?"

Judith winced. "I really don't think that's a good idea, Joe. Mrs. Burgess expects us to stick around. Besides," she went on, wincing some more, "I understand she often takes a bad turn in the mornings."

"Oh." The disappointment was palpable in Joe's voice. "Okay. Wednesday, maybe. Or you might be home by then. Call me first thing tomorrow morning."

After giving assurances of various kinds, including her undying love, Judith hung up just as Renie knocked several books off of a shelf.

"Oww!" she cried, doing a little dance. "This big brown one landed on my foot."

"Why," Judith demanded, "are you hauling books out of the bookcase? Do you think that's where the brandy is hidden, you idiot?"

Renie gave Judith a sheepish look. "No, of course not. But the glass door to this shelf wasn't quite closed and these blasted books weren't shoved all the way . . . Hey, look. There's a safe back here, behind the books."

Judith peered over Renie's shoulder. "You're right." She nudged Renie out of the way to take a closer look. "What's this?" she asked, pointing to something red and sticky on the door of the small safe.

"What? I can't see. I've only got one eye, remember?"

Judith hesitated before touching the crimson blob. "Dare I?" she asked Renie.

"Dare you what?" Renie's brown eyes widened. "Oh, no! You're not going to test your safecracking skills, are you?"

"No. I don't want to open the safe." She took a deep breath and slowly reached inside the shelf. "I'm not crazy about touching this red stuff because from here, it looks a lot like blood."

FIVE

"YOU CAN'T SEE so well yourself," Renie chided as Judith stood by the bookcase with a smear of strawberry pie on her index finger.

"Hunh," Judith muttered. "Whodunit?"

"Who cares?" Renie said. "Besides us, Mrs. Burgess and Peggy may have had strawberry pie for dessert. Ada Dietz made it. Maybe she or some of the other servants had a slice. What difference does it make? They all might have had some reason to get into the safe."

"Not the servants," Judith said, then added, "unless they were requested to do so."

"I don't see that it matters," Renie insisted. "Hand me the phone. I still have to call Mom."

While Renie talked to Aunt Deb, Judith studied the safe, wiped off the rest of the strawberry residue with a tissue, and put the books back in place. She could have read one of them in the time it took for Renie to finish the phone call:

"Yes, Mom, my eye is okay . . . No, I don't need to go back to the doctor . . . Yes, I remember when your former boss, Ewart Gladstone Whiffel, had Bell's palsy . . . No, I didn't remember that his depth perception was so bad he fell down an elevator shaft . . . Yes, it's a very big old house . . . No, I'm not in a draft . . . Yes, I'll leave a light on so I can find the bathroom . . . No, Mom, a flashlight isn't necessary. I was four years old when I had that accident because I couldn't find the toilet . . . Yes, Judith is fine, too . . . No, she didn't have to have Aunt Gertrude pried away from her with a crowbar . . . Yes, I know Aunt Gertrude can be unreasonable . . . No, I had no idea she put her dentures inside Alice O'Reilly's croissant at the last bridge club meeting . . . Yes, I'm sorry Alice passed out under the card table, but she does scare easily . . . No, I hadn't heard about your girdle stay popping out and stabbing you in the chin . . ."

Renie had made at least ten complete tours of the library before she finally got her mother off the line. Wordlessly, she handed the receiver to Judith and collapsed into one of the wingback chairs.

Gertrude answered on the seventh ring. "What do you want?" she rasped.

"Just checking to see if you're okay, Mother," Judith said.

"I'm okay. So what?"

"So I just wanted to wish you—"

"Ha!" Gertrude interrupted, though she wasn't speaking into the phone. "Trumped your trick, Mr. R. You're set by two. You thought I was out."

"—good night," Judith finished.

"What?"

"I said," Judith began, keeping a grip on her patience, "that I—"

"Hang on. Arlene just dealt a new hand. I'm in."

Judith waited.

"Two hundred," Gertrude said. "Two-twenty. Two-forty. Two-sixty. You surrender, Arlene? Let's see that kitty."

"Good-bye, Mother," Judith said wearily.

Gertrude's only response was, "Two aces in the kitty. Now I've got a hundred aces and a spread in clubs. Read 'em and weep."

"She's fine," Judith said, hanging up. "Shall we wander a bit?"

"You mean inside, I trust," Renie replied. "It's dark outside."

"Of course. Let's see how many other oppressive, over-decorated rooms we can find on this floor."

The cousins didn't get very far. They'd reached the entry hall when they saw a man coming from the direction of the main staircase. He was dressed in a dark suit and wore rimless glasses.

"Wayne?" Renie said out of the side of her mouth.

"Could be." Judith held her ground as the balding man with the slight paunch approached, looking out of sorts.

"Excuse me," he said, "I'm at a disadvantage. Are you . . . ?" A vague expression crossed his unremarkable features.

For what seemed like the hundredth time that day, Judith and Renie introduced themselves.

"Beverly's friends," Wayne Burgess murmured. "I hope she hasn't inconvenienced you. My half-sister sometimes gets a wild hare."

"Then your mother's fears don't trouble you?" Judith asked.

Wayne gazed up at the gesso ceiling. "No. You see," he continued in a very somber tone, "sooner or later, the mind begins to go. Loved ones don't want to see that happen, so they ignore it or pretend there's another cause. But I've been aware for the past two years that *Maman* has slipped." He offered the cousins a bland smile. "I'm afraid you're wasting your time here."

Neither Judith nor Renie felt they could argue with Wayne Burgess. "If that's the case," Judith said slowly, "then shouldn't someone be with her all the time? You know, to make sure she's not setting fires or drinking Drano?"

"I don't think we've reached that point," Wayne responded, smoothing what was left of his hair, which was such a rich brown that Judith suspected he dyed it. "Accidents do happen. And they always seem to come in bunches. Haven't you noticed that?"

Judith allowed that she had. Her own mother had practically set herself on fire the previous Friday. "Did you just see her now?" Judith inquired. "How was she?"

"She seemed . . . fine." The slight twitch at Wayne's mouth indicated otherwise. "She'll be down shortly, after her program is over. Oh," he added, turning around, "here she is now."

"Did you stop for another piece of pie?" Mrs. Burgess asked with a twinkle in her eye. "I thought you'd already left. You really should have stayed to see how the inspector solved the case. Most ingenious."

Wayne regarded his stepmother with amusement. "I'm sure it was very clever," he said, then clapped a hand to his head. "I left my raincoat in your room. I'd better get it. The wind's come up and it may rain by morning." He patted Mrs. Burgess's shoulder and went back to the main staircase.

"Wayne has a sweet tooth," Leota Burgess explained. "He shouldn't indulge it so much or he'll get fat. Come, let's go into the parlor. We'll have Kenyon bring afterdinner drinks. I prefer waiting for the food to digest before I have what actually constitutes a nightcap."

The parlor in the north tower was much smaller than the drawing room, but just as cluttered. Every chair, sofa, and settee was piled with silk and satin and velvet pillows. The potted plants, of which there were many, crowded the curved room. And there was yet more bric-a-brac, fashioned from gold, silver, crystal, and ivory.

Kenyon tottered in to take the drink orders. After he departed, Mrs. Burgess sat back on the dark blue settee and shook her head. "Wayne knows better than to interrupt me when I'm watching my programs. It's very distracting, and not the proper time to discuss serious matters. I almost missed the second killing."

The cousins commiserated until Kenyon returned with a snifter of brandy for his mistress and Drambuie for each of the guests. Breathing in the fumes from her glass, Judith finally brought up the question she'd been meaning to ask.

"A name keeps popping up," Judith said after taking a sweet, golden sip. "Suzette. Who is she?"

Mrs. Burgess's gnarled fingers tightened on the brandy snifter. She drew back against the settee, then visibly relaxed. "Suzette. Now there's a name from out of the past. I believe she was a servant here, long before I married Walter. Why on earth do you ask?"

Judith felt slightly embarrassed. "Her name came up a few times today, and everyone acted sort of strange. I was just curious."

"No need," Mrs. Burgess said calmly. "I certainly never knew Suzette. Do put her out of your mind and concentrate on the present."

The door flew open and a young man with red hair and a pizza box charged into the room. "Pizza delivery!" he cried. "Double cheese, Canadian bacon, pineapple, and mushrooms! Hot from the oven where we been shovin'!"

"Oh, Bayless," Mrs. Burgess said in an exasperated tone. "You know better than to do that. And you know I don't eat pizza."

"But *Grandmaman*," the young man called Bayless protested, "the staff can eat it." He glanced at Judith and Renie. "Or your guests. I miscounted the orders on the last delivery, and I can't take it back to the shop. It'll be all cold and gruesome."

"That's the second time in a week you've miscounted," Mrs. Burgess said testily. "Really, Bayless, you must pay more attention. How do you expect to turn a profit when you're so slipshod?"

The freckles on the young man's face merged with his blush. "I'm sorry," he said, hanging his head. "Don't get mad at me. I'm doing my best. Really."

Mrs. Burgess permitted herself an indulgent smile. "I know you are, but you—" She stopped, apparently realizing that family matters should not be discussed in front of guests. "Bayless, this is Mrs. Jones and Mrs. Flynn. They're friends of your Aunt Beverly's."

"Hi," Bayless said, coming back to life and giving the

cousins a lopsided grin. "Call me Bop. *Grandmaman* is the only one who can call me Bayless."

Taking in the red and white pizza delivery costume, Judith grinned back. "Your place is right out on the highway, isn't it? I saw it coming here this morning."

"Right," Bayless, now Bop, replied, his green eyes dancing. "It's a good location, but there's plenty of competition. Here," he said, holding out the box. "Try some. It's really good."

Judith and Renie each selected a piece. "It *is* good," Renie said, licking her lips. "Wonderful cheese. I like that. It doesn't taste processed."

"It isn't," Bop said proudly. "I use only real stuff. That Canadian bacon is first-rate. Can you tell the difference?"

"Yes," Judith said, "I can. It's thicker and richer. Thank you . . . Bop."

"Got to run," Bop said, blowing a kiss at his grandmother. "See you soon."

Mrs. Burgess shook her head after Bop left. "Such a sweet boy, really. But no business sense, no awareness of balancing books, no thought of economy. I'd always hoped that both he and Kenneth would go to work for the timber company, but neither of them has. It's very discouraging."

Briefly, the three women chatted about The Young and their frequent lack of focus. They were just finishing their drinks when Kenyon arrived, announcing, "Mr. Kenneth."

"Kenneth?" Mrs. Burgess's forehead creased. "Oh, dear. What does *he* want? And why doesn't he come in?"

Kenyon cleared his throat. "I believe he's having what he would call an anxiety attack. He seems quite upset, if I may say so."

Mrs. Burgess let out a heavy sigh. "Very well. Send him in. I suppose he wants to stay the night. Again."

Kenneth Ward staggered into the parlor, groping the walls for support. Kenyon was right—the young man was very agitated and his lanky body jiggled like Jell-O.

"It's horrible!" he cried. "I can't believe it!" Kenneth collapsed next to his grandmother on the sofa.

"For heavens' sakes, do calm down," Mrs. Burgess ordered, though not unkindly. "Please compose yourself. Meet your Aunt Beverly's friends, Mrs. Jones and Mrs. Flynn. And do look me in the eye."

Kenneth looked younger than what Judith had calculated, putting him at thirty or so. His long fair hair, pale blue eyes, and indistinct features added to his youthful appearance. Awkwardly, he nodded at the cousins, then turned back to his grandmother. "I can barely talk, it's so awful."

Apparently, Kenneth's ravaged face finally made an impression on Mrs. Burgess. "What is it?" she demanded, looking alarmed.

"I saw a fox," Kenneth blurted.

His grandmother seemed to relax. "Where?" she asked, then turned to the cousins. "We have quite a bit of wildlife around here, you know."

"Not in the woods," Kenneth responded with a jerky shake of his head. "On Mrs. Benson."

"Mrs. Benson?" Leota Burgess echoed. "From The Pines? Are you referring to her apparel?"

Kenneth nodded. "More than one fox, I swear. It was a very long coat. I drove by The Pines just now. I almost went off the road. Mrs. Benson was going somewhere with Mr. Benson."

"The opera, perhaps." Mrs. Burgess smoothed Kenneth's disheveled hair. "Now don't be upset. The foxes were already dead before Mrs. Benson put them on. Really, you can't get distressed every time you see someone wearing fur."

"But I do!" Kenneth wailed. "It's such a horrible thing, killing animals to show off. I want to create that sanctuary, to make them all safe."

"Now, now," Mrs. Burgess said. "We're not getting into that tonight."

Kenneth looked up into his grandmother's face. "You haven't done anything, have you?"

"Stop," Mrs. Burgess commanded as she put a finger to Kenneth's lips. "We're not going to talk about it now. Did you come here because you wanted to stay or are you going back to your apartment in town?"

Kenneth shook his head again. "I can't go back now. I'm too upset. Is it all right if I stay in my old tower room?"

"Of course," Mrs. Burgess said, patting Kenneth's arm. "You always do. Now take a nice warm bath and calm down. If you need me, you know where to find me. My next detective program comes on at ten."

"Thank you, *Grandmaman,*" Kenneth said, rising with some difficulty and then bending down to kiss his grandmother's hand. "You promise not to do anything?"

"Don't you fret," Mrs. Burgess said. "We've got plenty of time to make decisions."

"Gee," Renie said after Kenneth had left the parlor, "is it always this chaotic around here? I was thinking that Creepers must be a very quiet house."

"It can be," Mrs. Burgess allowed. "But in many ways, we live in and out of each other's pockets. As you may have noted, we're a close-knit family. I suppose you could say we Burgesses have a special bond."

Called money, Judith thought, and immediately chastised herself for being unkind.

Apparently Renie's mind was following the same track. "I can see how an interdependency might develop. I imagine the whole community here at Sunset Cliffs is very . . . close."

"Yes," Mrs. Burgess replied primly. "We keep ourselves to ourselves, as they say. After all, we share the same goals and interests."

Called money, Judith thought again, and this time spared herself chastisement. She could certainly understand how the residents of an exclusive gated neighborhood would tend to befriend and trust only one another. Assuming, of course, that they trusted anyone at all.

"Please excuse Kenneth," Mrs. Burgess was saying. "He's a very excitable young man, especially when it comes to animals."

"He'd like Clarence," Renie said. "We call him Mein Hare."

"What?" Mrs. Burgess looked puzzled. "Who is Clarence?"

Judith held up a hand. "Don't ask. Once Renie gets started on her bunny, you won't get out of here in time for your TV program."

Mrs. Burgess glanced at the diamond-studded watch. "You're right. It's nine-forty already. I must retire so that I can be in bed by ten to watch my show."

"You don't feel nervous about sleeping alone?" Judith asked, as she got to her feet.

Mrs. Burgess wore a sad little smile. "Oddly enough, I don't, now that I lock myself in. Only Sarah has the keys, and I trust her implicitly. Good night, my dears. Do sleep well."

A few minutes later, Judith and Renie wandered back toward the main staircase. Kenyon was at the door, peering outside.

"More visitors?" Judith inquired.

Kenyon closed the door. "Sarah thought she heard a car, but I don't see anyone. I might mention that we all retire when the mistress does. If there's anything you need, please let us know now." He sketched a little bow.

"We're fine," said Renie. "In fact, we're going to bed, too. Good night." The cousins ascended the wide, carpeted staircase.

"Bop and Kenneth," Judith said when they reached their suite. "What a pair of ill-matched cousins. We aren't like that, are we?"

Renie was pulling her red cashmere sweater over her head. "You mean poles apart in personality? Yes, I think we are, except that with us it's not readily apparent. Or so extreme."

"I wonder what Kenneth wanted to discuss with his grandmother?" Judith mused, slipping off her pumps and rubbing her tired feet.

"Fur," Renie said. "He's probably one of those people

who throws paint on mink coats and sable jackets. I don't wear fur, but I find that kind of protest not just loathsome, but criminal." Hanging up her black pleated skirt in the armoire, Renie announced that she was going to take a bath.

Judith nodded. "I'm going to watch the ten o'clock news."

"It's way too early for me to go to sleep," Renie called from the bathroom. "I brought a book, so I'll read for a while."

"Fine," said Judith. "I'll shower in the morning. That's what I do at home."

Judith found the remote control on the night table, next to a lamp with a beaded shade. The TV itself was enclosed in another, smaller armoire that looked as if it could have dated from the seventeenth century.

The news from the last part of the twentieth century was much more tawdry and inelegant. The President was having woman trouble, the Albanians were rioting, and the Serbs were hopping mad. However, the economy was strong, the sports news from spring training held the usual March promise, and the university's basketball team was going to the NCAA tournament. On the downside, the weather called for blustery winds and heavy rain.

Renie didn't come out of the bathroom until the anchorpersons were signing off. "I read in the tub," she said. "I often do, and that one is really comfortable."

Judith stared at her cousin. "You took off the patch."

Renie nodded. "I do, at night. I tend to keep my eyes closed when I sleep."

"Let's see." Judith propped herself up on one elbow. "The left eye looks . . . droopy."

"It is . . . dopey. That's the problem. But it's better," Renie said. "Maybe I'll try to read a little more. Will the light bother you?"

"No," Judith replied, settling down under the covers. "Joe often reads in bed. I know you're a night owl, but I think breakfast is served at eight-thirty. You'd better be fully conscious."

"I'm never fully conscious before ten, and you know it," Renie said. "Don't worry, I can fake it."

As Judith drifted off to sleep, she could hear the wind in the trees. Somehow, it was a cozy, comforting sound, as if Nature were playing a lullaby.

She was asleep when she felt Renie shake her. "Did you hear that?" Renie asked in an uneasy voice.

It took Judith a moment to figure out where she was—and why she was there. "What time is it?" She blinked, trying to adjust to the lamp that glowed on the night table.

"Not yet eleven-thirty," Renie answered impatiently. "I heard something that sounded like a scream or a moan. Twice, in the last minute or so."

Judith sat up. "You mean it's not the middle of the night? I must have just dropped off."

"You did," Renie said, giving Judith another shake. "Come on, grab a robe."

A minute later, the cousins were in the hall. It was completely dark, and they had to feel their way along the wall. After passing the first closed door, they saw a weak patch of light coming from Mrs. Burgess's room. Hurrying to the source, they found the door wide open.

"Mrs. Burgess?" Renie called.

There was no answer, except for the wind blowing in from the west. Slipping into the sitting room, Judith noticed that the light was coming from the boudoir.

Mrs. Burgess was nowhere in sight, but the bathroom door was closed. "Mrs. Burgess?" Renie called again as she tapped on the solid mahogany door.

This time, the cousins both heard something like a moan or a groan. It wasn't coming from the bathroom. They dashed out into the hall, but could see nothing in the darkness.

"There's got to be a light switch around here somewhere," Judith muttered as she felt the wall nearest to the central staircase. "Damn. I can't find it." She kept going, making circular motions with her hand.

They heard the sound again. "It's coming from downstairs," Judith breathed, then miraculously felt a switchplate beneath her fingers.

The lights came on. Judith and Renie rushed to the head of the central staircase. They looked down to the bottom, and saw a black heap on the floor. Judith jumped in surprise, then took Renie by the hand.

"Don't fall," she urged, hurrying down the stairs. "What on earth . . . ?"

The question hung on the air. At the bottom of the stairs they could see the black heap more closely. It moved, and another groan was heard.

"It's Dr. Moss," Judith cried. She started for the doctor, who was completely covered by the black cape and a big hat. Then, with a jolt, she saw the top of Mrs. Burgess's head. She was lying underneath the doctor.

"Help me," she gasped. "I think Dr. Moss is dead."

Before the cousins could do anything but suck in their breaths, Mrs. Burgess passed out.

SIX

"IS THIS ECSTASY or a nasty accident?" Renie whispered as the cousins tried to ease Dr. Moss's body off Mrs. Burgess. "Or, given their ages, both?"

"Hush," Judith hissed, getting a grip on Dr. Moss's shoulders. "One, two, three, heave-ho!"

The cousins moved the doctor just enough to free the unconscious woman. "We've got to call the police and the medics," Judith said, then heard the soft sound of sobbing from somewhere nearby. She turned swiftly and saw Kenneth, huddled next to a marble statue of Venus Rising from the Sea.

He pointed a shaking finger at his grandmother. "She's dead, isn't she?" Kenneth asked between sobs. "I feel terrible." He moved on unsteady legs from just inside the entry hall.

"She's not dead," Renie snapped, standing up. "Move it, I'm calling the cops." Brushing past Kenneth, she rushed toward the library.

"Not dead?" Kenneth asked in a toneless voice. "But . . ."

"Dr. Moss is dead," Judith said, feeling for a pulse and not finding one.

"Then we can't call him," Kenneth said.

"That's right." Judith gritted her teeth. "Get some brandy from the drawing room. Hurry up."

"I'll call Dr. Stevens from there," Kenneth said over his shoulder.

Judith didn't have any idea who Dr. Stevens was, but figured he must be someone known to the family. Mrs. Burgess, however, was starting to regain consciousness just as Renie returned.

"They're on the way," she said. "I gather it's the county sheriff's jurisdiction."

Mrs. Burgess was moaning again. "Ohh . . ." she gasped. "Ohh . . . What . . . ?"

Judith helped the older woman sit up. "Don't strain yourself," she said softly. "Here's Kenneth. He has some brandy."

"Kenneth?" Mrs. Burgess regarded her grandson with a strange expression. "Oh. That's right. You're here."

"Yes, *Grandmaman*," Kenneth replied, holding the brandy snifter to Mrs. Burgess's lips. "Drink this. It'll make you feel better."

"No!" Mrs. Burgess slapped at the snifter, sending it flying out of Kenneth's hand. It didn't break, but brandy spilled all over the Persian carpet.

"What's wrong, *Grandmaman*?" Kenneth asked in a pitiful voice. "I would never hurt you."

It was obvious that Leota Burgess was trying to compose herself. "No. Of course you wouldn't. But . . ." Her gaze strayed to the inert body of Dr. Moss. "Oh, my! I can't believe he's dead."

"I called Dr. Stevens," Kenneth said, still kneeling beside his grandmother. "He'll be here right away."

"Dr. Stevens," Mrs. Burgess murmured, her gnarled fingers kneading at the folds of her deep purple bathrobe. "Yes, of course. Oh, what will he think about Dr. Moss?"

"That he's dead?" Renie said under her breath to Judith, who was now trying to examine the dead man without touching anything.

"A heart attack?" Judith whispered. "It wouldn't be surprising. Dr. Moss must have been about ninety." Pointing to the medical bag at the doctor's side, she turned to Mrs. Burgess. "Did you call for him?"

Leota Burgess's eyes widened. "No. Why should I? I feel fine. Or did, until now. I believe I reinjured my ankle."

"What happened?" Judith asked. "You came downstairs and—what?"

Mrs. Burgess held her head. "I feel so queer. I'm not exactly sure . . . Let me think."

A silence fell over the little group. "Would you like us to help you into the drawing room?" Judith finally asked.

Mrs. Burgess looked again at Dr. Moss's body and shivered. "Yes. Please."

It was Kenneth who assisted his grandmother to a sofa in the drawing room just off the central staircase. She could barely walk, and her grandson staggered slightly under her weight. After making her as comfortable as possible, Kenneth returned to the entry hall to await the emergency personnel.

"Maybe I will have some brandy," Mrs. Burgess said with a heavy sigh. "You know where the liquor is. If you don't mind . . ."

Renie went over to the bar where Kenyon had served them before dinner. Judith tried to keep her expression blank as she sat down next to Mrs. Burgess. Apparently, the old lady had no qualms about drinking brandy that wasn't served by her grandson.

"Do you remember anything?" Judith asked.

"It's very vague," Mrs. Burgess replied. "I was about to go to sleep when my buzzer rang. Just outside the front door is a speaker so that I can be buzzed if someone should come to call and the servants don't hear. We put it in for Kenyon, really, because he's gotten so deaf."

Leota Burgess paused as Renie returned, juggling three brandy snifters. "Thank you, my dear," the old woman said, though her hand trembled as she accepted the drink. "Anyway, it was Dr. Moss. He has his own key—he's had it for years, in case of an emergency—and he let himself in. I got up and started downstairs, first turning on the lights with the switch near my door. I reached the top of the stairs and saw Dr. Moss. I was telling him that I'd come down when the lights went out."

"But you'd just turned them on," Judith put in.

Mrs. Burgess nodded. "So I had. But there's a second switch in the entry hall so that the lights can be turned on and off from both ends of the staircase. The next thing I knew, I fell. I must have been so startled that I tripped. I tumbled all the way downstairs and—"

She stopped, looking blankly at the cousins. "I'm very fuzzy about what happened next."

Though there had been no sound of sirens or flashes of red and blue lights, voices in the hall indicated that someone had arrived. Judith excused herself and went to investigate. Two sheriff's deputies were speaking to Kenneth, and the medics were hauling their equipment into the house.

"Dr. Moss is in there," Kenneth said in a nervous voice as he pointed to the staircase. "We think he had a heart attack. He was very old."

One of the deputies, a chunky man of forty whose name tag read "R. Sorensen," turned to Judith. "Are you a family member?"

Judith said she was a guest. "My cousin's here, too. She's with Mrs. Burgess in the drawing room. Should I call her in?"

Sorensen held up a hand. "Slow down, ma'am. We'd rather you and Mr . . ." He turned to Kenneth. "Ward, is it? Deputy Foster here and me would like you both to leave the staircase area."

Kenneth started to protest, but Judith knew from experience that when cops gave orders, they expected to be obeyed. Reluctantly, she headed for the drawing room, passing the medics on her way.

"Twenty—thirty minutes ago?" one of them said to the other. "He's still warm."

Mrs. Burgess's color had improved and her hands had

stopped shaking. "What's going on?" she demanded when Judith reentered the drawing room.

"Routine," Judith said in a soothing voice. "Do you want the medics to check you out?"

"No," Mrs. Burgess said firmly. "I'll wait for Dr. Stevens. He doesn't live far from here. Indeed, he and Dr. Moss share a large home about two blocks from the entrance to Sunset Cliffs."

"Dr. Stevens is Dr. Moss's partner?" Renie asked.

"Yes. Dr. Moss has had his offices in the house for some time," Mrs. Burgess explained. "When Mrs. Moss died a few years ago, he invited Dr. Stevens to move in with him. Theo Stevens was doing his residency at the time, and grateful for free room and board."

Renie set her brandy snifter down on a teak side table next to her big mohair chair. "So after his training was completed, he joined Dr. Moss's practice?"

"Yes." Mrs. Burgess's face tightened. "It made sense. Dr. Moss was in his eighties, and wasn't able to handle his patient load by himself."

"It sounds very convenient," Judith said. "Economical, too. I take it Dr. Stevens is single?"

"So far." Briefly, Mrs. Burgess looked away, then fixed Judith with a sharp gaze. "Where's Kenneth?"

Upon leaving the entry hall, Judith had assumed Kenneth would follow her back to the drawing room. "I . . . I don't know," she stammered. "The deputies sent both of us away. Shall I check on him?"

"Please," Mrs. Burgess said with that familiar regal air.

As she descended the central stairs, Judith saw Sorensen and Foster standing by Dr. Moss's body. "We've called in the detectives," Sorensen said in a grave voice. "This was no heart attack. We've got a homicide on our hands."

On the surface, Judith was shocked; deep down, she wasn't the least surprised. They had come to Creepers to prevent a murder. That they had failed was a terrible misfortune. Neither Judith nor Renie could have guessed that they were protecting the wrong potential victim. Still, she felt derelict in their duty, and full of remorse.

"How was he killed?" Judith asked in a hushed voice.

Sorensen shook his head. "Sorry, ma'am. We can't say anything until the coroner arrives. Maybe not even then. Would you please leave the crime scene?"

"I was looking for Kenneth Ward," Judith said. "Did you see where he went?"

The second deputy, Foster, gestured toward the entry hall. "I think he went that way."

"Thanks." Judith started to move, then stopped. The hat had been removed from the back of Dr. Moss's head. She saw the deep, bloody wound at the base of the skull and knew the cause of death: the proverbial blunt instrument.

An inch or so away from the body, Judith spotted some small clumps of dirt. She was about to say something when Sorensen took her by the elbow. "Please, ma'am, let's move along. This is now an official crime scene."

"I know," Judith said softly. *I know a crime scene when I see one*, she thought. *And I'm beginning to think I've seen one too many.*

Since Foster had pointed to the entry hall, Judith figured that Kenneth might have gone into the library. It seemed logical, and she was aware that it was time to delve into her reliable wellspring of logic.

Apparently, Renie had left the lights on in the library after calling 911. Kenneth, however, was not in sight. Just for good measure, Judith glanced at the bookcase that concealed the safe. Nothing seemed to have been disturbed; the glass-fronted door was firmly shut and the books appeared to be as the cousins had left them. The killer apparently hadn't broken into the safe.

She was turning to leave when she spotted a writing tablet on the desk. Almost certain that it hadn't been there while she and Renie had been making their phone calls, Judith glanced at the top page.

The handwriting was very irregular, large and loopy, as

if the writer had been out of control. With some effort, Judith finally made out the words:

"How did it go so wrong?"

Drumming her fingers on the desk, Judith waged war within herself. Was this someone's random scribbles—or some kind of evidence? Dare she tear off the top sheet and take it with her?

She dared not, but she committed the words to memory and left. Outside in the passageway, she paused at the door opposite to the library. She'd noticed it only vaguely on her earlier visits, and wondered where it led. Cautiously, she turned the decorated brass knob.

A winding flight of stairs met her eyes. This must be the way to the north tower, Judith thought, and closed the door. She didn't recall seeing a staircase leading out of the parlor in the tower. Perhaps Kenneth had used these steps to go up to his room to collect himself.

The detectives, a slim young Asian man and a middle-aged African-American woman on the plump side, were just arriving when Judith scurried through the entry hall. Not wanting to get herself in trouble, she kept going. Apparently, the medics had left. There was no sign of their equipment anywhere.

But there was another newcomer in the drawing room. A tall, dark-skinned man in his thirties was bending over Mrs. Burgess. "I'll give you a sedative," he said in a pleasant, soothing voice. "I'm sure nothing's broken, but we can X-ray that ankle tomorrow."

"Thank you, Dr. Stevens," Mrs. Burgess said. "You must be as upset as I am."

Dr. Stevens avoided Mrs. Burgess's gaze. Perhaps, Judith thought, he already knew that his partner had been murdered. "Yes," he replied. "It's a terrible shock."

Mrs. Burgess looked beyond the doctor to Judith. "Did you find Kenneth?"

Judith shook her head. "He must have gone back to his room."

Mrs. Burgess scowled. "That boy is useless in a crisis. I need him to help me get up to my room."

"We can manage," Dr. Stevens reassured his patient. "Perhaps if one of you ladies could give me a hand?"

"Sure," Renie said. "I'll help."

"No, you won't," Judith said. "You can't see. Stay here, I'll accompany Mrs. Burgess."

There was an odd glint in Renie's eyes as she watched Dr. Stevens get Mrs. Burgess on her feet. As he coaxed and steadied her, Renie sidled up to Judith.

"What's going on, coz? You look weird."

Judith half-covered her mouth with her hand. "Murder," she whispered. "Detectives on scene."

Renie stepped out of the way as Judith joined the doctor and his patient. "Why," Judith heard her cousin say as they half-carried Mrs. Burgess from the room, "would I ever expect natural causes?"

Now that she knew Dr. Moss had been killed, Judith could hardly wait to question her hostess. But Dr. Stevens was firm. Mrs. Burgess must have complete rest. After administering the sedative, he stood silently by the bed. Then, as the old woman's eyes began to droop, he guided Judith out of the suite.

"I know Aaron—Dr. Moss—was murdered," he said. "But there's no need for Leota Burgess to find out until she's had a good night's rest. And there's certainly no need to have the police question her. It's bad enough that all these emergency types have come to Creepers, but right now, she's in no condition to be grilled by them."

Judith nodded. "I understand. I also have the feeling that when she sees the detectives, she's going to have a small fit."

"Why is that?" Dr. Stevens asked with a frown.

"Because they're not lily-white," Judith replied.

Dr. Stevens's handsome face wore an expression of irony. "Neither," he said, "am I."

Embarrassed, Judith's hands flew to her cheeks. "I'm

sorry. I didn't mean . . . That is, I gather that Mrs. Burgess is rather . . . prejudiced."

The doctor nodded. "She's a product of her generation and social class. If you took a census of Sunset Cliffs, you wouldn't find a single non Anglo-Saxon. Unless you count the hired help, which no one does."

"Has it been difficult for you to treat patients in this community?" Judith asked as they paused in the sitting room.

"Yes," Dr. Stevens replied frankly. "I've been in practice almost three years, and some of the residents still refuse to let me see them. White blood tainted by black blood, no matter what the ratio, is inferior, and thus not qualified for the professions." He paused, his expression ironic. "That's one reason Dr. Moss couldn't retire."

"But Leota Burgess wasn't one of the holdouts," Judith remarked.

"No." Dr. Stevens's eyes shifted away from Judith. "Excuse me," he said, picking the phone up from a walnut demi-lune console, "I'm calling for a private duty nurse. Hopefully, Millicent Fritz is available. She's been to Creepers on other occasions."

Feeling dismissed, Judith went downstairs. The detectives had now been joined by the coroner, who had his bag of grisly tricks next to Dr. Moss's body.

"Ma'am," Sorensen called in a weary voice before Judith could reach the last two steps, "*please*. You can't keep coming through here."

"I have to," Judith protested. "It's the only way I know to get from one floor to the other."

The female detective looked up. "Are you the one who found the body?"

Judith nodded. "I'm Mrs. Flynn. My cousin Mrs. Jones and I did. That is, we found Dr. Moss's body lying on top of Mrs. Burgess."

The woman, who conveyed what Judith guessed was probably a deceptively affable demeanor, turned to her partner. "We'd better talk to them, Junior. You're almost through here, aren't you, sugar?" she asked the coroner.

"Just about," the coroner replied. "The ambulance is waiting outside."

"Good," the woman responded. "I'll get the deputies to bag as much evidence as they can find."

Judith stood off to one side, by the entrance to the drawing room. She glanced across the open area to the entry hall where she saw Sarah Kenyon and Ada Dietz looking bewildered.

"What's happening?" Sarah asked in a tense voice. "Is that Dr. Moss? What's that black and yellow tape?"

The crime scene tape was being unwound by the young male detective. "Step back, please," he said in a light, pleasant voice. "We have a homicide here."

The female detective went over to the two stunned staff members. "I'm Detective Edwina Jefferson," she said. "My partner's Danny Wong. Are you family?"

Sarah, whose eyes were riveted on the corpse, shook her head. "I'm the housekeeper, and this is Ada Dietz, the cook."

"Are there other live-in employees?" Edwina inquired.

Sarah replied that there were, naming Kenyon and Edna. "Our quarters are on the third floor. As I was going to bed, I happened to look out the window and I saw the emergency vehicles."

"We'd like to talk to them," Edwina said. "Could you bring them down and have them wait for us?"

The housekeeper nodded. "I'll take them into the library."

Thinking of the note on the library desk, Judith intervened. "The parlor would be better, Ms. Kenyon. It's more . . . cozy."

Sarah and Ada both gave Judith a curious glance, but didn't argue. The ambulance attendants entered with a gurney and began the removal of the body.

"Where's your sister, honey?" Edwina asked.

"She's my cousin," Judith corrected. "We're as close as sisters, though. Maybe closer. She's in the drawing room.

One of the grandsons is here, too. He must have gone back to his room."

Edwina nodded, then turned to her partner. "Junior, have one of the servants send for him. I'll start the inquiries and you can join us when everything's squared away out here." She stepped aside and let Judith lead the way.

Renie was nursing a second brandy and leafing through an old photo album. She put the hand-tooled book on the side table, stretched, yawned, and smiled somewhat sheepishly.

"This is like a fashion history of the last century or more," Renie said. "I've only gotten to the end of World War One."

"Good for you," Judith said. "We've gotten to the interrogation point. This is Edwina Jefferson. I believe she's the primary."

Edwina gave Judith a penetrating look. "You seem to know the drill, honey."

"I do," Judith replied. "My husband just retired as a homicide detective with the metro police force."

Edwina beamed. "Joe Flynn?" She shook Judith's hand. "I've met him on a couple of cross-jurisdictions cases. He's a great guy. The squad was sorry to see him go."

So was I, Judith thought. "You must know his former partner, Woody Price. He's teamed now with Sancha Rael."

"I haven't run into her yet," Edwina said, sitting down in a tan leather chair with armrests and legs made of ivory tusks. "But I do know Woody from working with Joe. He's also very good." She paused and let out a gusty laugh. "Even though he is 'colored.' They made a terrific team."

Renie was yawning again. "Can I go to bed? It's one A.M. and about five minutes past my bedtime."

"Sorry, honey," Edwina said, taking a legal-sized tablet out of her big black purse. "I have just a few questions. Let's start with the basics—names, addresses, and so forth."

The preliminaries took less than three minutes. By that

time, Danny Wong had joined them. Edwina jokingly referred to him as her junior partner.

"Danny was just promoted the first of the year," Edwina explained. "That's a big deal for him, since he only graduated from the law enforcement program at Sunset Community College three years ago. We've worked just two homicides together, and they were both cut-and-dried. When I don't call him Junior, I call him my Number Three Son. I've got two of my own at home." She poked him in the ribs and laughed again. "See how he shows respect to his other momma? I tell you, honey, this boy never pokes back."

Renie was smiling. "You remind me of the old days in Reno and Vegas, before the casinos got cold and corporate. Most of the dealers were very friendly and they called everybody honey."

Edwina gave Renie a shrewd look. "I call everybody honey—until I can trust them. Then, if they're real sweet, they might get to be sugar."

Judith's eyes widened. "You don't trust us?"

Edwina shook her head. "Not quite, honey. But I'll cut you some slack because you're Joe's wife. You probably know better than to try hoodwinking the cops."

"Somebody thinks they can," Judith noted.

"Somebody always does, " Edwina replied. "That's how Junior and I keep our jobs. Okay," she went on, getting down to business, "tell me why you were asked to stay with Mrs. Burgess."

Judith went into the events that had raised the alarm for both Leota Burgess and her daughter Bev. "We still haven't figured out if the attempts on her life were serious or not."

"Really?" Edwina said. "I think you have to take them seriously now. Wouldn't you agree that the intended victim wasn't Dr. Moss, but Leota Burgess?"

SEVEN

JUDITH SUPPOSED THAT in the back of her mind it had already occurred to her that the killer had made a terrible mistake. *How did it go so wrong?* The words on the notepad leaped in front of Judith's eyes, and she immediately informed the detectives about the scribbled question.

"Danny, will you have a look?" Edwina requested. "And see if the rest of the servants and the grandson are in the parlor."

Judith had turned to Renie. "Did you see the note when you called 911 from the library?"

Renie's forehead wrinkled. "I don't think so. But frankly, I might not have noticed. I grabbed the phone, punched in the number, gave the message, and came tearing back to the staircase." Giving a little start, she put a hand to her mouth. "There was one other thing, though—I thought I heard someone running outside of the library. It was probably just the wind."

Edwina had settled into the leather chair. "Are you sure?"

Renie shook her head. "I wasn't focused on anything but the phone call."

Edwina uttered a small sigh. "Okay, let's go over what led up to finding the body." She was still looking at Renie. "You definitely heard something from your bedroom, honey?"

"It was very faint," Renie replied, "but I was still awake. I suppose I was on the alert, too, since we'd been asked to watch for anything unusual. In fact, I'd heard something odd a moment or two earlier, a sort of cry or . . . I really can't describe it. I thought it was the wind, which started blowing about the time we came up to our rooms."

Edwina nodded. "Yes. It started to rain just before we got here. This place is hard to find in the dark. Go on, honey."

"Anyway, when I heard the next noise, I woke Judith and we went first to Mrs. Burgess's room because there was a light on and the door was open. We heard the noise again while we were in her boudoir."

"Do you agree?" Edwina asked Judith.

"Yes. I didn't hear it the first time—I was asleep. But I heard the second sort of groan or moan. There were no lights on in the corridor, so we had to search for the switch. When we turned it on, we saw what looked like a big pile of dark clothing at the bottom of the staircase."

"And then?" Edwina prodded.

The cousins exchanged glances, then Renie nodded to Judith. "We saw something move," Judith said, taking the cue, "and then we saw the top of Mrs. Burgess's head. I don't recall whether I checked Dr. Moss's pulse before or after we got Mrs. Burgess out from under him."

"Do you know why Dr. Moss was here?" Edwina inquired, as Danny returned from the library with the tablet.

"Mrs. Burgess didn't send for him," Judith said, explaining about the doctor's key to the house, the buzzer system, and how the lights had gone out just as the old lady started down the stairs.

Both detectives stared at Judith. "You mean," Danny began, "that someone was in the entry hall?"

"Yes," Judith agreed. "The other switch is just around the corner from the staircase area."

"So," Edwina said thoughtfully, "the killer attacked after

turning out the lights and popped the wrong person."

"That must be what happened," Judith said, though there was a note of doubt in her voice. "But what if Mrs. Burgess hadn't fallen downstairs? What if she'd remained at the top? How would the killer have known since the lights were out?"

Edwina gave a little shrug. "Whoever it was heard her fall. As you mentioned, Mrs. Jones, she cried out, which was the first sound that caught your attention. Obviously, the attack came after that."

Judith didn't want to seem argumentative, so she kept a kernel of skepticism to herself. Edwina, meanwhile, had taken the tablet from Danny Wong. "Hunh," she said after reading the single question. " 'How did it go so wrong?' That's curious. Do you recognize the handwriting?"

"No," Judith answered. "We really don't know these people."

"Along with fingerprints, we'll get samples from the household so a handwriting expert can analyze it," Edwina said, putting the tablet in a plastic bag. "What about the evening's events? Did anything unusual happen? Was anyone else in the house besides the people who are here now?"

"There were quite a few visitors," Judith replied, "but I gathered it wasn't unusual." She turned to Renie. "Who came first? Peggy?"

Renie nodded. "Peggy Burgess—I mean, Peggy Hillman, who is a stepdaughter, got here while we were having cocktails. She stayed to dinner."

"That's right," Judith agreed, thinking that dinner seemed like a very long time ago. "The stepson, Wayne Burgess, showed up after dinner to see Mrs. Burgess. He runs Evergreen Timber, which is the family business."

Danny took notes while Edwina continued to ask the questions. "You have any notion how Peggy and Wayne get on with their stepmother?"

"They seem to be on good terms," Renie put in, "at least as far as we could tell. The only complaint from Mrs. Burgess was that Wayne had interrupted one of her favorite TV programs."

"Then a grandson came by, Wayne's son," Judith continued. "He owns Bop's Pizza Palace out on the highway."

"What time was that?" Edwina asked.

Judith considered. "A little before nine. Bop had an extra pizza which he left at the house."

"Then came Kenneth," Renie said, rolling her eyes. "He was upset. He'd seen a woman in Sunset Cliffs wearing fur. Kenneth is one of those animal rights activists."

Edwina wrinkled her nose. "If you can afford it, flaunt it. I would, I'd have fur from the top of my head clear down to my heels. Does he live at Creepers?"

Renie shook her head. "He used to, I gather, but he has a place in town. Still, he sometimes spends the night here, judging from what his grandmother said."

"Anyone else?"

"Nobody we saw," Renie replied. "Mrs. Burgess retired before ten, and we went upstairs about fifteen, twenty minutes later."

Edwina paused, waiting for Danny to catch up. "Is there anything else you two can tell us?"

Judith looked at Renie who shook her head and yawned again. "I guess not," Judith began, then snapped her fingers. "Yes, there is one thing—I noticed some dirt by Dr. Moss's body. I assume you saw it?"

"Yes," Edwina nodded. "We bagged that, too."

Judith turned to Danny Wong. "Did you find Kenneth Ward?"

The young detective said that the housekeeper had found him out in the garden. "I guess he was pretty distraught." Danny winced. "In describing him, Ms. Kenyon used the phrase 'baying at the moon.'"

"Oh, great," Renie murmured.

"By the way," Judith said, rising from the sofa, "have you found the weapon?"

"No." Edwina's plump face showed no expression.

"There's plenty of heavy bric-a-brac around," Renie said.

"Maybe Dr. Moss was struck by a ceramic gopher."

Edwina chuckled. "That's the problem, honey. We're examining everything in the vicinity."

"You found nothing under the body?" Judith asked.

"That's right," Edwina replied, then added, "We'll ask the housekeeper for a list of family members who should be notified."

"Most of them live close by," Judith offered. "There's Beverly Ohashi, of course. Maybe my cousin should call her now. It must be daytime in Egypt."

"I meant Dr. Moss's relatives, too," Edwina said. "Do you know if he had any family?"

"His wife died a few years ago," Judith responded. "I've heard no references to children."

As they exited the drawing room, Renie gave Judith a sharp jab in the ribs. "All I want to do is go to sleep. It's damned awkward to have to be the bearer of bad news at one-thirty in the morning."

"But Bev has got to find out that somebody may have tried to kill her mother—again," Judith countered. "Goodness, the woman is like a cat—nine lives."

"You really think she was the intended victim?" Renie asked as they made their way around the crime scene tape.

Judith sighed. "I don't know. Doesn't it seem strange that Dr. Moss came to Creepers? He had his black bag, as if he were making a house call. If Mrs. Burgess didn't summon him, who did? And why?"

Just as they started up the staircase, Dr. Stevens began his descent. "Nurse Fritz will be here shortly. I've been in Mrs. Burgess's sitting room, standing guard." He paused and looked slightly sheepish. "Maybe that sounds silly, but you never know. Would you mind taking over for me until the nurse arrives? I've just been paged by the hospital."

Renie sagged against Judith. "Can I jump in bed with the old girl?" she asked. "I'm beat."

"I'll stay," Judith volunteered.

"Ooh . . ." Renie gave Judith another jab. "Okay, okay. I'll stretch out on the settee."

"Good." Dr. Stevens smiled at the cousins. "Oh, by the way, I should get Dr. Moss's key to the house. I suppose I'm now the official Creepers physician."

Judith didn't think he looked pleased by the prospect, but she made no comment. "The keys probably went with the body," she said. "You'll have to get them later, when you or whoever collect the rest of his belongings. Did he have family?"

Dr. Stevens looked away to the spot where Dr. Moss had been found. "No. He and Mrs. Moss were childless and his only brother died several years ago."

Danny Wong came through the entry hall and into the staircase area. "Forgot my pen," he mumbled, embarrassed.

"Detective," Dr. Stevens called after him. "When will I be able to retrieve Dr. Moss's keys?"

Danny turned around. "What keys?"

The doctor frowned. "Pardon?"

"There weren't any keys," Danny replied. "His wallet, credit cards, everything else was there in his cape pocket. But no keys. Odd, huh?"

Judith thought it was more than odd, it was downright suspicious.

The cousins peeked in on Mrs. Burgess, who was sleeping soundly. Renie flopped down on the settee by the phone and looked for a directory. "I know Bev's number, but I forget the international calling code." She leaned over and fished around in the side table drawers. "Here it is."

A few moments later, Renie was talking to Bev. "No," Renie said, "it's not bad news about your mother . . . Well, it's not exactly good news, either . . . Remember Dr. Moss? . . . Let me put it this way, remember the *late* Dr. Moss? He was killed this evening and . . . sort of fell on top of your mother . . ." This time, Renie's pause was longer. "No, of course not. If he'd been pushed off the roof, I would've said so. Somebody hit him in the back of the head, apparently while he was talking to your . . . No, I've no idea who did it . . . Yes, really, your mother's fine. Judith and I found them at the bottom of the . . ."

Judith stood by the fireplace and listened to the wind in the chimney while Renie finished her story. It took some time, with many interruptions from Bev. Finally, Renie ended the conversation.

"Yes," she said, her words a bit slurred from weariness, "they were going to notify Peggy and Wayne as soon as possible . . . Yes, I realize Kenneth may be unstable . . . What kind of animals? . . . Oh, *those* kinds of animals . . . No, I don't know how the servants are taking it . . . Please, Bev, don't worry so . . . No, don't think of coming home at this point. The police will sort it all out. Call me tomorrow, and I'll let you know what's happening, okay?"

Renie finally hung up and promptly assumed a fetal position on the settee.

"Aren't you going to tell me what Bev said?" Judith asked in an incredulous voice.

"No," Renie muttered. "It was nothing important." She burrowed her head into a trio of small satin pillows.

"How," Judith demanded, pacing the floor, "can you possibly sleep? I can't stand it. I feel as if I should be talking to the staff, or Kenneth, or whomever. Where were all the family members when the murder occurred? Virtually everybody lives close by. They're all recognizable by the guards at the gatehouse. Did Dr. Moss say anything to the guard when he was waved through? Did you really hear footsteps outside the library?"

"Mmm," Renie rolled over, her face against the back of the settee.

"What about the weapon? Surely it must be one of those statues or fireplace tools or another one of the dozens of lethal items in the entry hall and the staircase area. Why was there dirt on the floor? It hadn't started raining yet— the ground was dry. Are there footprints outside?"

Renie said nothing.

Judith went to the window and peered through the heavy drapes. "It's really blowing and the rain's coming down hard. But the storm didn't move in until after Dr. Moss was killed. Have any telltale footprints been washed away by the rain?"

Renie was snoring softly. Judith started moving away from the window, then noticed a faint light in one of the outbuildings to her far right. She tried to identify which one, but between her unfamiliarity with the garden's layout and the rain slashing against the windows, she couldn't tell.

But she could go look. A sleeping Renie wasn't as effective a watchdog as an alert Renie, but at least she was there. Judith left the suite and hurried down the hall to check from her own rooms where the angle was much better.

It took a minute, but Judith got her bearings. The light was coming from the pool house. Putting on her walking shoes and raincoat, she started back down the hall, then stopped. The back stairs had to be nearby. Judith didn't want to run into the detectives again, at least not just now. If the main staircase was outside Mrs. Burgess's suite, then the back stairs should be in the same area, only to the rear of the house. But there was just one more room before the hall dead-ended into a large linen closet. She retraced her steps, and suddenly an idea struck her: The back stairs must run behind Mrs. Burgess's suite.

Returning to the sitting room, Judith found Renie still sound asleep. There was a door on her left, which she hadn't noticed before. The doorknob turned easily to reveal a small well-organized office, complete with a brand-new computer. There was, however, no stairway, though it looked as if at one time there had been another door in the opposite wall. The outline remained, and the space had been painted over with a mural of tropical birds.

Judith tiptoed into the bedroom. A nightlight covered by a china seashell cast a soft glow over Mrs. Burgess, who also appeared to be in a deep sleep. The walk-in closet next to the bathroom didn't contain a stairway, either.

Standing at the foot of the big four-poster bed, Judith peered in every direction. Finally, she saw a Chinese screen in the far corner of the boudoir. Sure enough, there was a door behind it—and a stairway. She also saw the elevator to the right of the stairwell, but decided against using it. The last thing she needed was to get stuck between floors.

If there was a light switch, Judith couldn't find it. Treading carefully down the narrow wooden steps, she reached the bottom and realized she was facing another door. She reasoned that it had to be the one she'd seen when she and Renie had come in the back way after their tour of the grounds.

She was not, however, prepared for the bright lights that met her eyes when she opened the door. She could hear voices in the kitchen, but could distinguish only Ada Dietz's and Edna Thompson's. Perhaps they were preparing some food for the rest of the staff and the detectives. It looked like it was going to be a long night.

Judith scurried past the open kitchen door where she caught a few of Ada's words. "It's that Suzette, she's always brought trouble to this house. If you ask me, there's no end to it."

Judith froze in place, but Edna's response was too soft to hear. Then what sounded like the dishwasher was turned on, drowning out both of the women's voices.

Judith went outside. The wind whipped at her coat and the rain pelted her face. Head down, she followed the faint light that shone in what she thought was the pool house.

By the time she reached the door, her nightgown and her hair were soaked. Cautiously turning the knob, she went inside and found herself in what was the changing area where an overhead light had been switched on.

I'm an idiot, she thought. *Why on earth have I come out here in a big storm?* Probably someone had carelessly left the light on. For all she knew, they always kept a light burning in the pool house. But Judith couldn't just turn around and go to bed. She felt a need for activity, and, as usual, her curiosity got the better of her. Smiling grimly, she thought of herself as a racehorse, sniffing the finish line.

Judith couldn't stop in the home stretch; she had to keep going.

She passed by the dressing rooms and the bathroom, then went through a door that led to the pool itself. The smell of chlorine was strong in her nostrils. In the faint light that followed her from the dressing area, she could see the Olympic-sized pool as well as some chairs and tables.

Adjusting to the near-darkness, her gaze wandered around the edges of the pool. There were potted plants, too, and a bar in one corner. It looked like a very pleasant place for a swim.

Finally, she took in the area at the near end of the pool. Judith could hear the wind wailing through the trees. She hugged the raincoat closer, and shivered in spite of herself.

Then she saw it. Huddled in the corner was another pile of clothes. It was like a flashback to the scene at the bottom of the staircase.

Oh, God, she thought, *not another body*. Judith swayed slightly, then forced herself to approach. She got within two feet before she recognized the form of a young woman in a fleece jacket. Sucking in her breath, Judith reached out a trembling hand to feel for a pulse.

The young woman's arms flailed and her legs kicked. Then she let out a blood-curdling scream that was almost swallowed by the next gust of wind.

One of the flying feet caught Judith off-guard, and she tumbled backward. Losing her balance, she fell into the swimming pool, where the wet tangle of raincoat and night-gown weighed her down.

At least, Judith thought as her head struck the hard tiles at the pool's side, *this one's still alive. But am I?*

She sank to the bottom and everything suddenly went dark.

EIGHT

FROM OUT OF the depths and deep in the night, Judith felt hands tugging at her arms. *We've hit an iceberg*, she could hear the *Titanic*'s captain say. *We're going down.*

But Judith was coming up. The hands that pulled at her arms were strong. They must belong to the hiking boots she could see at the edge of the pool. Man? Woman? Leonardo DiCaprio?

Slowly, she looked up and tried to focus her eyes. The ship had stopped spinning. But there was no iceberg and the creature with the mass of frizzy strawberry-blond hair was no actor, but a young woman. Judith realized she was not in the North Atlantic, but in the Burgess swimming pool.

"My God!" the young woman cried. "I'm so sorry! Let me help!"

Judith felt that was only fair, since this must be the person who had knocked her into the pool in the first place. Sputtering, Judith clambered onto dry ground.

"You're all wet," her savior declared. "Can you forgive me?"

"I was half-wet before I fell in," Judith responded, brushing hair out of her eyes and trying to get her bearings. "Who did you think I was? And who are you?"

"I thought you were a fiendish rapist," the young woman answered in a high-pitched voice.

"Do I look like a fiendish rapist?" Judith retorted, wringing out her raincoat.

The young woman backed away. "No . . . no, of course not. But I was in Arcadia."

Judith gave a start. "Arcadia?" Seeing a faraway look come into the young woman's eyes, Judith held up a hand. She'd had enough fantasy for one night already. "Never mind. I'm Judith Flynn, a friend of Mrs. Burgess," she said, stretching the truth a bit as she rubbed at the bump on the back of her head. "Now please tell me who you are."

The dreamy expression turned wary. "Do I know you?"

"It doesn't seem so," Judith said, growing impatient and beginning to shiver from the cold, wet garments. "If you don't want to tell me, I'm going back to the house. My head hurts."

"Oh." The young woman gazed at the pool. She gazed at the ceiling. She gazed at the floor. She was almost as tall as Judith, but her thin figure and the untamed masses of reddish-blond hair lent a wraithlike air. After coming to what appeared to be an excruciating decision, she finally spoke: "I'm Caroline Flaherty."

The name Flaherty meant nothing to Judith, but Caroline rang a bell. "You're . . . a granddaughter?"

Caroline nodded. "My mother's Peggy Hillman now, but my father's name was Ward. Flaherty's my married name."

Judith gave an absent nod. As far as she could tell, Caroline didn't act as if she knew about any of the events that had transpired during the past few hours at Creepers. Judith could ask, but now wasn't the time. Her priorities were a throbbing head and a chilled body.

"I think we should go inside," Judith said, then pointed to a backpack that rested against the tiles. "Is that yours?"

Caroline frowned at the dark green item. "Is it? Oh— yes. I was using it for a pillow."

As the wind howled in the trees, Judith led the way to

the house. "We'll take the back stairs," she said. "We can go up to my room."

Caroline had stopped walking and stood staring up at the bulk that was Creepers. "Why are so many lights on? Isn't it still nighttime?"

"Yes, it must be around two-thirty. Come on, I'll explain when we get inside."

Caroline didn't budge. "Has something happened to *Gran'mère*?" she asked in an uncertain voice.

"*Gran'mère*? Oh—your grandmother. No," Judith assured the young woman, "she's fine. But she's asleep. Hurry, I'm frozen to the bone and I need some aspirin."

The kitchen had been vacated, and the dishwasher churned in the darkness. Judith and Caroline climbed the narrow back stairs. "You probably know the way better than I do," Judith said to her companion. "I assume you grew up around here."

"Yes," Caroline replied. "Kenneth and I sometimes stayed here when we were children, but my parents lived a few miles away, in a nice house overlooking the sound. After the divorce, Mommy and my stepdad stayed on, but then he got killed in Vietnam. Way back, when my parents got married, my real daddy didn't . . ." Her high-pitched voice trailed away.

"I take it he preferred not to be so near his in-laws," Judith remarked dryly.

"Yes . . . in a way," Caroline replied.

"Understandable," Judith said, opening the door to Mrs. Burgess's suite and signaling for Caroline to be quiet.

The mistress of the house was still sound asleep. Caroline tiptoed past the bed with a whispered, "*Cher Gran'mère*." As they reached the door to the sitting room, Judith heard low, angry voices. One of them sounded as if it belonged to Renie.

A rawboned middle-aged woman in full nurse's regalia stood with hands on hips, facing off with a pugnacious Renie.

"Listen, Glitz or Ritz or Ditz or whatever your name is,"

Renie snarled, "I don't take orders from anybody except Bill and even that's a sometime thing. If you want to get out of here with your appendages still somewhere in the vicinity of your torso, you'd better—"

She broke off, following the nurse's startled gaze. "Coz," Renie said, her jaw dropping as she took in Judith's appearance. "What happened?"

"Never mind," said Judith. "What's happening here?"

"Meet Nurse Zitz," Renie said, still staring at her cousin.

"Fritz," the nurse shot back, glaring at Renie. "Millicent Fritz." She transferred the glare to Judith, then hesitated as she saw Caroline quivering in the background. "My dear, is that you, Carrie?"

"Miss Fritz?" Tremulously, Caroline moved out from behind Judith. "Hi." She waved a thin hand in the nurse's direction.

"Well, now." Fritz beamed with apparent pleasure. "I haven't seen you since your grandmother had her gall bladder attack four years ago. I wasn't able to come when she sprained her ankle last fall. My, you really haven't changed."

"Too bad," muttered Renie, who was now standing next to Judith. "She could have used some improvement. Who's this one?"

"Caroline, Peggy's kid," Judith said between clenched teeth. "Are we unwanted in here?"

Caroline and the nurse had finished their friendly exchange. Fritz turned a gimlet eye on the cousins. "Mrs. Burgess's granddaughter is here. You two may go."

"That answers my question," Judith said. "Bye."

Renie let out an exasperated sigh. "Swell. Now I've lost face, not to mention sleep." She turned to the nurse. "I guess I can't send you to the OR after all, Pitz. We'll take up where we left in the morning, right where you called me 'a buck-toothed interfering nobody.' " Renie sashayed out of the sitting room.

"She really said that?" Judith gasped when they reached the hall.

"Sort of," Renie replied. "At least she was thinking it. Now tell me why you're all wet."

In their suite, Judith made a beeline for the pillbox she always carried in her purse. Before saying another word, she gulped down two aspirin. As she got out of her wet clothes, she rapidly summed up her adventures in the pool house.

Renie was already under the covers. "Your poor head. Did you really black out?"

"I sure did," Judith replied. "At least for a few seconds."

Renie gave her cousin a weary yet sympathetic smile. "I should have been with you."

"You were asleep," Judith said dryly.

Renie made a face. "I was at that." She paused to arrange the pillows. "So Caroline's the poet," she remarked. "How'd she end up out back?"

Judith sighed. "I've no idea. I never got a chance to ask her. How did you and Nurse Fritz get into it?"

"I'm not a Burgess," Renie said between yawns, "and in that old bat's mind, you might as well be a blister on the big toe of life."

Judith shrugged as she headed into the bathroom. "I assume Fritz will tell Caroline about Dr. Moss. I wonder when she arrived. It must have been before the medics and the police got here or she would have asked what was going on."

"Whatever." Renie had turned over on her side.

Judith took a hot shower, finally getting the chill out of her bones. Since she'd exchanged her bathrobe for her raincoat, she decided to sleep in the robe. The nightgown wouldn't be dry until morning. When she returned to the bedroom, Renie was out for the count.

But Judith wasn't sleepy. The events of the past few hours had started the adrenaline flowing. Or perhaps it was the fall into the pool. Whatever the cause, she felt wide awake. After about five minutes of staring into the darkness, Judith got up to get the book she'd brought along. She'd just taken it out of her suitcase when she heard a frantic pounding from somewhere in the vicinity. Going into the sitting room, she realized that someone was knocking on their door.

"Who is it?" she asked, her ear to the heavy oak.

"Caroline," came the reply. "Help me, please!"

"Just a minute." Judith dashed to the other end of the room and closed the bedroom door, then returned to let Caroline in. "My cousin's sleeping," she cautioned. "What's wrong?"

The younger woman fell into a damask-covered armchair. "It's Dr. Moss. He's been murdered, and the police will think I did it!"

"Why?" Judith asked, sitting down on the settee.

"Because," Caroline replied, putting her thumb in her mouth like a small child.

Trying to convey an aura of calm, Judith folded her hands in her lap. "Let's start from the beginning. When did you arrive at Creepers?"

Slowly, Caroline removed her thumb. Judith figured she must be in her thirties, but like her brother Kenneth, she looked and acted much younger. "I'm not sure," Caroline said vaguely. "The house was dark except for a light or two on the third floor in the servants' quarters. It was so quiet, like a crypt . . . the silence of sadness, the gloom of doom, the empty womb. I felt inspired to write a poem. I didn't think I should bother *Gran'mère*, so I went out to the pool house and fell asleep until you woke me up."

"You'd come from . . . where?" Judith asked, recalling only that Caroline lived somewhere north of the city.

"La Bido," Caroline replied. "I have a cottage there. We creative types band together in the town. It's quite an artists' community."

Judith knew the picturesque little town, which was on the edge of an Indian reservation. It was about an hour's drive from Sunset Cliffs, if traffic wasn't heavy on the interstate.

"Your husband lives there, too?" Judith asked, already knowing the answer.

Caroline shook her head, sending the wild frizzy hair flying around her shoulders. "Brett and I are separated. We used to live together in La Bido, but last summer he rented a place on the ocean. I haven't seen him since."

"What brought you here?" Judith inquired, trying to sound casual.

"I wanted to talk to *Gran'mère*." Caroline lowered her eyes. "I wanted to ask her about something."

"Why would anyone think you murdered Dr. Moss?"

Caroline's gray eyes widened. "Because. Because I was so mad at him when Daddy was killed."

Judith gave herself a little shake. "Why was that?"

"Dr. Moss was the one who found Daddy by the side of the road." Caroline paused, her eyes filling with tears. "I always blamed him for not being able to save Daddy."

"I thought your father was killed in a car accident," Judith said, feeling somewhat at sea.

Caroline wiped at her eyes and nodded. "He was. It was a hit-and-run, up by the golf course. Daddy's car broke down, and he'd gotten out, probably coming to Creepers for help. At least that's what we figured afterward."

"Goodness," Judith whispered, "I didn't know any of the specifics about the accident. Did they catch the person who hit him?"

"No." Caroline's hands twisted in distress. "It was about the time that night classes let out at the community college. The authorities figured it was a student who was in a big hurry to get home."

"How was it that Dr. Moss found your father?" Judith asked.

Caroline grimaced. "I don't remember exactly. It happened four years ago. I've written so many poems about it that I've lost sight of the actual facts. Imagery, emotion, meter—they're far more important than reality."

"Um . . . yes, I suppose so." Judith murmured. "I don't imagine you have any idea who'd want to kill Dr. Moss?"

Caroline shook her head very slowly. "Only me. But I've written my way out of that vengeful aura."

"That's good," Judith said, trying to smile. "Do you think the killer might have made a mistake?"

Caroline stared at Judith. "A mistake? How do you mean?"

Judith winced. "Well . . . Did you know your grandmother felt . . . threatened?"

The laugh that Caroline emitted was as high-pitched as her speech, but quite merry. "Of course! At her age, she's looking into the future, trying to penetrate the Other Side. Being *Gran'mère*, she enjoys a touch of drama. I've inherited that trait from her, but I use it in my poetry."

"But you're not a blood relation," Judith blurted.

The merriment died. "No," Caroline admitted. "I'm not. She's really my stepgrandmother. But I never think of her like that. She's the only grandmother I've ever known."

"Of course," Judith went on in a soothing tone, "traits can be picked up by environment and association. Her imagination no doubt rubbed off on you."

"Yes," Caroline asserted, her smile emerging again. "I'm sure that's how it worked. Anyway, I've never worried about anyone trying to kill her. In fact, I've encouraged her to come up with more ideas. Eventually, I'll work them into an epic verse. A kind of saga, you see."

"Mmm," Judith murmured, wondering if Caroline's talent was genuine. "Have you been published?"

"Oh, yes." Caroline nodded several times. "I had a poem published just last month by a small press in Japan."

"Japan?"

Caroline nodded some more. "It was haiku, and Uncle Tom translated it for me."

It took Judith a moment to recall that Uncle Tom was Bev's husband. "That's wonderful," she said as weariness suddenly overcame her like a big, dark cloud. "It's three A.M. I'm going to bed. Are you going to stay in the tower with your brother, Kenneth?"

Alarm enveloped Caroline, who began rocking back and forth in the armchair. "No! Kenneth can't be staying there. That's impossible."

"Why?" Judith inquired in a reasonable tone. "I gathered he usually stays there. Aren't those your old rooms?"

"Yes, yes," Caroline replied, nodding jerkily. "But they're haunted."

"They are? By whom?"

Caroline bowed her head, the wild hair covering her face. "By Suzette," she said in a barely audible voice. "I'll stay next door, between you and *Gran'mère*. I won't be frightened there."

Before Judith could pose another question, Caroline flew out of the sitting room.

The wind had died down by morning, and the rain had almost stopped. When Judith woke up a few minutes after nine, she could see patches of blue sky to the west. She could also see Renie, still buried under the covers. Since her cousin rarely became fully alert before ten, Judith decided to perform her own morning ablutions first. Thus, when she emerged from the bathroom, she was surprised to see Renie sitting up in bed with her feet dangling above the floor.

"Duty calls," Renie mumbled. "We have to check on Mrs. B."

"I can do that while you dress," Judith offered.

"Fine." Staggering to her feet, Renie made her uncertain way into the bathroom.

Leota Burgess was breakfasting in bed. A gilt-edged tray laden with several covered dishes and a silver coffee pot rested on her lap. Nurse Fritz was nowhere in sight.

"I sent her off to get her own breakfast," Mrs. Burgess said in answer to Judith's query. "I don't care for other people eating in my boudoir."

"Should I leave?" Judith offered, rising from the chair in which she'd just sat down.

"No, certainly not," Mrs. Burgess replied with a faint smile. "Just don't join me in my meal. Where's Serena?"

Judith explained that her cousin would be along soon. "I gather Nurse Fritz is something of a fixture at Creepers."

"She has been," Mrs. Burgess said with a glint in her eye. "She cared for my late husband during his final illness. Then she was with us when I had my gall bladder attack. I haven't seen her since. We asked for her when I sprained my ankle, but Fritz told Dr. Moss she was unavailable. I'm surprised that she showed up now."

"Well." Judith was at a momentary loss for words. "She must have a busy schedule."

"I'm sure she does." Mrs. Burgess spooned up some oatmeal.

"I really must ask you something," Judith began in an earnest voice. "I mentioned it earlier, but the name Suzette keeps popping up. Last night Caroline refused to stay with Kenneth in the tower because—"

Mrs. Burgess dropped her spoon. "Caroline? Is Caroline here?"

Judith had forgotten that Mrs. Burgess might not have been informed of her granddaughter's arrival. "Yes, last night. Oh, dear—I'm sorry. I thought Nurse Fritz would've told you."

"Indeed not," Mrs. Burgess retorted. "Where *is* Carrie?"

Judith gestured in the direction of the next room. "Between our suite and yours." She went on to explain about finding Caroline in the pool house.

Mrs. Burgess sighed. "Such a foolish girl. Carrie tends to show up at all hours. She has no concept of time. Or much else, for that matter. Would you see if she's awake? I'd like to speak with her."

Temporarily diverted from the matter of Suzette, Judith could only smile and obey. Caroline's door was locked, however, and there was no response to repeated knocking. If, Judith reasoned, the intervening suite was set up in the same way as her own room and Mrs. Burgess's, Caroline probably couldn't hear anyone at the door if she was still asleep or in the shower.

Back in the corridor, Judith saw Renie coming her way. "I was trying to rouse Caroline," Judith explained. "Mrs.

Burgess didn't know she was here. Hey, you left your eye patch off again."

Renie gave her cousin a quirky little smile. "It's better, if you don't mind the fact that my eyes don't match."

"You're right. The left one's still drooping. You look sort of stoned."

"I feel sort of stoned," Renie replied. "That was one short night's sleep." She kept going down the hall.

"I thought you wanted to see Leota," Judith called after her.

Renie didn't turn around. "I do. In time. Right now, I'm going outside to smoke."

Shaking her head, Judith returned to the master suite. Mrs. Burgess was leafing through a copy of *Forbes* while Edna collected the breakfast tray.

"Leave the coffee pot and my cup," Mrs. Burgess said without looking up.

Edna gave a single nod. Judith noted that the maid's eyes were red-rimmed and her hands shook.

"Let me help you," Judith offered, catching a china cream pitcher just as it was about to fall off the tray. "I'll take these things to the elevator."

"Oh, no, please, I can manage," Edna protested.

But Judith was already behind the Chinese screen. "That's okay," she said with a smile. "Maybe I can grab a piece of toast while I'm in the kitchen."

"Oh! Yes, of course. Breakfast is laid out in the dining room, though. Perhaps you'd like to sit down and eat," Edna said as the elevator doors opened.

"I'll wait for my cousin," Judith said as the small car creaked and groaned on its descent. "Are the police still here?"

Edna turned her familiar shade of pink. "I hope not! Imagine! Police at Creepers! And people of color, at that. Dear me."

"But Beverly's husband is Japanese, and Dr. Stevens is African-American," Judith pointed out as the elevator came to rest.

"That's different," Edna said. "Mr. Ohashi is seldom at Creepers, and Dr. Stevens is . . . only part Negro. I try to think of him as white. A dark white, of course."

Following Edna into the kitchen, Judith placed the tray on the counter and greeted Ada Dietz. The cook looked surprised, and none too pleased.

"We don't need extra help," she declared, giving the maid a sharp glance. "Despite the commotion, we're doing just fine. Aren't we, Edna?"

"Oh, yes, certainly," Edna replied, her small hands fluttering over the front of her uniform. "We're fine as can be."

As her stomach growled, Judith noted the gleaming four-slice toaster, but decided against making any unwelcome requests. "What a well-appointed kitchen," she said in her most ingratiating manner. Gazing around the big high-ceilinged room with its work island in the center, she took in the latest appliances, including a commercial-sized grill next to an old-fashioned green and cream–colored range. It was, she thought, along with the matching counter tiles, the only holdover from another era. "I run a B&B, and I don't have a quarter of this space."

"It's adequate," Ada responded through tight lips.

Edna nodded enthusiastically. "My sister has everything she needs. Why, in the old days, when everyone was living here, we—"

"Edna!" Ada waved a wooden spoon at the maid. "How many times do I have to tell you not to be indiscreet?"

Edna hung her head. "I'm sorry, Ada. It's just that those were such—"

"Edna . . ." There was a stern warning in Ada's voice.

"I didn't realize you were sisters," Judith broke in, still smiling. "How nice for the two of you to work together for so long."

Ada turned her back and faced the stove; Edna seemed to shrivel up and began removing the dirty dishes from the gilt-edged tray; Judith stopped smiling and headed back for the elevator. If she got stuck between floors now, at least someone would know where she was. They might not care, but they would know.

Renie was sitting with Mrs. Burgess when Judith returned to the master suite. She jumped in her chair when she saw Judith emerge from behind the Chinese screen.

"What is this?" Renie said, wide-eyed. "A secret passage?"

Judith explained about the back stairs and the elevator while Mrs. Burgess's shrewd gaze was fixed on her face. "I wondered about that when you left a few minutes ago," the old lady said. "You seem to have gotten well-acquainted with the house."

"It was a necessity last night," Judith said, on the defensive. "As I just explained, I wanted to see what was going on in the pool house. That's how I found Caroline."

Mrs. Burgess sipped coffee from her china cup. "Yes, of course. I'm having Jeepers drain the pool. He's not full-time staff, but he is one of our gardeners. We could have had another tragedy last night. I'm terribly sorry about Caroline's reaction. How's your head?"

Judith fingered the small swelling. "It's better, though I still have a headache."

"Don't we all?" Mrs. Burgess sighed. "Please, go eat your breakfasts. Fritz will be back any minute. I'll see if she can find out if Caroline's awake."

"Jeepers Creepers?" Renie said as they went out into the hall.

"It's no worse than that relative of your dad's, Mabel Frable," Judith retorted. "Anyway, Jeepers Creepers isn't his real name."

"I hope not," Renie said as they descended the main staircase and saw the crime scene tape still in place. "By the way, I just got better acquainted with the house myself. I decided to see if I could find a way to smoke out on the second-floor balcony. Not only did I do that, I went into the other tower, to the south. There's a sewing room on the second floor and part of a ballroom on the first. The round part looks as if it's where the orchestra would play."

"I wonder when they last held a ball here?" Judith mused as they circumvented the ominous black and yellow tape.

Renie shrugged. "Who knows? But from a design standpoint, I find the house intriguing. It gives me ideas."

"It gives me ideas, too," Judith said, "but not about art. I have to tell you about Caroline coming to our rooms last night." She dragged her feet through the entry hall and down the corridor to the dining room as she related Caroline's story about her father's fatal accident and her own fears of the tower bedroom.

Before Renie could respond, they reached the dining room, where they found Peggy Hillman and a tall, attractive man in his fifties, both drinking Bloody Marys. Judith guessed that the man was Peggy's third husband, Russell, the golf pro.

She was right. Peggy introduced them and then sat back down at the long table and waited for the cousins to fill their plates. When they were seated, Peggy placed both hands flat on the linen cloth, as if she were about to make a speech.

"I really appreciate having you two come here," she said, her husky voice sounding tense. "We all do, don't we, Russ?"

Russ nodded affably.

"But now that we've actually had a murder—even if it wasn't *Maman*, thank God—it's best that you leave. Since Dr. Moss was killed in this house, it's become a family matter." Peggy paused and grimaced. "Do you think you can be out of here within the hour?"

NINE

THE COUSINS DIDN'T argue. They merely exchanged surreptitious glances and continued eating. Given their apparent acquiescence, Peggy reverted to her more outgoing self.

"Tell them about the time Arnie and Jack played Sunset Cliffs, Russ. That's one of my favorite anecdotes."

Dutifully, Russ Hillman went into a well-rehearsed if entertaining story of Palmer and Nicklaus's adventures on the local links. Russ struck Judith as a charming man who had a spent a lifetime living off the scraps of the elite. Indeed, he reminded her of a big, friendly dog trying to please his mistress. Judith half-expected to see him wag his tail.

At Peggy's urging, Russ had just launched into a tale about Greg Norman and Tiger Woods when Wayne and Dorothy Burgess arrived. Wayne and Peggy locked gazes; the sister nodded once at her brother.

"I think Mrs. Jones and Mrs. Flynn are very glad to be leaving," Peggy said with a small laugh. "I'm sure they've had enough of us."

"We're awfully sorry that your visit wasn't more pleasant," Wayne remarked as he picked his way through the dishes on the sideboard. "Perhaps you can come back some time when things settle down."

Judith thought he almost sounded sincere, though she knew better. "That would be lovely," she said. "Maybe Bev and Tom will be back by then."

"Don't count on it," Dorothy said, lighting a cigarette. "Those two don't show up more than once every three years. Wouldn't you think they'd get sick of all that dust?" She blew out a cloud of smoke and flicked ash into a Limoges saucer.

Renie picked up the cue and lighted her own cigarette. Peggy, Russ and Wayne all looked startled. "Really," Wayne began, "my wife is the only one who is allowed to—"

"Stick it," Dorothy broke in. "What's one more butt around this place?" She glanced up as Kenneth came into the dining room. "Speaking of which . . ." She uttered a little laugh and eyed her nephew with something akin to contempt. "Well? You save any saber-toothed tigers this morning, Kenny?"

"Aunt Dorothy, please," Kenneth began in a ragged voice. "Don't you feel a kinship with all creatures great and small?"

"Only the great ones," Dorothy shot back. "The small ones don't count. Did you talk to your dear *Grandmaman* last night?"

"I didn't get a chance," Kenneth answered defensively.

"Lay off, will you, Dot?" Peggy said in a testy tone. "Kenny's not the only one around here who asks favors from *Maman*. What about Howdy-Doody and his pathetic pizza parlor?"

"Bop's doing just fine," Dorothy retorted. "At least he works. What about your Caroline and her lamebrained plan to start a women's writing center?"

"Hey," snapped Peggy, "I thought you were all for that. Aren't you the one who thinks women should have their own careers?"

"That's not a career," Dorothy countered, "that's a retreat, which is all Caroline's ever done—retreat from the real world. The last time I read something she wrote it was about an ant crawling around on a paper towel."

Wayne had gotten to his feet. "Peg, Dot—please. We have guests. *Please*." He sat down again, but not before giving his wife and his sister a reproachful stare.

Judith finished her scrambled eggs and stood up. "Don't worry about us." She nudged Renie under the table. "We're leaving. Thanks for everything."

The cousins got as far as the door when they almost collided with Edwina Jefferson and Danny Wong.

"Hold it," Edwina said, blocking their way. "We've got some questions for all of you."

"Who let *you* in?" Dorothy demanded, angrily stubbing her cigarette out in the Limoges saucer.

"Some old coot who was about to keel over," Edwina said in a vexed tone. "We're the law, remember?"

"I thought," Wayne said in a stilted voice, "you finished your inquiries last night."

Edwina poured herself a cup of coffee from the sideboard and sat down between Wayne and Kenneth. "Are you kidding, honey? We just got started." She turned to her partner, tugging at his sleeve. "Take a load off, Junior. There's tea, too. Chop, chop."

Danny, however, merely grinned, and sat by Judith and Renie, who had resumed their places at the table.

"Okay," Edwina said, her shrewd brown eyes taking in each of the others, "we started with a homicide. Now we've got another crime." She didn't skip a beat as everyone stared, including Wayne, who had clearly taken umbrage at being called honey. "I'm going to ask each of you where you were last night, and not just at the time of the murder but up until around five this morning," Edwina said. "Let's start with some introductions. Danny and I haven't met all of you."

As the family members identified themselves, Judith reasoned that neither the Wayne Burgesses nor the Hillmans had come to Creepers until morning. Or if they had, they'd arrived after the detectives had left.

"Let's start with you, honey," Edwina said to Wayne

Burgess. "Last night from eleven o'clock, if you please."

Wayne pursed his lips. "I prefer that you don't call me honey."

Edwina cocked her head. "Is that right? Go on, honey, where were you?"

"What is this other so-called crime?" Wayne demanded, getting red in the face. "We have a right to know."

"No, you don't," Edwina said calmly. "Come on, honey, where were you?"

"Now see here—" Wayne began, wagging a finger at Edwina.

"Junior," she said, turning to Danny Wong, "make a note that Mr. Wayne Burgess refuses to answer the question."

"What?" Wayne exploded. "Of course I'll answer the question!"

Edwina sat back in the chair, arms folded across her plump bosom. "Go ahead."

"I was home." Wayne glared at Edwina. "All night."

"Oh?" Edwina turned back to Danny. "Don't we have a couple of witnesses who said Mr. Burgess was at Creepers earlier in the evening?"

"Yes, we heard about that last night," Danny replied with a quick glance at the cousins.

"I thought," Wayne said stiffly, "that I was only to account for my time after eleven P.M."

"True," Edwina agreed. "We just don't want any blanket statements. Go on, honey."

Wayne grimaced. "I told you. I was at home."

"You live close by," Edwina remarked. "A few minutes ago, you and your wife gave your address as Evergreen. Isn't that another one of these big estates in Sunset Cliffs?"

"That's correct," Wayne replied.

Edwina gazed at Dorothy Burgess. "Will you confirm that, honey?"

Dorothy winced. "Yes. Of course."

"You were there, too?" Edwina asked.

"Certainly. I didn't leave the house all day."

Edwina turned from the Burgesses to the Hillmans. "You

were here earlier in the evening, too," the detective said to Peggy.

"That's right," Peggy replied. "I had dinner with *Maman.*"

Edwina smiled broadly. "*Maman,* huh? I like that. There's Creole blood in my family, and once in a while a French phrase slips in. Did you come back to the house later?"

"No." Peggy paused. "Actually, I drove out to the highway. Russ was going to be late, so I thought I'd do some shopping over at the mall. They don't close until nine-thirty."

"Your house is on the golf course?"

"Yes, not far from the chapel."

"What time did you finally get home?"

Peggy considered. "Eleven, eleven-thirty?"

Edwina frowned. "It's not more than ten minutes from Sunset Cliffs to the mall. If the stores close at nine-thirty, what took you so long to get home?"

"I was hungry by then," Peggy replied. "I stopped at Lenny's for a burger. *Maman* eats dinner early because of her TV programs."

Edwina turned her gaze on Russ Hillman. "When did you get home, honey?"

Russ didn't seem to mind the informality. "It was late. I had dinner and drinks with some club members. Eleven or so, I guess. Maybe later."

"Who got home first, you or your wife?" Edwina asked.

"Ah . . ." Russ gazed up at the crystal chandelier. "She did."

"Thank you." Edwina smiled at Kenneth. "I spoke with you last night. Where were you after Danny and I left Creepers?"

"Here," Kenneth replied a bit nervously. "I went back to bed. I just came downstairs before you arrived."

Edwina regarded Judith and Renie. "And you two?"

Renie answered first, relating how she'd dozed off on the settee in Mrs. Burgess's sitting room, and had been awakened by the arrival of Nurse Fritz. "After that, we went back to our rooms. I dozed off again and slept straight through."

Judith, however, had a much longer tale. As she related how she'd encountered Caroline in the pool house, Peggy gasped in surprise.

"Carrie's here?" she said. "I'd no idea."

At that moment, Caroline, looking dazed, appeared in the dining room. "Gosh," she said, "this is quite a crowd. Hi, Mommy. Hi, everybody. What's going on?"

"These people," Peggy said with a grimace, "are detectives. They—"

Before Peggy could get the words out, Caroline fainted.

As Kenyon was summoned to fetch smelling salts, Judith and Renie exchanged bemused glances. The butler was gone so long that Caroline came to before he got back.

"Do you want to lie down?" Peggy asked her daughter.

Caroline nodded. Wayne rose from the table. "I think we should adjourn this farce to the drawing room. Here, Carrie, I'll help you."

Kenneth took his sister's other arm, leading the way down the hall, through the entryway and past the central staircase. Caroline took one look at the crime scene tape and fainted again.

"Good grief," Renie muttered. "What is this? A nineteenth-century melodrama? When does the villain arrive, twirling his black mustache?"

"Maybe he—or she—already has," Judith said under her breath as the cousins made way in the entry hall for Kenyon, who was finally bringing the smelling salts.

Renie leaned one hand on a small round rosewood table that stood against the wall separating the entry hall from the staircase area. "We might as well linger here while our swooning heroine is revived." She fiddled with a bronze lamp featuring the figurines of two small children playing with a puppy. "How the heck do you turn this thing on, or is it just for decorative purposes?" She bent down and finally found the chain, which had gotten tangled up under the pink tulip shade. "Lights on, lights out. Caroline faints, Caroline comes to. Can we really go home now?"

"Of course not," Judith replied in an undertone as Peggy ministered to her daughter. "The cops won't let us. You know that, which is why I didn't argue. Hey," she said suddenly, "why doesn't that light turn on?"

Renie had still been idly pulling the chain. "You're right." She bent down to peer under the table. "Aha. My knowledge of things electrical has served me well. Lights don't turn on if they're not plugged in. This sucker isn't."

By the staircase, Caroline was coughing and choking from the effects of the smelling salts. Her uncle and her brother again picked her up and all but carried her in the direction of the drawing room.

Judith was leaning down next to Renie, who was reaching for the plug. "Hold it," Judith ordered, shoving her cousin's hand out of the way. "Is that dirt under here?" She stood up, pulling Renie with her. "Think this through. Why is that lamp unplugged? Is it usually left on at night to provide some light for the entry hall? Did the killer unplug it to make the hall completely dark? Or is it the weapon? What about these little bits of dirt? They look the same as the small clumps I saw by Dr. Moss's body."

"Dirt's dirt," Renie declared. "Why didn't the cops bag this lamp? They took away some of the other stuff, like that figure of Venus and the wrought-iron hat rack."

As Judith studied the entry hall, Danny Wong appeared from the drawing room. "Excuse me, ladies," he said in his soft, polite voice. "Would you mind joining us?"

"Take a look at this, Detective," Judith said, then repeated the same questions she'd put to Renie. "What do you think?"

Danny rubbed his chin. "You may be right. I'll go tell Winnie."

Winnie, Judith assumed, was Edwina's nickname. The cousins waited until the senior detective came out of the drawing room.

"Well, Mrs. Flynn," she said after she'd examined the

lamp and the floor, "Joe's knack seems to have rubbed off on you."

"I've had the opportunity to help him on a couple of cases," Judith said modestly. She didn't add that she'd solved a lot more on her own.

"I'll get Junior to take care of this right away," Edwina said, then put a hand on Judith's shoulder. "You're working your way up from honey, honey."

In the drawing room, Caroline had collected herself and then accounted for her whereabouts during the night. Edwina nodded after Danny summarized the young woman's statement.

"Good," Edwina said. "We'll talk to the servants now. You folks can go off and do whatever folks like you do. By the way, after we interview Mrs. Burgess, I'd like to talk to . . ." She took the notebook from Danny and flipped through the pages. "Bop, is it?" She looked at Wayne. "He's your son, isn't he, honey? Please let him know we want to see him here within the hour."

Wayne's eyes narrowed at Edwina. "Before I call my son or head for my office in town, I want to hear about this other so-called crime. You said earlier you'd tell us."

"I will," Edwina replied in an amiable tone. "Some time last night, Dr. Moss's home was entered. His office was rifled, his safe had been opened, and it appears that some of his records and papers were stolen. It's possible that the thief was the same person who murdered him."

Judith wasn't surprised.

Much to the family's dismay, Edwina had ordered Judith and Renie to stay at Creepers for at least the next twenty-four hours. She also warned the family not to leave the vicinity until further notice. Judith couldn't tell which directive angered them most.

With nothing better to do, the cousins poured themselves some coffee and retreated to the parlor. Edwina and Danny had assembled the staff in the dining room. Wayne had gone downtown where Evergreen Timber's head offices were located, Russ had headed for the clubhouse at the golf course, and Peggy and Dorothy had gone to their respective homes. When last seen, Caroline and Kenneth had been talking earnestly together in the drawing room. Bop still hadn't arrived.

"Edwina mentioned that Dr. Stevens phoned in the robbery report," Judith said, sitting in front of the empty fireplace. "Of course, it's his home, too. I suppose they had separate offices there. I wonder what time Dr. Stevens discovered the break-in?"

Renie took out her cigarettes, caught Judith's glare, and put them back. "It wasn't a break-in," she pointed out. "Edwina figured that the killer took Dr. Moss's keys, which is why they weren't on his person. What time did Dr. Stevens leave here?"

"Around one-thirty, maybe closer to two," Judith replied. "I have trouble recalling exact times and the sequence of events. So much happened so fast. But Dr. Stevens wasn't going straight home, remember? The hospital had just paged him."

"That's right," Renie agreed. "That widens the window of opportunity."

"Not really," Judith said. "The killer couldn't know Dr. Stevens would be paged. I'll bet whoever did it went straight to the doctors' place. It's not more than a few minutes from Creepers."

Renie didn't say anything right away. Finally, she regarded Judith over the rim of her coffee cup. "Okay, so who was the real victim?"

It was Judith's turn to become mute. At last, she gave a slow shake of her head. "I honestly don't know. Ever since the murder occurred, I've gone this way and that. My initial reaction was that it was a huge mistake. Look," she said, leaning forward in one of the matching chinoiserie armchairs, "the killer enters the house, or is already here. It's possible, if unlikely, that the killer followed Dr. Moss inside. Or maybe came in with him. He wouldn't suspect anything if it was someone he knew."

"I got it," Renie said with a droll expression. "The killer

is there, in the entry hall or by the staircase. Go on."

"Dr. Moss buzzes Mrs. Burgess. She turns on the lights and appears at the top of the stairs. Assuming the lamp was on, the killer unplugs it because he or she can't find the chain. It was tangled up, remember? Then the main downstairs switch is clicked off. It's right there, by that little round table. Didn't you see it?"

"No," Renie answered. "Not just now, but you're right."

"The killer then grabs whatever, maybe the lamp itself. Mrs. Burgess falls down the stairs. The killer attacks, but in the dark, he or she can't tell exactly who's getting smashed over the head. Even if a few seconds elapsed and the killer's eyes adjusted a bit, both the doctor and Leota were wearing dark clothing. It would be an easy mistake."

"Not if Leota was already on the floor," Renie pointed out.

"That's a problem," Judith conceded, "which is why I keep going back and forth. Certainly it's easy to think that Mrs. Burgess was the intended victim. But why go to Dr. Moss's house and steal his files? And which files were they? Something he kept on Leota and the alleged attempts at poisoning her?"

"Maybe," Renie suggested, "he'd become suspicious."

"In which case," Judith went on, "he'd have to be eliminated first, before he could point a finger at the would-be killer."

"Obviously, Mrs. Burgess still isn't safe."

"That's quite likely. Even if we weren't confined to Creepers, I doubt very much if Bev would want us to leave. She's probably over there in Egypt, worrying herself sick."

"She'll call today," Renie remarked. "Or I'll call her. Say, what about Joe and Bill and our mothers? How come we haven't heard from them? They must know about the murder and be pretty worried, too."

Judith nodded. "You're right. I should call Joe now." She glanced at the telephone on the mahogany end table. "I hate to do it. If he knows there's been a murder, instead of just an ailing old lady, he'll yell and bellow and insist I get the hell out of here. He might even pull rank and tell Edwina to send us home."

"That's a bad thing?" Renie said in a small voice.

"Yes, if Bev wants us here. That's why we came in the first place."

Renie ran her hand through her pixie haircut. "Why did I agree to do this? Why couldn't I be callous like everyone else and say no?"

"Because," Judith said as she dialed her home phone number, "you aren't callous. Underneath that prickly exterior, you have a heart of—Hi, Joe. How are you?"

"Jude-girl," Joe said, warmth running through his voice like honey on hot biscuits. "Has it ever been lonesome around here. When will you be home?"

Joe's reaction wasn't quite what Judith had expected. "Ah . . . tomorrow, maybe?"

"Tomorrow?" Joe's voice dropped a notch. "Not today?"

Judith offered Renie a puzzled shake of her head. "I told you it'd be a couple of days. Mrs. Burgess . . . still needs us," she added on a cautious note.

"I need you, too," Joe said, sounding glum. "But I'll survive. The guests have left for the day and the Rankerses have gone home. What should I do now?"

"Where's Phyliss?" Judith asked, referring to her daily help.

"Upstairs," Joe replied. "I keep my distance from her. I don't want to be saved by Phyliss Rackley. She's collecting for the missionaries in Minnesota."

"What missionaries?" Judith asked, increasingly baffled by Joe's lack of acknowledgment concerning the murder case.

"Who knows? You know Phyliss and her fundamentalist leanings. Her cousin Rip is one of the missionaries. He's saving souls in St. Paul."

"Good grief," Judith sighed. "Ignore her."

"I do. I will."

"How's Mother?" Judith asked, changing the subject.

"She went to St. Paul with cousin Rip." Joe sounded more cheerful.

"Joe . . ."

"She's fine." Joe paused. "Tomorrow, huh?"

"Probably," Judith said. "If you're at loose ends, why don't you clean out some of that old stuff in the basement? I'll call St. Vincent de Paul when I get home."

"I don't want to do that when you're not around," Joe objected. "I might toss the wrong stuff."

Judith suppressed a sigh. "What about the garage?"

"It's still there," Joe said blithely.

"I mean . . . Never mind. I'll call you tomorrow, okay?"

"Call later today. I'll be here." Joe had again turned glum.

"I will if I get a chance," Judith said, then added, "I love you."

"I hope so," Joe said on a wistful note.

Judith put the phone down and gazed at Renie. "He doesn't know about the murder. How can that be? He reads the paper every morning."

Renie had gotten up and was pacing the floor. "There's no point calling Bill or my mother. We all take the evening paper, and neither of them watches TV or listens to the radio during the day. Maybe Joe was busy helping with the guests and hasn't seen the paper yet."

Judith shook her head. "The guests are gone. He's bored. I don't get it."

Renie halted in mid-step. "I do. These people aren't like the rest of us unwashed masses. Wayne Burgess—and Leota, too—have the clout to keep this story out of the media. What do you want to bet that Wayne's on inter-locking boards, with enough influence to manage a total blackout?"

Judith considered Renie's words. "You're right. When we were at Mountain Goat Lodge, those phone company executives thought they could keep the lid on until things got completely out of control."

"It's crazy, it's wrong, but I'll bet that's what happened,"

Renie said, coming back to sit down by Judith. "These are the privileged people, and they don't play by the same rules as the rest of us."

"That's frightening," Judith said softly, "to think that the super-rich can get away with something like that."

"It's not the super-rich so much as the super-elite," Renie said. "The nouveaux riches, even with all their money and power, couldn't pull this off. For one thing, they're usually in high-profile businesses and actually seek the limelight as a professional tool. If something like this happened with them, I doubt they could turn it off. They need the media. But an old family like the Burgesses or the other people who live in Sunset Cliffs are icons. Often, they can avoid publicity."

Judith gave Renie a long, hard look. "But even they can't get away with murder."

Renie grinned at her cousin. "Not if you can help it."

Judith stood up. "Let's explore some more. How about this tower? I found the staircase last night. It's across from the library."

Renie was game. "Okay, let's go."

The stone steps made a semicircle around the first-floor parlor before the cousins encountered an open door. Peeking inside, they saw that the room was empty, though there were signs of recent occupancy.

"Kenneth's hideout," Judith remarked, taking in a stack of magazines and newspapers devoted to wildlife preservation. "This is kind of cozy. I wonder why Caroline was so terrified of staying in the tower?"

"Because she's nuts?" Renie retorted.

Judith smiled, but her attention was on the second-floor room itself. Three tall, narrow windows stood half-open, the morning breeze stirring white lace curtains. There were two single beds, one of which was unmade, a small fireplace, a bureau, and a dresser. The bathroom and a well-stocked closet were set into the wall that was attached to the rest of the house. A third door opened to reveal what had been the nursery where a rocking horse, a dollhouse,

Matchbox cars, a train set, and other toys were still strewn around the room.

The cousins proceeded up to the third floor. The door at the top of the landing was closed, but unlocked.

"Nobody home," Judith said as they looked at the tidy space with its single bed and other furnishings in the same dark, heavy style as the pieces on the floor below. There was another bathroom, an empty closet, and a door leading to a room that held tables, chairs, a chalkboard, a globe, and shelves of books.

"The schoolroom," Judith said, closing the door. She stood by the bureau, tapping one foot. "Okay, this is— was—Caroline's room when she visited Creepers. There's just one bed. Down one flight there are two beds which must be where Kenneth and Bop slept. I'll bet that in the previous generation, Wayne had this room, and Peggy and Bev shared the one below."

"An excellent deduction," Renie remarked. "So what?"

Judith didn't answer right away. "How many floors did you see in the tower from outside, not counting the daylight basement?"

Renie thought through the question. "Four. This tower is taller than the rest of the house. The top floor had dormer windows."

"Right. The stairs go up another flight, but not to the attic, which first occurred to me," Judith said. "What's missing in this picture?"

"TV?" Renie answered.

Judith grinned at her cousin. "No, really, coz. Think."

"I give up," Renie said, chagrined.

"The nanny's quarters," Judith responded. "Hasn't it dawned on you that all the Burgess offspring use French words to refer to Leota? *Maman*, *Gran'mère*, and so on. The name Suzette is French, and Mrs. Burgess told me that before she married Walter Burgess, Suzette had been a nanny here. So where did Suzette and subsequent nannies stay?"

"I love a hint like that," Renie said, grinning back at Judith. "On the fourth floor."

"Exactly. Let's go up there."

The cousins climbed the last flight of stairs. The door to the room on the fourth floor was padlocked. The padlock itself was rusty, and cobwebs clung to the door.

Judith looked at Renie. "So far, Creepers seems to have an open-door policy. But not up here. I wonder why?"

A sharp pounding noise startled the cousins before Renie could answer. They turned at the top of the stairs, but could see nothing unusual.

"It came from further down," Judith said, descending one step at a time.

"Here?" Renie asked, pausing at the third-floor landing.

"Maybe," Judith allowed, then jumped as the noise sounded again, this time closer.

"Go away!" a harsh voice cried.

"Who is *that*?" Judith whispered.

"Go away!" the voice repeated, louder and more shrill.

"Good idea," said Renie, scampering around Judith and starting down the stairs. "Oops!" Renie missed a step and almost fell.

Judith, sensing but not seeing another presence, followed on her cousin's heels. Then she stopped, listening to see if she could determine where the harassing voice was coming from.

"Somebody really wants us out of here," she murmured.

"I told you," Renie whispered back, "that's fine with me. Let's go."

But Judith still waited, her ears alert.

The cousins heard nothing except the wind, moaning in the tower.

TEN

"NOW WHAT?" RENIE demanded as they reached the ground floor and leaned against the wall in the passageway between the tower door and the library.

Judith shook her head. "I don't know. It sounded more like a woman than a man."

"But no one I could recognize," Renie said, finally catching her breath. "Of course whoever it was sort of shrieked. That could distort the voice."

Taking a last look at the door to the tower, which Judith had firmly closed behind them, she started for the main hall. "It could have come from the nursery, Kenneth's room, even the schoolroom. I couldn't get any sense of where it originated. It almost seemed to float."

"Brrr," Renie said with a shiver. "Let's not get fanciful, coz. I think we can deduce that we're not wanted around here."

"All the more reason to stick around," Judith said. "Somebody may feel we're onto something. In fact, we'd better check on our charge."

On their way through the entry hall they spotted Bop, heading for the door. He stopped and gave the cousins a lopsided grin.

"You sure picked a weird time to visit Creepers," he

declared. "Poor old *Grandmaman*. She thinks the killer was trying to put out *her* lights."

"Do you think so?" Judith asked.

Bop shrugged. He was wearing his pizza delivery uniform, complete with a red cap atop his red hair. "Who'd want to kill old Doc?"

"Somebody did, though," Judith responded. "By the way, Bop, does the name Suzette mean anything to you?"

"Suzette?" Bop's forehead wrinkled. "Did I date her?"

"I doubt it," Judith said. "She was a nanny here before your grandmother married your grandfather."

"I like older women," Bop said, then grinned some more. "Maybe not that old. Suzette, huh? I've heard the name, but I don't know anything about her. Should I?"

"Mentioning her seems to scare the wits out of your cousin Caroline," Judith remarked.

Bop shrugged again. "What wits? I didn't know Carrie had any. Everything scares her. One time she hung up her bathrobe on a clothesrack and woke up during the night, convinced a rapist was lurking in the corner. She got a knife from someplace and ruined a lot of chenille. Carrie's really strange."

"And Kenneth?" Judith prompted.

Bop laughed. "He's weird, too. My crazy cousins, I call them. But not to their faces. It'd make them cry. They both inherited some serious short circuits. Hey, gotta run. The pizza palace opens ten minutes from now, at eleven-thirty."

"You talked to the detectives?" Judith asked before Bop could get out through the front door.

"Yeah, not that I could tell them anything," Bop replied. "I spent the night at my folks' place. My apartment has a gas leak. See you."

"Bop," Renie said under her breath. "Semi-normal. I can guess why he hasn't gone into the family business."

"You're right, coz," Judith said. "If Maxwell Burgess handed over the company reins to Walter, and Walter passed them along to Wayne, why isn't Bop the heir apparent? I figure he's around thirty."

"Peggy told us why," Renie replied. "She said he wasn't suited for the task."

"I thought maybe she was being prejudiced," Judith said as they climbed the stairs. "Kenneth and Caroline certainly aren't suited for it, either."

"Which is why Wayne won't retire until he has to," Renie noted.

Nurse Fritz opened the door of the master suite and took one look at Renie. "Go away," she said and slammed the door.

"Butt," Renie muttered. "Shall I disappear?"

Judith grimaced. "I don't know. It's too bad you and the nurse didn't hit it off."

Renie was wearing a belligerent look. "Hit it off? Nurse Blitz is lucky I didn't hit *her*."

Judith stared at the closed door. "Maybe I should have my head examined."

"Probably. You really don't think I'm going to apologize, do you?"

"I spoke literally," Judith said. "I mean have the bump on my head examined. By a nurse."

"In other words," Renie said dryly, "I should disappear."

"Do you mind?" Judith looked apologetic.

"Of course I do," Renie said, heading for the cousins' suite. "I was the one who was invited here in the first place. When I talk to Bev, I'm going to tell her about Nurse Titz. I'll bet she'll put a flea in her mother's ear."

Judith knocked again. This time, it took quite a while for the nurse to come to the door. When she did, she peered out warily.

"I'm alone," Judith said with a sheepish smile.

"I should hope so," Fritz said, letting Judith in. "What is it?"

Having gained access to Mrs. Burgess's sitting room, Judith decided to skip the matter of the bump on her head. "I told Mrs. Burgess I'd be back to see her after breakfast. Have the detectives come and gone?"

"Yes, just minutes ago," Fritz responded, still regarding

Judith with suspicion. "Are you quite sure you're a family friend?"

Judith, who was almost as tall, if not as broad, as Nurse Fritz, stood within six inches of the other woman. "What did Mrs. Burgess tell you?"

"Very little," Fritz replied. "Mrs. Burgess isn't a common gossip."

The phrase, with the tiniest hint of resentment, caught Judith's attention. "You're right, she isn't. That makes it difficult, I imagine. I mean, if you have to pass the time with a patient who doesn't chat. I don't blame you for not coming when Mrs. Burgess sprained her ankle last fall."

Nurse Fritz bridled at the suggestion, reminding Judith of a large grouse, all puffed up with wings aflapping. "That wasn't my reason. I'm a professional. I never let a patient's idiosyncrasy deter me from accepting an assignment."

"Goodness," Judith said, trying to look aghast, "I didn't mean that. I assumed that you had another patient, perhaps one with whom the hours wouldn't drag."

The nurse seemed taken aback. "Well, yes, that was what happened."

"You'd think," Judith went on in a musing tone, "that this huge old house would have heard and seen so much over the last century. It seems a shame that a family like the Burgesses won't share its tragedies and triumphs, especially with someone like you who has been with them during their darkest hours."

"You hear things," Fritz said with an ambiguous expression.

"You should," Judith averred. "A nurse is a natural confidante. She's there in life and death situations. Who else can be trusted in such difficult times?"

"As I mentioned," Fritz said, preening a bit, "some things *do* come out. It certainly hasn't been all roses. Take those grandchildren, for instance. Ten years ago when I was caring for Mr. Walter all those months, they were barely out of their teens. Kenneth and Caroline kept dropping out of one expensive college after the other. I don't think either of them ever got a degree. And then Bop—such a dreadful nickname, so undignified—refused to go to college at all. Finally, his father coaxed—or should I say bribed?—him into attending the local university to major in business. Naturally, I assumed he was being groomed to follow in his father's footsteps at Evergreen Timber. Not so. He flunked out and enrolled at Sunset Community College just up the road. I never did hear if he graduated, but he certainly never went back to the university."

"My, my," Judith said in a doleful tone. "Think of squandering the chance at such fine schools. Have they no ambition?"

"Not when it comes to business," Fritz replied. "Unless you consider that pizza parlor a business, which I do not. It's a whim."

"Is it a success?" Judith asked innocently.

Nurse Fritz pulled at her long lower lip. "Well, now. I live over on the other side of the highway, so I go by there regularly. Bop opened the place about four years ago. I must admit that it always seems busy. I believe that it isn't delivery only, but has a small restaurant as well."

"Maybe," Judith suggested, "that's what Bop wanted. To have a successful business on his own."

"He hardly started from the ground up." Fritz sniffed. "After Mr. Walter died, he left each of the children and grandchildren a rather hefty sum in trust." The nurse leaned closer to Judith and lowered her voice. "I really shouldn't discuss this, but I know for a fact that Kenneth, Caroline, and Bop received at least a million dollars apiece. The parents got considerably more."

"My," Judith said, "that's a nice amount. What did Kenneth and Caroline do with their share?"

Before Nurse Fritz could respond, a knock sounded at the door. "Now who could that be?" the nurse asked in an irritated voice.

Judith didn't recognize the man in his forties with the shaved head. He was wearing striped coveralls and a denim jacket. Nurse Fritz knew him, however, and reluctantly let him into the sitting room.

"What is it, Jeepers?" she asked, still sounding irritable.

"It's these," Jeepers replied, handing over a bunch of keys. "I found them stuck in the pool drain just now."

Nurse Fritz stared at the keys. "I'll see to whom they belong," she said.

"Thanks," Jeepers responded and left.

Judith thought she knew who owned the keys, but decided not to say anything. Glancing at her watch, she asked Nurse Fritz if she could see Mrs. Burgess for a few minutes.

"Of course," the nurse replied. "Indeed, you'd better go in right now. It's well after eleven-thirty, and her program comes on at noon."

"That's what I thought," Judith said with a smile. "Shall I show her the keys?"

"Why not?" Fritz handed them to Judith, apparently glad to be relieved of the responsibility. "Really, people are so careless."

Mrs. Burgess had changed into a cream-colored bed jacket and matching negligee. Her hair had been combed and makeup had been subtly applied. She no longer looked as tired and pinched as she had earlier in the morning.

"I was wondering where you and Serena had gone," she said with the hint of a twinkle in her gaze. "In fact, where *is* Serena? Her eye's not bothering her, I hope."

Judith glanced at the door to the sitting room to make sure it had been firmly shut. "It's not the eye per se," Judith said with a smile. "It's that she and Nurse Fritz don't see eye to eye."

"Oh, bother Nurse Fritz," Mrs. Burgess said with a wave of her hand. "Millicent is a very rigid person. When she's on a case, she thinks she runs the whole show. I'll speak to her about Serena. What's that in your hand?"

Judith gave the keys to Mrs. Burgess. "Jeepers found these when he drained the pool just now. Do you recognize them?"

The old lady stared at the large ring with perhaps a dozen

or more keys of various shapes and sizes. "No, not really. Should I?"

"I wonder if they belonged to Dr. Moss," Judith said. "His keys were missing when the police searched his body."

Mrs. Burgess shuddered. "I can't tell you how awful I feel about his death. Aaron has been part of my life since I came to Creepers as a bride. I feel like a little of me has died with him." She gave Judith a pathetic little smile. "Please don't think me foolish, but in the last few years, I've lost so many people I cared about."

"Of course not," Judith assured her hostess. "Sixty years is a long time to know someone."

"Yes, it is." Mrs. Burgess leaned back against the pillows. "You might try those keys on the front door, then ask Dr. Stevens to see if they fit his house and office. Goodness, I can't think why anyone would want to get into Dr. Moss's office. The detectives just told me about the theft when they interviewed me a few minutes ago."

Judith sat down in the chair beside the bed. "I hope they didn't tire you."

Mrs. Burgess sighed. "No, it was reasonably brief. Goodness, where do all these people come from? Is this the result of equal opportunity employment?"

"Perhaps," Judith allowed, "along with ambition and hard work. So far, Detectives Jefferson and Wong seem very competent."

"I suppose." Mrs. Burgess seemed uncertain. "They have their work cut out for them. I must confess, I was very little help. All I remember is seeing Dr. Moss standing near the foot of the stairs, and then the lights went out. I fell, and must have fainted. The next thing I knew, you and Serena were trying to pull Dr. Moss off of me. And then I fainted again." She shook her head at the memory.

"You're sure you saw no one else?" Judith asked.

Briefly, Mrs. Burgess's eyes closed. "No one except Dr. Moss. He was quite alone."

"This may sound crazy," Judith said with an apologetic

smile, "but do you recall if that table lamp in the entry hall was turned on?"

Mrs. Burgess's carefully plucked eyebrows arched slightly. "It should have been. We leave it on at night in case anyone is moving about on the main floor. We also leave a few other lights on in the hallways, especially near the kitchen."

"But did you notice if it was on?" Judith persisted.

"No. Everything happened too quickly. Why do you ask?"

"Oh—no particular reason," Judith said, then grew thoughtful. "Did the detectives tell you if they have any idea who called Dr. Moss in the first place?"

"They didn't say." Mrs. Burgess adjusted the marabou collar on her bed jacket. "But he wouldn't have come here at that time of night without being summoned. He'd already stopped by during the day."

Again, Judith was silent for a few moments. "Mrs. Burgess," she finally said, "do you still feel that you're in danger?"

The old lady flinched. "Yes. More so than ever. You see," she said, turning a bleak face to Judith, "I trusted Aaron—Dr. Moss—implicitly. He would never cause me any harm, either physical or emotional. Somehow, as long as he was still here, I felt as if there was a buffer between me and whatever evil lay beyond. Now he's dead, and I don't know whom to trust."

"Not even your family?" Judith asked in a dismayed voice.

Mrs. Burgess turned away. "Least of all my family."

Dr. Stevens arrived a moment later to check on his newly acquired patient. Nurse Fritz joined him while Judith lingered in the sitting room. She knew he wouldn't stay long because Mrs. Burgess's soap opera was about to air.

Since Judith had last seen him, Theo Stevens looked older and more drawn. "How's the ankle?" she asked as he came out of the bedroom.

"It's still swollen," Dr. Stevens replied. "Nurse will keep icing it."

Judith produced the keys. "Do these belong to Dr. Moss?"

Dr. Stevens took them from Judith. "Yes. Where were they?"

Judith explained about Jeepers and the pool drain. "Doesn't that suggest," she said, "that the killer returned here to dump the keys?"

"Certainly." Dr. Stevens's expression was grim. "Which means the killer has access to the house and grounds."

"I think that can be assumed," Judith said.

"Why bring them back?" Dr. Stevens remarked, frowning as he pocketed the keys. "The killer could have thrown them anywhere into the woods around here. Or maybe not," he said. "I saw uniformed deputies combing the vicinity when I drove into Sunset Cliffs."

"You should turn those keys over to the police," Judith said. "Any fingerprints were probably destroyed when the keys were thrown in the pool, not to mention Jeepers and the two of us touching them. Still, the detectives must be told where they were found."

"Oh. Of course." Dr. Stevens looked a bit sheepish. "I'll do that on my way out."

"By the way, what time did you discover the theft?" Judith asked, hoping her voice sounded casual.

"Around four-fifteen this morning," Dr. Stevens replied, then smiled at Judith. "Are you playing detective, Mrs. Flynn?"

"Sort of," Judith admitted, then told Dr. Stevens about the summons that Renie had received from Beverly Ohashi. "It seems that Mrs. Burgess is still fearful for her life."

"I don't blame her," Dr. Stevens said, looking at his watch. "But there are deputies around the grounds. That should reassure her."

"This is a very high-profile murder investigation," Judith said. "Heads will roll if it's not solved promptly."

Dr. Stevens tapped his watch. "My head will roll if I

don't get to the Carruthers house at Beaux Arts. Mrs. Carruthers is having another asthma attack."

Judith followed Dr. Stevens out into the hall. "Does she live in Sunset Cliffs, too?"

"Yes, about a half-mile from here. They have remarkable gardens, though no one outside of the community gets to see them." He switched his leather briefcase from one hand to the other as he started down the stairs. "It's a pity, isn't it? The exclusiveness, the snobbery. I wonder how long I can last in this environment?"

"Do you want to?" Judith asked with a wry smile.

Dr. Stevens grimaced. "I have to," he said, and moved briskly down the stairs.

Peggy Hillman, carrying an overnight case and a garment bag, crossed paths with the doctor between the entry hall and the staircase area. After a brief exchange of greetings, she headed upstairs.

"I see we can't throw you out," she said to Judith, though not without humor.

"I'm afraid not," Judith responded. "It looks like you're moving in."

"I am." Peggy crossed over to the door just down the hall from Mrs. Burgess's suite. "I intend to keep an eye on *Maman*. Maybe we should've taken her fears more seriously."

"She's still very worried," Judith noted.

"Who can blame her?" Peggy set the overnight case and the garment bag down on the floor. "This door always sticks. Kenyon should oil it. Of course somebody should oil Kenyon. He creaks worse than anything else in this house. Ah—there we go." She picked up her belongings and turned back to Judith. "I understand Carrie has the room on the other side of *Maman*. I prefer it, but I guess I'm stuck with Papa's old quarters."

"Your father?" Judith said and saw Peggy nod. "He and your mother had separate bedrooms?"

"It's a family tradition, going back to the nineteenth century. I'm not saying that both bedrooms were always used,"

Peggy said with a wink. "Of course it was a necessity when Papa became so ill. At one time, there was a connecting door and a little hall between the two suites, but that was sealed off years ago when Papa was still married to my real mother. See you later." Peggy scooted inside and closed the door with her hip.

Judith remembered the small office just off Mrs. Burgess's suite. As she walked back to her own rooms, she wondered why the common door had been closed off. Age wouldn't have been a factor. If memory served, the first Mrs. Burgess had been a young woman when she died.

She was still thinking about Walter and Margaret Burgess when she found Renie smoking and doing a crossword puzzle from the morning paper.

"I filched this," Renie said, pointing to the rest of the newspaper sections. "We were right. No news is good news for the Burgesses."

Judith glanced at the front page, which displayed headlines from foreign capitals, Washington, D.C., and, on the local scene, the previous night's windstorm. "Amazing," she remarked. "But if the killer is caught, the trial will have to be covered by the press. Then all this secrecy is for naught."

Renie put out her cigarette and set the crossword aside. "What if the killer isn't caught? What if the family knows who did it, and they're closing ranks?"

"Coz." Judith plopped down next to Renie on the settee. "That's a terrible, if plausible, idea." She made a face at the three cigarette butts Renie had extinguished in a heart-shaped Belleek candy dish. "You know, I really wish you'd quit smoking and go back to eating like a hog."

"I may have to, if they keep raising the price of cigarettes," Renie said. "A carton costs more than a prime rib. By the way, what did you think of the interviews this morning with the family?"

Judith got up and emptied the candy dish in the fireplace. "I found it odd that the detectives didn't talk to each person separately," she said, sitting back down. "I wonder if that was a ploy to see how the two couples would answer in front of each other. Frankly, I didn't think they came off too well, especially Peggy and Russ."

"I agree," Renie said. "Peggy's story about going to the mall and stopping for a snack was particularly lame."

"Peggy moved into Creepers. She's worried about her mother." Judith remembered then to tell Renie about Dr. Moss's keys, and her conversations with Nurse Fritz, Dr. Stevens, and Mrs. Burgess. "I found it odd that Fritz knew so much about the money that Walter Burgess left for the grandchildren. She would have finished her assignment here when he died, and the will probably wasn't read right away."

"Maybe the old gargoyle stayed on to care for Leota," Renie suggested. "Widowhood might have temporarily sunk her."

Judith looked skeptical. "Leota knew her husband was dying. She's a very strong woman. I doubt that she collapsed after his death. It must have come as a relief—for both of them." Moving restlessly on the settee, Judith continued. "I keep wondering if the reason for Dr. Moss's murder goes back in time. Suzette's name keeps surfacing, and never in a positive way. Then, when I talked to Peggy just now, I realized how little the family speaks of Margaret Burgess. What happened to her?"

Renie shrugged. "She died when Peggy and Wayne were very young. They probably don't remember her. Cancer, I always assumed, though Bev never said so."

"Why would you seal up the door between your bedroom and your husband's?" Judith asked.

"Because Bill wanted to sleep in the closet with his favorite pair of orthopedic shoes?" Renie made a face at Judith. "Come on, coz, you know we don't have separate bedrooms."

"You know what I mean," Judith chided. "You'd do that if you didn't want to have sex."

"Maybe," Renie said, growing serious, "Margaret Burgess didn't want to have any more kids. Or maybe she couldn't. Birth control wasn't so reliable sixty-odd years ago."

"So my mother tells me when she calls me The Great Mistake," Judith said dryly.

"You're speculating," Renie said. "About Walter and Margaret, I mean."

"I guess. It's made my head hurt," Judith complained, reaching for her handbag to get her pillbox. "Oh, rats. I forgot, I took the last two aspirin this morning when I got up. We'll have to go out to the car. There's some in the first aid kit."

"They must have aspirin in the house," Renie said. "You should have asked Dr. Stevens."

"We could use some fresh air," Judith said, checking to see if her raincoat was dry.

"Okay." Renie sighed. "Get my coat while you're at it."

The cousins were out in the hall before they realized they'd have to ask the housekeeper to open the garage. At the bottom of the stairs, they met Kenyon, who was teetering around the crime scene tape.

"So ugly," he murmured in a disgusted tone. "It detracts from the décor, don't you think?"

"The body detracted a lot more," Renie replied.

Kenyon didn't seem to hear the remark. "So tiresome," he wheezed. "All this coming and going. By the time I get to the front door, the caller has gone to the back. The family knows better, though sometimes they forget, too. I do wish the police would leave us alone."

Just as Kenyon finished speaking, the front door opened. It was Kenneth, holding a baby raccoon.

"Is that a cat, Mr. Kenneth?" Kenyon asked, squinting at the animal.

"No," Kenneth replied, "it's a raccoon. I found him out by the greenhouse. He's hurt his left back paw."

The animal growled, swiped at Kenneth's nose, and jumped onto the floor. "Oww!" Kenneth wailed, as blood trickled down his face. "He scratched me. Doesn't he realize I'm trying to help him?"

"It doesn't look like it," Renie said as the raccoon ran off down the hall in the direction of the kitchen. "He doesn't seem to be limping."

Frantically, Kenneth tried to stanch the blood with a handkerchief even as he gazed every which way around the staircase area and the entry hall. "I need a cage, Kenyon. Hurry, please."

The butler cupped his right ear. "A what, Mr. Kenneth? Did you mislay your key again?"

"I . . . need . . . a . . . cage," Kenneth repeated, huffing and puffing between words. "And a bandage."

Screams erupted from the rear of the house. Judith and Renie whirled around and started down the hall. The last words they heard from Kenyon were, "I didn't quite catch that . . ."

Edna was cowering in a corner, her face white as a sheet. Ada was wielding a marble rolling pin, and had managed to box in the raccoon between the work island and a large carton. With one swift move, she overturned the carton and trapped the animal.

"Who let this beast in here?" she demanded, still waving the rolling pin. "I'm telling those policemen who are all over the grounds to take this thing away and shoot it."

"He belongs to Kenneth," Judith said. "He'll take care of it."

Ada backed away and set the rolling pin down on the island counter. "He'd better do it quick. That creature is trying to escape."

Indeed, the carton was moving, unfortunately toward Edna, who screamed again.

"Oh, be quiet!" Ada shouted, putting a firm hand on the carton.

"I think I'm going to faint," Edna said in a weak voice.

"Don't," Renie said. "It'll take Kenyon thirty minutes to get a cage and another twenty to fetch the smelling salts. You'll be devoured alive by the time he gets here."

"Ooh!" Edna's knees buckled and she fell to the floor in a heap.

"I don't believe this," Renie declared in a sharp, annoyed tone. "What's wrong with these people? We have raccoons marching through our yard all the time."

"Edna's absolutely hopeless," her sister said, as vexed as Renie. "Let her lie there. She'll come 'round. She always does."

Kenneth appeared with a large adhesive bandage plastered across his nose. "Where's Roscoe?" he asked, his head jerking in every direction.

"Roscoe?" Judith echoed.

"The raccoon. I already named him." Kenneth spotted Edna on the floor. "Did she fall on top of him? Is he all right?"

"Here," Ada said, slapping at the carton, which was still wriggling under her hand. "Get this thing out of here right now. How many times have I told you not to bring stray animals into the house? You know how they upset your grandmother."

"I don't have a cage," Kenneth said. "Kenyon's getting it."

"Then turn this box into a cage," Ada ordered. "Just take this animal away."

Kenyon appeared in the kitchen, bearing not a cage but a bottle of smelling salts. "Where is whoever it is?" he asked vaguely.

Kenneth, Ada, and the cousins stared at him. "You were supposed to get a cage," Kenneth said in a helpless voice.

"Oh." The butler spotted Edna. "There she is. I'll take care of this, Mr. Kenneth."

"I'm leaving now," Renie announced and walked out of the kitchen.

Judith decided that her cousin had the right idea. "Let's let them solve that problem," she said as they started down the hall. "Now where do you suppose we might find Sarah Kenyon?"

Renie paused where the hall opened onto another, narrower corridor. "We've never been this way. Let's check."

The first door was ajar. The cousins peeked inside and

saw an old-fashioned breakfast nook that looked as if it could accommodate eight or ten people. The second door revealed a bathroom. The third was shut tight.

Judith knocked. "Who is it?" came the response.

"Sarah?" Judith breathed.

Renie nodded. "It's Mrs. Jones and Mrs. Flynn," she called out. "May we come in?"

The housekeeper's office was much larger and more fully appointed than the small room off Mrs. Burgess's suite. Sarah Kenyon sat in front of the latest generation of computers, a telephone at her ear. She signaled for the cousins to wait.

"The chateau chart for the eighty-nines is incomplete," she said into the receiver. "You've included nothing from the area around Chambord. Please e-mail me at once or we'll go elsewhere to replenish our cellars. Thank you."

Sarah hung up and shook her head. "These wine merchants. They've become so careless since all the young people fancy themselves connoisseurs. Forty years ago, people of that age and class were lucky to drink beer off the grocery shelves."

Judith gazed around the office, which couldn't have been in greater contrast to the rest of the house. Everything was high tech and cutting edge, including the compartmentalized desk and the adjustable chair.

"This looks very efficient," she said.

"It is." Sarah offered the cousins a thin smile. "I couldn't work any other way."

"Did you hear all the commotion a few minutes ago?" Judith asked.

Sarah looked puzzled. "No. But then I probably wouldn't. This house has such thick walls and I've had this room soundproofed. What happened?"

Judith explained about the raccoon. Sarah dismissed the incident with a wave of her hand. "Kenneth is always trying to bring some animal into Creepers. Once, when he was around ten, he came home with an emu that had escaped from the zoo. Emus are very large, but they can't fly. Curious, isn't it?"

"Very," Judith said. "Mrs. Kenyon, we wanted to ask—"

"Ms. Kenyon," Sarah broke in, though she said it with another faint smile. "I'm not married."

"Oh?" Judith's expression betrayed her surprise.

Sarah laughed. "Did you think Kenyon was my husband?" She laughed some more. "He's my father. I was virtually raised here at Creepers."

"Really," Judith remarked. "Was that a good experience?"

The smile died on Sarah's lips. "It was my only experience. There was no other way."

For once, Judith was at a loss for words. So, apparently was Renie, who was examining the fax machine. "We have to get in the garage," she announced. "Can we use that automatic opener?"

Sarah looked apologetic. "You could if I knew where it was. I couldn't find it this morning when I first arrived in my office. That's why I've been on the phone all day. I wasn't able to get the car to run errands."

"Who else would have used it?" Judith asked.

"No one," Sarah replied. "Since my father stopped driving, I'm the only one who takes the cars out. Mrs. Burgess never learned to drive and the rest of the family have their own transportation."

"How strange," Judith commented. "Did you tell the police?"

Sarah regarded Judith with surprise. "No. Why should I?"

"Well . . . with the murder and all," Judith said a trifle lamely.

"I don't think anyone tried to escape in the Seville or the Rolls," Sarah said in an amused tone. She opened a drawer on the right side of the desk. "I always keep the opener right here, by my purse, and— Good heavens, here it is. Am I losing my mind?"

"You were upset last night after Dr. Moss was killed,"

Judith said in her most sympathetic voice. "Maybe this morning, you still were. Murder has that effect on people."

"That's a glib explanation," Sarah responded, "but I don't have a better one. Here," she said, handing the device to Judith. "Just bring it back as soon as you're finished."

All was quiet in the hallway as the cousins headed for the front door. Around the side of the house, they encountered a bored-looking Deputy Sorensen.

"How's it going?" Judith asked with a bright smile.

Sorensen snorted. "They could make better use of my time by letting me chase some crooks. What do they expect me to find, some guy running out of the house with a bag marked 'Loot'? This was an inside job if I ever saw one."

"You're right," Judith agreed. "Have the searchers found anything?"

"I couldn't say if they had," Sorensen replied. "But they haven't."

Judith kept smiling as she and Renie proceeded to the garage. The remote worked efficiently, and a moment later they were inside the large, neat area where only three cars were sheltered in four stalls.

"Wow," Judith breathed, "look at that Rolls. It must be a classic. Thirties, maybe?"

Renie studied the dark blue automobile, which shone like a sapphire. "Yes. A Silver Cloud, I think. That Cadillac's pretty spiffy, too."

Judith glanced at the big black sedan, which was also a vintage model. "Beautiful. Joe would love to see these cars."

The Subaru looked like a foster child as it stood in the third spot. Judith patted it with affection, then opened the trunk and got out the first aid kit. Renie, meanwhile, was wandering around by the tool bench, which was as well outfitted as a small service station.

"I wonder if Kenyon worked on these cars before he couldn't see so well," Renie remarked, moving toward the empty stall. "Somebody must have used all these tools. Oops!" She took a quick step backward. "Hey, coz, look.

I almost stepped in this puddle of oil. It seems fresh."

Judith replaced the first aid kit and closed the trunk. "Let's see." She peered down at the floor. "You're right. There isn't much of it, but it certainly hasn't been here long enough to saturate the cement." She stood up and gazed at the rest of the floor. "No tire tracks of any kind, no other oil stains. This spot looks as if it hasn't been used lately."

"Except for that," Renie said, pointing her foot at the small slick. "Like maybe last night?"

"Like that."

"Like the killer?" Renie said.

Judith was looking grim. "Also like that."

ELEVEN

As THE COUSINS went up to their suite, they heard shouting from somewhere along the hall. When they reached the second floor, they stopped to determine the source.

"It's coming from Mrs. Burgess's room," Judith said in alarm. "We'd better see what's happening."

Nurse Fritz was in the sitting room, her stiff white cap askew and her hands over her ears. She blanched when she saw Judith and Renie. "You'd better leave," she said, speaking in an abnormally loud voice. "This is a private quarrel."

"Quarrel?" Judith said. "It sounds like a knock-down-drag-out fight to me. Is Mrs. Burgess okay?"

"What?" Fritz cupped one of her ears.

Judith and Renie brushed past the nurse just as Kenneth came hurtling through the bedroom door.

"You can't do this to me!" he screamed, shaking a fist in the direction of his grandmother. "I can call a lawyer, too!" He gave Judith a hard shove and rushed out of the master suite.

"Well, I never!" Fritz declared.

Judith was already at Mrs. Burgess's bedside. The old lady had gone completely white under her makeup and was breathing heavily.

"Get in here, Twitz," Renie said, motioning from the

doorway. "Your patient is having the fan-tods."

"The what?" Fritz gasped.

"That's what we call it in our family," Renie said calmly. "You'd better earn your pay."

With an acid glance at Renie, Nurse Fritz went to Mrs. Burgess. "Are we distressed this afternoon?"

"Of course we are," Mrs. Burgess burst out, her voice shaking. "Where is my television remote? That wretched boy turned off my program!"

"But Mrs. Burgess," the nurse protested, checking her watch, "it's two minutes after one. Your show is over."

"My show wasn't over when Kenneth turned off the TV," Mrs. Burgess asserted. "There was almost ten minutes to go. How shall I find out what happened to Tiffany and the bogus drum major from the Ohio State marching band?"

"Tune in tomorrow," Renie said, sliding the remote out from under the bed.

The old lady gave Renie a withering look. "On tomorrow's episode, they may switch to Elliott trapped in that hot air balloon, or Dora May, out at the old Johnson farm with Uncle Jasper, who's not her real uncle, and in fact, isn't even Uncle—" Mrs. Burgess stopped, frowning at Nurse Fritz. "Where's Edna? Where's my luncheon tray?"

"I'll check," Fritz said, and left the room, her starched uniform looking a trifle limp.

"You're certain you feel okay?" Judith asked.

Mrs. Burgess sighed. "Yes, yes. But that set-to with Kenneth was most unpleasant."

"Was it about the raccoon?" Renie inquired.

The old lady's eyes narrowed. "You know about the raccoon? Well, yes, it was, in a way. Kenneth is so obsessed with animals. I hope he turned that creature out into the woods where it belongs. I simply won't allow them in the house. Why, he once brought a billy goat right into this very room. Imagine!"

Nurse Fritz returned to the bedroom. "Your tray will be up in just a few minutes. Edna had some sort of spell, but she's fine now."

"Edna." Mrs. Burgess shook her head. "Such a nervous person, so easily upset. She needs more spunk."

A knock sounded from the sitting room. Nurse Fritz trudged off again. "It's Kenyon," she announced. "Mr. Gibbons is here."

Mrs. Burgess scowled. "I thought I told him to come at two," she said, more to herself than to the cousins. "Very well, send him in. Shoo, everyone. You, too, Fritz. Have Edna bring up a big pot of coffee and an extra cup."

Kenyon was holding the door open for a tall, spare man of sixty. He wore a dark business suit and carried a briefcase. A hawklike nose dominated his face, and he seemed to have no lips. Nodding to the cousins, he passed noiselessly through the sitting room and entered the bedchamber.

"Close the door, Gaylord," Mrs. Burgess commanded.

Gaylord Gibbons did as he was told, but before the door was completely shut, Judith saw Mrs. Burgess reach for the drawer in the nightstand.

"Don't tell me," Judith said to Nurse Fritz when they were out in the hall. "Mr. Gibbons is an attorney."

"Yes," the nurse responded as the three women circumvented Kenyon, who was shuffling along at his own rate of speed, or lack thereof. "Gaylord Gibbons of Gibbons, Gibbons, and Crump. The family has retained the firm for over a hundred years."

Renie, whose mother had been a legal secretary, recognized the names. "I didn't know any of the Gibbonses were still around. Gaylord must be—what? The great-grandson of the founder, Garrison Gibbons?"

"I believe so," Fritz said grudgingly. It was clear that she still didn't care much for Renie.

"When did Mrs. Burgess summon him?" Judith asked as they proceeded downstairs.

"I don't know," the nurse responded. "She must have called him when I was out of the room."

At the bottom of the stairs, Danny Wong was removing the crime scene tape. Edwina Jefferson, sipping from a large convenience store cup, watched her partner from the entry hall.

"Hi, gals," she said, raising the cup in salute. "Junior and I just got back from lunch. Did we miss anything?"

"Just Kenneth, hosting Wild Kingdom," Renie said. "We, however, missed lunch."

Judith hastily explained about the raccoon, then humbled herself to ask Nurse Fritz if she'd mind having some food brought to the library.

The nurse wasn't pleased. "I'm an RN, not a lackey," she huffed.

"Sorry," Judith apologized. "I'll do it myself."

"Never mind." Fritz sighed. "I wouldn't mind a little something myself. I certainly hope they didn't bake the raccoon."

Turning to Edwina, Judith was still in her humble mode. "I don't want to interfere, but could we talk?"

"In the library?" Edwina grinned. "Sure. Junior here can keep himself occupied."

Seated in a circle near the desk, Judith related everything she knew to the detective, including the recent arrival of Gaylord Gibbons. "My cousin and I want to help," she said in conclusion. "We know the homicide has been kept out of the media."

"And," Edwina said with a bemused expression, "your sense of justice demands that rich folks should pay the piper? Honey, the problem is that rich folks can *pay off* the piper. I don't necessarily mean with bribes, either. When was the last time that anybody with money in this country got the death penalty or even a really stiff sentence?"

Judith's expression was unusually stubborn. "I know that. My husband's a retired cop, remember? I don't see you giving up. Why should the rest of us?"

Edwina rocked back and forth in the Chippendale-style chair behind the desk. "You're serious. I'm impressed."

After a timid knock on the door, Edna arrived with the food. She took one look at the detective and started to tremble. "Oh, dear. Are you arresting these ladies?"

"Not yet," Edwina replied with a twinkle.

Edna skittered out of the library, wringing her hands.

"She's been very helpful," Edwina said. "She hasn't meant to be, but she can't stop talking."

"I know," Judith said. "I've got some questions for her, too. By the way, did you check the safe in here?"

Edwina nodded. "Yes, and we found a trace of strawberry pie. As far as we could tell, the safe was in order. Several people had pie, including Wayne Burgess, Kenneth Ward, and most of the staff."

"Kenneth?" Judith said in surprise. "He didn't show up at Creepers until nine or later, and we found the pie traces some time after seven."

Edwina looked smug. "I know that's what he said. But Dietz, the cook, insists he was here a few minutes before seven. That's when he ate the pie. He wanted to see his grandmother, but her TV show was on."

Judith recalled Kenyon's remark to Kenneth about mislaying his key. "Did Kenneth come in via the back door?"

"I don't know," Edwina said, "but he was definitely here."

Renie gestured at the desk. "How about that note my cousin found on the tablet? Do you know who wrote it?"

"Not yet," Edwina replied. "We haven't got all the handwriting samples. We have, however, eliminated Caroline's husband, Brett Flaherty. He has an airtight alibi. Brett was attending some literary reading at a bookstore where he lives down on the ocean. They had a discussion afterward, and he didn't leave until after eleven. That's a two- to three-hour drive. He's out of it."

The three women turned silent for a few moments. Judith and Renie ate their shrimp salads and more of Ada's hot rolls. Edwina finished her soda with a slurp that sounded like a flourish.

"That's interesting about the oil stain in the garage," the detective finally said. "I'll have Danny check it out. Assuming, of course, that the opener hasn't disappeared again.

None of you should have handled it," she added with a reproachful look.

Judith grimaced. "You're right. But my head was pounding so hard at the time, all I could think of was getting to my aspirin. Anyway, don't you suspect whoever took it— if it was the killer—wore gloves?"

"That's likely," Edwina admitted. "Let's hope that there isn't more than one vehicle in the family with an oil leak."

Though she knew she might not get an answer, Judith had to ask the question "Is there any progress?"

Edwina made a face. "The only thing I can say is that some of these folks aren't being candid. Some, like Kenneth, are lying. And then there are those who are covering up for themselves, or somebody else."

"So you're stuck," Renie said.

"No," Edwina replied, very serious. "This case is only fourteen hours old. We're collecting evidence; we'll be conducting more interviews. The worst part is that the higher-ups insist we treat these people with kid gloves. That means it's going to take longer to wear them down."

"Dare I ask," Judith began, "if you believe the intended victim was Dr. Moss?"

Edwina took a deep breath. "What do you think?"

Judith didn't know whether to be flattered or to feel put off. "I'm leaning toward Dr. Moss. But it may have been necessary to get rid of him first before killing Mrs. Burgess. How seriously do you take the alleged earlier attempts?"

"When Danny and I talked to her this morning, we felt Mrs. B. was very sharp," Edwina said in a careful voice. "She reminded me of my Aunt Laura Lou. Ninety-four, and she can give you the roster of every baseball team in the American and National Leagues, plus the Atlanta Braves' farm clubs right down through Single A. The only weird thing she ever did in her whole life was to send love letters to Henry Aaron." Edwina laughed. "She lives in Columbus, Muscogee County, I might add. Anyway, I didn't get the impression that Mrs. B. was imagining things. Sure, she watches TV, but who doesn't?"

"I gather," Judith said, pouring more coffee, "that none of these alleged attempts was reported to the sheriff?"

"That's right," Edwina replied. "It's not surprising. We spoke earlier about how these people hate intrusion and despise publicity. Not to mention that Mrs. B. might be afraid of looking like a crank in the eyes of her peers."

"I wonder what they think of the family now?" Renie mused. "The word must have spread all over Sunset Cliffs that Dr. Moss was murdered here."

"I understand there've been quite a few calls, though not many visitors," Edwina said. "It's as if the other inhabitants think murder is contagious."

"I imagine Wayne Burgess has fielded a bunch of queries," Judith said. "Despite the media blackout, the homicide investigation must have leaked all over the city, including the corner offices downtown."

"Even snobs like to gossip, especially about each other," Edwina noted. "We're interviewing the neighbors, but nobody lives close by. That's the way it is in this place. Sunset Cliffs dwellers have acres of property and plenty of privacy. The closest house is Evergreen, which belongs to the Wayne Burgesses."

"You won't get much out of the other residents anyway," Renie said. "They'll close ranks, too. The only way they'll tell you anything is if they have a grudge or an old rivalry."

"Which," Edwina said, "is what we're hoping for. The rich may band together, but it doesn't mean they have to like each other. Since the Burgesses originally owned everything around here and still have a large amount of unsold property, there are bound to be some hard feelings. We'll just hope for a break. It's too bad so many of these people are vacationing someplace else this time of year."

"You mentioned evidence," Judith said. "Is any of it tangible?"

Edwina laughed. "You know better than to ask. You mentioned walking around the grounds yesterday. I didn't notice that hitching post out in front last night—it was too dark and stormy. Usually, those old-fashioned stereotypical representations of black people don't bother me. But this morning the first thing I saw was that poor little black footman, holding out his hand. He's there to do his master's bidding, but it looks as if he's begging. Which, of course he is." Edwina paused, her expression ironic. "Walking into this house, you can feel the prejudice, the hostility, the overwhelming sense of superiority. It's like the air is poisoned. Anyway, I stopped to look at the little guy. I wanted to tell him that the most recognizable face on the planet is a black man named Michael Jordan."

She stopped, looking sheepish. "Silly, huh? But while I was looking down, I spotted this." Edwina fished into her briefcase and displayed a plastic envelope that contained a tacklike object. "It's a marker, to show where your golf ball lands on the course. The uniforms didn't see this last night because it was probably covered by leaves and branches that blew down during the storm. Do you recall it from yesterday?"

"No," Judith said. "Renie fell over the hitching post when we got here yesterday morning. We had to straighten it up. I'm sure we'd have noticed it if only because the rest of the grounds are so pristine."

"Russ Hillman?" Renie suggested.

"Maybe," Edwina allowed. "I assume he's not the only golfer in this bunch."

"Russ said he wasn't here last night," Judith said. "Of course he might have dropped it this morning when he came to breakfast."

Edwina shook her head. "You can't see too clearly through the plastic, but there's mud on this marker. It stopped raining right after sunrise, at least an hour before the Hillmans arrived."

"So Russ may be lying," Renie remarked.

"Possibly," Edwina said. "Mr. Hillman just jumped to the top of the interview list."

Another knock sounded at the door, followed by Deputy Sorensen poking his head into the library. "We finally got hold of the guard who was on duty in the gatehouse between six and midnight," Sorensen announced. "You want to see him? His name's Jack Moody."

"Take him into the parlor," Edwina said, getting up from behind the desk. "Leave the door ajar in case Danny needs me." She winked at the cousins.

As soon as the deputy and the detective left, Judith grinned at Renie. "Edwina is my new best friend. I think she believes we can help."

"Why," Renie said in her best middle-aged ingenue's manner, "do I sense that Edwina has talked to Woody Price?"

Judith's eyes widened. "That didn't occur to me. I hope Woody didn't give me too much of a build-up. And I sure hope he hasn't talked to Joe."

"Woody," Renie intoned, "is the soul of discretion. Under that walrus mustache of his, nobody keeps a tighter or stiffer upper lip."

The cousins allowed three minutes before they crept out of the library, went down the hall, and posted themselves outside the parlor door. They had only a splinter view of the room, but they could hear perfectly.

"Okay, Jack," Edwina was saying, "how long have you been employed by the Sunset Cliffs community?"

"Seven years, come May," a deep, husky voice replied. "I hired on after I got out of the merchant marine. The six to midnight shift is all mine. I don't like working days."

"Tell me about the patrol that drives around the community."

"That's a separate bunch of guys," Moody responded. "It's a private security outfit that works some of the businesses around here. They drive through once, twice a day to keep an eye out for people who don't belong."

"How would those people get into Sunset Cliffs in the first place?" Edwina asked.

"It don't happen very often. But once in a while some Nosey Parker sweet-talks a resident or staff member to get 'em inside, just to look around."

"Do you know if the patrol came through last night?"

"Nope, not on my shift. If they show up at night, which they don't always, it's usually around two, two-thirty, after the taverns close and everything quiets down out on the highway."

"We tried to get hold of you last night about an hour after you got off work. Where were you?"

"I usually stop for a couple of beers and maybe a few hands of poker at The Ace in the Hole or The Flush Royale. You know, to unwind."

"You like this job?"

"You bet. It's pretty soft, if you don't mind putting up with a lot of guff from the swells. The pay's not bad, the Christmas bonuses are good, especially the ones that come in a big fancy bottle from the liquor store, and there are some other bennies, too, if you know what I mean."

"Like what?"

"Oh—I guess you could call 'em tokens of appreciation. No big deal, but it's the thought that counts, right?"

"So tell me about last night. Is that your log?"

"Yeah. The deputy told me to bring it along. Wanna see it?"

"That's the general idea," Edwina said sarcastically.

There was a pause, apparently for the transfer of the log. Judith twisted around, trying to get a different view. She saw the partial outline of a hefty man in jeans and a denim jacket.

"I see several names I don't recognize," Edwina said. "Apparently, they went to other homes in Sunset Cliffs."

"Yeah, visitors. I don't log the regulars, I just wave 'em through."

"Can you recall which members of the Burgess family came through the gatehouse during your shift?"

Another pause ensued. "Mr. Burgess—Wayne Burgess—came in about six, a little earlier than usual. He works late downtown most nights. He had his driver and the limo. The limo went back out about ten minutes later."

"Without Wayne Burgess?"

"I guess. It's got those tinted windows. It's hard to tell, especially after it starts getting dark."

"Who else?"

"The young guy, Mrs. Hillman's son, walked through a few minutes after the limo went out. That must've been about six-thirty."

"Walked through?"

"Right. He don't drive. He takes the bus when he comes from his place in town. Hell, the bus stop ain't that far from here."

"Did he go out again last night?"

"Nope."

"Who was next?"

"Um . . . the redheaded kid with the pizza truck. That was later, eight, eight-thirty. Bop, they call him. Real friendly, not all snooty like the rest of 'em. Oh—and the girl. She lives up north. I forget her name."

"She drove?"

Jack chuckled, a rumbling sound that ended in a cough. "Would you believe it? She doesn't drive, either, so she hitchhikes. I always wonder if somebody who picked her up would find out how much money there was in the family and hold her for ransom."

"Hitchhiking is dangerous," Edwina allowed. "But it does explain why we never found her car. What time did Caroline Flaherty arrive?"

"That's her name? I guess I still think of her as Carrie Ward. I remember when her dad got killed by that hit-and-run driver. She was real tore up."

"The time?" Edwina persisted.

"Time? Oh—Carrie. Ten, ten-thirty, maybe? I'm not real sure. I was getting kind of beat."

"Anyone else?"

"The doctor. He don't live here, but he might as well. I always wave him through, just like family."

"What time?"

"Uh—eleven-thirty, eleven-forty-five?"

"No. That's wrong. Dr. Moss was dead by then. Think again."

"Well, then it must have been more like eleven-fifteen." A truculent note had edged into Moody's voice.

"Do you recall anybody else?"

"The cops. The medics. All those emergency types. Then Hank Ferguson came along for the midnight to six shift, so I took off."

"Mr. Moody, there are no entries in your log after tenthirty. Was it really that quiet?"

"I don't log people goin' out." The mulish tone was still in Moody's voice.

"You didn't log the emergency personnel, either."

"That's different. They ain't visitors as such."

Edwina's sigh was audible in the hallway. "Okay, just a couple more questions. Who, if anyone from the Burgess family, left Sunset Cliffs while you were on duty?"

"The pizza guy. He went out around nine and came back later. He gets off after eleven when the place closes down."

"And?"

"Nobody."

"What about Mrs. Hillman?"

"Never saw her."

"Come on, Mr. Moody, Peggy Hillman told us she went over to the mall. You must have seen her, both coming and going."

"Maybe I was taking a leak."

"Do you always take a leak when Mrs. Hillman comes and goes?" Edwina's voice had turned harsh.

"Hell, I don't know. Look, sometimes I get sleepy. A half-hour, an hour'll go by and no action. I nod off. So what? The folks who live here know how to trip the barricade. I ain't no cop."

"You certainly aren't," Edwina said. "For the last time, do you recall Mrs. Hillman leaving or returning to Sunset Cliffs last night?"

"Aww . . . Okay, maybe she did come through around seven or so. Maybe she didn't come back till after midnight.

Yeah, that must have been it. Check with Fergie. He'll know."

"We have. He didn't." There was a brief pause before Edwina spoke again. "Okay, you can go. But not too far. Get it?"

"Yeah, yeah, I got it. Anyways, I gotta work tonight."

As Judith and Renie heard the movement of a chair, they scooted out into the entry hall. Russ Hillman, looking tired and bewildered, was pacing the floor.

"What's going on?" he asked. "That young detective called to say I had to get over here pronto."

Jack Moody came stomping through the entry hall, muttering to himself. He barely looked at the cousins or Russ before he slammed out of the house. Edwina strolled in and greeted Russ.

"Let's talk," she said, and beckoned the newcomer in the direction of the parlor.

Judith and Renie waited until they were sure that the pair had settled in for the interview. But this time when they went to the parlor door, they found that it was closed tight.

"Drat," Judith breathed. "I guess she doesn't like us anymore."

"This interrogation is different," Renie pointed out. "Moody wasn't a suspect."

"True. All the same, I wouldn't mind chatting with him. He might be more forthcoming when he's not talking to a cop," Judith said as they headed back to the entry hall where Kenyon was showing Gaylord Gibbons out and letting Dorothy Burgess in.

Dorothy took one look at Gaylord and grabbed him by the lapels. "Let me warn you," she said in an angry voice, "if you make trouble for me, I'll sue your ass."

The startled lawyer reeled on the threshold. "But Mrs. Dorothy . . ."

Throwing Gaylord one last stinging look, she marched into the house and headed straight for the main staircase. "Don't worry about announcing me, Kenyon," she shouted.

"By the time you get upstairs, I'll be leaving this place. Forever."

"Ma'am?" Kenyon said, cupping his ear.

But Dorothy was already out of sight.

TWELVE

THE RAIN WAS slanting down against the old wavery glass in the guest suite windows. Judith sat on a Regency bench and stared outside. She could see two uniformed deputies wearing dark slickers and heading in the direction of the garage.

"We're not doing our job," Judith stated, turning away from the window. "We hardly see Mrs. Burgess, and we haven't any idea if she was the intended victim, let alone who killed Dr. Moss. There has to be a connection of some kind between his death and the attempts on Leota's life, either by accident or design." She sighed in frustration. "I'm more confused than when we got here."

"That makes two of us," Renie said, tossing aside the magazine she'd been perusing on the settee. "What did you think of Moody?"

"He's either lying about who he saw or didn't see, or he sits in that gatehouse and gets drunk. Both, maybe. Those 'bennies' he mentioned are probably bribes," Judith declared. "Think about it—you live in Sunset Cliffs, and your every move is monitored. These people don't lead blameless lives. If you've got a vice, especially if it's sex, you don't want anyone to know all your comings and goings."

"This whole place gets more prisonlike all the time," Renie said.

"You bet it does," Judith responded, getting up from the bench. "I honestly don't know why people would want to live here. Oh, it has privacy, it has snob appeal, and it's a beautiful setting, but I'd go nuts."

"It's not normal," Renie agreed. "It reminds me of a big castle, where you have to pull up the drawbridge."

"And what's up with Dorothy Burgess?" Judith asked. "What was she talking about when she said she was leaving here forever?"

"Leaving here means leaving Wayne, wouldn't you guess?" Renie also stood up and went over to the fireplace. "It's cold, since the wind's come up again. I wonder if we could get somebody to build us a fire?"

"Like Kenyon? It'll be summer before he can do it. Besides," Judith added, going to the door, "we need to do our own interviewing. I still want to get Edna alone."

"Call for her," Renie said, pointing to the speaking tube by the bedroom door. "Tea would be nice, especially with some lovely finger sandwiches."

Judith sniffed the air. "This place doesn't smell like a pool hall anymore. You haven't had a cigarette since we got back here twenty minutes ago. How come?"

"I thought about what you said," Renie replied. "I'm fond of food. When my eggnog diet failed me at Christmas a couple of years ago and I gained a few pounds, I started smoking instead of eating so much. I lost the weight, but now I keep losing it. Instead of being just right, I've gotten too thin. As of now, I'm a pig again."

"Hooray!" Judith cried, rushing over to give Renie a hug. "I thought there was less of you, but I hated to mention it."

"I know, I know," Renie said, hugging Judith back. "It's always galled you because I don't have to watch my weight. But maybe my metabolism has changed, and I *will* have to cut down a bit. For now, though, I'm going to give it my best shot. Hand me that speaking tube."

Ada Dietz was on the other end, taking Renie's order in a less than gracious manner.

"Heck," Renie said, putting the speaking tube aside, "it's after three, a good time for tea. Why should she be grumpy?"

"It's her nature, I guess," Judith replied, back at the window. "There's Danny Wong. They must be checking that oil spot. At least we found out why Caroline's car wasn't parked around here."

"I hadn't thought about it," Renie admitted.

"I had," Judith said, moving away from the window. "But from what I know of Caroline, she might have parked it anywhere along the road and walked here in a daze. The storm didn't start until after she arrived."

Fifteen minutes later, Edna showed up with the tea cart. The cousins oohed and aahed over the finger sandwiches and admired the Royal Worcester teapot and matching cups.

"I hope this wasn't a bother," Judith said to the little maid. "Did you have to bring tea up for Mrs. Burgess and Dorothy as well?"

"Oh!" Edna put a hand to her lips. "I shouldn't think so. Mrs. Dorothy has already left. In such a temper, too. Nurse Fritz had to give the mistress a sedative."

"Really," Judith said in surprise. "Do you know why?"

The maid shook her head. "My, no. I just happened to be going by the mistress's suite when Mrs. Dorothy came out. She seemed very angry."

"Here, Edna," Judith said in her most kindly voice, "sit for a minute. Perhaps you'd enjoy one of these lovely sandwiches your sister made for us."

"Oh, no, I couldn't," Edna protested, though she gingerly sat down on the edge of the settee. "I'll rest my feet for a minute, though."

Renie, who had scooped up four of the sandwiches, nudged Edna with her elbow. "Come on, dive in. The salmon ones are really terrific."

"Tea?" Judith proffered the pot.

Edna held up her hands. "Thank you, but I—"

"M-m-mm," Renie sighed, licking her lips as she gobbled up a cucumber sandwich. "Sinfully delicious. Here, take one. I insist."

"Well . . ." Edna's small body seemed convulsed by a mammoth struggle. "Dear me, I suppose it would be rude to refuse."

"Very rude," Renie remarked with a devilish smile. "Take two."

"Poor Mrs. Burgess," Judith said as she sipped her tea. "She's had nothing but trouble the last two days. I wonder what Dorothy said that was so upsetting."

Edna daintily chewed her sandwich. "I couldn't say, of course. Though about a quarter of an hour before I saw Mrs. Dorothy leave, I came up the back stairs to fetch the mistress's luncheon things. It seemed to me that they were arguing. Just as I was about to enter the mistress's bedroom from behind the Chinese screen, I thought I saw a pin on the floor. You know what they say, 'Pick up a pin and have good luck all day.' Or something like that." Predictably, Edna was turning pink. "While I was searching for the pin, I couldn't help but overhear. They were rather loud, you see." The little maid gave the cousins an apologetic glance.

"Of course," Judith soothed.

"Anyway," Edna continued, "Mrs. Dorothy said something about the mistress refusing to give her money for her Jim. Naturally, I was shocked. I've never heard of anyone named Jim, and it occurred to me that Mrs. Dorothy was talking about another man."

"My, my," Judith exclaimed.

"Have another sandwich," Renie offered.

"Thank you." Edna paused to take a bite and chew very slowly. "The mistress was horrified, and said she'd have no part of such folly. Then Mrs. Dorothy said if that was so, then she'd have to file for divorce. The mistress got very distressed, saying in no uncertain terms that Burgesses did not divorce. Then Mrs. Dorothy said they did so, too. Mrs. Peggy had divorced Mr. Charles, and Miss Caroline was going to divorce Mr. Brett. The mistress said that was different, Mr. Charles was no good, and Miss Caroline was only separated. That's when I bumped my head on the screen, and they realized I was there. Naturally, they stopped arguing."

"Did you find the pin?" Renie asked with a straight face.

Edna looked away. "No. It must have been a trick of the light. So shadowy by the back stairs passageway."

"Are you sure you don't want some tea?" Judith asked.

"No, please," Edna responded, rising from the settee. "I must get back to the kitchen. Ada will wonder why I've been gone so long. She doesn't like me chatting with people. Please don't tell her that we had a little visit."

"Of course not," Judith assured her. "One small question, Edna. Why is the top floor of the north tower sealed off?"

The little maid looked stricken. "Oh, Mrs. Flynn, you don't want to know! Not that I can really tell you, but it's something terrible that happened a long, long time ago. I swear, it's better not even to think about it." With a jerky little curtsy, Edna left the room.

"Who's Jim?" Renie asked, eating the last sandwich.

"Dorothy's boyfriend, I guess," Judith replied. "I wonder if Wayne knows about all this?"

"It sounds as if he'll soon find out," Renie remarked. "I suppose this explained Dorothy's threat to Gaylord Gibbons. She doesn't want him messing up her divorce settlement."

"Bop might know what's going on with his parents," Judith said. "Would you like to order a pizza?"

Renie groaned. "It's four o'clock, and dinner's at six. Even I don't want to gorge."

"Dinner needn't be at six," Judith pointed out. "Leota will have a tray sent to her room. Plus, we could save the pizza for later, and have Ada Dietz microwave it."

"Let's wait," Renie said, puffing out her cheeks. "I feel like a blimp."

Judith gave in. "Okay." Restless, she began to prowl the room, finally stopping by the magazine rack. "Not much choice here. Mostly business magazines, and a *Country Life* I've already seen. The only thing left is what looks like a community newspaper." Fishing the tabloid out of the rack, she noted the date. "Last week's edition. What do I need to know about the north section of the county?"

"Nothing you couldn't read in the daily papers," Renie said, pouring more tea.

But Judith was transfixed by the front page. "Speaking of Bop, here he is. 'Bop Burgess,' " she read from the caption under the young man's photo, " 'founder of one of the community's most successful new businesses.' It says here that three local entrepreneurs were honored at a Chamber of Commerce dinner February twentieth for their contribution to the local economy. Listen to this—'Burgess's Bop's Pizza Palace began turning a profit after only four months. The youthful owner has been credited with astute management, innovative advertising, and shrewd financial skills.' Here's a quote from Bop—'That's high praise, but I honestly believe that the reason we're making money is because we don't stint on ingredients or service. We also use imagination, not only in how we make our pizzas, but what we call them. Mozzarella Bella, Fisherman's Friend, The Wild Side—we think these names add a lot more excitement than just saying cheese, anchovies, or mushrooms.' "

Renie sat with her chin on her hand. "Who said Bop had no business sense?"

Judith thought for a moment. "Peggy? Mrs. Burgess?"

"Whoever it was, was wrong," said Renie.

Replacing the newspaper, Judith went back to the window. "The wind's really blowing. We must be in for another storm." She walked to the fireplace and leaned down. "I can hear it in the chimney. It almost sounds like someone crying." Pausing, she listened more closely. "It *is* someone crying. It's very faint, but I'm sure of it."

"Caroline," Renie said, getting up. "She's in the room next door."

Without another word, the cousins went out into the hall

and knocked on Caroline's door. There was no answer.

Judith knocked again. "Caroline?" she called.

Renie reached around Judith and turned the knob. The door was unlocked.

The suite in which Caroline was staying had been designed to accommodate the dual fireplaces and shared chimney. Caroline was lying on the rug in front of the hearth, sobbing uncontrollably.

"Caroline," Judith repeated, touching the girl's shoulder, "stop, please. You'll make yourself sick."

"Should I get Nurse Fritz?" Renie asked as Caroline sobbed on.

"Wait," Judith said, firmly grasping Caroline's arms and hauling her into an upright position. "Hush! You're hysterical. What's wrong?"

Caroline began to hiccough between sobs. Renie went off to fetch some water.

"Shh, shh," Judith soothed, propping Caroline up. "If I help, can you get to the sofa?"

"I . . . should . . . have . . . died . . . too," Caroline gulped.

"What?" Judith struggled to get some leverage under Caroline's arms.

"Death . . . is . . . sweet," the girl gasped.

"Speak for yourself," Renie snapped, holding out a glass of water.

Caroline, still hiccoughing, tried to push the glass away. "No . . . no . . ."

"It's poison," Renie said in a cheerful voice. "Cyanide. Yum, yum."

"Please, Caroline," Judith begged, "you really are going to be ill. We'll have to call Dr. Stevens."

The sobs began to subside. At last, Caroline accepted the water. "Is it really poison?" she whispered.

"No such luck," Renie said. "Just drink the damned thing."

To the cousins' relief, Caroline drank half the water, then shifted her weight away from Judith but remained seated on the floor. "Four years ago tomorrow," she murmured. "March fourth. It was stormy then, too."

Puzzled, Judith tried to make herself comfortable. "What are you talking about?"

"My daddy. He was killed March fourth, four years ago, the night *Gran'mère* had her gall bladder attack."

"Is that why you said you should have died, too?" Judith asked gently. "To be with your father?"

Caroline nodded. "Nothing's gone right for me since. He was my anchor. That's why I married Brett."

"You mean Brett was a father figure?" Renie inquired, taking a big fringed pillow from the sofa and sitting down on it next to Judith. "Was he much older?"

"Not really," Caroline replied. "Only eight years. But he was someone I could lean on. Brett's smart, talented, clever. He's published two novels already. I thought because he was a writer, he could help me with my poetry. But Brett doesn't know anything about poetry. And I guess I never really loved him."

"That's a terrible shame," Judith said with a pang. She remembered all too well her rebound marriage to Dan McMonigle. Unlike Caroline, Judith had managed, at great cost, to hold on until Dan's death nineteen years later.

"I came to Creepers last night because I wanted to be here for the anniversary," Caroline said as the hiccoughs subsided and the tears began to dry up. "I heard there was going to be a storm, so I decided to start out before the weather changed."

"Were you at Creepers when your father was killed?" Judith asked.

"Yes. I was still living at home, with Mommy and Russ. They'd only been married about two years," Caroline explained, then paused to take another sip of water. "Mommy encouraged me to spend the night with *Gran'mère* because she wasn't feeling well. Kenny couldn't come—he was out rescuing beavers from some pond."

"How did you learn about the accident?" Judith inquired.

"The police told us," Caroline said, starting to tear up

again. "It was around nine o'clock. Mommy had just stopped by on her way from having dinner with Russ at the club. She came to see *Gran'mère* because she'd had another spell. Then the sheriff's deputies showed up and told us about Daddy. Mommy went to pieces and Dr. Moss had to give her a sedative."

"Dr. Moss was at Creepers?" Judith asked.

"Yes, I'd sent for him," Caroline replied. "He was arranging for *Gran'mère* to be taken to the hospital. I had to ride along in the ambulance with Nurse Fritz because Mommy was so distraught and Dr. Moss wasn't feeling well, either. That's the first time I realized how old he really was. He'd been around for so long and his hair was always white, I guess I never noticed."

"But you were okay?" Renie asked, slightly incredulous.

"I was numb." Caroline looked away from the cousins, as if she could picture herself moving silent and robotlike through the vast rooms of Creepers. "With *Gran'mère* ill and Mommy upset, I kept the news about Daddy at a distance. It was only the next day, after *Gran'mère* got through her surgery, that I collapsed."

"In spite of the divorce," Judith said in a thoughtful tone, "your mother must still have been fond of your father."

Caroline frowned. "I suppose. They didn't get along very well, though. It was always a hassle when he wanted Kenny and me to spend time with him."

"Did he live close by?" Renie asked.

Caroline nodded. "North of here, in a condo by the ferry dock. He'd remarried after the divorce, but that only lasted a few years. I'm not sure Daddy was the marrying kind."

"What did he do for a living?" Renie asked.

"When Mommy first met Daddy," Caroline said with a tremulous smile, "he worked at the yacht club marina. Later, he got interested in repairing and restoring antique automobiles. Then, after they divorced, he hurt his back and couldn't work, at least not at the jobs he liked." The smile faded, and the tears were about to fall again.

Judith patted Caroline's arm. "You mustn't dwell on his death. If your father was such a source of strength for you while he was alive, you must know that he wouldn't want you to give in to grief."

Caroline offered Judith a pitiful little smile. "I realize that. But I think it's because I didn't fall apart the night he was killed, so I've had to make up for it since."

"It's four years later," Renie asserted. "We all have to move on."

Wiping at her eyes, Caroline sighed. "Maybe it would have helped if they'd caught whoever killed him. Then there'd be closure. It was different with Zane."

"Zane?" Judith said, frowning.

"Mommy's second husband," Caroline replied. "Zane Crowley. His body was never found after he went off into the jungle and got blown up. Zane was nice, and all that, but he and Mommy were only married for a couple of years, and he was always off on some assignment. Anyway, after he was killed, Mommy got a nice note from the President or somebody. But with Daddy, there was nothing official. The wound feels like it's still open."

"That's understandable," Judith said, "but after all this time, it's not going to happen. If I were you, I'd try to stop mourning so much, and refocus your poetry on other subjects."

"I thought," Caroline said in a hollow voice, "if I wrote about Daddy's death, I could find some meaning in it. The way it is now, it's only a random, senseless act. Whoever killed him just drove on. For all I know, that person didn't even realize what happened. It was such a stormy night, he or she may have thought they'd hit a bump or a branch. The police told us that visibility was very poor."

The door opened to reveal Peggy Hillman, who stared at the trio on the floor. "What's this? The Three Stooges?"

Renie stood up. "I used to be Curly, but my perm grew out. We were talking to your daughter. She was upset because her father was killed four years ago tomorrow. How do you feel about that, Peggy?"

Peggy looked affronted. "How I feel is none of your damned business. How Carrie feels isn't your business, either. Come on, Carrie, let's go downstairs. It's time for the cocktail hour."

"We're still on schedule?" Renie asked.

"We're on *my* schedule," Peggy retorted. "The cocktail hour will be two hours long. Get up, Carrie. Let's go."

Slowly, Caroline got to her feet. "I don't think I want a cocktail, Mommy. Is it okay if I just stay here in my room?"

"No, it's not. You need to mingle." Peggy tapped her foot.

"Mingle?" Caroline echoed, sounding bewildered. "Who do we mingle with? There's nobody here but us."

"There's a bunch of people coming over," Peggy said. "I invited some of the neighbors. They won't admit it, but they're dying to find out what happened here."

"People?" Caroline looked alarmed. "What kind of people?"

Peggy's foot tapped faster. "The Bensons. The Fredericks. The Morris sisters, Mrs. Wiggins and her son, Harold. Really, Caroline, you need to mix more."

"Okay," Caroline said without enthusiasm. "Let me change and wash my face."

"Good," Peggy responded. "I'll see you in the drawing room."

"Cocktails," Renie murmured as the cousins followed Peggy from the suite. "Does that include appetizers?"

"Cocktails don't include you," Peggy retorted over her shoulder. "This is strictly a Sunset Cliffs gathering. If you want a belt, send for Kenyon."

Before Renie could retaliate, Edna appeared at the top of the stairs. "There's a phone call for you, Mrs. Jones. You may take it in your suite. I believe it's Mrs. Beverly."

"Bev!" Peggy whirled around. "What's she doing calling you? Does she know about the mess we're in?"

"Sure," Renie replied. "She's checking with me for recent developments. Such as you being a big jerk." Sticking her thumbs in her ears, and wiggling her fingers at Peggy, Renie flounced off down the hall.

"How many people have you alienated here so far?" Judith inquired as the cousins entered their suite.

"Not enough," Renie snapped as she went to pick up the phone.

Judith sat down on the settee next to Renie, hoping she might overhear some of the conversation at Bev's end. Unfortunately, the connection wasn't strong, and she could catch only a few words.

"Yes, the police are making progress, albeit slowly," Renie said into the receiver. "Well, your mother had to be sedated this afternoon. There was some kind of dust-up with Dorothy, which followed on the heels of a row with Kenneth and his raccoon . . ."

Judith closed her eyes as Renie and Bev continued talking. Finally, as the conversation was winding down, Renie asked Bev if she knew anyone named Jim.

"No?" Renie said, nudging Judith. "He seems to be the other man in this divorce thing. Yes, I realize you've been away a great deal. One more question, Bev. Who's Suzette?"

Once again, Judith tried to hear Bev's response. She caught only a couple of words, which meant nothing out of context.

"Okay, Bev, thanks. That's the first concrete information we've had," Renie said, making a circle with her thumb and forefinger for Judith's benefit. "And by the way, your sister, Peggy, is treating us like garden pests. She tried to throw us out this morning." There was another pause before Renie spoke again. "Good. Thanks, we'd appreciate that. We'll keep in touch. Bye."

"Well?" Judith said as Renie hung up.

"Bev's going to call Peggy and tell her to knock it off," Renie said. "If that doesn't work, she'll talk to Wayne. Bev feels more strongly than ever about us sticking around to watch Leota."

"As if we see much of her," Judith groused. "Okay, so tell me what she said about Suzette."

"Suzette," Renie began, "was the French-speaking nanny who was hired to care for Peggy and Wayne. As far as Bev can tell, she left shortly before Margaret Burgess died. A new nanny was hired, Brewster was her name, and she stayed on until Bev was nine or ten. After that, Leota felt the kids didn't need a nanny, because they were all in school and old enough to look out for themselves. Brewster left about the same time that Kenyon and the rest of the current staff were hired, which, as Bev reflected on the wholesale changes, seemed strange. It seemed natural that the nanny would be let go, but not everybody else. No one ever explained any of it to her, and she'd sort of forgotten about it over the years. Brewster—Ellen Brewster—by the way, is still alive and living in a nursing home, but she's completely gaga."

"That's it?" Judith said, faintly disappointed.

"That's it," Renie said, "except that when Kenyon joined the household, he'd been widowed and brought Sarah with him."

"She mentioned being raised here," Judith remarked. "It must have been an odd life for her, growing up among the rich kids with her father as the family butler."

"That would be tough," Renie allowed. "Sarah has never left this place. I wonder if she ever tried."

Sadly, Judith shook her head. "While we might see Creepers as a prison, others might see it as a refuge."

"Possibly," Renie said, getting up. "What do you think of Bev's information regarding Suzette?"

Judith shrugged. "I don't know what to think. It sounds innocuous. Maybe there are too many lively imaginations in this house. Leota, Caroline, Edna. Hey, where are you going?"

Renie was at the door. "Down for cocktails. Are you coming?"

"But Peggy told us we weren't welcome," Judith protested.

"Peggy be damned," Renie retorted. "Bev told us to hang in there. So that's what we'll do. Let's go. Maybe some of the guests will have insights about Leota's near-death experiences, or Dr. Moss's real one."

"I don't know," Judith quibbled. "We should probably visit Leota."

"She's still out of it, I bet," Renie countered. "We can check in with her after we've been snubbed by the neighbors."

With misgivings, Judith trailed after Renie, but insisted on stopping at Mrs. Burgess's suite. Nurse Fritz opened the door a scant two inches.

"How's the patient?" Judith inquired.

"Worn out," Fritz replied. "Dr. Stevens gave me orders to keep everyone away, which certainly didn't sit well with Mr. Wayne. I had to send him packing not more than five minutes ago. No visitors means no visitors. I reminded him that this isn't Evergreen Timber. Dr. Stevens is in charge here."

"Is Dr. Stevens here now?" Judith asked.

"He left," said Fritz. "Doctor's on the ragged edge, too. This has been a very difficult day for him, not to mention the fact that he was up virtually all of last night."

Judith agreed, adding that Nurse Fritz must also be tired. "Can you rest a bit?"

"Not until Mrs. Burgess settles in for the night," Fritz said. "I'm fine. I'm accustomed to long hours."

The cousins continued downstairs. They could hear subdued voices in the drawing room. Upon entering, they saw a dozen or more well-dressed, decorous men and women drinking cocktails and talking in small groups of twos and threes.

Peggy Hillman took one look at Judith and Renie, then marched straight toward them. "Listen," she said, her voice low, her face flushed, and fire in her blue eyes, "I told you to butt out. Do I have to get nasty?"

"You already did," Renie shot back. "We're here on a mission, remember? If you don't lighten up, Bev's going to fly home to find out what's really going on."

"Bev!" Peggy sneered, clutching her Scotch and soda. "She stays away for years on end, then thinks she has a right to lord it over the rest of us. She's been an intruder at Creepers since the day she was born."

"Bev's my friend," Renie asserted. "Unless you want a scene in front of all these clannish moneybags, move your butt so we can watch Kenyon mix our drinks in slow motion."

Eyes still flashing, Peggy started to say something, but stopped and stepped aside. "You win this round," she hissed, "but watch yourself. Those big front teeth of yours better not bite off more than they can chew."

Renie smirked, but said nothing further until she and Judith reached the bar. "Did we once say Peggy was ever so human? I retract that statement."

"Don't," Judith responded, aware that some of the guests were staring discreetly. "It's because she's so human that she's so mad at us."

"Is that supposed to make me feel better?" Renie retorted.

Judith shrugged. "No, but a good stiff shot might. Let's drink."

The cocktail hour, which lasted until almost seven as Peggy had promised, proved a disappointment to the cousins. As Renie had flippantly predicted, they were indeed snubbed by the residents of Sunset Cliffs. Even Judith, with her friendly manner, struck out when it came to making conversation. Not once did either of the cousins get past the introduction stages. Aside from chatting briefly with Kenneth, they ended up talking to each other.

"I get the impression we aren't welcome at dinner," Judith said as they took what was left of their drinks into the parlor. "Who do you think will be there?"

Renie ticked off names on her fingers. "Peggy, Wayne, Kenneth, Caroline, maybe Russ. I doubt Dorothy will show up after that scene with Leota. Mr. Wayne and Mrs. Dorothy, as they're known here, can't be on good terms. You know, I can't imagine being called Mrs. Renie."

Judith smiled. "Then I won't call you that. I was thinking, it might be nice to get out of here for a while. Are you
hungry for pizza yet?"

"For dinner?" Renie grimaced. "Okay, if you insist. But
it's still blowing and raining like mad. Are you sure you
don't want to eat in?"

"Very sure," Judith said, finishing her drink. "Let's find
Sarah Kenyon and get the garage opener so we can take
out my Subaru."

Sarah wasn't in her office down the hall, which wasn't
surprising since it was after seven.

"Her quarters are on the third floor with the other servants," Judith mused, "but a housekeeper is in a little different category. Maybe she has a sitting room on this floor."

"There's that room we've never seen right here across
from the breakfast nook," Renie pointed out.

"We can but try," Judith said, and opened the door. It
was a game room, complete with pool table, bar, jukebox,
big game trophies, and two people writhing on the floor.

As quickly and as silently as possible, Judith closed the
door and grabbed Renie. "Let's get the hell out of here."

"Who was that?" Renie panted as they raced through the
hallway and back toward the parlor.

"I'm not sure about the woman," Judith gasped as they
reached sanctuary, "but the man was definitely Wayne Burgess."

THIRTEEN

SUDDENLY OUT OF the mood to drive over to the highway, Judith and Renie had asked Kenyon to bring them a third drink. "We aren't driving," Judith said as they waited for the butler to show up in the parlor.

"Are you sure it was Wayne Burgess?" Renie asked.

"Yes," Judith declared. "What little light there was from the wall sconces shone right on the back of his head. I'll bet he dyes his hair. Anyway, his glasses were lying on the pool table."

"It could be Dorothy, in a reconciliation attempt," Renie said, though she sounded uncertain.

"Dubious," Judith replied. "Unless we've got incest going on here—heaven forbid—it wasn't Peggy or Caroline."

"Nitz Furse?" Renie suggested.

"Get serious," Judith said. "Even if Wayne was really desperate, Fritz wears white stockings. The lady in heat did not."

"Who's left?" Renie asked.

"The neighbors, obviously. There were a couple of women there—Mrs. Benson and Mrs. Frederick—who were fairly attractive. They were wearing skirts, but then all the women dress for cocktails around here. Whoever it was had decent-looking legs. Or indecent, given the situation."

"No wonder Dorothy wants to run off with Jim," Renie said. "Hanky-panky all over the place. I suppose you could expect it in a closed community like Sunset Cliffs. Do you think Wayne and Whoever knew we were there?"

"They wouldn't have noticed if Minnesota Fats was trying to play a game of pool in the same room," Judith said. "You would have thought they'd have locked the door."

"Maybe they went in to shoot some pool and were suddenly overcome with mutual desire," Renie remarked. "Personally, I find Wayne more of a dud than a stud, but you never know."

Kenyon finally appeared with the drinks. "Will you be dining later?" he inquired.

"Yes," Judith replied. "Probably in here. What's on the menu?"

"A clear soup, spinach salad with a hot bacon dressing, beef Wellington, garlic mashed potatoes, fresh broccoli, and a white chocolate mousse for dessert. Of course if you prefer something else . . ."

"Bring it on," Renie interrupted.

"Half an hour," Judith said, smiling. "We'll finish our drinks first."

"As you wish, ma'am," said Kenyon, and creaked out of the parlor.

"Food." Renie sighed. "I'm glad I'm back."

"With a vengeance," Judith murmured. "You know," she went on, "when I saw those stuffed animal heads in the game room, I had to wonder if Kenneth wasn't reacting to them. His grandfather or great-grandfather must have hunted. Maybe he grew up feeling sorry for the lions and tigers and bears, oh, my!"

"I could eat a bear," Renie said.

Judith didn't comment. For a few minutes, the cousins sipped their drinks in silence, though they could hear the wind and rain howling outside.

"I want another look at the tower rooms," Judith said suddenly.

"Why?"

"I'm not sure," Judith admitted, "but our previous visit was pretty cursory."

"What if Kenneth's up there, feeding Roscoe the Raccoon?" Renie asked.

"He won't be," Judith replied, getting up. "Kenneth's at dinner with the rest of the family."

"Okay." Renie sighed. "Let's go, but I can do without the invisible weirdo telling us to go away. Peggy's bad enough doing that in person."

Climbing the tower staircase, the cousins could feel the wind. "Not well-insulated in this part of the house," Judith noted as they entered Kenneth's room.

"It's a tower," Renie said. "What would you expect?"

Judith really hadn't expected to see Roscoe, but there he was, standing on his hind legs in a commodious cage. The bandit eyes gazed soulfully at the cousins.

"Hey," Renie said, kneeling down, "from the looks of that food dish, you've eaten more than we have this evening. You'll have to wait for dessert."

Judith, meanwhile, was studying the small fireplace, peeking into drawers, looking under the bed. "Nothing," she said, opening the door to the nursery. "Just the kind of things you'd expect Kenneth to keep on hand for his frequent visits to Creepers."

Renie said good-bye to Roscoe and followed Judith into the nursery. "How long," Renie mused, "do you suppose it's been since any kids played in here?"

Judith calculated. "Fifteen years, maybe more?"

"Do you think they're keeping it for grandchildren?" Renie asked in a wistful tone.

Judith gave her cousin a sympathetic glance. So far, none of the three grown Jones offspring had acquired mates or produced children. "That's possible," Judith said. "You shouldn't give up hope, especially these days when kids marry so late."

Renie didn't respond. Instead, she contemplated the train set. "This is a Marx, the same vintage as mine. I don't think they make them anymore. Uncle Corky gave it to me when I was two."

Judith shot Renie a wry look. "He'd given cousin Sue a Lionel before that. I was next in line, but the war came along, and I never got mine."

"You'd have stepped on yours," Renie said, grinning. "I was so excited because I got a freight and Sue only got a passenger model. It didn't have as many cars."

"I liked dolls better anyway," Judith said, though the envy still lingered in her voice. "Some of these are much older," Judith said. "They're porcelain and bisque. Lovely clothes, too."

"They probably belonged to Bev's Aunt Ginny," Renie replied. "She married a man from back east and died about the time I met Bev. Ginny wasn't old, only late fifties, I'd guess."

"These toys run the gamut," Judith remarked. "From hand-carved wooden soldiers to plastic Barbies. And look at this dollhouse. I'll bet this dates back to Aunt Ginny, too. The furniture is the same style as many of the pieces in this house."

"Hey," Renie said, joining Judith at the shelf where the dollhouse was displayed, "this looks like a cutaway replica of Creepers itself. There's even a tower room on this one side and it's—" Renie blanched and let out a little gasp.

"What's wrong, coz? Are you okay?" Judith asked in alarm.

A gust of wind blew the door to the nursery shut, making both cousins jump. "Yeah, right, I'm just fine," Renie said in a startled voice. "But look at this. How creepy can Creepers get?"

Judith followed Renie's finger. In the top floor of the half-version of the tower was a bed, a chair, a table, and a tiny doll in a long dark dress. The doll was lying facedown on the floor in what looked like a pool of blood.

The lights in the nursery went out.

* * *

Scrambling over each other, the cousins groped for the door. Judith found the knob first and moved cautiously out of the nursery. She was trying to find the stairs when she felt something soft and fluttery brush against her cheek. "What was that?" Judith asked in sudden panic.

"What was what?" Renie asked back.

Judith started to shake. "I felt something touch my face. Are you sure it wasn't you?"

"I'm behind you," Renie said, her voice tense.

"It felt like . . . hair," Judith gulped.

"What?" Renie sounded hoarse.

"Listen." Judith stood motionless, straining her ears. "I heard something, a hollow sort of noise."

Neither Judith nor Renie moved for almost a full minute. The silence, like the darkness, was absolute and suffocating.

"It's gone," Judith finally said. "My God, what was it?"

"A cobweb?" Renie offered.

"No. It felt thicker. Heavier."

"Don't hurt me!" shrieked a voice from somewhere on the stairs below them.

Judith and Renie clutched at each other, teetering dangerously.

"Jeez," Renie breathed, "what now?"

"It's that same voice we heard before," Judith said, shaken to her toes. "I still don't recognize it."

"Let's get out of here," Renie urged.

Still clinging to each other, the cousins made their way down the stone steps. They heard nothing else. At the second-floor landing, Judith fumbled for the door to Kenneth's room, but the knob seemed stuck.

"I can't get in," she said.

"Why do you want to?"

"I thought we might find a candle in there," Judith said. "You try it."

Judith rattled the doorknob. "It's stuck."

"Oh, for—" Renie pushed Judith out of the way. She

yanked, she tugged, she pulled, she swore. "You're right. It's stuck." For good measure, she gave the door a hefty kick.

It swung open, but Kenneth's room also lay in darkness. Roscoe could be heard, stirring about in his cage.

"There should be a candle around here," Judith said, feeling her way across the small, round room. "Maybe by the fireplace."

"Forget the candle," Renie said. "We can get out of here by following the wall next to the stairs. It's only one floor."

Judith, however, was running her hand across the mantel. "You're right. I can't find a candle. But I found a coin. If it's a penny, we're in luck."

"Like Edna and her nonexistent pin? Come on," Renie urged, "take my hand. I can see as well in the dark as I can in broad daylight. Let's go."

Renie led Judith down one step at a time. The wind grew louder; something rattled and crashed outside. Judith almost fell over Renie, who had stopped when she'd heard the unexpected noise.

Judith prodded Renie. "Keep moving."

"I can't," Renie said in a strange voice.

"Why not?"

Renie gulped. "There's somebody standing in front of me."

Judith let out a little squeak, then summoned up her courage. "Who's there?" she called over Renie's shoulder.

The response materialized from out of the dark: "Pardon?"

"Kenyon?" Renie gasped. "It's us. Mrs. Flynn and Mrs. Jones."

"Pardon?" Kenyon repeated.

"It's the visitors," Renie yelled.

"Ah. I've been searching everywhere for you." Kenyon's soft, slow footsteps went before them. "Dinner is served."

Fumbling and stumbling, the cousins finally reached the parlor. Kenyon had disappeared, but a small pedestal table had been set with a half-dozen lighted tapers and several covered dishes.

"Holy St. Joseph," Renie exclaimed, collapsing into one of the matching chinoiserie armchairs. "I'm limp. Where's what's left of my bourbon?"

Judith picked up both cocktail glasses from the mahogany and walnut credenza. "Drink up. We need to settle our nerves. What do you think is up there in that blasted tower?"

Renie was still goggle-eyed. "Maybe Caroline's right. It's haunted."

"Don't say that," Judith retorted. "It won't take much to convince me."

"The speaking tubes," Renie said suddenly. "Could there be one on the staircase and somebody's using it to scare us?"

Between gulps of Scotch, Judith considered. "No. They've been removed. I noticed a place in Kenneth's room where there used to be one, but it's gone now. Besides, whoever brushed against my face didn't come out of a speaking tube."

"No," Renie said thoughtfully. "I guess not."

Judith tried to get a grip on her composure as she gazed around the parlor where the candles cast an eerie amber glow. "The power must be out all over the house. Maybe the whole area."

"Hardly surprising with all this wind," Renie said, relaxing a bit and tasting her soup. "Remember the year cousin Sue was having Thanksgiving dinner and a big windstorm blew everything out? She tried to cook the turkey in her barbecue and set their deck on fire."

Buttering another of Dietz's delicious rolls, Judith nodded. "That was too bad. It was a nice deck, though it didn't have much of a view."

"It had a better one after all the trees burned down," Renie noted. "But I thought it was mean of your mother to tell the firefighters that my mother was out of the house when she was still inside in her wheelchair."

"That's what your mother gets for always saying, 'Don't worry about me.' Nobody did."

"*I* did," Renie declared, lapping up the fresh spinach in her salad. "I about choked to death rescuing her. It's a wonder Mom and I didn't have to be treated for smoke inhalation."

Judith chuckled. "Our mothers," she said with a shake of her head.

In the glow of the candlelight, the cousins stared at each other. "*Our mothers*," they exclaimed in unison.

Judith reached for the phone. "We'd better call now. I'll go first, then you can call yours. Then I'll call Joe and you can— Rats, there's no dial tone." Judith replaced the receiver. "The phones must be out, too."

"I'm getting a cell phone," Renie asserted. "I hate it when people use them on the road, but they can be a big help in an emergency."

"Go for it," Judith murmured, taking a bite of the flaky crust on her beef Wellington. "Strange sensations and odd noises aside, were we hallucinating in the nursery?"

"You mean the figure in the dollhouse?" Renie said, spearing broccoli. "No. But of course it wasn't real blood. It was some sort of red plastic, like the kind I use to mask photos in a layout."

Savoring the perfectly done beef, Judith nodded. "A childish joke, I suppose. Except that the real tower is sealed. I think we should mention this to Edwina. She could get a search warrant to see what's up there."

Renie made a face. "On what grounds? Because some kid, maybe years ago, played a gruesome little prank? Or because someone's trying to scare us to death?" And what does any of it have to do with Dr. Moss's murder?"

Judith, however, gave her cousin a canny look. "That's a good question. I'd like Edwina to find out."

"You *are* hallucinating," Renie said, putting extra butter on her mashed potatoes.

"Maybe," Judith said, picking up the coin she'd found in Kenneth's room. "I'm feeling lucky. I practically had to pry this sucker out from between the bricks. It must mean something."

"You're desperate," said Renie between mouthfuls of beef.

"I don't think so." Judith held the penny under one of the candles, then frowned. "This isn't a penny. It's . . ." She paused, peering in the dim light. "It's a centime, from Haiti."

"Haiti?" Renie said. "Oh, good grief, now we're into voodoo."

"This is really old," Judith said, still gazing at the coin. "It's dated 1928."

"So sell it to a collector," Renie said, cutting into her beef Wellington. "You might get a U.S. penny in exchange."

"I wonder if I should call Edwina," Judith mused.

"You can't," Renie said. "The phones are dead, remember?"

"Drat."

Kenyon reappeared, carrying a flashlight and a tray. "Dessert," he murmured. "May I remove your soup and salad plates?"

"Yes, thanks," Judith said, moving a few inches away from the table and speaking in a loud voice. "How did you find us in the tower, Kenyon?"

"It seemed logical, ma'am," Kenyon replied. "I'd looked everywhere else. Unfortunately, the batteries went out just as you emerged from the second floor." He tapped the flashlight.

"What," Judith asked, still speaking loudly, "do you know about Haiti?"

"Haiti? I believe they've had some problems there over the years, ma'am. Dictators and such. At one time, the United States occupied the island, but that was many years ago, when I was quite young."

"Yes," Judith agreed, "that sounds right. Do you recall if any of the family ever visited there?"

"Not in my time," Kenyon replied. "However, Mr. Max-

well and Mr. Walter were both world travelers. They might
have done. Mr. Walter in particular was always gadding
about. East Africa, India, the Argentine. He and his father
were both great hunters. The mistress never cared for
roughing it, which, I understand, is required when one is
seeking okapis and dik-diks. Tents. Mosquito netting.
Boiled water. The mistress would be put off. Will that be
all for now? I'll bring coffee in a few minutes, and whatever choice of after-dinner beverages you'd prefer."

"A couple of Drambuies would be nice," Renie said.

"Very good." Kenyon bowed himself out.

"He's right," Renie remarked. "Leota in a tent doesn't
ring true."

"Why Haiti?" Judith said.

"Huh?" Renie looked up from her almost-empty dinner
plate. "Why not?"

"Because, as Kenyon pointed out, it's been a trouble spot
for quite a while," Judith explained. "It wouldn't be my
first choice as a travel destination."

"Forget it," Renie said. "Maybe nobody went there.
Maybe somebody found that coin. Heck, maybe there's a
numismatist in the family."

Judith didn't comment. Indeed, her attention was caught
by voices in the hall outside the parlor. Apparently Kenyon
had not quite closed the door behind him.

"Who's that?" Judith whispered to Renie.

Renie, who had her back to the door, turned around, then
shook her head. "I can't see anybody," she whispered back,
"but it sounds like Wayne and Peggy."

"You wouldn't dare," Peggy shouted. "Not after all these
years!"

"Do you think I want to?" Wayne retorted, his voice also
raised, though still under control. "My hand is being forced.
I have only two choices."

"*Maman* won't allow it," Peggy declared. "Think of the
disgrace!"

"*Maman* will see there's no other way," Wayne said dog-
gedly.

There was a pause, and then Peggy's voice dropped. "Have you talked to her?"

"Not exactly," Wayne replied, also speaking in a more normal tone. "I tried to bring it up last night, but she was watching one of her programs. This morning, of course, was inappropriate. She was still asleep when I left for the office."

"She'll never approve," Peggy said, her voice now further away. "My God, Wayne, how did you ever get yourself into such a . . ."

Brother and sister passed out of earshot.

"The divorce," Judith said. "Wayne must know about Dorothy and Jim."

"Maybe Dorothy knows about Wayne and whoever was in the game room," Renie said, attacking her white chocolate mousse.

Sadly, Judith shook her head. "They must have been married for over thirty years. Why can't people work things out?"

The lights went on.

"Thank goodness," Judith said in relief. "I'll call Mother."

But the phone was still dead. Judith was still staring at the receiver when Kenyon came in with the coffee service and two small balloon glasses filled with Drambuie.

"Why doesn't the phone work now that the electricity is back?" Judith inquired of the butler.

Kenyon cleared his throat. "We have an auxiliary generator out back, ma'am. Mr. Jeepers has managed to turn it on. Unfortunately, it doesn't restore the phone lines."

"Oh." Judith looked disappointed.

The butler staggered out with a tray filled with glasses, silver serving dishes, dinner and butter plates, and eating utensils.

Judith winced. "That poor old guy. It's a wonder he and Edna don't collapse, what with all the fetching and carrying they have to do. There's a lot of ground to cover in this house."

"I don't think there's a retirement plan at Creepers," Renie said cynically.

"Why did they all come at once?" Judith said, seemingly from out of nowhere.

"Who? What are you talking about?"

"The staff. Remember, Bev said that Kenyon and the rest of them were hired about the same time, after World War Two. Which," Judith continued, "means that the rest of the servants, including Nanny Brewster, must have all left at the same time."

"That's not too hard to figure," Renie reasoned. "The war was over, it was a time of great transition. They probably found other jobs."

Judith shook her head. "All the veterans were back. There was inflation and strikes and, as Mother so often tells me, if Harry Truman hadn't given 'em hell, there wouldn't have been any boom during the Eisenhower years."

"That's true," Renie remarked. "How easily we forget. So what's your point?"

Judith gave Renie a sheepish grin. "The more I hear about this house and this family, the more I think of the period from the mid-1930s to the late 1940s as the Dark Ages. What really went on here?"

"Specifically, you mean what went on with Margaret Burgess," Renie said. "Is that the key?"

"Now that you mention it," Judith responded, "maybe it is. But I'll be darned if I know what it has to do with Dr. Moss's murder."

"Where's your logic?" Renie asked, sipping Drambuie.

"What?"

"Your logic. Why would anyone kill a doctor, especially an old guy who's been devoted to this family for sixty years?"

"We've been over that," Judith said, but caught the gleam in Renie's eyes. "Okay, because he knew something. He had something in his medical records or private papers that someone couldn't afford to have exposed. Maybe he took Leota's fears seriously, and he knew who was trying to kill her."

"Go on."

"But why wait all these years if it goes back to Margaret, who died circa 1937? What happened in the last few days to goad someone into killing Dr. Moss? Frankly, the connection with Margaret makes no sense. And yet I feel there must be something."

"The next time I talk to Bev," Renie said, "I'll ask her how her father's first wife died."

"Good," Judith said. "The next question is, why try to kill an old lady like Leota?" Judith was on her feet, circling the parlor, glass in hand. "This old lady is in excellent health, but she has tons of money. She could live another ten, even twenty years. Money is always an excellent motive. Who desperately needs money? Dorothy and Jim? Who else?"

There was a rap at the door, which was still ajar. Dr. Stevens peeked in. "May I?" he asked.

"Of course," Judith said. "What brought you out on such a stormy night?"

Theo Stevens smiled. "The storm." He sat down in the chair Judith had pulled out for him. "Since the phones were out, I thought I'd better check on Mrs. Burgess in case Nurse Fritz had been trying to reach me. She wasn't, and my patient is better this evening, though she's had a rough twenty-four hours." He paused to gaze at Judith. "Mrs. Burgess said you got a nasty bump on the head last night."

Judith's hand automatically touched her scalp. "I did, but it's better."

Dr. Stevens got up to examine the slight swelling. "You're right, it's coming along. Headache? Double vision? Dizziness? Nausea?"

"Just a headache," Judith replied.

The doctor turned to Renie. "How's the Bell's palsy, Mrs. Jones?"

"Droopy, still a little numb by my ear, but improving,"

Renie said. "This is the first day I haven't had to patch the eye."

Dr. Stevens smiled. "Good. It just takes time. By the way, Dr. Moss's funeral is set for Thursday at eleven in the chapel. Will you attend?"

Judith and Renie exchanged glances. "We don't know," Judith finally said. "It depends on the police—and other things. About our staying on, I mean. Will Dr. Moss have any family at the services?"

Theo Stevens shook his head. "His only relatives are distant cousins who live in California and the Midwest. I don't think Aaron had seen any of them in years."

Renie uttered a little snort. "So some shirttail relations will inherit whatever the poor man saved up all these years, and count themselves lucky because he had the grace to get himself killed. I've seen that often—my mother was a legal secretary. Let's hope Dr. Moss left everything to charity."

Theo Stevens's dark skin grew even darker. He coughed in a nervous manner. "Actually, Mr. Gibbons told me today that Aaron left everything to me. It's no secret, of course. The will has to be made public when it's filed for probate."

Renie beamed at the doctor. "That's great. Certainly you should get the house because you and Dr. Moss shared both living and work quarters there."

"Congratulations," Judith said, putting out her hand. "Not having to find a new situation must be a big help when you're just starting your practice. Dr. Moss must have thought a great deal of you."

Dr. Stevens avoided Judith's gaze. "It seems so," he murmured.

Renie was nodding agreement. "Whatever savings he had will come in handy. Somehow, though, I don't see Dr. Moss charging enormous fees, even if his patients were rich."

"You're right," Dr. Stevens replied, once again looking at the cousins. "Aaron began his practice in the Depression when even some of the wealthy residents of Sunset Cliffs were facing financial disaster. He was grateful to the ones who could afford to pay him, and he never felt right about raising his fees the way other doctors did over the years. That's why," he went on, as if in a daze, "I can't believe his estate is valued at over three million dollars."

FOURTEEN

JUDITH AND RENIE couldn't quite believe the size of Aaron Moss's holdings, either. The amount was actually closer to four million, Dr. Stevens explained, because it didn't include the house.

"It's not a large or lavish house," he said, "but it's very nice, and of course any property that abuts Sunset Cliffs is expensive. Mr. Gibbons estimated that it was worth another half-million on today's market."

"Did Dr. Moss play the stock market?" Renie asked.

"No," Theo Stevens replied. "But he lived a rather spartan life, especially after his wife died. Like all doctors, Aaron had to pay huge premiums for malpractice insurance. Frankly, I can't figure out how he accumulated so much money. In all the years I've known him, he never even hinted at such a thing."

"Does Mr. Gibbons know?" Judith inquired.

"I'm not sure," Dr. Stevens said. "Lawyers are so closemouthed. I got the impression, though, that he might know more than he let on."

"Maybe," Renie said, draining her glass, "some grateful patient either gave or left Dr. Moss the money. Maybe several of them did, and he invested it."

Theo Stevens frowned. "I don't think so. Just three or four years ago, while I was completing my residency and living with Dr. Moss, he complained about the high cost of new equipment. In fact, he didn't replace most of the items he already had, because he felt he wouldn't be around forever, and that when I took over, I could choose what suited my needs best."

"Do you have a nurse or a receptionist?" Judith inquired.

"Dr. Moss's wife, Isabel, was a nurse," Dr. Stevens replied. "She did everything until she became ill about five years ago. Dr. Moss hired an older woman to replace her, but I think it was too hard for him to make the adjustment. He let her go, and then there was a series of younger nurses, none of whom cared much for such a restricted practice. After I joined him, we got Ms. Parker. She's middle-aged, very capable, and a recent graduate of the local community college. She'd gone back to school after her divorce. Of course she's an LPN, but that's all we really needed. The receptionist work is the biggest part of her job."

"Does she know about Dr. Moss's death?" Judith asked.

"No." Dr. Stevens gave Judith a rueful smile. "She's in Hawaii for two weeks. Aaron is—was—very good about giving her time off. She'll be back Sunday. Laura—Ms. Parker—will be devastated."

"So she wouldn't know where Dr. Moss got all his money," Renie commented. "If it was a recent windfall, wouldn't he have told you, especially since you're his heir? How long have you known Dr. Moss?"

Dr. Stevens took a deep breath, as if steeling himself. "Since the day I was born. He delivered me."

"Oh." Renie looked a little embarrassed. "Your mother lived in Sunset Cliffs?"

"No," Theo Stevens replied, standing up. "My parents lived in the city. Excuse me, I'd better head home. I'm pretty tired myself. Good night." Ducking his head, he hurried out of the parlor.

"Logic," Judith intoned, "tells me something odd is going on with Dr. Stevens and his background. He's at least a quarter, maybe half, African-American, which means he's the product of an interracial marriage. His mother and father were inside the city, and since it was going on forty years ago, they may have lived in a primarily black neighborhood. As I understand it, Dr. Moss's practice was restricted to Sunset Cliffs and part of the adjacent upscale neighborhood. Now why was Dr. Moss attending a mixed-race couple ten miles away?"

Renie looked guileless. "Because they lived somewhere else since our city is usually ahead of the times when it comes to social issues? Because plenty of minorities have lived wherever they wanted including in our own neighborhood? Because it was around 1960, and Dr. Moss was making a civil rights statement?"

"The last reason isn't as dopey as it sounds," Judith said. "And yet," she continued, going over to the window and peering through the damask draperies, "I don't think it's the explanation. No matter where they lived, Dr. Stevens's parents were singled out, not just then, but later, when Theo was finishing his medical studies. Where's the link?" She paused, noting that the wind had died down, but the rain was still pouring. "Intervals," she said, turning back to Renie. "What we were talking about before Dr. Stevens showed up. We've got something strange going on sixty-odd years ago with Suzette, the French-speaking nanny. We've got something else that happened here after the war. Then Theo Stevens is born thirty-five or more years ago, and Dr. Moss treated him like his son and heir."

"Dr. Stevens is his heir," Renie put in. "Could he also be Dr. Moss's son?"

Judith stared at Renie. "It's possible—but I don't quite see it. Or do I? Dr. Moss is then in his fifties. He and his wife have no children. Maybe Mrs. Moss was incapable of child-bearing. Aaron Moss meets an attractive black woman and has an affair. She gets pregnant, and he takes care of her. Yes, it could fit, but it'd mean that Dr. Moss didn't mind flaunting his illegitimate son in the face of Sunset Cliffs. That's the part that doesn't ring true."

"I kind of like it," Renie said.

Judith looked doubtful. "Let me get back to my chronology. Thirty-five or so years later, Dr. Moss is murdered. What does that suggest?"

"Confusion," Renie replied, putting the Drambuie glasses and coffee cups on the tray that Kenyon had delivered. "Does it do something for you?"

Judith grabbed the sugar bowl, the cream pitcher, and the silverware. "Yes, it does. Generations, that's what. Not all precise, but if you skip the postwar episode, you've got three generations."

"So?" Renie said, opening the parlor door with her elbow.

"Calamitous events," Judith said, following Renie out into the hall. "Suzette, who worked for Walter and Margaret Burgess. Kenyon, arriving with a whole new passel of servants circa 1946. Dr. Moss delivering Theo Stevens. The threats to Leota and Dr. Moss's murder."

"You forgot something," Renie said as they headed for the kitchen. "Charles Ward's hit-and-run death. Doesn't he count, too?"

Judith wrinkled her nose. "Should he?"

"Maybe," Renie said. "All the usual suspects were involved, including Dr. Moss."

"But he was at Creepers to see Leota," Judith reminded Renie. "Her gall bladder attack, remember?"

"I know," Renie said as they entered the kitchen. "But it's still a tragedy involving this whole crew. Hi, Ada," she said brightly.

To the cousins' surprise, Ada Dietz was crying. She looked up from a stool next to the work island and stared dumbly at Judith and Renie.

"What are you doing here?" she demanded in a hoarse voice.

"Helping," Renie replied, setting the tray down. "What's wrong?"

"Nothing," Ada barked. "It's almost ten, I've had to do without power for half the evening, this household is in chaos, and I won't be finished here until midnight. The dishwasher's backed up by three loads."

"Then we'll pitch in," Judith said. "What needs to be done right now?"

Grudgingly, Ada indicated a stack of plates in the sink. "They need to be scraped. The garbage has to be taken out. I wouldn't do it during that storm. I have to box up some leftovers to send to Mr. Bop when he gets off work. Between all the visitors and the police, I feel like I've been feeding an army. No offense," she hastened to add, apparently remembering that Judith and Renie qualified as guests.

"I take out the garbage at home," Renie said. "Where does it go?"

"There's a brown Dumpster off the back porch," Ada said, then got down off the stool and wiped her eyes. "See here, there's no need . . ."

"Ta-da!" Renie shouted, picking up a plastic bag in each hand. "I can use the fresh air. Be right back."

"You're guests," Ada said, looking worried. "The Mrs. better not hear about this."

"Don't tell her," Judith said, turning on the sink and rinsing off plates. "You and Edna must have been very young when you came to Creepers. How long has it been, Ada?"

Ada sighed. "Close to fifty years. I was barely twenty, but my husband was killed right at the end of the war in the Pacific. Edna had been in service with a family in the city. They divorced and broke up housekeeping, so she had to find another position. The Burgesses needed a maid and a cook, and I'd been working at a restaurant downtown. Edna's always been timid, and she was afraid to take on a big place like Creepers, so she insisted I come along, at least for a while."

Ada stopped, and scowled at Judith. "Why am I telling you all this? I don't even know you."

"Yes, you do," Judith replied cheerfully. "I cook for a living, too. It's a big part of my job as a B&B hostess. We're both working girls, Ada. The lifestyle at Creepers is as foreign to me as Xanadu."

"You have a kind face," Ada murmured. "It isn't often

I get to talk to somebody of my own class who's sensible."

"You mean solid middle class." Judith smiled.

"Do I?" Ada's own smile was grim. "I guess you're right. I used to get out more when I was younger, but these days, it's all I can do to keep up with everything around here. You'd think that once the children were grown, they wouldn't be around so much."

"Ha!" said Renie who had reappeared in the kitchen. "Our kids are never leaving. When Bill and I die, they'll just stick us somewhere down in the basement, along with all their other castoff belongings. They're not much younger than these kids, either."

Ada regarded Renie with curiosity. "Who's Bill?"

"My husband," Renie said. "Our three are in their twenties."

"I wasn't talking about the younger generation," Ada said. "I meant the older ones. Mr. Wayne, Mrs. Peggy. Mrs. Beverly is the only one who had the nerve and the ambition to get away from Creepers. Oh, Mr. Wayne and Mrs. Peggy may have separate houses, but they're so close you could spit on them. Now I could see it if Mrs. B. had all the money. But Mr. B. left them each a tidy sum. And still they never move away. It's like they're chained to Creepers."

"But not Bev," Renie noted.

"No," Ada said thoughtfully. "Not Mrs. Bev. She's different than the other two. Always was independent. And always a bit of an outsider. She was about ten when I came here, and I felt sorry for her. Wayne and Peggy were so mean to her. It was always like they knew some big secret and they weren't going to let her in on it. I don't care if she did marry a Japanese man, he's a fine fellow, and it just showed them all up. It serves Wayne Burgess right. Now the Japanese are all over him."

"They are?" Judith said in surprise.

"You bet," Ada said with a decisive nod. "They want to buy out Evergreen Timber, and judging from what I hear—not that I'm one to eavesdrop, that's Edna's style—I say, good. And never mind that the Japanese killed Homer—

that was my husband. These big shots didn't sink his ship, they were still in diapers, or whatever Japanese babies wore back then. Wayne is no businessman, and never was."

Judith perched on the stool that Ada had vacated. "So a Japanese company is trying to buy out Evergreen Timber?"

"That's right, you heard it here," Ada asserted. "He's gotten himself and the company in a real hole, and the Mrs. is wild. She won't hear of such a thing, but it's either that or go bankrupt." Ada gave the cousins a sly look. "The phone rings in here, you see, and sometimes when Sarah isn't around to answer it, I have to pick it up."

And sometimes when Sarah *is* around, Judith thought, and stifled a smile. "I can see why Mrs. Burgess is upset. Evergreen was founded by Maxwell Burgess. It's been around for over a hundred years."

"They should have let Peggy run it," Ada averred. "Peggy was the firstborn, and might have had a better head for business than Wayne. But Mr. Walter couldn't see a woman being an executive, not in those days, and Wayne got the job. Then Wayne passes over Mr. Bop, his own son, who has twice as much business sense. Though," she added, "I don't think he wanted to do it. He'd rather have his little pizza parlor. I've often wondered why."

"Pressure," Renie suggested. "It's one thing to own a small restaurant, and another to run a huge corporation like Evergreen Timber."

"I suppose," Ada allowed.

"Poor Wayne," Judith said, feigning sympathy. "This certainly comes at a bad time for him. Or maybe it's the reason for his . . . domestic troubles?"

Ada's gray eyes widened. "You know about that?"

Judith gave a sad shake of her head. "Oh, yes."

Ada uttered a little snort. "A long time brewing, if you ask me. Mrs. Dorothy has never been a happy woman. She never wanted to stay home and just be an executive's wife. If he'd let her have that gym, they wouldn't be in this mess."

Renie was frowning. "Do you mean Jim—or gym?"

"A gym," Ada replied. "You know, one of those health clubs. Dorothy has been wanting to start one out on the highway for the past several years. Wayne was dead-set against it, and the Mrs. wouldn't give her a dime for it. 'Common,' that's what the Mrs. called it."

Judith and Renie exchanged quick glances. "So that's at the heart of this divorce?"

"Partly, anyway," Ada said. "I'll be frank, I'm on Dorothy's side. She's had a bad time of it. I didn't much mind telling the police that Wayne was here last night."

"They knew that," Judith put in.

"I don't mean early in the evening," Ada said. "I mean late, around eleven-fifteen. Not that that's unusual for him." She paused and the corners of her mouth turned down. "Anyway, I saw him come to the house. I was getting ready for bed and watching the TV news. They said a storm was coming, so I went to the window to see if it had started to rain. It hadn't yet, but I saw him, sneaking around out front."

"What did the police say?" Judith asked, trying to hide her excitement.

Ada shrugged her broad shoulders. "Not much. You know how they are, though that black woman is kind of nice. She calls me honey."

"Yes, she's very nice," Judith said absently. "Did Wayne actually come inside?"

"I don't know," Ada answered. "My bath was running. As soon as the weather forecast was over, I turned the TV off and headed for the tub."

"So you didn't see Dr. Moss arrive?" Judith queried.

"No." Ada opened the dishwasher, which had finished its cycle. "I was half asleep when the next thing I knew, I heard someone running along the hall and then a couple of minutes later, Sarah was at my door, telling me there were a bunch of emergency vehicles out front. That's when Sarah and I came downstairs to see what was happening."

"Did the rest of the staff wake up then?" Judith asked.

Ada made a face. "Kenyon's so deaf he wouldn't have

heard an atom bomb go off, and Edna snores like a loco-
motive. Her room is next to mine, but I didn't rouse her
then. She would've passed out from all the excitement."

"Is Sarah's room near yours?" Renie asked, pitching in
to help Ada put the dishes away.

"Being the housekeeper," Ada said with a captious expression, "means she gets an actual suite, front and center,
with my rooms at one end and Kenyon's at the other.
Edna's next to me, but on the north side of the house. The
rest of the third floor is pretty much used for storage, since
there aren't any extra maids or footmen these days. There's
not much space left over, because the third floor is mostly
dormer rooms."

"What about the nannies?" Judith asked. "Were they also
on the third floor?"

"No, they were in the tower, above the children's
rooms," Ada replied, starting to reload the dishwasher with
Renie's assistance. "I'm told they had speaking tubes running between the tower floors, in case the kiddies got sick
during the night. They were taken out after the last nanny
left because Peggy and Wayne used the tubes to wake up
poor Beverly and scare her half to death."

Sarah Kenyon entered the kitchen, also looking tired. She
bit her lip when she saw Renie hard at work. "You don't
have to earn your keep, Mrs. Jones," she said, though it
was impossible to tell from her tone if she was being hu-
morous.

"I'm compulsive about dishwashers," Renie replied. "I
think of them as ferry boats. You load them up, and off
they go, with water, water everywhere. Then they get un-
loaded when they've completed their run, and sure enough,
there are always more passengers waiting to come aboard."
She offered the housekeeper her most disingenuous smile.
"I have a lot of fun in the kitchen."

A bit uncertainly, Sarah smiled back. "If Ada needs help,
I'll take over. Actually, I was looking for you ladies. Mrs.
Burgess wanted to see you before she went to sleep, but
it's well after ten now, and she's watching one of her pro-

grams. If you could time it just right, you might slip in just after it's over at eleven."

"Of course," Judith said. "By the way, are the phones working?"

"Not yet," Sarah replied, carefully placing two crystal goblets into the top rack of the dishwasher. "It's a nuisance, but Kenneth said there was a problem in the local central office. I believe he heard it on his transistor radio."

"Joe must be worried sick," Judith said as the cousins trudged down the hall.

"He'll figure out the phones are screwed up," Renie said in reassurance. "What do you suppose he did all day?"

"Who knows? Brooded, maybe." Judith halted in mid-step. "You said you heard someone running outside last night when you were in the library calling 911. Could that have been Wayne, taking off?"

Renie's eyes widened. "Sure. But it could have been somebody else, too."

Judith sighed. "I know. Unless Wayne killed Dr. Moss. But why?" She grabbed Renie's arm as her cousin turned to go into the parlor. "We might as well go back upstairs. It's almost ten-thirty, and we have to check in with Leota at precisely eleven-oh-one."

"Bear with me," Renie said, shaking Judith off and proceeding into the parlor where she went to one of the windows to pull aside the drapes. "I found this by the Dumpster when I took out the garbage."

Judith stared at the crowbar. "The weapon?"

Renie stared at Judith. "Shoot. I didn't think of that. I got it because I thought we might use it to pry open the fourth-floor tower room door."

Judith grimaced. "I'm not sure I want to do that tonight. In the dark. With the power going out. Hearing strange voices. Anyway, we should turn this over to the police."

"Well, phooey," Renie said. "I thought I was on to something."

"I suppose you got fingerprints all over it?" Judith said.

Renie made a face at Judith. "Do you think I carried it

in with my teeth? Besides, it was out back, not out front. Don't you think the police would have spotted it when they searched the grounds?"

Renie was making sense. "Yes, probably. If it was there then." Using her skirt to wrap around the crowbar, Judith picked it up. "We still ought to mention it to Edwina. Come on, let's head upstairs."

Kenneth met them in the entry hall. "What's that?" he asked, pointing to the crowbar.

"We . . . need it to open the fireplace damper," Judith fibbed. "It's stuck."

"This house," Kenneth said in a dreamy voice, "has flaws, but that's because it's so old. It makes Creepers all the more wonderful, don't you think?"

"It's a matter of taste," Renie said firmly.

"Creepers should last forever," Kenneth went on, as if Renie hadn't spoken. "I'd keep it the same, I swear I would. But not the grounds. Gardens are a waste."

"I beg your pardon?" Judith said, puzzled.

"I'd let it all go wild, tear down the outbuildings," Kenneth continued, his eyes drifting around the entry hall. "If I could, I'd evict everyone in Sunset Cliffs, and raze all the houses. *Grandmaman* doesn't understand."

"Kenny?" Russ Hillman stood in the doorway. "I've come to take you home."

Slowly, Kenneth turned to face his stepfather. "I changed my mind." His voice grew shrill. "I'm staying on again tonight."

"But your mother told me you wanted to go back to your place in town," Russ said.

"No!" Kenneth stamped his foot like a child. "I'm not finished here. Go away."

"Kenny . . ." Russ began, his hands outstretched.

"No, no, no!" Kenneth shouted. "I'm going to my room." He wheeled around and practically ran in the direction of the north tower.

Russ shook his head. "Sorry, ladies. He's in one of his

moods. Peggy tells me he's already had at least one row with his grandmother."

"He has," Judith said, moving the crowbar behind her back. "Did Peggy say why they quarreled?"

Russ groaned. "The usual. Kenny wants to turn Creepers into an animal preserve."

Judith let out a strange little laugh. "In the middle of Sunset Cliffs? No wonder he was talking about getting rid of the rest of the residents."

"It's not really a joke," Russ said. "The Burgess family not only still owns about a third of the undeveloped property in Sunset Cliffs—excluding the golf course—but Maxwell, the patriarch, retained certain rights in . . . I forget the term."

"En perpetua?" Renie put in.

"Something like that." Russ cocked his head to one side and gave Renie his engaging grin. "Anyway, it means the Burgesses—at least Leota—can make certain rules about land usage."

"Like turning somebody's three-car garage into a tropical bird aviary?" Renie asked.

"Not quite," Russ said. "It's more about what they can and can't complain about with regard to their own property. If Leota wanted to build a ten-story condo that cut off somebody's view, she could do it, and they'd have no recourse. Or put a stream through somebody's land. Things like that."

"Like letting the deer and the antelope roam through the rose garden?" said Renie.

"Exactly." Russ grinned again.

"It all sounds hypothetical," Judith noted. "Leota would never allow such a thing."

"Well . . ." Russ scratched his head. "I'm not so sure about that. I think she's leaving Creepers to Kenny."

"Really?" Judith said in surprise. "How come?"

"Nobody else wants it," Russ responded, taking an imaginary golf swing. "Peggy and I have our place on the links, Wayne and Dorothy live at Evergreen."

"Has none of you ever thought of moving?" Judith asked.

Something flickered in Russ's hazel eyes. "No. Why should we?"

"There've been . . . rumors," Judith said with a little shrug.

"About what?" Russ's gaze hardened.

"Oh—changes," Judith said vaguely. "I'm not sure. We don't know the rest of the family well. What were you saying about Creepers?"

Russ cleared his throat. "You mean about only Kenny wanting the house?" Seeing Judith nod, he seemed to relax. "Well . . . Bop has his apartment just off the highway near the pizza place, and Carrie likes that artists' community up north where she wants to start some kind of women's writing retreat. Peggy talked Kenny into getting a place in town to wean him away from Creepers, but it hasn't worked." He paused to take another swing, his gaze following the invisible ball. "Kenny and Carrie got shuttled back and forth between Peggy's marriages. They spent so much time at Creepers that they felt like this was their real home. At least Kenny does. I'm not so sure about Carrie, but then who is? She may be my stepdaughter, but she's kind of an odd duck."

"And Kenny isn't?" Renie broke in.

"Oh—he's just got this mania for animals," Russ replied, now bending over to concentrate on the imaginary ball. "I'll admit he's a little immature, they both are, but they've had a rough time growing up. Peggy was a single mom for quite a while after her second husband died in 'Nam." He paused, watching the unseen ball travel what seemed to be a rather short distance. "Hey! I birdied that hole. How about that?"

"Terrific," Judith enthused. "You must be a very fine golfer."

"I do okay," Russ admitted. "This course here is a good one, but I prefer Pebble Beach. Peggy and I usually go down there in March, but things are kind of up in the air right now."

"You mean because of Dr. Moss's murder?" Judith asked.

"Well . . . that and other things." Russ gave the cousins an off-center smile. "Guess I'd better go. It's going on eleven. Peggy's staying here again tonight, so somebody ought to keep the home fires burning."

"Russ," Judith said, holding out a hand to stay him, "what kind of a father was Charles Ward? Don't think I'm snoopy, but you mentioned that Caroline and Kenneth had a rough upbringing. Did he do his share?"

Russ scratched his head again. "I don't really know. Peggy always complained about him when he was still alive, but the kids, especially Carrie, seemed nuts about him. I met him a few times, but Peggy and I'd only been married a couple of years before he got killed. He seemed like an up-front kind of guy, but we didn't have much in common. My world's golf, and Charlie didn't play. He'd hurt his back. I wouldn't call him an invalid, but he was pretty screwed up by the time I met him."

"It doesn't sound as if his last years were very happy," Judith remarked.

Russ chuckled. "You wouldn't have known it to meet him. He was one happy-go-lucky sonuvagun. I suppose that's what drew Peggy to him in the first place. She's always liked a good time. Catch you later." Russ went out through the front door.

"Does he or doesn't he know about the trouble between Wayne and Dorothy?" Judith asked Renie as they started up the stairs.

"Does," Renie answered. "If Peggy knows, and I assume she does, then Russ knows."

"Why not say so?"

"We're not family," Renie said as they reached the second floor.

"He blabbed everything else to us," Judith argued. "Besides, he's not one of The Rich. None of Peggy's husbands was, it seems."

"Her rebellion," Renie said. "Or her need to be better

than somebody. Bill would say the latter, that she was dominated by her parents, especially Walter. Her mother—stepmother, that is—has both beauty and class, neither of which Peggy has in nearly the same quantities. Bill would describe her as—"

"Not now," Judith said in a whisper as she pointed to her watch. "It's two minutes to eleven."

"Then I can finish telling you what Bill would say," Renie whispered back.

"No, you can't." Judith smiled meaningfully at Renie. "I'm thinking."

"Thinking," Renie said in a vexed tone, "that you never like hearing Bill's psychological insights because they don't always agree with yours and he usually has them first."

"That's not true," Judith retorted. "Not exactly, anyway. Bill's approach is clinical, mine is based on experience. I don't claim to be an expert like he is, but I think I have a pretty good knowledge of how people behave."

"You do, it's just that you never want to hear me out when—" Renie stopped and Judith jumped at the sound of a heavy thud on the other side of the door. "What was that?" Renie asked, looking apprehensive.

"Let's find out." Holding the crowbar in one hand and turning the knob with the other, Judith entered Mrs. Burgess's suite.

Nurse Fritz was lying facedown in a large mushroom, pepperoni, and tomato pizza.

FIFTEEN

"QUICK!" JUDITH CRIED. "Check on Leota. And try to call 911!"

Renie rushed into the bedroom while Judith attempted to rouse Nurse Fritz. The stricken woman was still breathing, but she didn't stir. Feeling panicky, Judith tried to remember the first aid instructions she had learned in order to handle emergencies at the B&B. She could only recall how to apply a tourniquet, which didn't seem appropriate since Nurse Fritz wasn't bleeding. The red blotches on her face were tomato sauce.

"Leota's sipping tea and fit as a fiddle," Renie said, breathless. "I called 911; they're on the way. Should I call Dr. Stevens, too?"

"No, go down and let the medics in," Judith said, still trying to bring Nurse Fritz around.

Renie raced out of the master suite. Feeling helpless, Judith went to the bedroom door. "Did Renie tell you Nurse Fritz collapsed?"

"Of course," Mrs. Burgess answered querulously. "Really, people today have no stamina."

Not wanting to alarm Mrs. Burgess, Judith murmured something about a stomach disorder, which triggered a question in her own mind about the pizza. "Was Bop here this evening?"

"Yes, he watched my program with me," Mrs. Burgess replied. "He just left, via the back stairs. He brought pizza for the staff. I gather Dietz is working late. You know," she added, pointing to an empty cardboard box on the nightstand, "it's rather tasty. I've never had pizza before."

"Excuse me," Judith said, "I'd better check on Fritz."

"She'll be fine," Mrs. Burgess asserted. "Nerves, that's all. I'd like to have just one member of the medical profession not fall apart on me in a time of crisis."

Judith, however, couldn't listen to the old lady's complaints. She rushed back to Millicent Fritz, whose breathing had grown more shallow. The crowbar still lay on the floor where Judith had left it. Again using her skirt, she carefully placed the tool behind the settee.

The sitting room seemed in order, except for Nurse Fritz. Judith noticed an empty teacup, a teapot, a half-filled glass of milk, and the remnants of white chocolate mousse. The medium-sized pizza box, with two missing slices, was marked with a hand-lettered "M," presumably for mushroom. Nurse Fritz, Judith concluded, was either finishing a late dinner or having an early snack when she passed out.

The door to the sitting room opened, revealing Peggy Hillman. "What's going on? I thought I heard somebody running around up here. Oh!" Peggy spotted Nurse Fritz and retreated a step. "Is she . . . ?"

"No," Judith replied in answer to the unfinished question. "But she's not good. The medics are on their way."

Drawing her green satin robe closer to her body, Peggy moved cautiously toward the unconscious woman. "Has she had a heart attack? A stroke?"

"I don't know," Judith responded. "My cousin and I found her like this. Don't alarm your mother. She thinks Fritz merely fainted."

"Maybe she did," Peggy said. "Did you throw water on her or use smelling salts?"

"I'm leaving the emergency measures to the pros." Judith didn't want to add that she'd had enough experience to know when someone suffered from something more sinister than a simple faint.

"I'll go see *Maman*," Peggy said, giving Nurse Fritz's crumpled form a wide berth as she headed into the bedroom. "God knows she seemed just fine when I left before her TV show came on."

Since Peggy hadn't closed the door to the suite, Judith could hear Renie explaining what had happened as she accompanied the medics up the stairs. Without further word, the emergency team went to work while the cousins stood near the windows and kept their mouths shut.

Judith tried to overhear what the two men and one woman were saying to each other, but they might as well have been speaking in code. She recognized them from the previous night, and wondered what they must think of the people who lived at Creepers. Whatever it was, she decided, they'd be pressured to keep it to themselves. The medics and their supervisors weren't dealing with trailer park trash.

"We're taking this one to the hospital," the female medic said as one of her companions used a cell phone to alert the emergency room staff. "Who's coming along?"

"I am," said Peggy, coming out of the bedroom. "I'll follow in my car as soon as I get dressed. I've got to notify Dr. Stevens first. That's Theo Stevens, got it?"

The female medic nodded. "Okay, see you there. Let's move out."

An IV had already been inserted in Nurse Fritz's left hand. With military precision, the trio put her on a gurney and wheeled her out of the room. Peggy followed.

At the door, one of the male medics, a young man with prematurely white hair, called back to Judith and Renie. "Don't touch any of those food and beverage items, okay? The police should be here any minute."

Renie shot Judith a wry look after the medic had left. "Does he expect us to be surprised?"

"Fritz isn't the fainting type, and she looked healthy as a horse," Judith declared. "We've had one murder and several attempts prior to that. How could we be surprised?"

"That's what I meant," Renie said. "Shall I go see Mrs. B. while you wait for the cops?"

"Sure," Judith said, then stared at Renie, openmouthed. "The phone! It works. You got through to 911."

"That's right," Renie said in wonder. "Are you going to call Joe? It's too late to ring Bill. He's in bed by now."

Judith grimaced. "I'd better not. I don't want to be talking to him when the police get here."

The words had barely gotten out of her mouth when they heard Edwina Jefferson's voice float up from the bottom of the main staircase. A moment later, she and Danny Wong were in the sitting room.

"The cook let us in," Edwina said, shaking the raindrops from her jacket. "What have we got now?"

"We don't know," Judith said, "but we're willing to suspect the worst."

Edwina nodded. "That's what the medics said. Possible poisoning." She scanned the leftover foods and beverages. "You haven't been tinkering, have you, sugar?"

"We know better." Judith smiled. "And I'm glad to hear I finally graduated to the rank of sugar."

Edwina gave a nod, then told Danny to bag the evidence. Judith remembered the crowbar and pointed to the back of the settee. "What do you think?"

Edwina frowned. "As a weapon? Where'd it come from?"

"Out back by the Dumpster," Renie answered, then hung her head. "And yes, I touched it. I didn't even think about it being the weapon."

"Then you're still honey, honey," Edwina said with a vexed expression. "What were you doing with a crowbar?"

"That's a long story." Renie sighed. "We wanted to get into the top floor of the north tower."

Edwina looked perplexed. "Why?"

Judith explained, but not before she had closed the door between the sitting room and the bedroom. The sealed door didn't seem to perturb Edwina, but the dollhouse discovery made her wince.

"That's ugly," she asserted. "Who'd do a nasty thing like that? And why?"

"That's the reason we wanted to get into the fourth-floor room," Judith said.

Danny was placing the crowbar in a large plastic bag. "The uniforms couldn't have missed this," he said. "It's too obvious. It must not have been there when they searched the grounds."

"In other words," Judith said dryly, "you still haven't found the weapon."

"Hey, Number Three Son," Edwina said to Danny, "stop giving information away. We haven't put these two on the payroll yet."

Standing by the fireplace, Renie pouted. "I want to be a sugar, too."

Edwina ignored her. "Okay," she said, sitting down on the settee, "tell me what happened with the nurse."

"There's not much to tell," Judith said. "We came up here about eleven to say good night to Mrs. Burgess when her TV show was over, and when we got to the door, we heard a big thump. We dashed in and found Nurse Fritz, lying in the pizza."

"She didn't say anything?" Edwina prodded.

"Nothing," Judith replied. "She was out like a light."

As Danny started to bag the remains of Fritz's meal, Edwina took another quick look. "What's that white pudding stuff?"

"White chocolate mousse," Judith answered. "It was the dessert *du jour*."

"Where'd the pizza come from? That redheaded kid's place?"

"Yes. Bop was here until eleven, watching Mrs. Burgess's show with her." Judith stopped and slapped a hand to her cheek. "Leota ate some of that pizza, too. I wonder if she should be checked by a doctor."

"How is she?" Edwina asked, glancing at the closed bedroom door.

"Fine," Judith replied. "She doesn't know that anything serious happened to Nurse Fritz, though."

"We aren't positive ourselves," Edwina said. "Okay, so who else has been around here this evening?"

"Everybody," Judith said, making a face. "Peggy's spending the night again, but she's gone off to the hospital to be with Nurse Fritz. I think most of the family came to dinner. I haven't seen Caroline, but I'm sure she's staying over. Kenneth is here. Russ Hillman stopped by around ten-thirty." Judith glanced at Renie. "Who else?"

"Dr. Stevens," Renie said, still pouting at Edwina. "I shouldn't tell you that. I'm not a sugar."

"What about Wayne and Dorothy Burgess?" Edwina queried, again ignoring Renie's complaint.

"Wayne was here earlier," Judith said slowly. "We saw him in the game room. With a woman."

"What woman?" Edwina asked.

"We couldn't see much of her," Judith said. "She was sort of under Wayne."

"Oh." Edwina burst into laughter. "You're kidding me. *Wayne?*"

Even Danny was smiling. "The woman wouldn't have been his wife, I take it?"

"Dubious," Judith replied. "Dorothy is threatening divorce. Did you know that the Japanese are trying to take over Evergreen Timber?"

"Yes," Edwina said. "We've been checking into the company. Evergreen's in big trouble. It'd take more money than even Mrs. Burgess has to bail out the firm at this point."

"Let's see," Judith ruminated. "What else did we learn? Oh—Dr. Moss left an estate of—"

"We know that, too." Edwina grinned. "We haven't been sitting on our hands, sugar. The young Dr. Stevens is now the wealthy Dr. Stevens, complete with a three-million-dollar motive for murder."

Judith flinched. "That's true, but you don't really think—"

Edwina broke in again. "We're keeping an open mind. Aren't we, Number Three Son?"

"We have to," Danny replied. "So far he's the only one with a clear-cut motive for killing Dr. Moss."

"But he wouldn't break into his own house and office," Judith protested.

"He might if he were clever," Edwina said. "And he *is* clever. The robbery would throw suspicion away from him."

Renie moved off the hearth. "He didn't know about the money. He seemed genuinely shocked."

Edwina said nothing until she started for the bedroom. "I'm going to talk to Mrs. Burgess. Come on, Danny, bring the notebook."

The cousins were left surrounded by evidence bags and a sense of gloom. "Does Edwina seriously suspect Theo Stevens?" Renie asked.

"She suspects everybody," Judith said glumly. "Maybe even us. By humoring us, she may be setting a trap. Who knows?"

Renie started to sulk again. "She called you sugar."

"That's in deference to Joe," Judith replied, then gazed at the phone. "I feel terrible that I didn't call him earlier today. What's wrong with me? There was a time when Joe was always uppermost in my mind."

"Eight years of marriage and twenty-four hours of daily togetherness will do that," Renie said. "You needed some time apart. Your resentment was showing."

"Not to him, I hope," Judith said with fervor. "Goodness knows, I still love him like mad."

"Of course you do. I still love Bill like mad, but we aren't joined at the hip," Renie contended. "Married or not, we're still individuals, and since we arrived at Creepers, we've had plenty of distractions. I do believe that around four o'clock this afternoon, I forgot I had children."

"I didn't," Judith said. "I wonder how Mike and Kristin and little Mac are doing."

"Probably just fine," Renie responded as Edwina and Danny reentered the room.

"We got a call from the hospital," Edwina said. "All they

can tell so far is that it's some kind of gastrointestinal distress. We'll gather up our goodies and go downstairs to talk to the cook." She motioned at Danny to collect the evidence bags, and then they were gone.

Judith led the way into Mrs. Burgess's bedroom. The old lady was looking tired, but otherwise none the worse for wear.

"What's going on with Millicent Fritz?" she demanded. "That colored woman wouldn't tell me a thing."

"Maybe," Renie broke in, "that's because she wasn't the right color."

"What?" Mrs. Burgess said. "I don't understand."

"I know you don't," Renie said quietly. "Never mind."

"Nurse Fritz may have food poisoning," Judith hedged. "Peggy's with her at the hospital, and Dr. Stevens has been called."

Mrs. Burgess frowned. "Whatever did Millicent eat this evening?"

"Pizza, for one," Judith said. "What kind did you and Bop have?"

Mrs. Burgess handed Judith the empty box. "The ingredients—I believe they're called toppings—are marked here," she said, pointing to the lid which, like Nurse Fritz's box, bore a handwritten "M."

Judith scanned the small squares that had been checked on the printed list: Mozzarella, Canadian bacon, pineapple with a regular crust. "This is different from the one Fritz had," she murmured, showing the box to Renie. "Mrs. Burgess, are you sure you feel okay?"

"I'm just fine," the old lady snapped, "despite a rather tumultuous day. But if Fritz is gone, I need someone to spend the night in here. I still can't walk on my ankle. Where's Caroline?"

Judith replied that they hadn't seen her for several hours. "Shall I see if she's in her room?"

"Please," Mrs. Burgess said. "She can sleep here on the chaise longue."

"I'll go get her," Renie said.

Offering Mrs. Burgess her most sympathetic expression, Judith sat down next to the bed. "You have great inner strength. I don't know many women who could go through what you have and still be so . . . chipper."

"Older women, you mean," Mrs. Burgess said with a shrewd glance at Judith. "Is your mother still living?"

In a way, Judith wanted to say, but didn't. "Yes, and she's quite a bit older than you are."

"How would she react?" Mrs. Burgess seemed genuinely interested.

The truth was that Gertrude would have exhibited her usual tough-as-nails demeanor. "Mother is a forceful personality," Judith responded. "She would probably be up to the task." *As in chewing up anyone who opposed her and spitting them out like so many pistachio nuts*, Judith thought. Which, she recalled, Gertrude had recently done, and spit out her dentures along with the pistachio shells. It had taken two days to find her mother's teeth because they had landed in a wastebasket that Phyliss Rackley had emptied into the Dumpster. A terrible scene had ensued, with Phyliss trying to save Gertrude's soul while Gertrude jammed the empty wastebasket over Phyliss's head.

But Judith didn't care to go into maternal-related details with Mrs. Burgess. "You mentioned a few minutes ago that you were . . . ah . . . fed up with medical people who . . . fell apart during a crisis. I was curious. Had Nurse Fritz done this before when she was caring for your husband?"

Mrs. Burgess shook her head. "No, Millicent was a rock all those months. At the end, no one could have been more stalwart or more kind. Of course, she had her reasons," the old lady added enigmatically.

"Oh?" Judith evinced casual curiosity. "You mean a sense of duty?"

"Not exactly." Mrs. Burgess stared straight ahead, her mouth fixed in a rigid line.

Judith had the feeling that Leota wasn't going to say any more on the subject. "Then you must have been referring to Dr. Moss. I can't imagine him losing his composure. Of course, I really didn't know him."

"Well, he did. Just once, I'll admit. I still don't know why . . ." Mrs. Burgess broke off as Renie reappeared with a very sleepy Caroline, who was wearing flannel PJs decorated with Porky and Petunia Pig. "My dear," the old lady said in greeting, "go back to sleep on the chaise longue. Mrs. Jones will get a pillow and blankets from the cupboard."

But Caroline made straight for the bed and crawled in next to her grandmother. "G'night," she mumbled, and buried her head in the pillow.

"Well." A faint smile touched Mrs. Burgess's mouth. "I suppose we can manage. It's a big bed."

Judith and Renie took their leave. Out in the sitting room, Judith reached for the phone book. "It's almost midnight. Let's see if we can get hold of Jack Moody at the gatehouse. I saw a number for it scrawled in the margin someplace. Ah—here it is."

"You're kidding," Renie said, her mouth agape. "Can't we go to bed like normal people? Sleep was short last night, in case you've forgotten."

"I told you earlier today I wanted to talk to Moody," Judith said. "We'll invite him over for drinks. That ought to lure him into our lair."

"Sheesh," said Renie, leaning against the wall.

Judith reached the security guard on the first ring. Her ploy worked, though it took some coaxing and a great deal of blarney: Moody would stop by Creepers as soon as he finished his shift.

"We'll entertain him in the drawing room because that's where the bar is," Judith said on her way out of the master suite. "Nobody else should be up and about except the detectives and maybe Ada Dietz."

Renie, however, balked. "You entertain him. I'm going to bed. My left eye feels like it's drooping down to my chin."

Judith examined Renie's face, and immediately felt sympathetic. "You don't look so good now that you mention it. Okay, see you later."

The entry hall was empty, and except for the soft sighing of the wind, Judith couldn't hear a sound inside the house. Wall sconces still burned in the hallway that led to the library, the game room, and the kitchen. Instead of the table lamp, which had been removed as evidence, a torchiere lamp glowed near the door that led to the parlor. The main lights also remained on.

Judith's gaze wandered from the entry hall to the open area at the bottom of the central staircase. She tried to envision the scene from the previous night: Presumably, Dr. Moss had let himself in with his own key, then used the intercom to call up to Mrs. Burgess. She then would have switched on the main lights from the second floor. The table lamp might or might not have been on. The doctor would have started for the stairs. At about the halfway point, the lights would have been turned off from the first-floor switch. Judith searched the wall for the panel and found it just inside the main entrance.

Where had the killer been standing when Dr. Moss entered the house? Probably just on the other side of the short wall that jutted out some three feet between the entry hall and the area at the bottom of the staircase. The doctor wouldn't have seen him—or her—because his back would have been turned as he headed for the stairs.

A quick reach around to the switch on the other side of the wall would have plunged the entire area into darkness. The killer must have advanced, weapon in hand. The blow was struck, with Leota Burgess hurtling down the stairs. She crashed to the floor as Dr. Moss fell down on top of the her.

Something was wrong with the scenario. There had to have been a second or two when the staircase area was in full light. If the killer had stood by the inside wall, Leota could have seen him—or her. If the killer had stood on the other side of the wall, she would have seen only Dr. Moss. That meant that as he entered the house and used the intercom, the doctor saw his murderer. It was someone he knew, probably the person who had summoned him to Creepers. Perhaps he had chatted with his would-be assailant. They might have talked about why he'd been called. The other person might have reinforced the idea that Mrs. Burgess was ill.

That made sense. Judith shivered as she thought of the kindly physician speaking to the person who was about to kill him. He trusted whoever it was. The face was familiar, and it masked a deadly intention.

But another possibility was equally plausible. Dr. Moss never saw the killer—but Leota Burgess did. If that was the case, she was protecting someone. It had to be a family member, Judith reasoned. Mrs. Burgess wouldn't lie for an outsider, particularly for someone of inferior social class. Loyalty was reserved for shared blue blood.

For the first time, Judith was convinced that Dr. Moss had been the intended victim all along. Why else lure him to Creepers?

But Mrs. Burgess was still in great danger. The reason for the doctor's killing might also be the motive for getting her out of the way. A person who deliberately killed had crossed the line. Judith knew from her own experience, as well as what she'd learned from Joe, that once that line had been crossed, there was no going back. It might be difficult, even agonizing, to kill the first time. To kill again was almost easy.

If the alleged attempts on Leota Burgess's life had only been imagined, Judith now knew that any threat to the old lady must be taken seriously.

The problem was that the next time might very well prove fatal.

SIXTEEN

JUDITH COULDN'T REMEMBER the last time she'd gotten drunk. Maybe it had been when she'd found out that Joe had eloped to Vegas with Herself. Perhaps it was on her wedding night with Dan. Or it could have been the morning after her wedding night with Dan. She honestly couldn't recall. The days and weeks and months of abandonment by Joe and the rebound marriage to Dan were a blur. For all she knew, she might even have been sober the whole time, and wished she'd been drunk.

But if Jack Moody didn't loosen up after two stiff drinks, Judith was going to start watering down her Scotch. She should have started with vodka. That way, Moody couldn't have known if she was drinking along with him or not.

"Awful nice of you to invite me in," Moody said from his place in one of the loden club chairs. "You sure picked a bad time to come visit."

Judith had embroidered her story about how she and Renie had been invited to Creepers. In her revised version, they were distant, impoverished kin, having been taken in by a kindly Mrs. Burgess. The fib, Judith felt, would make Jack Moody feel more at ease.

Her ploy seemed to work. Moody looked relaxed as he guzzled his gin and tonic. "These are great smokes," he remarked, waggling a long cigar between his teeth. "Cuban, huh?"

"I think so," Judith said. For all she knew, they could have come from Moose Jaw, Saskatchewan. She'd found the box in a glass-fronted cabinet in back of the bar.

"I've never been inside one of these fancy houses until today," Moody said for the fourth time. "Seven years on the job, and not one invite. Then some poor old coot gets whacked, and here I am, in and out like a freakin' yo-yo."

Judith offered Moody a tight little smile. "Still, you must have gotten to know the residents quite well. Seven years is a long time."

Moody chuckled. "You can't say as if we're chummy. But yeah, sometimes you get to shoot the breeze, especially if they're not being driven by a chauffeur. Take Mr. Hillman. He's almost a regular guy. I don't golf, see, but when the big names come here to play, I get to wave 'em through. Then Mr. Hillman tells me stories about 'em, like who's a good egg and who's a jerk. Two years ago, they had this celebrity tournament, and some of those Hollywood types came up to . . ."

Moody droned on. Judith had already heard about various big names who had birdied, bogeyed and boogied around the golf course. Her eyelids were getting heavy. She saw that Moody was almost done with his third gin and tonic. Maybe, just maybe, by number four, he'd loosen up so that she could learn something pertinent to the case.

"So as a rule," Moody continued, apparently having wound down his account of actually seeing Kevin Costner and Charles Barkley in the flesh, "I get off work and head for the highway. It's my way, ya see—my way's the highway."

"Ha-ha," Judith laughed lamely. "Would you like another G&T?"

Moody held out his glass. "Sure, why not? I probably won't hit the highway tonight. I usually stick to beer when I play cards."

Judith went behind the bar. She was drinking icewater

this time, and hoping Moody wouldn't notice. "Poker?" she asked in a tired voice.

"I would if I could." Moody chuckled richly. "You can meet some foxy ladies at some of those places. Not real young, but who wants 'em just out of kindergarten? I like a woman who's a real woman. You're not so bad yourself, Mrs. Finn."

"Flynn," Judith said absently, handing Moody his fresh drink. "I'm afraid that's the last lime."

Moody began to hum. "The last lime I saw Paris . . ."

Judith held her head. "Uh . . . Do you often win? At cards, I mean?"

Moody nodded. "Texas Hold 'Em—that's my game. I do just fine. In fact," he went on, lowering his voice and leaning closer to Judith, "last night, I cleaned out Carrot Top."

"Who?" Judith didn't understand the reference.

"You know—the redheaded rich kid, Bop Burgess. I won over three hundred bucks on one hand. Bluffed him out of his jock. He had a straight flush, too." Moody chuckled uproariously.

"Bop plays poker out on the highway?" Judith asked.

"Damned near every night," Moody answered, the chuckles turning into a cough as he took a deep drag on his cigar. " 'Course I don't usually play with him. He tries to get into the high-stakes games. That's outta my league."

"Is Bop lucky?" Judith inquired, finally sensing that she was about to get some interesting, if irrelevant, information out of Jack Moody.

Moody, who was still coughing, shook his head. "No," he finally managed to say. "The kid's a lousy poker player. He's got one of those faces that telegraphs everything in his hand. Jeez, he even grins when he gets the hole card he wants. But he loves the game. I'll say that for him."

"Compulsive?" Judith suggested.

"Huh?" Moody stared. "Oh—you mean he can't quit. That's right. He's one of those guys who never knows when to fold. When he gets good cards—which ain't often—he freezes. No killer instinct. That's how I beat him last night. A straight flush, for God's sake, and when I raise him, he throws in the hand."

"But he doesn't fold when he gets poor cards," Judith noted, wondering how long she could stay awake.

Moody nodded. "You got it. Seven-card stud, and he don't ever fold till the last damned, card. You got nothin' after the third card, you're out. That's my rule, anyways. He ain't lucky, he's a chump." Leaning down to rummage in a large paper bag that sat beside his chair, Moody pulled out a pizza box. "But Bop's a nice guy, considering. He's always giving me free pizza. Want some? I didn't quite finish it tonight."

"No, thank you," Judith said, eyeing the box, which had a large letter "F" written on the front. "What kind do you like?"

"Most any kind," Moody replied, returning the box to the bag. "This one's anchovies and onions."

Something tripped in Judith's brain, but she was too tired to grasp its significance. Besides, she had one last, important question to put to Jack Moody.

"I know that rich people have a reputation for being tight with their money," she said, forcing a smile, "but I'll bet they can be generous in some ways. If you know what I mean." Somehow, she managed a wink.

With a sly look, Moody set his cigar down in a marble ashtray. "You bet. See, these folks have one thing more precious than their money. And you know what that is."

Judging from the vague expression that suddenly came across Moody's face, he knew, but couldn't come up with the word.

"Their reputations?" Judith offered.

"That's it. Their reputations." Moody took a long sip from his drink. "They got secrets, see. They come in, they go out. Mostly, it's innocent stuff, but not always. I could tell you some tales, Mrs. Flinch."

"Flynn," Judith said under her breath. "You could? Please do. I'm all ears."

"Take this bunch," Moody said, making a circular motion with his index finger to include the entire household. "That Mrs. Burgess, for instance. The younger one, I mean, who lives at Evergreen. She and Mr. Hillman have something going, if you ask me. See, I didn't let on to the cops about it, 'cause it's none of their beeswax. But last night, just before I went off my shift, the two of them headed out in his car. They done that before, maybe a dozen times since Christmas. Fergie—he's the guard who takes over from me at midnight—says he's seen 'em come back around four, five in the morning. But I think Mrs. Hillman is on to them—she was hot on their trail last night, and I'll bet she followed 'em out to one of the motels on the highway. I'd hate to have been in Mr. Hillman's shoes—Mrs. Hillman's got quite a temper."

"Dorothy Burgess and Russ Hillman," Judith murmured. "That's extremely interesting. Are they the only ones from the family who . . . ah . . . carry on?"

"That depends," Moody replied, removing the lime from his glass and placing it in the ashtray next to the cigar. "Bop has girlfriends, but usually he takes them to his own pad. At least as near as I can tell, since I've seen him pick up a babe now and then at the card rooms. 'Course he's single, so what? I'll tell you one thing, though—I don't think he wants his folks to know he goes to those card rooms. He slips me a few bucks now and then to make sure I don't let the cat out of the bag." Moody paused, apparently collecting his thoughts which, judging from his unfocused eyes, were scattered in several directions. "I can't speak for Mr. Burgess. Wayne Burgess, that is. Or Mrs. Hillman. The young one—Caroline or Carrie or whatever—hasn't had any men friends since she and her husband split up. The only female Kenny Hillman ever brought in was a bear he rescued from the circus. Name was Daphne."

Judith was hardly surprised, but Moody's hilarious reaction jarred her. "This bear, see, looked kinda like Mr. Van Buren from Twelve Cedars, over by the creek. He's a real hairy guy with a big beard. Face it, I'd had a coupla swigs—it was early March, and Mrs. Hillman had given me a case of Wild Turkey as a late Christmas present. I was freezin' my nummies off, and that hundred-and-one proof went down real good. Anyways, I shouldna been surprised—the night before Kenny came through with three beavers."

"You certainly have the lowdown on the people in Sunset Cliffs," Judith said, fighting back a yawn. "I mustn't keep you. I'm sure you need to get your sleep."

Moody picked up the cigar and finished his drink. "It's early by my clock. One, one-thirty? I'm usually just getting settled in at the table by now."

"Maybe you can still find a game," Judith suggested with what she hoped sounded like enthusiasm. "Oh, by the way—when Dr. Moss drove through last night, did he say anything to you?"

Moody shook his head. "Nope. I knew the poor old guy real well. I always let him cruise right by. Dirty rotten luck, him getting killed. Do they know who did it?"

"I'm afraid not," Judith said, inching her way to the edge of the chair.

Moody stretched and yawned. "Maybe I will hit the hay. It's been kind of a rough day, talking to the cops, being extra careful on my shift tonight. In fact, this is the worst thing that's ever happened to me on this job since the night Charlie Ward got himself run over."

"That's right," Judith said. "You would have been working at Sunset Cliffs then, too."

The security guard stood up, his paunch bulging over a wide leather belt with a Longhorn buckle. "That was a mess. Poor Dr. Moss, he found Charlie out there beside the road. Mrs. Burgess was sick, and he'd come tearing over from the hospital to see to her, and about a quarter-mile up the public road by the golf course, there was Charlie, lying in the ditch like a pile of dirty laundry. I never seen Doc so upset."

"I don't blame him," Judith said, also on her feet. "It must have been a shock."

"It was one damned thing after another," Moody murmured, swaying slightly. "I always figured it was some drunk coming from one of the taverns on the highway. Some people don't know when to quit." He took three steps and tripped over an ottoman.

"Maybe you shouldn't drive," Judith said, feeling guilty.

"Maybe I should," Moody replied, picking himself up. "I sure as hell can't walk."

"Please," Judith begged, "let me call a cab."

Moody hesitated. "I got a better idea. I'll get Fergie to come get me. I only live a half-mile from Sunset Cliffs."

"But he's on duty," Judith protested.

"It won't take fifteen minutes," Moody insisted.

"Won't he get in trouble for leaving the gatehouse untended?" Judith asked.

"Naw." Moody wove his way out of the drawing room. "It's late, it's a weeknight, it oughtta be quiet."

There was no point in arguing. Judith couldn't wrestle a two-hundred-pound tub into submission. But she did wonder how often the gatehouse guards were derelict in their duty.

After Moody had been picked up by the other guard, Judith went back into the drawing room to empty the ashtray and collect the dirty glasses. The pizza box lay on the floor next to Moody's chair. Judith was hungry. She decided to warm up the leftover pieces in the kitchen.

Ada Dietz was no longer at work, but Sarah Kenyon was sitting on one of the stools at the counter, drinking a cup of tea.

"You're up late," Judith said with a tired smile.

Sarah turned on the stool. "So are you. Don't tell me you're keeping a twenty-four-hour vigil now that Nurse Fritz has gotten sick."

"No, I'm headed for bed after I have a snack. Care for some pizza?" Judith put the highball glasses in the dishwasher, then showed Sarah the box. "Tell me—what does the 'F' stand for?"

The housekeeper refused the pizza offer but studied the

handwritten letter. "Oh. Is that anchovies?" She saw Judith nod. "Then 'F' is the menu code for Fisherman's Friend. That's how Bop marks the boxes—a different letter for each pizza type. 'S' is Sassy Sausage, 'P' is Pepperoni No Baloney, 'A' is All There Is and More, which is the works. I forget the rest."

"What's 'M'?" Judith asked.

"Let me think—Mozzarella Bella."

"There's only one 'M'? What about mushrooms?"

"There's only one kind of pizza for each letter," Sarah explained, looking somewhat puzzled at Judith's line of questioning. "The mushroom pizza is something else. Really, I can't remember them all."

Judith put the two remaining pizza slices in the microwave. "That's okay, it's not important. I was just curious."

Neither woman spoke while the microwave buzzed off the seconds. Then, as Judith put the pieces on a plate, she asked Sarah why she was keeping such late hours.

"I've been busy up until now," the housekeeper replied. "In fact, I'm not done yet. I still have to pack."

"Pack?" Judith stared.

Sarah never changed expression. Indeed, now that Judith was watching her closely, she noticed that the housekeeper looked pale, even haggard.

"Yes," Sarah said in a dull voice, "my father and I are leaving on a six o'clock flight to Boston. There's not much point in going to bed. It's going on two already."

Clumsily, Judith sat down on the other stool. "I don't understand. Why are you leaving? How can you leave, with the homicide investigation still going on?"

"We're leaving because we should have left thirty years ago," Sarah said with bitterness. "We're not coming back."

"But . . ."

"As for how we can leave," Sarah continued with a tight little smile, "we're not suspects. My father is too feeble to have killed Dr. Moss, and I have an airtight alibi."

"You do?" Judith couldn't stop staring.

Sarah nodded. "Yes. I was upstairs in my room screwing the executive hosiery off of Wayne Burgess."

Somehow, Judith managed to keep from falling off the stool. It wasn't the revelation that shocked her so much as Sarah Kenyon's blunt language. But Sarah wasn't a blue-blooded aristocrat. She was a middle-class working woman, and despite being penned up in Creepers for most of her life, her job ensured that the outside world would rub off on her.

Or so Judith figured, but she was only partly right.

"It's late, I'm tired, and I've kept up a façade for so long that I can't stand it," Sarah declared. "I don't have to do that anymore. I'm leaving, and I should feel like the most liberated woman on earth. Unfortunately, I feel awful."

"Why is that?" Judith asked, finally regaining her composure and no longer staring unabashedly at Sarah.

"It's a long story," the housekeeper said with a grim smile. "You've caught me with my defenses down, but holding everything in doesn't matter anymore. It all began with my grandfather, Anthony Kenyon. He and my grandmother, Olivia, lived in Sunset Cliffs. They had a house about a mile from here that was known as The Chateau."

Nibbling pizza, Judith leaned back against the counter and listened to the Kenyon saga. Anthony Kenyon had been a successful banker until the '29 crash. He had lost everything, and committed suicide with his hunting rifle. Sarah's father, Edward Kenyon, had been away at Bowdoin College at the time. He had to quit school and come home to help his mother, who had been forced to sell The Chateau and move into an apartment. Not only had Olivia Kenyon's health declined after her husband's death, but her mental condition had become unstable. She died exactly six years to the day of her husband's suicide.

"My father had no brothers or sisters," Sarah explained, her strong, attractive features looking bleak. "It was the Great Depression, and jobs were hard to find. He found work wherever he could, but it was a hand-to-mouth existence."

In 1939, Edward married a woman named Frances Anderson, a clerk at the Belle Epoch department store. Despite the hard times that Edward had been through since his father's death, he and Frances had been shaped by different worlds. Sarah was born in the spring of 1941, but the marriage was already foundering. When the Japanese attacked Pearl Harbor, Edward joined the navy the next day.

"My father served in some of the most terrible campaigns in the South Pacific," Sarah said, pouring herself another cup of tea. "He was wounded twice. I hardly ever saw him when I was small, and my mother had to work despite the fact that she wasn't in good health."

When Kenyon was finally discharged in late 1945, he came home to a wife who was suffering from kidney disease and a daughter who was almost school-age. He'd hoped to take advantage of the GI Bill to finish his college education, but Frances's medical expenses were piling up. She could no longer work, and jobs for veterans were scarce.

"Mom died two days after I started kindergarten," Sarah recounted. "It was really strange—I'd grown up so far with only my mother, and then I was left with a father I scarcely knew."

Judith was sympathetic. "The war took a horrible toll, and not just in battle casualties. I don't think the younger generation has any idea what it was like."

Sarah nodded agreement. "Anyway, at this point Dad was desperate. You see, he'd always blamed the Burgesses—Maxwell, in particular—for the family's ruin. In the mid-1920s, my grandfather had made a huge loan to Maxwell Burgess so that Evergreen Timber could buy a vast parcel of forest land up near the Canadian border. Maxwell defaulted on that loan, and it helped bring on our family's financial disaster. In Dad's mind, he had not only lost both parents, but the house in which he was raised, his financial security, and a chance for a college education. Consequently, my father went to see Walter Burgess. Maxwell had just died, and his wife had been dead for several years.

"Dad demanded—not asked—that he be given a job," Sarah continued with a faint smile. "Because of old Mr. Burgess's death, the family was in the middle of a staff upheaval, and Walter Burgess offered Dad the position of butler. He was insulted at first, but then he set out his conditions. He would accept the job if the salary was double what other butlers were being paid, and if I could live with him at Creepers. To his surprise, Walter agreed. Then Leota stepped in, and said that when it came time for my father to retire, he and I should have the cottage out on the grounds. Mrs. Burgess has a conscience, or at least a sense of justice, I'll say that for her. The problem was that my father never wanted to retire. He actually likes being a butler. It's his little joke on the world, bowing and scraping to the nabobs, and knowing inside that he's as good as they are."

"Interesting," Judith murmured, and meant it. People's stories always fascinated her. "So what convinced your father to give it all up now?"

"Me." Sarah set her teacup down with emphasis. "I have to get away. Because of Wayne."

"But I've heard that he and Dorothy may be divorcing," Judith noted.

"It's not as simple as that." Sarah sighed. "Wayne and I fell in love when he was twenty-one and I was seventeen. We'd been raised together, and while I wasn't part of the family, I was part of the household. Do you see the difference? And the affinity?"

Judith did. She could picture the young Sarah joining in the games, sharing the secrets, swimming in the pool, playing on the tennis courts—but never really belonging.

"It wasn't puppy love," Sarah asserted. "Wayne had dated a number of girls by then, mostly debutantes his mother presented to him. I'd had a boyfriend when I was sixteen, a fellow I'd met in high school. We were pretty serious for a while. I was old for my age, probably because of never having had a two-parent family or much of a real home." She paused, taking a deep breath. "And then, one

June morning, Wayne came home from college for the
summer. It was like I'd never seen him before. He wasn't
a boy, he was a man. He told me later he had a similar
reaction—I was all grown up and looked like I'd been waiting for him my whole life."

Judith smiled softly. "I can practically see it. What happened?"

Sarah's mouth turned down. "What you'd expect. By the
end of the summer, we wanted to get engaged. His parents
wouldn't hear of it. Mrs. Burgess felt rather bad about it, I
think, but she held firm with Mr. Burgess. I simply wasn't
suitable."

"But your family had originally lived in Sunset Cliffs,"
Judith pointed out.

"Of course. But I hadn't, except as a servant's daughter.
I was the granddaughter of a man who committed suicide
because he'd been ruined financially. I might have had better luck if I'd been a rollerskating carhop from out on the
highway."

"So Wayne ended up with Dorothy," Judith remarked.

"Yes, but not right away. Wayne hadn't finished college,
so he went off again in the fall, and I tried to get over him.
But when he returned for the holidays, nothing had
changed. Nothing ever did, not even after he married Dorothy." Sarah gave Judith an ironic glance. "Most people
would scoff, but you absolutely cannot kill true love. You
can stuff it in the closet, lock it in a vault, bury it in the
backyard—but it's still there no matter how many years
and how many obstacles keep you apart."

"I know," Judith said softly, thinking of the quarter-
century without Joe and how time had changed nothing
between them. "I know all about that."

Sarah surveyed Judith with interest. "Yes. Yes, I think
you do. Maybe that's why I'm telling you all this. But what
it comes to now, even though Wayne and I have continued
our affair off and on for all these years, is that I won't be
part of the reason he and Dorothy end their marriage. I've
never married, but I consider the union sacred. If I leave

Creepers, and five years from now Wayne is free and asks me to marry him, I might consider it. But this is all wrong now. Wayne's having terrible business problems, Dorothy's hell-bent on divorce, we've had a murder at Creepers—everything's a mess. Dad is unhappy with my decision, but I won't leave him behind. He's so frail, and I'd worry about him constantly. We have distant cousins in Boston, and there'll be an entire continent between us and this place. We're going, and that's it."

"Does Mrs. Burgess know?" Judith asked.

"No," Sarah replied, getting up from the stool. "I stopped by her suite earlier this evening, but I just couldn't work up the nerve to tell her. She's had a rough time of it lately. Anyway, I've left a letter explaining everything. I hate leaving the family in the lurch, but if I give notice and wait for my replacement, I might change my mind. I can't do that."

"I understand," Judith said simply. "I wish you and your father the best of luck. By the way, you mentioned that he came here at a time of staff upheaval. Were all those changes made only because Maxwell Burgess had just died?"

"That's what I always heard," Sarah said, looking mildly surprised. "But I was just a little kid when Dad and I moved in."

"What did you ever hear about Suzette?" Judith asked.

Sarah broke into a grin. "Suzette, the Creepers ghost. She was a nanny to Peggy and Wayne. There was some kind of scandal, I think. They were never sure what it was because they were both so young. In fact, it happened not long before their mother died. You can imagine for kids who were say—three, in Peggy's case, and Wayne wasn't yet two—that scandal didn't mean much to them. In fact, Wayne doesn't remember his real mother at all. In some ways, I think we were drawn together because we'd both lost our mothers so young."

"Suzette was French, right?" Judith said, not wanting to get sidetracked.

"French-speaking," Sarah replied. "She was Haitian."

Judith recalled the coin. "Was she black?"

"I believe most Haitians are," Sarah said dryly.

"Yes, of course." But Judith's mind had raced ahead. "You don't know what happened to her?"

"No. The kids used to tell each other terrible tales about her. Voodoo and all that. I used to feel sorry for Beverly, because they were always trying to scare her to death. For all I know, Suzette quit in a huff and went to work for the Boring Airplane Company."

Judith smiled at the suggestion. But she didn't believe it.

"I've got to pack," Sarah said. "I feel better. Thanks for hearing me out. Maybe, since I'm about to turn my back on all this, I needed to tell my story."

"I was glad to listen to it," Judith said. "I think you're very brave."

"Am I?" Sarah gave Judith a half-smile. "Or am I a coward? By the way, that was you and your cousin who came into the game room today, wasn't it?"

Judith grimaced. "Yes. Sorry."

"Don't be. It was our farewell fling. The rest of the leave-taking is mundane. Now I'll have to find some suitcases."

Sarah disappeared into the hall. No doubt she'd find suitcases easily enough, Judith thought. The problem was that Sarah Kenyon was carrying more baggage than one person should bear.

SEVENTEEN

SO MANY THINGS were darting around in Judith's brain that she thought she'd have trouble getting to sleep. At precisely two A.M. she switched off the bedside lamp and climbed under the covers. Renie was just a mound in the bed, dead to the world. Judith envied her cousin's ability to sleep so soundly.

The next thing she knew, it was ten minutes after nine. Renie was still a mound in the bed. Hurriedly, Judith got up and headed for the bathroom. After a quick shower, she went into the sitting room and called Joe.

Arlene Rankers answered the phone. "Goodness, Judith," she said in a breathless voice, "I'm just serving the last batch of guests. Can you call back later?"

"Where's Joe?" Judith asked.

"Joe?" Arlene said in a voice that sounded as if she'd never heard of him.

"Where did he go?" Judith persisted.

"I've no idea," Arlene said crisply. "Call me back. The scrambled eggs and ham are about to scorch."

Vexed, Judith clicked off, then dialed her mother's number. As usual, Gertrude didn't answer until the ninth ring.

"Where are you now?" her mother demanded in a crabby voice. "Pismo Beach?"

"Of course not, Mother," Judith said. "Why would I be in Pismo Beach?"

"Because somebody on TV is from there," Gertrude said illogically. "It sounds like the kind of place you'd go."

"I'm out in the north end of town," Judith responded. "Renie and I are staying with friends."

"That's dumb," Gertrude grumbled. "Why would you stay with friends in the north end when you can be with your family in your own house? Or," she asked, a sly note creeping into her voice, "are you and Lunkhead separated?"

"Of course not," Judith retorted. "I explained all this to you before I left Monday. We're helping out. One of Renie's friends has a problem."

"Any friend of Serena's is a problem," Gertrude snapped. "That girl has no sense. What does she do with all her time? Draw stupid little pictures, right? Cartoons, I bet, like the Katzenjammer Kids and Maggie and Jiggs."

"Not exactly," Judith said, running an agitated hand through her wet hair. "Look, I just wanted to see if you're okay. We might be home today or at the latest, tomorrow."

"Okay? Are you kidding?" Gertrude huffed. "Three of my ten toes fell off. My chest feels like an elephant sat on it. I'm so stiff from arthritis that the St. Vincent de Paul thought I was a hat rack."

"Yes, Mother." Judith sighed. "Have you had breakfast?"

"As a matter of fact, I have," Gertrude said smugly. "Arlene knows how to treat me. She made little pigs."

"That's nice," Judith said. "Arlene's a terrific cook."

"Better than some," Gertrude said in her raspy voice. "I gotta go, kiddo. The exterminator's here."

"What exterminator?" Judith asked, feeling an onset of panic.

"His name's Marbles," Gertrude replied. "He's here to get the possums. So long, Toots."

Gertrude hung up.

Renie was staggering out of the bathroom when Judith returned to the bedroom. "Whazzup?" she mumbled.

"Have you ever had possums in your yard?" Judith asked.

"Sure." Renie focused her eyes. "Twice. Found one on the back porch a year ago. Ugly suckers." She blinked and made an effort to become alert. "I told you about it at the time."

While the cousins dressed, Judith recounted the phone calls she'd just made. "I wonder where Joe went," she said, going over to the speaking tube.

"Out for breakfast, maybe," Renie said. "Bill does that every so often, especially if he attends weekday Mass. What are you doing?"

"Husbands and possums aren't the only things I have to discuss," Judith said, switching on the tube. "Let's eat up here, so we don't have eavesdroppers. What do you want?"

Renie recited a long list, which, to Judith's dismay, included lamb kidneys. "Good luck," said Judith. "This isn't England."

Judith considered waiting to divulge her information until after Renie had her first cup of coffee, but couldn't contain herself. She disposed of Jack Moody before Kenyon delivered their trays.

"Kenyon!" Judith exclaimed in surprise. "I thought you left."

"Haven't you heard, ma'am?" the butler replied. "The heavy winds blew away the rain and brought in a thick fog. The airport is closed, at least until this afternoon."

Renie, naturally, was bug-eyed. "What was that all about?" she demanded after Kenyon had toddled off.

"I was just getting to that," Judith said, and promptly went into the story about Edward and Sarah Kenyon. She paused only when Renie lifted one of the silver lids and uttered a delighted cry at the sight of four lamb kidneys on the plate.

"But now," Judith said in conclusion, "it seems the Kenyons are stuck at Creepers, at least for a while. Coz, how can you eat innards?"

"Easy," Renie responded. "I already ate them." She

pulled back from the table and patted her stomach. "Yum, yum."

"Innards and carrots mashed up with rutabagas," Judith murmured with disgust. "You have some queer tastes."

"What do you mean?" Renie countered. "You eat liver and onions. Liver is—are?—innards. I can't stand liver. Giblets are good, though."

"Giblets are good," Judith agreed. "Giblets in dressing, giblets in gravy, just plain giblets. And speaking of food, hear me out on the pizza issue."

"Huh?" Renie looked up from her almost-empty dishes. "Pizza?"

Judith recited the information Sarah had given her about the pizza box markings. "One letter for each specialty item—got that?" She saw Renie nod. "But there was an 'M' on Nurse Fritz's box and another 'M' on the one we saw in Mrs. Burgess's bedroom. How come? They were two different kind of pizzas."

Renie looked blank. "A simple mistake? Or," she said, gathering steam, "you were looking at one of the boxes upside-down. One of the 'Ms' might have been a 'W.'"

"Brilliant, coz," Judith said excitedly. "Your designer's eye has done it again. So, do we conclude that the boxes got mixed up, and the pizza for Nurse Fritz was the one intended for Mrs. Burgess?"

"As in an attempt to poison the old girl?" Renie said with a skeptical expression. "We don't know that the pizza was poisoned. Nurse Kitz ate and drank some other things last night. Besides, wouldn't it be extremely stupid of Bop to poison his own pizza?"

"Bop's a risk taker, remember?"

"But," Renie put in, "according to Jack Moody, Bop has no killer instinct."

Judith grew solemn. "I know. That bothers me. Of course Moody was referring to playing cards, but poker is often a metaphor for life. All the attempts—if they were real attempts—on Leota's life have failed. Is that by accident or by design?"

"In a really weird, oddball kind of way, you're making sense," Renie declared. "Will you mention this to Edwina and Danny?"

"Sure," Judith said, finishing her coffee and standing up. "Let's find out what's happened while we slept."

"What about Leota?" Renie asked. "Shouldn't we check on her?"

Judith snapped her fingers. "You're right. I'm being derelict in my duty. Let's go."

Mrs. Burgess had long since finished breakfast and was sitting up in bed reading a romance novel. Caroline was nowhere to be seen, though the remnants of a meal for two remained on a large tray by the Chinese screen. Apparently, Leota's rule against others eating with her in the boudoir didn't apply to kin.

"Nurse Fritz is improving," Mrs. Burgess announced. "Food poisoning can be dangerous, though."

"Do you know what they think caused it?" Judith asked.

"If so, I haven't heard," the old lady replied. "I do hope Fritz can come back on duty soon."

Renie had sat down in a chair next to the bed. "You feel okay, though? I mean, it wasn't the pizza?"

"Of course not!" Mrs. Burgess huffed. "Bop wouldn't use substandard ingredients. He and I both ate all of ours, and as far as I know he's fine. So am I. Except for my ankle. It still pains me."

"Bop certainly has a flair for naming his pizzas," Judith remarked. "What was yours called?"

"Wild something-or-other," Mrs. Burgess answered. "The names are clever indeed. I believe I haven't given Bop full credit for his business acumen. But all things considered, that's understandable." She frowned and looked away.

Judith started to say something about the Kenyons' imminent departure, but thought better of it. Perhaps Mrs. Burgess didn't yet know.

"You're staying on for the funeral tomorrow, I trust?" Mrs. Burgess's gaze shifted away from the window where the outer world was shrouded in heavy fog. "I'm sure Beverly would want you to stand in for her."

"Yes," Renie replied, though there was a reluctant note in her voice. "We'll be there. To be honest, I'm not sure the police want us to leave just yet."

"Twaddle," said the old lady. "You're scarcely criminals, and they know it." She paused as Edna entered the room, announcing Dr. Stevens.

"Good morning," he said in greeting as Edna bustled around the room and collected the big tray. She could barely balance it as she passed behind the Chinese screen to the backstairs area.

"Well?" Mrs. Burgess said to the doctor. "How long am I to be incapacitated?"

"Through the weekend, at least," Dr. Stevens replied with an encouraging smile. "Don't worry, we'll get you to the funeral in a very comfortable wheelchair."

Mrs. Burgess made an impatient gesture with her right hand. "I'll hate that. It shows weakness. Don't you think I could put my weight on it just long enough to get in and out of the chapel?"

The cousins decided to withdraw. Murmuring excuses, they left the master suite.

"Where do we find another crowbar?" Judith asked when they reached the hall.

"Huh? Oh—you mean to get into the tower room?" Renie considered. "Are you sure you want to go up there again?"

"Yes," Judith declared. "I don't know who's trying to warn us off, but we can't give up."

"Your call," Renie said without enthusiasm.

"Sarah Kenyon referred to Suzette as a ghost haunting the place," Judith said. "That's nonsense, of course. I don't think Sarah meant it seriously."

Renie looked askance. "I suppose not."

"You don't believe in ghosts," Judith said, surprised at her cousin's reaction.

"No," Renie said after a pause. "Not really. But if ever a house had them, it'd be Creepers."

"True," Judith admitted. "Let's forget about ghosts and get some tools."

"Kenyon will know where they are," Renie said. "Let's ask him."

The butler was in the dining room, polishing silver.

"You don't seem to be surrendering your duties even though you're leaving," Judith remarked with a smile.

"As it turns out," Kenyon said, squinting at a silver cream pitcher with his half-blind eyes, "we won't be leaving now until Friday. I felt quite strongly about staying on until after Dr. Moss's services. Naturally, my daughter is disappointed. She had her heart set on leaving this morning."

Renie inquired about tools. Keeping his expression impassive, the butler suggested they try the shed nearest the house.

"Mr. Jeepers is doing some repair work necessitated by the storm," Kenyon said. "I believe you'll find him nearby."

Mr. Jeepers's real name was Arnie Norberg. "Bop nicknamed me when he was a kid," Arnie explained. "It stuck. I suppose anybody who was called Bop felt everybody else should have a nickname, too."

In the well-organized toolshed, Arnie supplied the cousins with another crowbar, a hammer, a chisel, and an axe. He couldn't resist asking to what purpose the tools would be put.

Judith opted for candor, explaining that the top floor of the north tower was sealed. They were curious. Arnie merely smiled.

"Friends of Miss Bev's, huh?" he remarked. "She's a peach. I've been working at Creepers off and on since she was in college."

"But not full-time?" Judith said.

Arnie shook his clean-shaven head. "No thanks. I started out doing odd jobs for the Van Burens, then some of the other families asked me to work for them. I like it better if

I'm not tied down to just one household. Frankly, these people give me the creeps. Excuse the expression."

" 'These people'?" Judith quoted. "You mean the Burgesses?"

"All of them." Arnie waved a hand, taking in the expanse of Sunset Cliffs. "They aren't like other people. They aren't real."

Judith didn't disagree. The cousins cautiously made their way through the thick fog to the rear of the house. At one point, Renie collided with the wishing well.

"Look out, coz," Judith said, unable to help because her hands were full. "Is your eye worse this morning?"

"No," Renie replied, rubbing her knee. "It's better. It's just the fog and my depth perception. I guess I should throw a coin in this thing and wish for improved vision."

Judith paused to smile at what she could see of the charming little stone well with its wooden bucket and lacy wrought-iron arch. "You wouldn't get your wish," she said. "The well's been sealed off, probably to keep kids from jumping into it."

The cousins were lucky in one respect, however. They didn't encounter anyone who might express curiosity about the clutch of tools they carried. The passageways were empty as they walked to the door that led to the north tower.

"Maybe we should have asked Arnie to help us," Judith said as they ascended the winding staircase.

"Let's see how we manage on our own," Renie replied, then stopped. "What's *that* noise?"

It sounded like a low, rolling moan. Climbing the last three steps, they saw that the door to Kenneth's room was open. Kenneth was lying on the bed; the moans were coming from him.

"Kenneth!" Judith cried, hurrying to the young man. "Are you ill?"

He kept moaning. Judith grabbed his arm and gave it a sharp shake. "Say something, please. What's wrong?"

"Everything," Kenneth wailed, his eyes closed and his

expression wretched. "I hate my family. I hate everyone. I hate myself."

A half-empty glass of juice sat on the nightstand. Judith picked it up. "Drink this, and tell us why you're so upset."

Kenneth waved the glass away, but struggled to sit up. "I love Creepers," he declared. "Isn't that enough?"

"You tell us," Renie said, leaning against the fireplace mantel.

"No." Kenneth shook his head several times. "I feel sick."

"Kenneth," Judith said quietly, "did you go into the safe the night before last?"

Kenneth's jaw dropped. "How did you know?"

"Logic," Judith replied. "You came here earlier in the evening, around seven while your grandmother was watching TV. You knew she was occupied, and you had another purpose. Ada Dietz said you ate some strawberry pie. Then I suspect you came into the library where you opened the safe, and left not only a smudge of strawberry, but your fingerprints. Whatever you found in the safe didn't alarm you too much, because the discussion you had later that evening with your grandmother was fairly tame. Then yesterday the two of you quarreled violently. Supposedly, you fought over the raccoon. But I don't think that was the main issue."

Kenneth's narrow shoulders sagged. "I'd looked for her will in the safe. She'd been threatening to change it. She hadn't." He winced as he tried to sit up straighter on the bed. "*Grandmaman* promised I'd inherit Creepers when she died because I was the only one in the family who loved the house. Monday night, I talked to her about my plans for an animal sanctuary here. She just laughed, as she's done before. I didn't tell her I'd already looked at the will to make sure she hadn't changed it." Kenneth flushed and ducked his head. "I mean, it's not really a secret, is it? We're all family."

"I'm not sure that counts," Judith said. *Especially*, she thought, *with this crew*.

"Then, when I brought Roscoe up to visit her yesterday," Kenneth continued, "she got very angry. She said she'd already talked to Gaylord Gibbons about adding a codicil or something to the will which would state that if I brought any animals into Creepers after she died, I'd have to forfeit the house. Isn't that outrageous?"

"No," Renie said calmly. "Sunset Cliffs isn't a zoo. Keeping animals around here could be dangerous." She paused, glancing around the room. "Where *is* Roscoe?"

"I set him free," Kenneth replied, on the defensive. "His paw seemed all right this morning."

Judith sat down in a railback chair. "I understand why you're upset. But that's no reason to hate your family."

"Yes, it is," Kenneth asserted. "They all want money when *Grandmaman* dies. All I want is the house. I still have most of my money from the trust that my grandfather left me. I haven't thrown it away like the rest of them."

"Do you mean spent—or squandered?" Renie put in.

"Both." Kenneth was looking petulant. "Bop used his to set up his pizza parlor. Carrie just frittered hers away, mainly on her husband, Brett. The dumb thing was that he didn't want expensive cars and designer clothes. Brett just wants to write his books. He should never have married my sister. I think he felt sorry for her."

"But Bop has been very successful," Judith pointed out.

"Oh?" Kenneth looked askance. "Then why is he always begging *Grandmaman* for loans?"

The cousins exchanged quick glances. Behind Kenneth's back, Renie made card-dealing gestures with her hands. Judith gave an almost imperceptible nod.

"What about your parents and the Wayne Burgesses?" Judith said. "Have they used up all their money, too?"

"I don't know about Uncle Wayne," Kenneth replied. "Somebody said the family business has gone sour. That's his problem. Nobody ever asked Bop or me to work for Evergreen. I wouldn't have anyway—all they do is chop down trees and ruin the animal habitat."

"Why weren't either of you asked?" Judith inquired.

"Maxwell, Walter, Wayne—three generations, and then . . ." She threw up her hands.

"I'll tell you why," Peggy Hillman said from the doorway. "Kenny, what's wrong? You look God-awful."

"I don't feel so good, Mom," Kenneth replied as his mother entered the tower room and put a hand to her son's forehead. "Do I have a temperature?"

"I don't think so," Peggy said. "You're just upset. Is it about that blasted raccoon?"

"In a way," Kenneth replied, peevish.

"I'll go get Dr. Stevens just to make sure," Peggy replied. "He's still with your grandmother." She stopped, then looked at the cousins. "You two have certainly managed to invade our lives in record time. Did Bev send you to watch *Maman* or to find out what she's been missing while she and Tom are rooting around in some pharaoh's tomb?"

Judith tried to detect if there was any humor behind Peggy's words. But the other woman seemed serious. Indeed, she looked as haggard as her son. The tinted blond hair seemed to have lost its luster, and there were dark circles under her eyes.

Judith evaded the question. "How long did you have to stay at the hospital with Nurse Fritz last night?"

Peggy shrugged. "A couple of hours, maybe more. I wanted to make sure she'd pull through. She will, but it was a near thing."

"Do they know anything more about what caused her illness?" Judith asked.

"Not that I've heard," Peggy said. "Fritz won't get out of the hospital until tomorrow. I guess she wants to go to Dr. Moss's funeral. She worked a lot of cases with him over the years."

"Tell them, Mom," Kenneth said suddenly. "You started to, then you stopped. They ought to know."

Peggy looked blank. "Tell them what? Don't you think they've heard too much?"

Kenneth shook his head. "About how people get passed over or ignored in the family business. Especially you."

"Oh." Peggy's face fell. "That's not . . . What the hell, why not?" She gave her son a feeble smile. "Kenny's proud of his old lady. That's nice, don't you think?" she asked of the cousins.

"My kids think I'm an idiot," Renie said.

Peggy's glance at Renie indicated that she probably agreed with the Jones offspring. She made no comment, however, and began speaking of herself.

"I'm almost two years older than Wayne. As the first-born, I should have gone into the family business—except that I came along a generation too soon. When we grew up in the late fifties, women weren't supposed to work outside the home."

"Bunk," Renie muttered. "All the women in our family did."

Peggy ignored the remark. "I always knew I was smarter than Wayne. Oh, he's not stupid, just average. You can't be average and run a big corporation like Evergreen Timber. And you can't be timid, either. You need nerve, and plenty of it. Wayne is inclined to be wishy-washy."

Peggy must have seen the look that passed between the cousins. She let out an exasperated sigh. "Good Lord, so you know about my brother and Sarah, too?"

"Um . . . well . . ." Judith mumbled.

"We're like termites," Renie said. "We come into a house and eat up all the information like it was cheap wood."

"Worms would be more like it," Peggy said, but this time there was a spark of something that might have been amusement in her blue eyes. "The liaison between Wayne and Sarah is no secret, at least not within the family. Dorothy's put up with it because, believe it or not, she loves Wayne. Or did, until lately. Now she wants a fresh start, before she gets too old. I don't blame her. She's another rich woman who hasn't been able to do what she wanted with her life because of social and family pressure. Wayne can't deal with it, not when he's up to his wire-frame glasses with Evergreen Timber troubles."

"I understand all that," Judith allowed, "including the part about you being passed over because the fifties were a different era for most women. But what about Bop? He was actually in line for the corner office at Evergreen, and we know he's got good business sense."

Peggy nodded. "That wasn't the problem. Bop would have been ready to enter the business about seven or eight years ago, shortly after my father died. Wayne had recently taken over, and the company was already in trouble. I think Wayne looked down the road and didn't want to saddle his son with the demise of Evergreen Timber. He's never said so outright, but that's the impression I've gotten over the years."

Judith gave Peggy an ironic look. "Nor did he want to admit you or even Bop might have done a better job. That's really sad."

"Sad, but true," Peggy said, biting off the words. "Excuse me, I'm going to try to catch Dr. Stevens before he leaves."

Kenneth laid back down in the bed. "Mom's got it all together. I really admire her."

"That's very sweet," Judith remarked.

"That's very weird," Renie said. "Say, what about Bev? Has she used up all her money?"

Kenneth grimaced. "I guess so. She used it to finance her husband's digs. Talk about pouring sand down a rat hole."

"That's not fair," Renie countered. "Tom Ohashi is doing important work."

Seeing an argument brewing, Judith intervened. "That's good news about Nurse Fritz. I hope she can attend the funeral tomorrow if it means so much to her."

"Nurse Fritz," Kenneth said in disgust. "She's nothing but a money-grubber."

Judith was surprised. "How do you mean?"

Kenneth laughed with a cynicism that ill-suited him. "She thought my grandfather would be so grateful to her for nursing him through his last illness that he'd leave her some kind of legacy. He didn't. Somehow, Dr. Moss coaxed her into taking care of *Grandmaman* when she was sick with her gall bladder, but she wouldn't come when *Grandmaman* sprained her ankle. I was really surprised to see her here yesterday."

Judith was silent for a moment, lost in thought. Fritz's knowledge about Walter Burgess's will obviously stemmed from personal interest. No doubt she had read the document after it had been filed for probate. Before Judith could comment further, Dr. Stevens appeared.

"We'll get out of the way," Judith volunteered.

Dr. Stevens smiled. "That's fine. By the way, what are those tools doing outside the door?"

With only a hint of embarrassment, Judith confided that she and Renie were going to try to get inside the top floor of the tower.

"Why?" Kenneth asked, his eyes wide.

"We like to keep ourselves occupied," Renie responded.

To Judith's surprise, Dr. Stevens was looking almost as dumbfounded as Kenneth. "What do you think is up there?" the doctor asked in a voice that sounded strained.

"We don't know," Judith said truthfully. "We're just curious."

Dr. Stevens gave a single nod. "I see. Maybe I'll join you as soon as I've checked out Kenneth here."

"Be our guest," said Renie.

Without speaking, the cousins trudged up the next two flights. They heard no odd sounds, felt no strange sensations. The bar across the solid oak door and the heavy padlock looked formidable. Judith went first, using the crowbar.

"Oof," she gasped. "This thing's rusted to the wood."

"You try one side, I'll use the hammer on the other," Renie suggested.

Judith pried and Renie swore. It occurred to Judith that her cousin couldn't perform a manual task without swearing, a trait she'd inherited from her father, who had been a seagoing man.

After the tenth or eleventh ear-scalding curse, Judith felt

compelled to upbraid Renie. "Coz, please. These people are going to think we crawled out of the sewer."

Renie let out one more string of curses that would have made public access TV viewers blush. But even as she wound down, the bar came free at one end and fell to one side of the door.

"Can I keep swearing?" Renie panted.

Also out of breath, Judith could only nod and point to the axe. Renie waited a few moments to catch her breath, then let loose with a mighty swing.

The axe made only a small dent. "We should have gotten a wedge from Jeepers," Renie said. "Let's try hitting the axe with the hammer."

It took several blows and a few more curses from Renie, but the door finally budged. Between gasps, Renie nodded to Judith. "Strut your stuff, coz."

Judith reached into the pocket of her beige slacks and removed a manicure kit. Dan McMonigle had had his own kind of life insurance: He had hidden away IRS notices, collection agency letters, promissory notes, and other incriminating pieces of paper so that Judith couldn't find them and thus try to kill him. To preserve her sanity, which she'd succeeded in doing, and to save the house, which she'd failed to do, Judith had learned to pick locks and open safes. Like riding a bicycle, it was not a skill she would ever lose.

The padlock was easier than she'd expected. The old Yale lock was more challenging, apparently because of the rust. It took Judith over three minutes to loosen the inner workings.

The door creaked open, revealing a room like the other two in the tower, except that the dormer ceiling was at steep angles. There was another small fireplace, and the furnishings had been left intact. The air smelled stale and damp. Cobwebs and dust covered the single bed, the bureau, the dressing table, and two chairs.

As Judith coughed, Renie sneezed. But the cousins approached the other door in the room and opened it. They assumed it led to an adjoining room, like the bedrooms on the second and third floors.

They were wrong. It was a wardrobe, the far wall rounded to indicate that this was the other side of the tower. There were clothes hanging inside, moldy and dust-laden.

Renie carefully pulled out a long navy blue dress. "The thirties," she said in awe. "Ankle-length, lace collar at the neck. Goodness."

Judith reached for a more colorful garment, streaked with faded blues, reds, and yellows. "Haitian?" she breathed.

Renie nodded. "Everything in here is sixty years old."

"So are we," Judith remarked dryly. "Almost, anyway."

They turned back to the bedroom itself. On a small side table next to the bed was a tin plate, a tin cup, and several tin utensils.

"Not the family silver," Renie remarked.

"Nor is this," Judith said, bending down. "What do you think?" She held up a rusty chain that was attached to the wall.

"Mother of God," Renie whispered. "What went on here?"

Dr. Stevens was at the door. "Have you found anything?" he asked in a not-too-steady voice.

"Yes," Judith said dumbly. "Come in."

With a tentative step, Dr. Stevens crossed the threshold. "Oh, my God!" he murmured. "What are you holding?"

Judith jiggled the chain. "Do you think this was used on Suzette?"

Dr. Stevens took two steps forward, staggered, and fell to the floor in a dead faint.

EIGHTEEN

"WE CAN'T CALL the family doctor when he *is* the family doctor," Renie asserted as Judith bent over Dr. Stevens. "What'll we do?"

"He'll come around," Judith said hopefully, "unless you want to go fetch some smelling salts."

"No thanks," Renie retorted, then gazed meaningfully at Judith. "Are you thinking what I'm thinking?"

"I'm wondering why we didn't think of it before," Judith said in wonder. "Somehow, Theo Stevens is related to Suzette."

"Grandson," Renie said. "What else?"

Judith nodded as the doctor began to stir and groan. "I'm sure you're right." She touched Dr. Stevens's forehead. "Are you okay? It's us. The cousins."

Theo Stevens's eyes began to open. He looked as if he were in pain. "My God," he moaned. "I . . . what . . . why?"

"Was she your grandmother?" Judith asked, supporting Dr. Stevens's head with her arm.

He gave a faint nod. "I shouldn't have come to the tower."

"We shouldn't have, either," Judith admitted. "The Burgess clan won't be happy about this."

"Damn the Burgess clan!" Dr. Stevens burst out. He

sat up, his anger fueling his strength. "How could they? How could she?"

"She?" Judith stared at the doctor. "Who? Mrs. Burgess?"

Theo Stevens held his head. "Not Leota Burgess. Margaret Burgess. Walter's first wife."

Judith gazed quickly around the room. There was fog outside the dirty windows; there was a different kind of fog inside, with its patina of dust and sad old memories. The cobwebs hung like the gauzy veil of a woman in mourning.

"Let's go downstairs," Judith said hurriedly. "This place is playing havoc with my allergies. I'm all choked up."

"So am I," Theo Stevens said in a plaintive voice. But he got to his feet and led the way down the steps, never looking back. "Kenneth is fine," the doctor said in his professional voice as they passed the second-floor bedroom. "His nerves are acting up. He's highly strung, like his sister, Caroline."

By the time they reached the library, Dr. Stevens seemed to have regained his composure. He apologized for passing out. "I knew," he said with a shake of his head, "but I never saw that room until now. Aaron told me it was closed up. I guess I was afraid to see it for myself."

"Do you want to talk about it?" Judith asked after the doctor had settled in behind the desk and she was seated in one of the wingback chairs. "Shall I send for coffee— or something stronger?"

"I'm all right," the doctor replied. "And no, I don't want to talk about it."

"Fine," Judith said in a pleasant tone, then turned to Renie, who was sitting in the other wingback chair. "See if you agree, coz. Suzette—and I'm sorry I don't know her last name . . ."

"Saint-Etienne," Dr. Stevens put in.

"Thanks. Suzette Saint-Etienne came to this country in the early thirties, probably because the Americans had withdrawn from Haiti, and she—"

"She came with Walter Burgess," Dr. Stevens interrupted.

"Really?" Judith said, wide-eyed. "Did they meet on one of his foreign travels?"

"Yes." Theo Stevens looked pained.

"He must have taken to her," Judith smiled. "Were they in love?"

"He was," the doctor replied. "Look, I told you I didn't want to discuss . . ."

Good-naturedly, Judith wagged a finger at him. "You don't have to. I'm just putting forth my theory."

"You're doing fine," Renie asserted. "So Walter was smitten with the beautiful Suzette and brought her to Creepers, right?"

"Exactly," Judith agreed. "He gave her a position here as nanny to his children. Though perhaps there was only Peggy at first. I have to assume that Margaret Burgess was suspicious of the affair from the start. She must have hated Suzette, and after Wayne was born, I'm guessing that she had the passage between the master suites closed up. The marriage, in effect, was over."

"But no divorce," Renie said. "That would have been scandalous in the thirties. Maybe Margaret was still in love with Walter. She must have been insane with jealousy. Literally."

Judith nodded, though she glanced at Dr. Stevens out of the corner of her eye. "I imagine. Who wouldn't be, in her position? She was a young woman with a faithless husband. Her social position was secure, but he was in love with another woman. Not only was she of an inferior class, but she was foreign—and black. I can imagine how galling all that was to Margaret. Like so many people of her generation, particularly, of her social standing, Margaret must have been a bigot."

Judith glanced at Theo Stevens, who seemed to bristle at the comment. He remained silent, however, his face set in a hard line.

"The final blow must have come when Suzette got preg-

nant," Renie mused. "I wonder if she flaunted her condition
in front of the mistress. Maybe there was a terrible scene.
Margaret must have gone to Walter and demanded that Suzette be sent packing."

"No." Dr. Stevens spoke quietly but firmly. "It didn't
happen that way. Or so Dr. Moss told me."

"What did happen?" Judith asked in a mild voice.

Dr. Stevens's shoulders slumped. He took a deep breath,
edged forward in the chair, and folded his hands on the
desk. "Margaret imprisoned Suzette in that tower room. It
was a prison—you saw that for yourselves. Suzette stayed
there until her baby was born. Then—" The doctor's voice
broke. "—Margaret murdered her."

"Dear God," Judith gasped. "I'd never have guessed
that."

Theo Stevens sat back in the chair. "According to Dr.
Moss, Margaret strangled her. Suzette was weak from
childbirth, and couldn't fight back. Margaret was a tall,
strong woman, and motivated by hatred and jealousy. The
baby was given to Dr. Moss to do with what he would. He
and his wife raised the child, and changed his name to
Stevens."

"Saint-Etienne," Renie murmured. "St. Stephen or
Steven."

"Yes." Dr. Stevens smiled faintly. "It wasn't easy for a
half-black boy to grow up in the all-white neighborhood
that existed around Creepers sixty years ago. Dr. Moss had
honored Suzette's request that he be named Toussaint, for
Toussaint L'Ouverture, the great Haitian patriot. The other
children called him Toast—for more than one reason."

"Kids are so cruel," Judith remarked. "What happened to
him later in life?"

"Dr. and Mrs. Moss decided to send him away to military
school," Theo Stevens explained. "They thought it might
be easier on him. It was, and he fell in love with the military way of life. He joined the army and rose to the rank
of major before dropping dead of a heart attack at the age
of thirty-eight, the same age I am now. As you've no doubt

guessed, he was my father. Dr. Moss felt he had to tell me about my history, especially if I was going to practice here."

"I assumed you were the son," Judith said. "Let's see—you were fourteen. That's a very bad age to lose a parent."

Dr. Stevens's smile was ironic. "It is. At the time, we were stationed at Wiesbaden where I'd learned to speak German. My father was just four months short of putting in his twenty years, which meant that my mother didn't get his full retirement. We moved back here after he died. It was a real shock in some ways. Growing up in Germany on the base, I was fairly insulated. Not that there still wasn't prejudice—but as an army brat, there was also a sense of family. Except for the Mosses and my maternal grandmother, who was quite elderly, my mother and I had to start all over. It was hard. I was just entering high school, and though we'd moved into a racially mixed neighborhood, I was bused to a school that was virtually all white. It wasn't easy fitting in, especially since I'd grown up in a foreign country. I wasn't 'cool'—I was merely strange."

"A stranger in your own land," Judith murmured.

"I've lived most of my life that way," Theo Stevens said ruefully, "including out here by Sunset Cliffs. Maybe that's why I'll stay on. Not only do I owe Aaron a huge debt, but my real roots are here. I'm determined to finally fit in somewhere. Being of mixed race, at least in my experience, means you don't belong as black or white. You feel like you're in some never-never land."

"Was your mother mixed, too?" Renie asked.

Dr. Stevens nodded. "She'd had a white ancestor a couple of generations back, though she felt more comfortable as a black woman." His expression grew grim. "My mother died four years after we returned to the States. Someone broke into our house, and she surprised the thief. He bludgeoned her to death with an African carving my father had picked up in his travels."

Renie was looking somber. "You've had more than your share. How have you managed to keep your sanity?"

"Dr. Moss," Theo Stevens said simply. "He was always there for me. When my father was stationed in Europe while my mother was pregnant, Aaron insisted on having her fly home so he could deliver the baby. Then, after my parents were dead, he and Mrs. Moss paid for my education. They were surrogate grandparents. I'd just turned eighteen when my mother was killed. If it hadn't been for Aaron and his wife, I never could have gone to medical school."

Renie had inched forward in the chair, chin on fists. "Who knows that you're aware of what happened to Suzette?"

"No one," Dr. Stevens replied. "I wouldn't have told you, except for your discovery of the tower room. I've wondered about talking to the police, but I can't see what good it would do. Surely there's no connection between my grandmother's death and Aaron's." He smiled weakly. "Maybe I needed to talk to somebody. Besides," he added, his eyes misting a bit, "now that Aaron's gone, these old secrets don't seem to matter, do they?"

"They don't show the family in a good light," Judith remarked.

Renie concurred. "Jealousy. Infidelity. Even murder— but all in the past. Still, the Burgesses wouldn't want the story broadcast, even though all the people involved are dead."

The doctor gave the cousins a pitying look. "You really don't understand how these people think, how they see themselves. The fact that Margaret Burgess murdered my grandmother—it would rock the world of Sunset Cliffs."

"She got away with it, though," Renie said. "Was that because of her wealth and social status?"

Theo Stevens rose from the chair and turned his back to the cousins. He parted the heavy drapes to peer out at the fog-shrouded garden. "She didn't get away with it," he said, finally facing Judith and Renie. "Two weeks later, Margaret Burgess killed herself."

*   *   *

Dr. Stevens told the story as he had learned it from Dr. Moss. It was simple enough: Walter Burgess had been on a big-game hunting expedition for almost two months when he came home to find his mistress locked away in the tower. He was fearless in the board rooms of the city's largest industries, brave as any lion while on the scent, bold as a bandit in his corner office.

"But," Dr. Stevens went on with an ironic twist to his mouth, "he couldn't stand up to his wife. Years later, Dr. Moss told me how Margaret would bully and humiliate him. It happened at least twice in front of Aaron, and he was horribly embarrassed for Walter."

"That kind of public—or even private—behavior will drive any man into the arms of a more sympathetic woman," Renie said. "My husband Bill has a name for that syndrome. He calls it—"

"Worse than nagging," Judith put in, trying to head Renie off before she started in on Bill's theories. "Go on, Dr. Stevens. We're . . . fascinated." Horrified, too, Judith thought. It was a terrible, tragic tale.

"Margaret threatened to expose her husband's affair and promised to release Suzette after the baby—my father—was born," Theo Stevens continued. "She kept Walter away from Suzette the last few weeks of the pregnancy. Only Dr. Moss was allowed in, and he'd come away physically ill."

The young doctor paused, passing his hands over his face as if he could see the horror for himself. "Then, when the baby was born, Margaret struck. Walter was undone. He suffered a nervous breakdown and took to his bed. No one knew about Suzette's murder except Margaret, Walter, and Dr. Moss. There had been no question of going to the police. What happened inside Creepers was private, a law unto itself. In an agony of conscience, Aaron agreed to keep silent. He had no choice, you see." A pitying smile touched Theo's mouth. "A young doctor, just starting out—it would have been his word against the mighty Burgess clan. Maxwell was still alive, and though Aaron was never sure how much the old man knew, he exerted enormous influence not just in the community, but the state."

"Some things don't change," Judith murmured. "Look at the media blackout on Dr. Moss's murder."

Dr. Stevens gave Judith a bleak look. "This was even worse, because none of it ever came to light." He cleared his throat before resuming his account. "Two weeks later, Margaret Burgess hanged herself in the tower, in the same tower room where she had murdered Suzette. The official word was that Margaret died of heart failure. Dr. Moss was compelled to sign the death certificate."

"Poor man," Judith sympathized. "What a burden he carried all those years."

"Indeed," Dr. Stevens replied. "I know that when he finally confided all this to me, it helped a little. He'd felt a moral obligation to write it all down and lock it away in his safe, to be opened only after his death."

"That must be what the thief was after," Renie put in.

"Of course," Theo Stevens agreed. "But I couldn't say as much. Suzette may have been my grandmother, but it still wasn't my secret. It belonged to Dr. Moss."

"Not anymore," Judith asserted, her face set. "Eventually, this will all come out."

"If the killer is caught," Dr. Stevens said, his high forehead creased. "Back then, even when Aaron knew who was guilty, there was nothing he could do. He told me he signed the death certificate because Margaret's heart had, in fact, stopped, and the scandal would have killed Walter, or at least driven him over the edge. Aaron was fond of Walter, who was, I gather, a decent man. In any event, Walter had two small children. It didn't seem right to deprive them of both parents. In fact, it struck Dr. Moss as too cruel to allow Peggy and Wayne to grow up by themselves at Creepers."

Judith and Renie were silent for several moments. Dr. Stevens was still standing, his eyes cast down on the smooth surface of the desk.

"This may sound callous," Renie finally said, "but what did Walter and Margaret do with the body?"

Sadly, Dr. Stevens shook his head. "I don't know. Neither did Aaron."

"I can guess," Judith said, still overcome by the enormity of his revelations.

Dr. Stevens looked up sharply. "What do you mean?"

Judith winced. "Do you really want to know?"

The doctor put a hand to his mouth, then paced back and forth behind the desk. "I'm not sure I do." He paused, leaning a hand on the back of the leather chair. "Yes. My grandmother's remains deserve a decent burial."

"Check with Jeepers, the handyman," Judith said. "I may be wrong, but ask him how long the wishing well has been closed up."

"So Theo Stevens is really a Burgess," Renie remarked after the doctor had left. "Do you agree that mixing bloodlines is a very good thing?"

"Inbreeding, even among tight little social circles is never a good idea," Judith said, still feeling unsettled.

"You end up with the Hapsburg lip," Renie said, "along with some other more ghastly things."

"Like insanity?" Judith murmured.

"Sometimes," Renie responded. "Margaret must have been insane, and not just with jealousy."

"Probably," Judith replied, doing some pacing of her own in front of the glass-enclosed bookcases. "But is it a motive for murder?"

"What?" Renie looked puzzled.

"A secret from so long ago," Judith said. "As we mentioned, none of the current family members was involved. Oh, sure, it'd be a big scandal if word ever got out, but not the sort of thing that would be ruinous to any of these people."

"It's no wonder Caroline wouldn't sleep in that other bedroom," Renie said. "That's where her grandmother hanged herself."

"True," Judith said, rather absently. "But who put that gruesome doll in the dollhouse? Certainly not Dr. Moss."

"You're right," Renie responded. "Did someone else know?"

Judith stopped pacing. "Leota? Would Walter have told her everything?"

"Maybe," Renie said. "She certainly would have wondered about his first wife. I don't see Leota as the second Mrs. de Winter in *Rebecca*."

"I also don't see her setting up a ghoulish exhibit like the dollhouse," Judith declared. "If she knows—and I suspect she does—she'd go out of her way to keep the secret. What bothers me is that when I asked Dr. Stevens if he thought Dr. Moss had been paid off to keep quiet, he said he didn't think so. Remember, he remarked that while Dr. Moss never complained about paying Dr. Stevens's medical school bills, it seemed to be kind of a squeeze financially."

"So the three million or whatever came later?" Renie said. "That doesn't make sense."

"It might," Judith said slowly, "if . . ." Her voice trailed off.

"If what?" Renie demanded.

"If . . ." Judith threw up her hands. "I don't know. If there was something else Dr. Moss knew. He certainly seems to be the family confidant. Sixty years ago, people tended to operate on a code of honor. Today it's money, money, money, and discretion is as old-fashioned as the bustle. Theo Stevens hasn't been out of medical school all that long. If Dr. Moss was being paid to keep quiet, then whatever the reason for the hush money must have happened more recently, say in the last ten years."

"Paid by whom?" Renie asked. "Walter? Leota? Wayne? Who?"

"I haven't a clue," Judith admitted. "For all I know, Dr. Moss's sizable estate has nothing to do with the Burgesses. He attended many wealthy families. We may be completely off the track."

"Why the loyalty to the Burgesses?" Renie pondered.

"That's easy," Judith replied. "Didn't someone tell us that they were the first ones to hire Dr. Moss?"

"Why?" Renie asked. "Look, sixty-odd years ago, Sunset Cliffs was miles beyond what was then the city limits. Why did Aaron Moss set up a practice so far out in the county?"

Judith considered. "For that very reason. It was the Depression. There were probably plenty of doctors in town. But you're right—why hire a young physician just out of medical school?"

"Leota might know," Renie suggested.

Judith sprung for the door. "Let's ask her, before she starts watching her TV programs."

Leota Burgess was sitting up in bed, playing gin rummy with Peggy.

Peggy barely looked up. "They're back," she said in an unenthusiastic tone and drained a glass that appeared to have contained her standard Scotch and soda.

Judith decided to humble herself. "Mrs. Burgess, we're curious. How did your husband and his first wife become acquainted with Dr. Moss?"

The old lady folded up her cards and set them facedown in front of her. "My, my, you do ask some peculiar questions. I can't imagine what the answer has to do with poor Aaron's murder."

"Now they're detectives," Peggy murmured. "Where will it all end?"

"It's quite simple," Mrs. Burgess said. "The previous family doctor took Aaron into his practice. Simmons, I think, was his name. Unfortunately, he died shortly afterward. Dr. Moss took over from him, which seemed like a good idea to my husband, because Dr. Simmons wasn't particularly up-to-date. Or so Walter told me." She picked up her cards and nodded at Peggy. "Your play, dear."

The cousins retreated into the hall. "We flunked that one," Renie noted. "The explanation is logical, and therefore, worthless."

"But we found out that they don't know we broke into the tower room," Judith said in a low voice. "They will, of course, and they'll be furious."

Renie glanced over the railing. "Jiggers, it's the cops."

She waved. "Hi, Edwina, Danny. It's me. Not a sugar."

Edwina motioned for Judith and Renie to come downstairs. "Is the library available?" she asked when the cousins reached the first floor.

Judith said that it was, but felt the detectives should have
a look at their discovery.

Edwina balked. "What's this Suzette business got to do
with the homicide investigation? We don't need to get sidetracked."

Judith admitted that there might not be a connection.

"Fine," Edwina said, waving an impatient hand. "You
can tell me about it later. We need to talk. That is, if you're
still having fun playing sleuths." She turned to Danny. "Get
us some coffee, Number Three Son. Please," she added
with a wry little smile.

On this visit to the library, it was Edwina who sat behind
the desk while the cousins resumed their places in the wingback chairs. "First off," the detective began in a no-
nonsense manner, "we think we know who wrote the note
that was left here." She tapped the desk. "Have you figured
it out yet?"

"Well . . ." Judith grimaced. "It's just a guess, but the
melodrama of it—the 'How did it all go so wrong?' or
whatever—sounds like Caroline."

Edwina chuckled. "Ain't you the one? Our handwriting
experts agree. But it wasn't that hard, was it? Caroline—
or maybe her brother, Kenneth—would be the only fools
who would leave something like that lying around in plain
sight. No reason for Kenneth to write that, not Monday
night, at any rate."

"Unless," Judith put in, "he killed Dr. Moss."

Edwina sat back in the leather armchair and sighed.
"There's always that. But it doesn't quite wash, does it?
The note could mean that the killer did in the wrong victim.
We don't think so, not with the robbery at Dr. Moss's
house. We're more inclined to think that if Caroline wrote
that note—and we're going to ask her that—she was referring to something else."

"Her marriage?" Judith suggested.

"Could be," Edwina allowed.

"Caroline must have come into Creepers before she went to the pool house," Judith said. "She realized her grandmother was watching TV, so she went outside to wait and got caught up with her latest poetic inspiration."

Edwina nodded. "Now tell me what you've managed to dredge up since Danny and I saw you last."

It took almost half an hour and two cups of coffee to get through the cousins' recital, which concluded with their discovery of the former prison in the tower room, the murder of Suzette, and the suicide of Margaret Burgess. Edwina's initial reaction to the sixty-year-old secret was anger.

"This is old news in a lot of ways," she said bitterly. "A sister gets it in the neck for playing games with a white man. I'll have Danny check the tower room later, then we'll see if we can connect any dots."

"We've shown you ours," Renie said, "now show us yours."

"You're on, Danny," she said to her partner. "Let's see how much information you can spill without completely tipping our hand. Remember, these are a couple of amateurs."

Clearing his throat, Danny Wong opened his notebook. "First, we just got the report from the hospital lab on Millicent Fritz's poisoning. Her tea had been laced with rat poison."

"Rat poison?" Judith echoed.

"Tea?" Renie repeated.

"I know," Edwina put in. "You were hoping for the pizza. But it isn't that straightforward."

"Dare we ask who might have done it?" Judith inquired.

"Ask away." Edwina shrugged. "Ada Dietz made the tea, her sister, Edna, brought it up to the master suite, Peggy Hillman came through the sitting room, so did Bop Burgess. Kenneth and Caroline had been in and out of the kitchen about the same time that the tea was being made. The only persons we can rule out are Dorothy and Wayne

Burgess, Russ Hillman, and the rest of the staff."

"Not much help there," Judith said, "except that Fritz must have been the intended victim. But why?"

"Good question," Edwina muttered. "This case is full of them."

"But you're making progress," Judith said in a hopeful tone. "You say you know that several people went in and out of Sunset Cliffs late Monday night and early Tuesday morning?"

"Yes," Edwina replied. "We put the squeeze on Jack Moody and the other guard, Ferguson. They didn't want to lose their jobs, but they don't want to go to jail for obstructing justice, either. The truth is," Edwina continued, her expression turning gloomy, "you could get in and out of this compound without a car, if you knew where and how to do it. I suspect just about everybody who lives around here knows that."

"And Russ and Dorothy alibi each other?" Judith asked.

"Of course," Edwina said, "but that's meaningless. If not in love, those two are mutually dependent. Dorothy Burgess has had a half-dozen affairs over the years, and who can blame her, given Wayne's long-term relationship with Sarah Kenyon. As for Russ, I gather he and Peggy haven't been very happy lately. Marry in haste and repent in leisure—isn't that the old saw?"

"Yes," Judith said absently. "What about the weapon? I can't believe you haven't come up with it."

"Believe it," Edwina said grimly. "The crowbar was clean. Sarah Kenyon used it to try to get the garage open when she couldn't find the remote control. She couldn't budge the door and left it out back. We think the killer took the remote to stash in a car while the murder was being committed."

"Reaffirming the insider theory," Judith remarked. "Maybe the killer took the weapon away."

"Maybe," Edwina allowed. "The uniforms have searched all over the area, but it's vast, and heavily wooded. The only good thing is that the groundskeepers or whatever they call them are constantly clearing away debris, especially after all the wind we've had lately."

"Hold on," Judith said. "If you don't put much faith in Russ and Dorothy's alibi, what about Wayne and Sarah Kenyon?"

"Same thing," Edwina replied, pouring more coffee. "But Danny and I are feeling some pressure. We were told late yesterday that we couldn't keep these people under wraps any longer. They're officially free to leave whenever they want, as long as they don't flee the country."

"Us, too?" Renie asked.

Edwina smiled slyly. "Do you want to?"

"We said we'd stay for the funeral," Judith hedged.

Edwina nodded. "In that case, you're covered, should any of them—such as Peggy—try to throw you out. Look, I really appreciate what you've been doing. You realize you're putting yourselves at risk."

"We've done it before," Judith admitted.

"We're doing it for Bev," Renie declared. "That's why we came in the first place. And frankly, we have no answers for her."

"You're not alone," Edwina said grimly. "What we've accomplished so far is strictly procedural—checking fingerprints, alibis, the handwriting on that note. Premeditated murder—which this must have been—is unusual."

"I know," Judith put in. "Joe's told me that a thousand times. What's worse in this case is that the killer is probably smarter than your average bear."

"What's worse," said Edwina, standing up, "is that the killer is richer than any bear. A conviction—let alone a stiff sentence—is going to be hard to get. I feel like I'm beat before I start." She paused and laughed as she led the others out of the library. "Look at it from my point of view— black female from lower-class background works her way up in the world, only to be tromped on by upper-class white social structure. Sometimes I wonder how far we've really come from that little black guy out front, waiting for Massa to arrive home at the old plantation."

They had reached the double doors at the entrance. "You know better," Judith admonished. "But I don't blame you for feeling down."

"We're off to question Russ Hillman," Edwina said. "I want to show him that golf marker again. He insists it could have been there for days."

"I wonder," Judith said, walking Edwina and Danny through the front doors. "What do you bet he came by Monday night, looking for Peggy? He might have wanted to know where she was before he headed out on his tryst with Dorothy."

Edwina cocked an eye at Judith. "Which means Peggy wasn't home when he got back from the golf course?"

Judith's expression grew puzzled. "Russ said she got home first. Maybe I'm wrong about why he came to Creepers so late. If he actually did."

"That's why we're going to talk to him again," Edwina said, surveying the front of the house. "Thank God, the fog's lifting."

It hadn't lifted quite enough for Renie, who once again stumbled over the figure of the footman. Swearing out loud, she regained her balance and made a face.

"I'll be glad when I can see again. This depth perception thing drives me nuts."

Judith bent down to straighten the small, sturdy little figure. Suddenly, she stood up. "Edwina—what about him?" She jabbed a finger at the ceramic statue whose once-colorful silks had faded with age.

"I told you," Edwina began, "I have to look at him as part of another era, when the insensitive white community regarded—"

With emphasis, Judith shook her head. "Never mind that. I understand completely. What I'm saying is that maybe you shouldn't look at him as a social statement. Instead," she went on with a curious expression, "how about thinking of him as a murder weapon?"

NINETEEN

"PREJUDICE CAN BLIND our eyes in many ways," Edwina murmured, then gazed at the cousins in embarrassment. "Of course you may be wrong. But we should have checked it out. All I could see when I looked at that little figure was a racial slur."

"That's okay, Edwina," Danny said in consolation. "If it had been wearing a long gown and a pigtail, I'd have felt the same way."

Edwina glared at her partner. "Then why didn't *you* figure it out?"

Danny backpedaled a couple of steps. "Well . . . I mean . . ."

Edwina laughed and grabbed Danny by the arm. "Never mind. Just pull the little guy out of the ground and bag him. We'll let the lab see if Mrs. Flynn is right or merely crazy."

Judith and Renie watched the unmarked county car disappear into the fog. "Which are you?" Renie asked in a wry voice.

"Neither," Judith replied, turning to go back inside, "but I sure am stupid. I should have figured that out a long time ago. So much attention was called to the little figure, but it always came from a completely different direction and diverted me."

"Don't feel bad," Renie said as they closed the double doors behind them. "It put Edwina off the track, too."

"But I don't have the same emotional response to such things," Judith said. "I should have been more objective. Of course, we may be wrong. It might not be the murder weapon. Still, it's the last potentially lethal object anyone would see before they entered Creepers. It's also a fixture, and as such, could be overlooked."

"Lunch can't be overlooked," Renie said. "It's ten to one. Where do we eat?"

There was a considerable pause before Judith answered. "How about Evergreen?"

"Huh?" Renie stared at Judith. "The company or the house?"

"The house," Judith replied. "Haven't we been neglecting Dorothy Burgess?"

Renie, however, balked. "She won't feed us. She'll sit there in that jungle solarium or whatever with all those plants and smoke like a faulty fireplace and the next thing you know, I'll be smoking, too."

Judith's face fell. "You're right." Again, she paused, then snapped her fingers. "Let's treat her to lunch."

"Why? She's rich. We're poor. Are you nuts?"

"Right again." Judith frowned. "Let's go to the country club anyway."

"Who said anything about a country club?" Renie asked.

"That's where I was thinking we could take Dorothy," Judith replied, heading up the central staircase. "Let's get our coats."

"Are we walking? Tell me we aren't walking. The golf course and the country club are clear over on the other side of Sunset Cliffs. It must be five miles away."

"It's not that far," Judith countered as they reached the top of the stairs. "A mile, at most. Do you want me to get the car out of the garage?"

Renie stopped and turned to face Judith. "Yes. Otherwise, when on a forced march, I collapse from hunger."

Sarah Kenyon was on the phone when the cousins went

to get the garage door opener. Judith mouthed the request; Sarah merely nodded, then produced the device.

Five minutes later, they were driving along the winding road that led from Creepers. "It's probably a good thing to start the car," Judith allowed. "It shouldn't sit for more than a couple of days. I wonder if the detectives ever found out anything about that oil leak."

"Edwina didn't mention it," Renie said as Judith slowed the Subaru down through a patch of fog. "But she did caution Danny not to tell us everything."

"So she did," Judith replied. "It's a long-shot, though. I'm not sure if you can match oil to a specific . . . Oh, no!"

Judith braked for a figure that had darted out through the fog. The car didn't quite stop in time: There was a sickening thud, a piercing scream, and a flurry of motion across the Subaru's hood. To Judith's horror, Dorothy Burgess's face stared at her through the windshield.

"Are you okay?" Judith cried, leaping out into the road.

Dorothy, clad in an off-white raincoat and matching slacks, clung to the hood. She made no response. With her heart sinking, Judith put a hand on the other woman's shoulder.

"Dorothy . . . ?"

"You moron!" Dorothy shouted, rolling over and slipping to the ground. "You could have killed me!"

"I'm so sorry," Judith apologized. "I was just creeping along and . . . Oh, please, I don't know what to say. Are you sure you're not hurt?"

Apparently, Dorothy wasn't sure. She wiggled both arms and both legs in turn, then twisted her torso around. Finally, bobbing her head up and down, she declared herself whole.

"But," she added, still angry and shaken, "I could have injuries that'll develop later. I hope you're insured up to your somewhat less than first-class haircut."

"Of course," Judith said, too upset to be indignant. "Believe it or not, we were thinking of inviting you to lunch."

"I don't believe it," Dorothy said angrily. "But as long

as you're here and I'm still shaking like a leaf, you might as well drop me off at the country club."

"You know," said Renie, who had gotten out of the car and was leaning against the roof, "you might consider not dressing up like Casper the Ghost when you walk in the fog. That outfit is kind of hard to see."

Dorothy didn't deign to respond, but with a swing of her head got into the backseat and slammed the door. In the few minutes that it took to reach the country club, she spoke only to give terse directions.

The clubhouse itself was what Judith would describe as California Missionaries Retire to Beverly Hills. The two-story cream-colored stucco building had a traditional red tile roof, arched windows, and a large verandah.

An attendant in a white jacket raced down the stairs when Judith pulled to a stop. He paused in mid-step when he saw Judith and Renie in the front seat. Before he could ask any embarrassing questions, Dorothy Burgess got out of the car.

"It's all right, Jason," she said. "They're with me. Why don't you park this crate where nobody can see it?"

Judith and Renie stared at each other in surprise. "We're allowed?" Renie said in her meekest voice.

"I guess." Judith left the key in the ignition and gave Jason a big smile.

"Sorry," Renie called to the attendant as she got out of the passenger seat. "We left the Edsel parked with the rusty pickup in the front yard."

Dorothy was already on the verandah. She didn't look back until the cousins had joined her in the clubhouse lobby.

"Well?" she demanded, handing her raincoat to a young woman dressed in maid's attire. "Are you satisfied? I assume you want to see every nook and cranny of Sunset Cliffs before you get thrown out."

"Very impressive," Judith murmured, glancing around at the wood and leather Spanish-style furniture. "But really, we wanted to talk to—"

Dorothy waved a hand, silencing Judith. "Come along, I

have a table that overlooks the seventh green. We can watch some crazy fools try to sink a six-inch putt in the fog."

"You don't golf?" Judith asked as they headed for the dining room.

"Actually, I do," Dorothy replied, nodding at the platinum-haired hostess and marching straight to a corner table. "But not in this kind of weather. I work out for exercise."

"I heard you were going to open a gym," Judith said innocently as the three women sat down.

Dorothy's fine eyebrows lifted. "You did, did you? My, but you do pick up the scuttlebutt."

"I think it's a great idea," Judith enthused.

"It is," Dorothy said. "I could make a go of it just off the women who live in Sunset Cliffs. Most of them sit around on their dead butts all day anyway." She paused as a chubby young waitress with perfect skin came to the table. "We'll have the Dungeness crab louies, thousand island dressing on the side, rolls, coffee, and three glasses of lemonade. Thanks, Melanie."

"It's a good thing we like crab louies," Renie murmured.

"Most people do," Dorothy said in a brisk voice. The bored, almost languid air that she had exuded upon her first meeting with the cousins seemed to have been put aside. "I don't like to waste time, especially with people I don't know well." She brushed the graying red hair away from her face and leaned forward in the chair. "Now tell me what you're up to. Why lunch? Why me?"

Judith fidgeted a bit, then decided to be candid. "You're an intelligent woman, Dorothy. Observant, too. Who do you think killed Dr. Moss?"

The green eyes, which were so much like her son Bop's, grew wary. "How should I know?"

"You must have a theory," Judith said, "especially since the suspects are pretty limited to Creepers."

Dorothy sighed heavily. "That's why I don't try to think about it. The possibilities are frightening."

"But you know these people," Judith pressed. "You've been in the family for—what? Almost forty years?"

"Almost," Dorothy said. "You think you know people after all that time. But do you—really?"

"Good point," Renie allowed. "Are you talking about a dark horse?"

Dorothy uttered a sharp little laugh, but didn't respond immediately. Melanie had arrived with the lemonade and a sunny smile. Judith glanced around the dining room with its open rafters and whitewashed walls. At a few minutes after one, there were only a handful of other members still eating. They looked prosperous and self-satisfied, a far cry from the rag-tag clientele to whom she once served well drinks and rib-eye steaks at the Meat & Mingle.

"Dark horse?" Dorothy repeated after Melanie had left. "If you mean someone who would be the last person I could imagine killing someone else, no. Edna, for instance. Kenyon. My mother-in-law. It's not just because they're old and physically hampered. It sounds as if this murder was planned, and if any of them wanted to kill somebody, they could use poison. Whoever struck down Dr. Moss was making a statement. Subconscious, maybe, but a statement nonetheless."

Judith was impressed by Dorothy's reasoning. "You may be right. But what kind of statement?"

"In-your-face," Dorothy replied. "Revenge. Righteous anger. Whatever. Not knowing who, I can't say what."

Finality. The word sprung to Judith's mind. Nothing was more final than death. She became lost in thought, and only a phrase from Renie brought her back into the conversation:

". . . not going to sue us?" Renie was saying to Dorothy.

Dorothy regarded Renie with a wry smile. "Probably not. But it was a stupid stunt. And not just on your part," she added, wagging a finger at Judith. "I should have been walking further off the road."

"I really do feel awful about it," Judith said earnestly. "I honestly thought I was just creeping along."

"You probably were," Dorothy acknowledged, "but I was

woolgathering. I've had a lot on my mind lately." She paused and eyed the cousins with an ironic expression. "No doubt you've heard something about that, too."

"There was a mention of some . . . domestic dispute," Judith hedged.

"We heard you threaten Mr. Gibbons," Renie put in. "It's also hard to keep a secret when you announce in front of God and everybody that you're leaving forever."

"True." Dorothy expelled another sigh.

The crab louies arrived, and Renie dove into hers like a rabbit let loose in Falstaff's produce section.

"Anyway," Dorothy continued, looking askance at Renie, who had an olive slice on her chin, "at least I was sober."

The forkful of crab that Judith was holding stopped midway to her mouth. "Sober? I don't understand."

"Oh." Dorothy smiled weakly. "I was thinking of Charlie Ward. I don't know if you've heard about him, but he was Peggy's first husband."

"Yes," Judith said, hastily swallowing the mouthful of crab. "He was killed in a hit-and-run accident."

Dorothy gave a little shrug. "I've heard that he was drunk at the time. It's plausible. He and Peggy used to get sauced fairly often. You'd almost have to be drunk to get killed along that stretch of road by the other side of the golf course. There must be ten, twelve feet, including a little gully for runoff, between the road itself and the golf course fence."

"Who told you he was drunk?" Renie asked, unaware that the olive slice had slipped onto her bosom.

Dorothy averted her gaze. "I forget. The accident happened a long time ago."

"Did you like Charlie?" Judith asked.

Dorothy hunched her shoulders. "He was passable."

"But not one of you," Renie remarked, finally discovering the stray olive and popping it in her mouth. Two older women, one with upswept silver hair and the other with a platinum pageboy, stared in distaste. Renie stared back and stuck out her tongue.

"No." Dorothy's expression was ironic. "Definitely not one of us. Charlie was strictly middle-class, and frankly, on the make. That roguishness appealed to Peggy. In fact, Leota found him fascinating, in a raffish, scapegrace kind of way. She's never taken to Tom Ohashi like that, though. To be frank, he came from a better class of people, and—unlike Charlie—is ambitious and hardworking. But he isn't a WASP. That puts him on a whole different level."

"That's too bad," Renie said, ducking around Dorothy and making an obscene gesture at the women who were whispering behind their bejeweled hands. "Tom's the perfect mate for Bev. I take it that the only marriage the Burgesses endorsed wholeheartedly was yours."

Dorothy smiled rather grimly. "I was a Prescott. My father was Judge Joshua Cole Prescott. Perhaps you've heard of him."

Judith hadn't, but Renie nodded. "He almost made it to the Supremes. My mother—she was a legal secretary—held him in high esteem." Again leaning to one side so Dorothy couldn't see her, Renie put both index fingers in her mouth and made a hideous face.

"A wise man," Dorothy said with a fond smile. "He opposed my marriage to Wayne from the start, but my mother pushed it. I suppose it seemed like a perfect match at the time."

"You've stayed married a very long time," Judith noted, finally catching on to what her cousin was doing and giving her a quick, hard look. "There must have been some happy years."

"There were," Dorothy responded. "Wayne knocked himself out to be a good husband. It wasn't until much later that I found out why. There was always Sarah, right from the start."

"But you persevered," Judith noted, relieved to see that the two outraged women were flouncing out of the dining room.

"If you can't beat 'em, join 'em," Dorothy replied. "At least that was my motto until recently. Time's running out, if I want a future." She put down her fork and placed her napkin on the table. "Are we done here?"

Judith was somewhat startled by Dorothy's abruptness. "Well . . . yes. Can't we treat you?"

Dorothy shook her head. "We don't have bills as such at the club. Everything goes on our monthly tab. This isn't Lenny's out on the highway. Besides," she added dryly, "I ought to pay. It's my penalty for speaking indiscreetly just now. Ordinarily, I don't discuss private matters with virtual strangers. I suppose it's Dr. Moss's death and the murder investigation. The last few days have been rather rugged."

"Plus," Judith said, "you have your own problems."

"So I do," Dorothy said as she pushed her chair away from the table. "Let's see if I—and the rest of the family— can get out of this alive."

The cousins left the clubhouse alone. Renie wondered if Dorothy was staying on to see Russ Hillman. Judith wondered if the detectives had already interviewed him about the golf marker.

"Do you think Dorothy's innocent?" Renie asked as they drove slowly along the twisting roads that were now free of fog.

"Of murdering Dr. Moss? Probably," Judith said in a thoughtful tone. "Her attitude seemed somewhat objective, if unhelpful. She was a bit evasive, though. I wonder if she's shielding someone."

"Like Russ?"

"Russ, Bop, even Wayne," Judith said. "I also think there may have been a reason behind having lunch with us."

"Such as?"

"To see if we had a favorite suspect. Dorothy Burgess may look down at us as socially inferior, but she doesn't think we're complete morons," Judith said as they passed Evergreen and headed on to Creepers. "She may also think we've heard something from the police."

Renie look unconvinced. "Dorothy didn't ask us a single question about what we thought."

"She wouldn't. That's not her style. She'd expect it come out in the course of the conversation."

"It didn't," Renie asserted. "So what use was our luncheon date to any of us?"

"I'm not sure," Judith said, still in a thoughtful mood. "But something she mentioned reinforced an idea I've had all along."

"What?"

"About events, and how the Burgesses react to them." Judith slowed down as they reached the circular drive. "What do these people talk about in terms of life passages? Not weddings and babies or even ordinary deaths. There are certain topics—let's call them leitmotifs as you opera fans would say—that keep recurring. Suzette. Leota's gall bladder attack. Charles Ward's fatal accident. Dr. Moss's murder."

"So what are you saying?" Renie asked.

"Maybe I'm trying too hard because I'm stumped," Judith admitted, pulling the Subaru to a stop in front of the multiple-car garage, "but I wonder if there isn't a link between all those things."

"How can there be?" Renie inquired. "No one is still around from the days of Suzette's demise, not even Dr. Moss."

"That's my point," Judith said. "He was around then. And so were two other people who are still with us."

"Who?" Renie asked, looking puzzled.

"Peggy and Wayne."

"You're nuts. They were babies."

"Not quite," Judith countered. "Peggy was three and Wayne was going on two."

"That's ridiculous," Renie scoffed. "How could they remember anything?"

"You do." Judith gave Renie a smug look. "Weren't you telling me the other day how excited you were when you got the electric train from Uncle Corky? You were two, but you remembered, because it was a big event in your life."

Renie frowned. "You're right. I remember quite a bit,

really, from my extreme youth. But I don't think everybody does."

"Maybe not, but the tension, the horror surrounding Suzette's tragedy would touch even a small child. Oh, there'd be no talk in front of the children, at least not by Margaret and Walter Burgess. But you never know about servants. And having Dad collapse with a nervous breakdown and Mom hang herself would definitely make an impression."

"That's so," Renie finally agreed. "It'd be traumatic. But will either of them talk about it? Or would they repress those memories?"

"You couldn't blame them if they did," Judith said. "I wonder what happened to those servants. I'm almost willing to bet that there was more than one wholesale discharge of staff. I'll bet whoever worked at Creepers at the time of the tragedy was let go, if not by Walter Burgess, then by Leota, when she married him a year or so later."

"She might tell us," Renie mused.

"I doubt it," Judith responded, then gazed at Renie. "Are you going to go get the garage opener or shall we spend the afternoon in the car?"

After the Subaru had been returned to its place, the cousins went into the house through the rear entrance. Edna was just coming out of the kitchen. She gave a start when she saw Judith and Renie appear in the hallway.

"How fortunate!" the little maid exclaimed. "The mistress has been asking for you. Do you mind?"

"Of course not, Edna," Judith replied, smiling kindly. "Tell me something, if you would. When you and Ada came to Creepers, had the departing staff been here a long time?"

"Oh, dear!" The query seemed to dismay Edna. "Let me think—yes, at least through the war. Except for Brewster—the nanny—they were mostly refugees. When the war ended, they wanted to go home."

Judith frowned at Edna. "Refugees?"

The maid nodded, making her white cap slip sideways. "From Europe. I believe they were mostly from the same family. Austrians, I think. They taught the children to waltz."

"Interesting," Judith said, still smiling. "Thank you, Edna."

"Certainly." Edna beamed at the cousins. "Would you like to take the elevator? It's much closer than the main stairs. It saves me so many steps."

With a wave for Ada, who was taking out the garbage, Judith and Renie climbed into the small car. "How come Bev never mentioned this Austrian family?" Judith queried.

"Because I didn't ask her about the Von Trapp family servants," Renie said. "We only talked about Suzette and Brewster. And don't tell me—Walter Burgess canned all the servants who were here when Suzette and Margaret met their fateful ends. The departing crew were probably bought off. Then Walter brought in these refugees who may or may not have understood English. End of in-house gossip."

The elevator groaned to a halt. "That's about it," Judith agreed. "It was shrewd. And when they went back to Austria after the war, they took whatever bits and pieces of information they might have learned with them."

Judith rapped on the Chinese screen and called Mrs. Burgess's name.

"Why," the old lady demanded as the cousins appeared from behind the screen, "are you coming from that direction?"

"Our feet hurt," Renie answered, dropping into a chair by the bed. "How are you this afternoon?"

"Improving," Mrs. Burgess replied, though she looked dispirited. "I wanted to let you know that after the funeral tomorrow, you're perfectly free to leave. I've already encroached far too much on your time."

Grimacing, Renie pulled the chair closer to the bed. "Mrs. Burgess, the danger to you may not be over. I hate to mention this, but has it occurred to you that the poison in Nurse"—Renie grimaced some more as she forced herself to pronounce the name properly—"Fritz's tea may have been meant for you?"

"The detectives alluded to that possibility this morning," Mrs. Burgess said. "It was very naughty of you not to tell me straightaway that Fritz had been poisoned."

"We weren't sure," Renie responded. "Besides, we didn't want to upset you."

Mrs. Burgess waved a hand. "Never mind. If I may say so without being offensive, it's become clear that you can't stop the attempts on my life, let alone discover who is making them. It's not your fault. The police aren't doing much better. Consequently, I've hired a private detective. I probably should have done so in the beginning, but I didn't want an outsider at Creepers. Now, after Dr. Moss's murder, there have been all sorts of intrusions. One more will scarcely matter, especially if he's competent. He'll arrive this afternoon and attend the funeral tomorrow. I spoke to him only a few minutes ago, and he wants to see how the mourners react at the service."

"That's smart of him," Judith put in. "My husband always did that when he was working a murder investigation. But I have to say that we feel terrible about being such failures."

"Nonsense," Mrs. Burgess retorted. "You're not professionals."

"Bev's going to be disappointed in us," Renie remarked. "I should be hearing from her some time today."

"No, you won't," Mrs. Burgess said. "She called earlier, apparently while you were unavailable. I spoke with her and explained everything. She's only upset because she put you to so much trouble. Now run along and enjoy the sunshine. It's gotten to be a nice day now that the fog's lifted."

"We flunked," Judith said glumly as they headed back downstairs. "I feel like a big fat zero."

"So do I," Renie said. "What's the point of staying for the funeral? We might as well go home now before Bill and the kids wind up eating pet food for dinner."

"You may be right," Judith said as they reached the main

floor. "Hey!" she cried, grabbing Renie's sleeve. "Leota didn't mention the tower room. Do you suppose they don't know what we did?"

Renie stared at Judith. "Maybe not. Nobody goes up there, not even to the third floor, let alone the fourth."

"But someone has," Judith said, pacing around the expanse in front of the central staircase. "Again, who put that doll and the phony blood in the dollhouse? When? Why?" She motioned to Renie. "Let's have another look."

"Coz . . ."

But Judith was already headed for the tower.

"What do you expect to find that you didn't see before?" Renie asked in a cross voice as she dutifully trudged along behind Judith.

"I don't know," Judith said. "I wonder if Edwina's checked out the tower yet."

To Renie's surprise, Judith stopped on the second floor. The door was ajar. Peeking inside, the cousins found no sign of Kenneth. Judith headed straight for the door that led to the old nursery.

The unfortunate doll still remained facedown in the plastic blood. Judith began searching other parts of the room, looking behind shelves of children's books, moving board games, inspecting every possible hiding place.

"I'd help, but I'm in ignorance," Renie said in an annoyed tone. "What are you trying to find?"

"I've no idea," Judith admitted, pounding on the walls.

"Great. Maybe I'll play with the electric train. It brings back fond memories. Oops!" Renie tripped over the rocking horse, falling hard on one knee. "Damn! I tore my good slacks. Look, this stupid floor is rotting."

"It is over a hundred years old," Judith noted, then studied the board that had broken in two. "What's that, underneath?"

"Don't ask me," Renie snapped. "I'm blind, remember? Damn, damn, damn. I paid almost two hundred bucks for these slacks."

Judith knelt down, carefully pulling at the pieces of

wood. To her surprise, they moved easily. "Bottles," she said in amazement. "Empty liquor bottles. What do you think, coz?"

"I think I wish they were full," Renie retorted. "I could use a drink."

"Who drank up here and stashed the evidence?" Judith said, excitement rising as she wrestled to free some of the bottles. "Look, some of these are labels that haven't been sold since I was working at the Meat & Mingle. Here's one that first came out around ten years ago. We can pinpoint the time frame from these," she went on, holding two of the bottles aloft. "They're all Scotch. Who does that point to?"

"You?" Renie said in a vexed voice.

Judith shot Renie a scornful look. "Mock me, if you will, but I think I finally see the light."

"Okay," Renie said ambiguously. "Let's get out of here."

Judith agreed. She was on her feet when they heard the shrill, piercing voice.

"Spare me! Spare me!"

The cousins exchanged swift, startled glances. "It's not in here," Judith said. "It's coming from down the stairwell."

They heard nothing until they reached the stairs. "Save me! Help me!" the strange voice cried.

"It's above us," Renie said, craning her neck to peer into the deep recesses of the stairwell.

But it was a noise from below that suddenly caught their attention. The cousins whirled around and looked down. Kenneth was standing in the curve of the tower wall.

"Was that you calling out?" Judith demanded.

Kenneth looked at Judith and Renie with wide, innocent eyes. "No. Of course not."

"Didn't you hear it?" Renie asked, taking a downward step.

"Oh, yes," Kenneth replied, seemingly undisturbed.

"What the hell is it?" Renie shouted.

Kenneth retreated on the stairs. "It's Suzette," he said, and disappeared around the corner.

TWENTY

"SUZETTE?" JUDITH ECHOED, racing after Renie who was chasing Kenneth. "What are you talking about?"

The cousins trapped him outside his room. "Suzette's been dead for sixty years," Renie declared. "There are no such things as ghosts." She grabbed Kenneth by the front of his shirt. "Out with it, tell us what's going on or I'll have to hurt you."

"She's not a ghost," Kenneth said, now looking frightened. "She's real. She's in great danger. I want to save her."

"Over the edge," Renie said out of the corner of her mouth. "Should we get help?"

Before Judith could respond, a series of squawks and a flurry of wings appeared from out of the stairwell shadows. Judith let out a startled cry and Renie let go of Kenneth. The young man darted out between his would-be captors and ran down to the bottom of the stairs.

"Now you've scared Suzette," Kenneth called out in an accusing voice.

Slowly, Judith and Renie followed him around the winding steps. They saw Kenneth by the door, a brightly colored parrot on his shoulder. "I've taught her to defend herself," he said, looking indignant. "Creepers isn't safe for my wild friends anymore, so I'm taking her somewhere that is." With a parting glare for Judith and Renie, Kenneth went through the door and into the passageway, the parrot leaning her head against her protector's.

"A damned bird," Renie muttered. "How could we be so dumb?"

"It was feathers I felt against my face," Judith said in exasperation. "Shoot."

"No wonder Leota doesn't want Kenneth bringing his menagerie to Creepers," Renie said, trudging down the rest of the stairs.

"I'll bet he sneaked that parrot in Monday night when he came the first time via the back door," Judith said. "Remember how the windows in his room were open when we first peeked in there? Suzette, as he calls her, must have been flying in and out like Superman."

"Too bad Roscoe didn't eat the damned thing," Renie said as they entered the parlor.

"Roscoe was in a cage," Judith reminded Renie, "which is where Suzette should have been, too." She sank into one of the chinoiserie chairs. "Want to hear my theory before I forget what it is?"

Naturally, Renie was all ears. "It's not bad," she said when Judith had finished. "But you—and maybe the detectives—haven't got a shred of evidence."

"The police might," Judith said. "They just aren't telling us. Or maybe they haven't put it all together."

"Are you going to share your theory with Edwina and Danny?" Renie asked.

Judith frowned. "I'm not sure. I don't want them to laugh at me."

"Maybe you should, though," Renie said. "Aren't we leaving?"

Judith glanced at her watch. It was going on three o'clock. "I suppose we should. Leota didn't sound as if she wanted us hanging around anymore. But," Judith added, her eyes narrowing, "you can see why she feels that way."

"Only if you're a threat to the family's reputation," Renie said.

Judith got up from the chinoiserie chair and began to pace, a habit that seemed to be growing since her arrival at Creepers. "I'd like to talk to at least a couple of people before we go. Maybe we can stall." She stopped to stare at the telephone. "I should call Joe. Maybe he's back from wherever he went by now."

Once again, Arlene answered the phone. "Joe just left again," she said, laughter bubbling up in her voice. "Oh, Judith, your mother is such a sketch. We brought her into the house—really, I think it's so unfair that she can't live in what really is her home—and we're playing charades. I'm on her team, and Vivian and Carl are on the other."

"Vivian?" The name thudded out of Judith's mouth. "She's back from Florida?"

"Yes, she got in yesterday, with such a gorgeous tan that I can hardly stand it," Arlene went on, "and you know how fond she is of your mother, but of course who wouldn't be unless they had *a heart of flint.*"

Judith ignored the implied barb. Perhaps the return of Joe's first wife explained his absences from Hillside Manor. Despite everything, including eight happy years of marriage, Judith could still feel pangs of jealousy. Vivian Flynn was much older, but she still possessed a certain hard-edged glamour that Judith envied.

Still, it was Arlene's needling about Gertrude's self-imposed exile that rankled most. "You know perfectly well that Mother refused to—"

"You'll never guess," Arlene interrupted, "what your mother did to win the last round. Cambridge, Massachusetts! She got to take out her teeth twice. It was hilarious!"

"I'll bet," Judith murmured.

"And for the first syllable of Massachusetts, she did 'sounds like' and wiggled her—"

"I'm sure she was terrific," Judith cut in. "Just tell Joe I might be home later today. If not, I'll be there around noon tomorrow, okay?"

"Don't rush on our account," Arlene said. "We're doing just fine. The rooms are all booked for tonight. Oh, my goodness," she continued, lowering her voice to a whisper, "I just got Woody Woodpecker. Well, that ought to be easy with Carl around. Bye, Judith."

Looking dazed, Judith hung up. "They're playing charades, with Mother and Herself."

Renie held up a hand. "Say no more. Please. Where's Joe?"

"I suspect he couldn't stand the idea of Mother coming into the house and lording it over him with me not there," Judith said. "As for where he's been, I assume you heard."

"The Return of Herself," Renie said, and couldn't hold back a smile. "Now do you want to go home or did I hear you correctly when you hedged about our ETA?"

In the middle of the room, Judith was turning this way and that. "I don't know. I wish I knew if the little footman really was the weapon."

"Would it change your mind about who killed Dr. Moss?" Renie asked with a puzzled expression.

"No." Judith rubbed her temples, wrung her hands, and shuffled her feet. Then she gave herself a good shake and eyed Renie with determination. "Come on, let's go find somebody."

"Who?" Renie asked, following Judith out of the parlor.

"Caroline, for one," Judith called over her shoulder. "Let's hope she's in her room."

Caroline, however, didn't respond to Judith's knock. Frustrated, Judith paced the hallway, but stopped abruptly when Kenyon came out of Mrs. Burgess's suite.

"Do you know where we could find Caroline or Kenneth?" Judith asked the butler.

Kenyon cupped an ear; Judith repeated the question.

"Miss Caroline and her mother went back to Mrs. Peggy's residence at The Willows," Kenyon replied. "Mr. Kenneth has left."

"Left, as in gone?" Renie asked.

Kenyon nodded solemnly. "I believe he's rather disturbed by the events of the past few days. Sarah is taking him to his place in town. They just went out through the back way. Mr. Kenneth was carrying a large bird."

"Thanks, Kenyon," Judith said, rushing past the old man and down the staircase. "Come on, let's head 'em off at the drive," she called to Renie.

The Cadillac was just pulling out of the garage. Judith stood in the driveway, waving her hands. Sarah Kenyon braked, then opened the window and leaned out. "What is it?" she asked, looking slightly annoyed.

"Could I talk to Kenneth for just a second? Please?" Judith begged.

After a brief discussion between the housekeeper and Kenneth, the young man got out of the car. Suzette could be seen sitting on the passenger headrest. "I'm never coming back," he declared, lower lip thrust out. "Not until *Grandmaman* says I can keep my animals here."

"How about getting a job?" Renie muttered under her breath.

With a warning glance at her cousin, Judith approached Kenneth. "Have you considered," she began in a gentle tone, "using your inheritance to buy land in a less populated area for your sanctuary?"

Kenneth's blue eyes widened. "But then I couldn't live at Creepers."

"Yes, actually, you could," Judith asserted. "Many people live in one place and work in another."

"Do you?" Kenneth asked, his head lowered so far that his chin almost touched his chest.

"Well . . . no, but that's because—"

The young man pointed to Renie. "Does she?"

"Ah . . . no, but . . . Never mind." Judith shook her head and waved a hand. "Forget it. Tell me something, Kenneth, why is your sister Caroline so frightened of the tower rooms?"

Kenneth took a step backward. "Because she's silly," he replied, though there was an uncertain note in his voice.

"She's not silly," Judith insisted. "She's scared, and I think I know why. Who told her stories that made her think the tower was haunted?"

Jamming his hands in his pockets, Kenneth twisted and turned in place. "Oh," he finally sighed, "it doesn't matter. It was a long time ago, when we were little kids. Carrie heard Aunt Bev talking about how my mom and Uncle Wayne used to scare her. She asked Aunt Bev, but she wouldn't tell Carrie. I guess it was because she didn't want her to be scared, too. But Carrie started having nightmares and getting stomachaches. Finally, she was told some tale about a servant named Suzette from a long time ago who'd died in the top part of the tower. That's why I named my parrot Suzette. I guess that's why the room was sealed up. But Carrie never got over it. In fact, she got worse. She built it up in her mind and wrote poems about it."

"Who told her?" Judith asked as Sarah honked the horn.

"My dad," Kenneth replied. "He and Carrie were always real close."

Sarah honked again. Kenneth turned and hurried back to the Cadillac.

"That," said Judith to Renie, "is what I figured."

"What now?" Renie asked, watching the big sleek sedan disappear.

Judith tapped her foot on the pavement. "I'm thinking. We don't want to do anything foolish."

"Like getting ourselves killed?"

"Like that." Suddenly, Judith snapped her fingers. "I've got it. Let's make a phone call."

Fifteen minutes later, Judith and Renie were back in the parlor. "It's three-twenty," Judith said, checking her watch for the fourth time. "I set our little meeting for four o'clock. Should we have a drink?"

"It might be a good idea," Renie said. "Dutch courage, I believe it's called. Let's head for the bar in the drawing room. I'd hate to have to wait for Kenyon to serve us."

Kenyon, however, was at the door of the drawing room. To the cousins' surprise, he barred the way with a feeble arm. "I'm sorry, ladies. Mr. Wayne is in here, speaking with the private detective. Would you mind waiting or may I help you?"

"We could use a drink," Renie said bluntly. "Would you mind?"

"Certainly." Kenyon lowered his arm, and Judith swore she could hear his joints creak. She could also hear low, masculine voices inside the drawing room. "That would be bourbon for you, Mrs. Jones, and for Mrs. Flynn, it's . . ." His face went blank.

"Scotch-rocks," said a voice from behind Kenyon.

Judith gaped as Joe Flynn came through the drawing room door.

Judith's knees all but buckled. "Joe! What are you doing here?"

He patted the breast pocket of his navy blazer. "I got my license. I'm a certified private eye. I come highly recommended." The green eyes sparkled with the old familiar magic.

"Joe . . ." To Kenyon's astonishment, Judith fell into her husband's arms. "I had no idea . . . When . . . ? How . . . ?"

"I've been thinking about it ever since I retired," Joe said between kisses. "I picked the license up yesterday. The local agency that Mrs. Burgess contacted this morning couldn't send anybody right away, so they called me."

Judith was speechless. Renie, however, was grinning. "Did Bill help talk you into this?"

Releasing Judith, Joe nodded. "He said it was a good idea to keep busy outside the house. Otherwise, you end up doing all sorts of horrible things, like cleaning out the basement. That's a lot harder than working part-time."

There were tears in Judith's eyes. "I can't believe you're here. I can't believe you're a private eye. I can't believe you didn't tell me."

"I wanted to surprise you," Joe said simply as Wayne Burgess joined them. "By the way," Joe went on, "Wayne knows we're married. In fact, he knows the story of my life about now. He seemed to like it."

Wayne looked sheepish. "I'm sorry. I didn't mean to pry, but I was intrigued when I found out that you two had married later in life after unhappy first marriages. It's a . . . heart-warming tale."

Kenyon cleared his throat. "Should I mix four drinks?"

Surreptitiously, Judith looked at her watch. It was going on four. "Um . . . Maybe we'd better skip ours. Believe it or not, we have . . . an appointment."

Joe regarded his wife with skepticism. "I don't believe it. But I'll let you play your little game. I still have to meet Mrs. Burgess upstairs."

Judith avoided Joe's eyes as she pushed Renie in the direction of the entry hall. "I feel like an idiot," she murmured. "Here I've been criticizing Joe, and all the time he was considering how to spend the rest of his life."

"Until he retires again," Renie said dryly. "Are you sure you want to go through with this now that he's arrived on the scene?"

"We have to," Judith said as they turned into the hallway that led to the tower stairs. "Our guest is probably waiting for us. It's almost four."

"I'm having misgivings," Renie said as they started up the winding stone steps. "Are you sure your so-called guest will show up?"

"Fairly sure," Judith replied as they reached the fourth floor. "My offer was irresistible."

"Your offer implied blackmail," Renie said, dropping her voice as they stood outside the battered tower door.

"I had to think of something," Judith murmured as she cautiously opened the door.

The only sound was the creaking of rusty hinges. The circular room was empty. Judith checked the closet, while Renie looked under the bed. They appeared to be all alone. Clouds had settled in again, and the small, dirty windows provided little illumination on this afternoon in late winter. Shadows crept across the floor, as if seeking to merge with the dusty cobwebs.

"Well?" Renie said as Judith sat down on the small cushioned seat between the two dormer windows. "Now what?"

"We wait. It's exactly four o'clock." Judith sounded confident but her dark eyes darted in every direction. "We have to put in a few more pieces to finish the jigsaw."

"I feel better standing up," Renie said, planting both feet firmly in front of the fireplace.

"Fine," Judith said, and then, despite herself, gave a start when the hinges groaned and the door swung open. With a swagger, Peggy Hillman entered the room.

"Hi," Judith said from the window seat. "We're glad you're here."

"Let's skip the chitchat," Peggy said, her voice huskier than usual. "How much is it going to cost us to keep you two quiet and why should we pay you a red cent?"

"It's like this," Judith said with a faint smile. "You've kept some deep, dark secrets for a very long time. We know all about Suzette, and what happened with your mother, Margaret Burgess. You were named for her, weren't you?"

"So?" Peggy's eyes narrowed as she perched uneasily on the narrow bed. "Why are you stirring up the past?"

"I told you," Judith asserted. "We know what happened here, in this very room. So do you."

With an abrupt swing of her head, Peggy turned away. "Let it be."

"We'd like to," Judith admitted. "It's a terrible story. But I think it has links to the present. That's what we want to find out from you."

"No," Peggy said, still staring off into the shadows. "You want money. Just like everybody else."

"That was only a lure," Judith said patiently. "We aren't blackmailers. All we want is the truth. You're the key, Peggy. You're a witness to what happened here over sixty years ago. I knew you wouldn't speak up unless I resorted to drastic measures."

Slowly, Peggy turned to face Judith. "I honestly don't remember much about what happened with Suzette. I was very, very young."

"You remember that your mother killed her," Judith said softly.

Peggy's eyes widened and her nostrils flared. "I remember no such thing. It was never mentioned."

Judith hesitated, trying to gauge Peggy's state of mind. "You knew, all the same. You must remember your mother's death two weeks later."

The hostility in Peggy's manner faded as she leaned her head back and closed her eyes. "Yes. Yes, I remember that." She swallowed hard and stared at Judith, then at Renie. There was a glint in her blue eyes, a fire that seemed to consume rather then light up Peggy's face. "My mother hanged herself here." She made a vague gesture with her hand. "There are no chairs, you see. There was one in this room then, an oak railback chair that was part of an old kitchen set. My mother stood on it and put a noose around her neck and tied it to that hook in the ceiling."

Judith and Renie stared at the sturdy iron hook that had probably once held a lantern.

"Then," Peggy went on, now staring at the floor, "she kicked the chair out from under her."

Judith nodded. "Yes, I see how that could have happened."

Peggy twisted around and glared at Judith. "No. You don't see anything. You can imagine it, but you don't see it. I do—because I found her."

Judith let out a little gasp. "I'm sorry. I didn't know."

"You do now." Peggy's face had hardened. "Isn't that what you wanted to find out? All the grisly, humiliating details?"

"Not exactly," Judith said, looking abject. "Goodness, you were—what? Two, three?"

"Three," Peggy answered. "Just three, the week before. I'd gotten a dollhouse for my birthday. I was alone. Our nanny—Suzette—had died, and my tower room was next to the nursery. Even though Wayne was barely a toddler, I didn't want him wrecking my dollhouse, so I brought it into my room. I was playing with it when I heard the thud from just over my head." She stopped, staring up at the ominous iron hook. "I was kind of a bold little thing. I came up the stairs to see what made the noise. Maybe I thought it was Wayne. He'd just learned to walk, but he was timid. I knew I could scare him away."

Peggy paused again, a hand over her eyes. "The door was unlocked. I never thought it odd at the time—you don't reason things through when you're only three. I went inside and . . ." The hand pressed against her mouth.

"I am sorry," Judith said, a miserable note in her voice. "If you don't want to talk about it anymore, we'll change the subject."

Peggy didn't speak right away. At last, the hand slipped into her lap. "I smashed the dollhouse to pieces. I took one of the fireplace tools and beat on it until it was destroyed."

"Then the dollhouse in the nursery . . . ?" Puzzled, Judith let the question hang.

"That dollhouse," said Renie, moving away from the hearth, "is an older one, which didn't belong to you. Your Aunt Virginia's, maybe?"

Peggy nodded. "Aunt Ginny played with it when she was a little girl. It had been specially made, a replica of Creepers itself. I wanted a new dollhouse, all my very own. Papa ordered it just for me."

"Ah," Judith said, grateful for Renie's visual perception. "But you didn't quite abandon your aunt's dollhouse, did you, Peggy?"

"What do you mean?" Peggy snapped. "I never played with a dollhouse again. Not anybody's, not even at my friends'."

"I think you did," Judith said deliberately. "I think you and Charlie Ward used to come up to the nursery and drink. I'm not sure why. Maybe it was a form of rebellion, maybe you were drawn to it because of what happened to your mother and Suzette. The nursery wasn't used by the younger generation, because you and your brother had your own houses. Anyway, you'd stash your Scotch bottles under the floor. One time, you must have gotten very drunk.

"Excuse me," Judith said quickly as she saw the protest on Peggy's face, "please let me finish. You told Charlie the whole story. You even made a ghastly little joke out of it, with a doll and some plastic blood. Afterward, you realized what a huge mistake you'd made. But Charlie was your husband, you'd sworn him to secrecy. Married couples shouldn't keep secrets from each other—except this was different. It revealed that your mother was a murderess."

"You're making this up," Peggy declared angrily. "What's your point?"

"The point is," Judith replied, "that you and Charlie didn't remain husband and wife. You divorced, and both of you remarried. Charlie and the second Mrs. Ward didn't make a go of it. You were widowed by Zane Crowley when he was killed in Vietnam. Then you married Russ Hillman."

Sliding off the bed and waving her arms, Peggy started for the door. "I don't need to hear my marital history. I know it by heart. Spare me."

"I can't," Judith said helplessly. "I wish I could."

Halfway across the room, Peggy stopped. "What do you mean?" The husky voice was breathless.

"Charlie Ward wasn't an ambitious man, and he claimed to have hurt his back so he couldn't work. You inherited a large sum of money when your father died. Charlie wanted his piece of the pie. He threatened to expose the family. So," Judith concluded, her voice breaking slightly, "you ran him down with your car."

Peggy burst out laughing, though there was no mirth in the sound. "What a crock! Some kid from the college or a drunk from the riffraff on the highway ran poor Charlie down. Everyone knows that."

"Not quite everyone," Judith said sadly. "Dr. Moss knew better. That's why you had to kill him, too."

Judith hadn't known what to expect. Out of the corner of her eye, she caught Renie searching the hearth, perhaps in search of one of the fireplace tools that Peggy had used to destroy her precious dollhouse.

But Peggy merely laughed some more. "You're a real pair of loons. Do you have any proof? And even if you had some ratty little scraps of evidence, who'd believe you?

You're nobody. I'm a Burgess." Her eyes narrowed at Judith and Renie. "Do you know what that means?"

"It means," Judith said slowly, "that your mother got away with murder. But that doesn't mean you will."

"Doesn't it? You're a fool." Peggy turned on her heel and left the tower.

"Is she right?" Renie asked, looking shaken.

Judith's shoulders sagged. "I don't know. Anything's possible when you're rich. But I certainly intend to tell Joe. And Edwina, of course."

With heavy steps, Judith and Renie left the tower. As they came from the passageway that led into the hall, they could hear raised voices in the entryway. Mystified, the cousins looked at each other, then hurried toward the commotion.

Edwina Jefferson was putting handcuffs on Peggy Hillman, who was swearing at the top of her lungs. "I'm arresting you for the murder of Dr. Aaron Moss. Anything you say may be held against you in a court of law . . ."

"How dare you?" Peggy screamed. "I'll sue! I'll see that you lose your job! You can't do this to me! You're . . . black!"

Edwina chuckled, but her usual good humor was absent. "Honey, I could bust you if I were purple," she said, propelling Peggy across the entry hall. "Maybe it's more fun because I *am* black. You know how lackadaisical and fun-loving we all are in the watermelon patch."

Arms crossed and leaning against the far wall was Joe Flynn, looking bemused. Judith hurried to join him.

"What happened?" she whispered as Peggy was dragged through the front entrance, where an incredulous Kenyon stood sentry.

Joe shrugged. "The perp went down. That's how it works."

"But . . . How did Edwina figure it out?" Judith asked, utterly bewildered.

"Let's get you that drink from the drawing room," Joe said. "Wayne's in there, having a second or maybe a third stiff shot, which I gather is unusual for him."

"He can use it," Renie murmured, as she trudged along behind the Flynns.

Wayne Burgess was slumped on the sofa, a glass in one hand, the other holding his head. "Are they gone?" he asked in a toneless voice.

"They are," Joe said, going to the bar. "Do you mind?"

Wayne shook his head, but said nothing.

Judith waited until Joe had poured the drinks. Feeling sorry for Wayne, whose troubles ranged from filial to marital to financial, she sat down beside him.

"So tell us," Judith urged as Joe and Renie seated themselves in two of the silk-covered armchairs.

"The usual. Hard work and plenty of interviews." Joe paused to sip his Scotch. "But it wasn't just Edwina. It was Danny Wong."

"Danny?" Renie echoed. "Number Three Son always seemed like the silent partner."

"Maybe," Joe grinned, "but that's what Woody was sometimes called when we partnered. Keeping your mouth shut doesn't mean you can't solve crimes."

"So how did Danny solve it?" Judith asked, her curiosity rampant.

Joe settled back in the chair. "When Charlie Ward was killed, Danny was enrolled in law enforcement classes at Sunset Community College. I don't know if you've checked out the road between the golf course and the campus, but it's a long, straight two-lane stretch. Now remember, Danny was just a kid, eighteen, maybe nineteen. He'd finished his class and just pulled out from the college. Danny got behind an old clunk that was going too slow for his teenage taste. He wanted to pass it, but there was a big Lincoln Town Car coming in the opposite direction at an extremely slow speed. Danny was temporarily stuck behind the clunk. A minute later he saw another car pulled off to his side of the road. There weren't any flashers on it, so he didn't stop. Danny, I should point out, had a late date that night."

"So far, I'm following you," Judith commented. "Go on."

"The following quarter," Joe resumed, "Danny's class was using case histories of certain types of situations, including hit-and-run accidents. It was only natural that the instructor chose the Ward fatality, since it had occurred so close to the campus. They could walk to the scene for their field trip."

"You mean they solved it?" Judith asked, gaping at Joe.

"No, no," Joe chuckled. "Nothing so simple. The point is, Danny vividly remembered the incident and even the Lincoln, which he recognized when he and Edwina went over it for possible evidence."

"Dr. Moss's Lincoln," Renie put in. "How did he know it was the same one he saw that night?"

"He didn't," Joe replied. "But it seemed like more than a coincidence, especially when he realized that Peggy Hillman's ex had been the hit-and-run victim. That got him to wondering, and of course Edwina jumped on it when he told her."

Judith felt her stomach lurch. "Wait a minute. You don't mean that Dr. Moss was the one who . . . ?"

Joe shook his head. "No. It turned out that, according to Kenyon, of all people, Charlie Ward was coming to see Peggy at The Willows. Charlie jokingly mentioned to Kenyon that he might end up walking from his place up north because he was having car problems."

"Real—or manufactured?" Judith asked.

Joe shrugged. "Unless Charlie's car is still around somewhere, only Peggy can answer that."

"I understand now why Peggy had to get Caroline out of the house that night," Judith said. "She couldn't afford to have her daughter know that Charlie was coming to blackmail her mother."

Joe gave a faint nod. "Anyway, Dr. Moss had been going south, to Creepers, and had seen the hit-and-run. When Danny saw his car, the doctor had turned around and was going back to the accident scene which was why he was driving so slowly. Danny and Edwina came to the conclusion that Moss had seen the accident and knew who was at fault."

Judith relaxed. "Exactly. Dr. Moss recognized Peggy's car, maybe Charlie's as well. The doctor had been on his way to see Mrs. Burgess, who'd had a gall bladder attack. By the time he got there, he was at the point of collapse. That's what put me onto Peggy's trail. What had upset Dr. Moss so badly before he even reached the house? Peggy had just arrived, which meant her alibi was iffy for the time of her ex-husband's death. I began to see a connection then, not only between the accident and Dr. Moss's murder, but going back to Suzette's death and Margaret Burgess's suicide."

Wayne's head jerked up. "You know?" he asked in a stricken voice.

Judith nodded. "I'm sorry," she said apologetically. "If it's any consolation, your mother must have been mentally unstable. It's likely that your sister inherited those genes."

"I don't remember my real mother," Wayne said, his voice thick. "But Peggy has always been . . . volatile."

"As in unbalanced?" Renie asked bluntly.

"No." The word was emphatic. "Peggy's not crazy. Neither was our mother."

Judith, Joe, and Renie all looked at each other. They shared a single thought: It was useless to argue with Wayne. Insanity wasn't acceptable for a Burgess, perhaps not even as a legal defense.

"Your sister was very human," Judith said, more gently. "We noticed that from the start. Perhaps because of that, the barriers that wealth and privilege provide were more fragile."

Wayne looked anguished. "Peggy was always less inclined to keep things to herself. She wasn't always . . . discreet."

Judith nodded. "Her indiscretion about how the rest of the family needed money and therefore might want to harm your stepmother also made me wonder. I realize now that it was deliberate. She was trying to steer us away from the real victim and the real motive, both of which were behind her need to silence Dr. Moss."

Edna, all aquiver, entered the drawing room. "Mr. Flynn? Mrs. Burgess would like to see you, please."

"Again?" Joe shrugged and stood up, then turned to Judith. "I guess I won't be home for dinner. Will you?"

Judith grimaced. "It's after five. I assume Arlene's managing?"

"As far as I know," Joe replied, crossing the room. "You and Renie might as well eat dinner somewhere out on the highway."

"But . . . Shouldn't we say good-bye to Leota?" Judith asked, reluctant to let go.

Embarrassed, Wayne cleared his throat. "*Maman* would prefer not to see you again."

Judith couldn't help but look annoyed. "Why? Does she feel she's lost face?"

Wayne hung his head. "I never question *Maman's* motives."

The implication was obvious. Judith had no right to question them, either. "But the case is closed, isn't it? Why are you staying, Joe?"

"One case is closed," Joe answered from the doorway. "The other isn't. Mrs. Burgess still wants to know who's been trying to kill her."

"Damn!" Judith breathed. "It wasn't Peggy? You mean Renie and I flunked detection?"

"Afraid so, Jude-girl," Joe said, growing impatient. "Don't worry about it. You're not detectives." He disappeared from the drawing room.

Judith and Renie went upstairs to pack.

Two days later, just as Judith was trying to convince Phyliss Rackley that Satan hadn't put a catnip mouse in the laundry detergent, Edwina Jefferson arrived at Hillside Manor.

"Peggy Hillman has entered a not guilty plea," she told

Judith as they sat down to coffee at the kitchen table. "Naturally, she's hired the best criminal lawyers available, including some dude from L.A."

"Do you think she'll get off?" Judith asked with a sinking feeling.

Edwina shrugged. "Who knows? Danny and I did our jobs. You did yours, too. I wanted to thank you and your cousin for your help."

"We didn't do much," Judith said bleakly. "In fact, you and Danny had it solved before we did."

"That's our job," Edwina said, accepting Judith's offer of cookies from the sheep-shaped jar on the kitchen table. "To make you feel better, you were right about Peggy taking the garage remote and putting the car in the garage. It had an oil leak, I might add. Anyway, that's why Russ Hillman didn't think she was at Creepers when he came looking for her the night of the murder."

"And dropped that golf marker?" Judith asked.

Edwina nodded. "He couldn't figure out where she was, and he wanted to make sure the coast was clear before he took off with Dorothy Burgess. The Hillmans have separate bedrooms, you know. So do Wayne and Dorothy."

"A family tradition," Judith murmured. "And a sad one. Tell me, did the dirt on the floor and under Dr. Moss's body come from the garden where the footman statue was planted?"

"So it seems, but the forensics folks found enough hair, skin particles, and fiber to clinch it as the weapon. Hey," Edwina said as Renie came in through the back door, "it's honey. What's up?"

"My blood pressure," Renie said, surprised to see the detective. "I just finished a presentation with some dunderheads at KINE-TV. Their ideas of public service suck. I ended up telling them the best public service they could render would be to go off the air. I think I lost the account."

Edwina laughed as Renie poured herself a mug of coffee. "Tact doesn't seem to be your strong suit. How do you stay in business?"

"Because I'm damned good," Renie replied. "Modest, too."

Judith looked askance at Renie. "Sometimes my cousin bugs me," she said to Edwina. "Frankly, I feel like a big flop."

"You shouldn't," Edwina said. "Your insights and your way with other people were invaluable. You were right about that wishing well." She winced. "While everyone was at Dr. Moss's funeral yesterday, the well was opened up and we found skeletal remains which were identified as belonging to Suzette. Dr. Stevens is very grateful. By the way, did you figure out where Dr. Moss got his money?"

Judith nodded vaguely. "Sort of. After Charlie Ward's accident, Aaron Moss told Peggy that he suspected her. For the sake of the family, especially Leota, of whom he was extremely fond, maybe even in love with, he agreed to keep quiet. Peggy paid him off with part of her inheritance from her father. But four years later, Dr. Moss was sensing his mortality. He could no longer keep the secret and live with his conscience. He was also afraid for Leota. He may have known that the attempts on her life were real, and somehow feared that Peggy had snapped, just like her birth mother, and was trying to kill Mrs. Burgess. I suspect he warned Peggy, which was a fatal mistake. She had to lure him to the house where she could kill him to keep him quiet. Then, to make sure her secret was safe, she took his keys and removed any evidence he might have saved at his office. She returned the keys the next morning, tossing them in the pool where she knew they'd be found. In a weird way, I think it was a thoughtful gesture. Peggy had caused her stepmother's fall. She felt bad about it, and wanted to make sure Dr. Stevens had a key to get into Creepers."

Edwina was nodding agreement. "One other thing—Caroline wrote those words on the tablet in the library. She was proud of them, and insisted I read the rest of it which she'd written later. It was a poem about her failed marriage.

A thirty-two-page poem." Edwina held her head, then asked if Joe had come home yet.

"No," Judith said. "He called earlier this morning to say he might be winding things up there by late this afternoon. Have you talked to him?"

"Yes, about an hour ago," Edwina replied, then looked apologetic. "He's solved the rest of the case."

"He has?" Judith almost dropped her coffee mug. "You mean it really was Peggy who was trying to knock off Mrs. Burgess?"

Edwina shook her head. "No. It was Bop."

"Bop," Judith murmured. "I certainly considered him, along with Kenneth. Dorothy seemed to be shielding somebody, so it had to be her husband, her son, or Russ Hillman. How did Joe find out?"

"Nurse Fritz," Edwina replied. "She's had it in for the family ever since she didn't get the legacy or whatever it was that Walter Burgess allegedly promised her. The other night, Edna brought up tea for Mrs. Burgess and Nurse Fritz. Bop was already there, having delivered the pizzas. Apparently, he was nervous—because of his intentions— and he mixed up the boxes. Fritz became suspicious. She guessed that something was amiss, but she didn't notice him tampering with the tea. Then she made the mistake of taking the cup that was meant for Leota."

"Gambling debts," Judith stated. "The motive was that he couldn't wait for his inheritance?"

"That's right," Edwina said. "His business is doing fine, but he's not making a sufficient profit to cover his losses. Bop's gambling wasn't limited to cards. He bet on every-thing—horses, sporting events, table games. Compulsive, of course."

Judith was looking bemused. "He didn't really want to kill his grandmother, though. Maybe he just wanted to scare her. How many times did he try? And fail? I remember hearing someone say Bop had no killer instinct. I should have taken it literally. Did you arrest him?"

"No," Edwina said with an ironic smile. "Mrs. Burgess refused to press charges. Instead, she handed over the money and insisted he start attending Gamblers Anonymous meetings."

"Leota couldn't take any more family embarrassment," Judith said. "It'll be very hard on all of them when the trial is held. You know," she went on, "I have a theory about why Leota didn't want to see us again before we left Creepers. I'll bet she saw Peggy in the entry hall just before the lights went out and Dr. Moss was struck from behind. She'll never admit that, not even if she's called to the stand. But after Peggy was arrested, Leota didn't dare look Renie and me in the eye. She's basically an honest woman and she was too ashamed."

"Honest," Renie noted, "except when it comes to upholding her family."

"Very likely," Edwina said, standing up. "If—a big if—Peggy's convicted, and goes to prison, it'll be a terrible disgrace. I can't imagine how she'll endure a life sentence."

"I don't know about that," Renie said, gobbling up sugar cookies. "She's already done a lifetime stretch. If Creepers looks like a prison, feels like a prison, then . . ." Renie shrugged.

"True," Judith said. "Wealth, especially inherited wealth, is imprisoning. What's worse is that it cuts you off from other people. You aren't whole, you're just a shadow of a real human being. It seems like a hollow life."

"And one we don't have to worry about," Edwina declared, hands folded in a prayerful gesture. "Thank you both. I've got to finish the paperwork." She turned to Renie. "You did good—sugar."

Renie's eyes grew wide as she grinned at Edwina. "I'm a sugar? Finally?"

Edwina didn't reply. Instead, she hugged Judith. "Don't beat yourself up. You've been one terrific amateur sleuth. So long—sister."

As Edwina's solid figure exited through the front door, Judith felt her spirits rise. "I really like her," she said.

"You like everybody," Renie said, pouting. "*Sister*—I

didn't know there was yet another level of endearment."

"It's because I'm married to an ex-cop," Judith said, hoping to salve Renie's feelings. "By the way, are you going to see Bev while she's in town?"

Beverly Ohashi had flown in from Cairo to help the rest of the family weather the storm in the wake of Peggy's arrest. "Probably," Renie replied as the cousins returned to the kitchen. "I guess if we couldn't figure out who was trying to kill Leota, it's a good thing Joe could."

Judith agreed, though with some reluctance. It still galled her that she'd been stumped by the attempts on Mrs. Burgess's life. Before she could say as much, Phyliss appeared, carrying an empty laundry basket.

"I'm sorry I won't be around when that church group gets here," she said, referring to the visitors who were arriving around five. "But I'll see cousin Orval and his wife, Radella, at the conference tomorrow morning. I told 'em Hillside Manor was the best B&B in town. Lots of extras, at a sensible price. They'll see things around here they never could imagine in Grundy Center, Iowa."

"That was very kind of you to recommend us," Judith said. "We'll be full up through the weekend."

Phyliss turned to Renie. "Hallo, Mrs. Jones. Have you been saved yet?"

"Not recently," Renie replied, flipping Phyliss off as the cleaning woman turned her back to empty a hamper of dirty clothes into the basket.

"Mend your ways," Phyliss said ominously. "By the way," she went on, looking at Judith, "your dryer's on its last legs. Something nasty's leaking out of one of those pipes by the old coal bin. Oh, and the hot water isn't really hot today. In fact, it's been getting worse all week."

Judith rolled her eyes. "Great. That sounds like at least a grand in repair bills. We're barely going to squeak by this month."

Renie shot Judith an ironic glance. "Do you wish you were rich?"

Judith started to open her mouth, caught herself, and

grinned at Renie. "No. I really like being poor."

"I thought so," said Renie. "So do I."

Phyliss looked mystified, then shrugged. "It's a good thing," she remarked. "The sink's backed up in the bathroom between guest rooms five and six. You better call a plumber."

By four o'clock, Judith was anxious for Joe to come home. They'd hardly seen each other in the past five days. She was turning on the oven when he came through the back door.

Judith rushed to meet him and threw her arms around his neck before he could close the back door. "I'm so glad you're home! Are you finished at Creepers?"

"Right," Joe said between kisses. "Hey, why the warm welcome?"

Judith smiled. "Because you're here."

"I thought I was driving you nuts," Joe replied, looking bewildered.

"I prefer it when you drive me crazy," Judith said, leaning back to unloosen his tie. "If you know what I mean."

The golden flecks danced in the magic eyes. "I think I do. But won't the guests start arriving any time?"

Judith shook her head. "Our visitors are from that Midwestern church tour that's in town for a big conference. Some of them are Phyliss's relatives. They'll arrive from the airport by van about five."

"Then we have time to be crazy," Joe said, pulling Judith over to the kitchen table.

"Joe!" Judith exclaimed. "Not here!"

"Why not?" Gently, he pressed her back against the table. "I never want you to think I'm dull or annoying."

"You're not." Judith sighed as Joe slipped his hands under her cotton sweater. "Crazy, maybe. Poor. Broke. Oh, Joe," she said, as they shed their clothes, "I'm so happy!"

As they writhed in rekindled passion, Joe and Judith

were oblivious to everything but each other. They didn't hear the open back door swing wide or the cheerful voice of a man they didn't know.

"We got here early!" he cried. "Praise the Lord!"

We hope you have enjoyed this Avon mystery. Mysteries fascinate and intrigue with the worlds they create. And what better way to capture your interest than this glimpse into the world of a select group of Avon authors.

Tamar Myers reveals the deadly side of the antique business. The bed-and-breakfast industry becomes lethal in the hands of Mary Daheim. A walk along San Antonio's famed River Walk with Carolyn Hart reveals a fascinating and mysterious place. Nevada Barr encounters danger on Ellis Island. Deborah Woodworth's Sister Rose Callahan discovers something sinister is afoot in her Kentucky Shaker village. Jill Churchill steps back in time to the 1930's along the Hudson River and creates a weekend of intrigue. And Anne George's Southern Sisters find that making money is a motive for murder.

So turn the page for a sneak peek into worlds filled with mystery and murder. And if you like what you read, head to your nearest bookstore. It's the only way to figure out whodunnit . . .

Abigail Timberlake, the heroine of Tamar Myers' delightful Den of Antiquity series, is smart, quirky, and strong-minded. She has to be—running your own antique business is a struggle, even on the cultured streets of Charlotte, North Carolina, and her mean-spirited divorce lawyer of an ex-husband's caused her a lot of trouble over the years. She also has a "delicate" relationship with her proper Southern mama.

The difficulties in Abby's personal life are nothing, though, to the trouble that erupts when she buys a "faux" Van Gogh at auction . . .

ESTATE OF MIND
by Tamar Myers

YOU ALREADY KNOW that my name is Abigail Timberlake, but you might not know that I was married to a beast of a man for just over twenty years. Buford Timberlake—or Timbersnake, as I call him—is one of Charlotte, North Carolina's most prominent divorce lawyers. Therefore, he knew exactly what he was doing when he traded me in for his secretary. Of course, Tweetie Bird is half my age—although parts of her are even much younger than that. The woman is 20 percent silicone, for crying out loud, although admittedly it balances rather nicely with the 20 percent that was sucked away from her hips.

In retrospect, however, there are worse things than having your husband dump you for a man-made woman. It hurt like the dickens at the time, but it would have hurt even more had he traded me in for a brainier model. I can buy most of what Tweetie has (her height excepted), but she will forever be afraid to flush the toilet lest she drown the Ty-D-Bol man.

And as for Buford, he got what he deserved. Our daughter, Susan, was nineteen at the time and in college, but our son, Charlie, was seventeen, and a high school junior. In the penultimate miscarriage of justice, Buford got custody of Charlie, our house, and even the dog Scruffles. I must point out that Buford got custody of our friends as well. Sure, they didn't legally belong to him, but where would you rather stake your loyalty? To a good old boy with more connections than the White House switchboard, or to a housewife whose biggest accomplishment, besides giving birth, was a pie crust that didn't shatter when you touched it with your fork? But like I said, Buford got what he deserved and today—it actually pains me to say this—neither of our children will speak to their father.

Now I own a four bedroom, three bath home not far from my shop. My antique shop is the Den of Antiquity. I paid for this house, mind you—not one farthing came from Buford. At any rate, I share this peaceful, if somewhat lonely, abode with a very hairy male who is young enough to be my son.

When I got home from the auction, I was in need of a little comfort, so I fixed myself a cup of tea with milk and sugar—never mind that it was summer—and curled up on the white cotton couch in the den. My other hand held a copy of Anne Grant's *Smoke Screen*, a mystery novel set in Charlotte and surrounding environs. I hadn't finished more than a page of this exciting read when my roommate rudely pushed it aside and climbed into my lap.

"Dmitri," I said, stroking his large orange head, "that 'Starry Night' painting is so ugly, if Van Gogh saw it, he'd cut off his other ear."

Some folks think that just because I'm in business for myself, I can set my own hours. That's true as long as I keep my shop open forty hours a week during prime business hours and spend another eight or ten hours attending sales. Not to mention the hours spent cleaning and organizing any subsequent purchases. I know what they mean, though. If I'm late to the shop, I may lose a valued customer, but I won't lose my job—at least not in one fell swoop.

I didn't think I'd ever get to sleep Wednesday night, and I didn't. It was well into the wee hours of Thursday morning when I stopped counting green thistles and drifted off. When my alarm beeped, I managed to turn it off in my sleep. Either that or in my excitement, I had forgotten to set it. At any rate, the telephone woke me up at 9:30, a half hour later than the time I usually open my shop.

"*Muoyo webe*," Mama said cheerily.

"What?" I pushed Dmitri off my chest and sat up.

"Life to you, Abby. That's how they say 'good morning' in Tshiluba."

I glanced at the clock. "Oh, shoot! Mama, I've got to run."

"I know, dear. I tried the shop first and got the machine. Abby, you really should consider getting a professional to record your message. Someone who sounds . . . well, more cultured."

"Like Rob?" I remembered the painting. "Mama, sorry, but I really can't talk now."

"Fine," Mama said, her cheeriness deserting her. "I guess, like they say, bad news can wait."

I sighed. Mama baits her hooks with an expertise to be envied by the best fly fishermen.

"Sock it to me, Mama. But make it quick."

"Are you sitting down, Abby?"

"Mama, I'm still in bed!"

"Abby, I'm afraid I have some horrible news to tell you about one of your former boyfriends."

"Greg?" I managed to gasp after a few seconds. "Did something happen to Greg?"

"No, dear, it's Gilbert Sweeny. He's dead."

I wanted to reach through the phone line and shake Mama until her pearls rattled. "Gilbert Sweeny was never my boyfriend!"

From nationally-bestselling author Mary Daheim, who creates a world inside a Seattle bed-and-breakfast that is impossible to resist, comes Creeps Suzette, *the newest addition to this delightful series . . .*

Judith McMonigle Flynn, the consummate hostess of Hillside Manor, fairly flies out the door in the dead of winter when her cousin Renie requests her company. As long as Judith's ornery mother, her ferocious feline, and her newly retired husband aren't joining them, Judith couldn't care less where they're going. That is until they arrive at the spooky vine-covered mansion, Creepers, in which an elderly woman lives in fear that someone is trying to kill her. And it's up to the cousins to determine which dark, drafty corner houses a cold-blooded killer before a permanent hush falls over them all . . .

CREEPS SUZETTE
by Mary Daheim

"As you wish, ma'am," said Kenyon, and creaked out of the parlor.

"Food," Renie sighed. "I'm glad I'm back."

"With a vengeance," Judith murmured. "You know," she went on, "when I saw those stuffed animal heads in the game room, I had to wonder if Kenneth wasn't reacting to them. His grandfather or great-grandfather must have

307

hunted. Maybe he grew up feeling sorry for the lions and tigers and bears, oh, my!"

"I could eat a bear," Renie said.

Climbing the tower staircase, the cousins could feel the wind. "Not well-insulated in this part of the house," Judith noted as they entered Kenneth's room.

"It's a tower," Renie said. "What would you expect?"

Judith really hadn't expected to see Roscoe the raccoon, but there he was, standing on his hind legs in a commodious cage. The bandit eyes gazed soulfully at the cousins.

"Hey," Renie said, kneeling down, "from the looks of that food dish, you've eaten more than we have this evening. You'll have to wait for dessert."

Judith, meanwhile, was studying the small fireplace, peeking into drawers, looking under the bed. "Nothing," she said, opening the door to the nursery. "Just the kind of things you'd expect Kenneth to keep on hand for his frequent visits to Creepers."

Renie said good-bye to Roscoe and followed Judith into the nursery. "How long," Renie mused, "do you suppose it's been since any kids played in here?"

Judith calculated. "Fifteen years, maybe more?"

"Do you think they're keeping it for grandchildren?" Renie asked in a wistful tone.

Judith gave her cousin a sympathetic glance. So far, none of the three grown Jones offspring had acquired mates or produced children. "That's possible," Judith said. "You shouldn't give up hope, especially these days when kids marry so late."

Renie didn't respond. Instead, she contemplated the train set. "This is the same vintage as the one I had. It's a Marx, like mine. I don't think they make them any more."

"Some of these dolls are much older," Judith said. "They're porcelain and bisque. These toys run the gamut. From hand-carved wooden soldiers to plastic Barbies. And look at this dollhouse. The furniture is all the same style as many of the pieces in this house."

"Hey," Renie said, joining Judith at the shelf where the

dollhouse was displayed, "this looks like a cutaway replica of Creepers itself. There's even a tower room on this one side and it's . . ." Renie blanched and let out a little gasp.

"What's wrong, coz? Are you okay?" Judith asked in alarm.

A gust of wind blew the door to the nursery shut, making both cousins jump. "Yeah, right, I'm just fine," Renie said in a startled voice. "But look at this. How creepy can Creepers get?"

Judith followed Renie's finger. In the top floor of the half-version of the tower was a bed, a chair, a table, and a tiny doll in a long dark dress. The doll was lying facedown on the floor in what looked like a pool of blood.

The lights in the nursery went out.

*Carolyn Hart is the multiple Agatha, Anthony, and
Macavity Award-winning author of the "Death on
Demand" series as well as the highly praised Henrie
O series. In* Death on the River Walk, *sixtysomething
retired journalist Henrietta O'Dwyer Collins must
turn her carefully-honed sleuthing skills to a truly
perplexing crime that's taken place at the luxurious
gift shop Tesoros on the fabled River Walk of San
Antonio, Texas. See why the* Los Angeles Times *said,
"If I were teaching a course on how to write a
mystery, I would make Carolyn Hart required
reading . . . Superb."*

DEATH ON THE RIVER WALK
by Carolyn Hart

SIRENS SQUALLED. WHEN the police arrived, this area
would be closed to all of us. Us. Funny. Was I aligning
myself with the Garza clan? Not exactly, though I was
charmed by Maria Elena, and I liked—or wanted to like—
her grandson Rick. But I wasn't kidding myself that the
death of the blond man wouldn't cause trouble for Iris.
Whatever she'd found in the wardrobe, it had to be con-
nected to this murder. And I wanted a look inside Tesoros
before Rick had a chance to grab Iris's backpack should it
be there. That was why I'd told Rick to make the call to
the police from La Mariposa.

The central light was on. That was the golden pool that
spread through the open door. The small recessed spots

above the limestone display islands were dark, so the rest of the store was dim and shadowy.

I followed alongside the path revealed by Manuel's mop. It was beginning to dry at the farther reach, but there was still enough moisture to tell the story I was sure the police would understand. The body had been moved along this path, leaving a trail of bloodstains. That's what Manuel had mopped up.

The sirens were louder, nearer.

The trail ended in the middle of the store near an island with a charming display of pottery banks—a lion, a bull, a big-cheeked balding man, a donkey, a rounded head with bright red cheeks. Arranged in a semicircle, each was equidistant from its neighbor. One was missing.

I used my pocket flashlight, snaked the beam high and low. I didn't find the missing bank. Or Iris's backpack.

The sirens choked in mid-wail.

I hurried, moving back and forth across the store, swinging the beam of my flashlight. No pottery bank, no backpack. Nothing else appeared out of order or disturbed in any way. The only oddity was the rapidly drying area of freshly mopped floor, a three-foot swath leading from the paperweight-display island to the front door.

I reached the front entrance and stepped outside. In trying to stay clear of the mopped area, I almost stumbled into the pail and mop. I leaned down, wrinkled my nose against the sour smell of ammonia, and pointed the flashlight beam into the faintly discolored water, no longer foamy with suds. The water's brownish tinge didn't obscure the round pink snout of a pottery pig bank.

Swift, heavy footsteps sounded on the steps leading down from La Mariposa. I moved quickly to stand by the bench. Iris looked with wide and frightened eyes at the policemen following Rick and his Uncle Frank into the brightness spilling out from Tesoros. I supposed Rick had wakened his uncle to tell him of the murder.

Iris reached out, grabbed my hand. Rick stopped a few feet from the body, pointed at it, then at the open door.

Frank Garza peered around the shoulder of a short policeman with sandy hair and thick glasses. Rick was pale and
strained. He spoke in short, jerky sentences to a burly policeman with ink-black hair, an expressionless face, and one
capable hand resting on the butt of his pistol. Frank patted
his hair, disarranged from sleep, stuffed his misbuttoned
shirt into his trousers.

When Rick stopped, the policeman turned and looked
toward the bench. Iris's fingers tightened on mine, but I
knew the policeman wasn't looking at us. He was looking
at Manuel, sitting quietly with his usual excellent posture,
back straight, feet apart, hands loose in his lap.

Manuel slowly realized that everyone was looking at
him. He blinked, looked at us eagerly, slowly lifted his
hands, and began to clap.

*Nevada Barr's brilliant series featuring Park Ranger
Anna Pigeon takes this remarkable heroine to the
scene of heinous crimes at the feet of a national
shrine—the Statue of Liberty. While bunking with
friends on Liberty Island, Anna finds solitude in the
majestically decayed remains of hospitals, medical
wards, and staff quarters of Ellis Island. When a
tumble through a crumbling staircase temporarily
halts her ramblings, Anna is willing to write off the
episode as an accident. But then a young girl falls—
or is pushed—to her death while exploring the Statue
of Liberty, and it's up to Anna to uncover the deadly
secrets of Lady Liberty's treasured island.*

LIBERTY FALLING
by Nevada Barr

HELD ALOFT BY the fingers of her right hand, Anna dangled
over the ruined stairwell. Between dust and night there was
no way of knowing what lay beneath. Soon either her fingers would uncurl from the rail or the rail would pull out
from the wall. Faint protests of aging screws in softening
plaster foretold the collapse. No superhuman feats of
strength struck Anna as doable. What fragment of energy
remained in her arm was fast burning away on the pain.
With a kick and a twist, she managed to grab hold of the
rail with her other hand as well. Much of the pressure was
taken off her shoulder, but she was left face to the wall.
There was the vague possibility that she could scoot one

hand width at a time up the railing, then swing her legs onto what might or might not be stable footing at the top of the stairs. Two shuffles nixed that plan. Old stairwells didn't fall away all in a heap like guillotined heads. Between her and the upper floor were the ragged remains, shards of wood and rusted metal. In the black dark she envisioned the route upward with the same jaundice a hay bale might view a pitchfork.

What the hell, she thought. *How far can it be?* And she let go.

With no visual reference, the fall, though in reality not more than five or six feet, jarred every bone in her body. Unaided by eyes and brain, her legs had no way of compensating. Knees buckled on impact and her chin smacked into them as her forehead met some immovable object. The good news was, the whole thing was over in the blink of a blind eye and she didn't think she'd sustained any lasting damage.

Wisdom dictated she lie still, take stock of her body and surroundings, but this decaying dark was so filthy she couldn't bear the thought of it. Stink rose from the litter: pigeon shit, damp and rot. Though she'd seen none, it was easy to imagine spiders of evil temperament and immoderate size. Easing up on feet and hands, she picked her way over rubble she could not see, heading for the faint smudge of gray that would lead her to the out-of-doors.

Free of the damage she'd wreaked, Anna quickly found her way out of the tangle of inner passages and escaped Island III through the back door of the ward. The sun had set. The world was bathed in gentle peach-colored light. A breeze, damp but cooling with the coming night, blew off the water. Sucking it in, she coughed another colony of spores from her lungs. With safety, the delayed reaction hit. Wobbly, she sat down on the steps and put her head between her knees.

Because she'd been messing around where she probably shouldn't have been in the first place, she'd been instrumental in the destruction of an irreplaceable historic structure. Sitting on the stoop, smeared with dirt and reeking of bygone pigeons, she contemplated whether to report the disaster or just slink away and let the monument's curators write it off to natural causes. She was within a heartbeat of deciding to do the honorable thing when the decision was taken from her.

The sound of boots on hard-packed earth followed by a voice saying: "Patsy thought it might be you," brought her head up. A lovely young man, resplendent in the uniform of the Park Police, was walking down the row of buildings toward her.

"Why?" Anna asked stupidly.

"One of the boat captains radioed that somebody was over here." The policeman sat down next to her. He was no more than twenty-two or -three, fit and handsome and oozing boyish charm. "Have you been crawling around or what?"

Anna took a look at herself. Her khaki shorts were streaked with black, her red tank top untucked and smeared with vile-smelling mixtures. A gash ran along her thigh from the hem of her shorts to her kneecap. It was bleeding, but not profusely. Given the amount of rust and offal in this adventure, she would have to clean it thoroughly and it wouldn't hurt to check when she'd last had a tetanus shot.

"Sort of," she said, and told him about the stairs. "Should we check it out? Surely we'll have to make a report. You'll have to write a report," she amended. "I'm just a hapless tourist."

The policeman looked over his shoulder. The doorway behind them was cloaked in early night. "Maybe in the morning," he said, and Anna could have sworn he was afraid. There was something in this strong man's voice that told her, were it a hundred years earlier, he would have made a sign against the evil eye.

Sister Rose Callahan, eldress of the Depression-era community of Believers at the Kentucky Shaker village of North Homage, knows that evil does not merely exist in the Bible. Sometimes it comes very close to home indeed.

"A complete and very charming portrait
of a world, its ways,
and the beliefs of its people,
and an excellent mystery to draw you along."
Anne Perry

In the next pages, Sister Rose confronts danger in the form of an old religious cult seeking new members among the peaceful Shakers.

A SIMPLE SHAKER MURDER
by Deborah Woodworth

AT FIRST, ROSE saw nothing alarming, only rows of strictly pruned apple trees, now barren of fruit and most of their leaves. The group ran through the apple trees and into the more neglected east side of the orchard, where the remains of touchier fruit trees lived out their years with little human attention. The pounding feet ahead of her stopped, and panting bodies piled behind one another, still trying to keep some semblance of separation between the brethren and the sisters.

The now-silent onlookers stared at an aged plum tree. From a sturdy branch hung the limp figure of a man, his feet dangling above the ground. His eyes were closed and his head slumped forward, almost hiding the rope that gouged into his neck. The man wore loose clothes that were neither Shaker nor of the world, and Rose sensed he was gone even before Josie reached for his wrist and shook her head.

Two brethren moved forward to cut the man down.

"Nay, don't, not yet," Rose said, hurrying forward.

Josie's eyebrows shot up. "Surely you don't think this is anything but the tragedy of a man choosing to end his own life?" She nodded past the man's torso to a delicate chair laying on its side in the grass. It was a Shaker design, not meant for such rough treatment. Dirt scuffed the woven red-and-white tape of the seat. Scratches marred the smooth slats that formed its ladder back.

"What's going on here? Has Mother Ann appeared and declared today a holiday from labor?" The powerful voice snapped startled heads backwards, to where Elder Wilhelm emerged from the trees, stern jaw set for disapproval.

No one answered. Everyone watched Wilhelm's ruddy face blanche as he came in view of the dead man.

"Dear God," he whispered. "Is he . . . ?"

"Yea," said Josie.

"Then cut him down instantly," Wilhelm said. His voice had regained its authority, but he ran a shaking hand through his thick white hair.

Eyes turned to Rose. "I believe we should leave him for now, Wilhelm," she said. A flush spread across Wilhelm's cheeks, and Rose knew she was in for a public tongue thrashing, so she explained quickly. "Though all the signs point to suicide, still it is a sudden and brutal death, and I believe we should alert the Sheriff. He'll want things left just as we found them."

"Sheriff Brock . . ." Wilhelm said with a snort of derision. "He will relish the opportunity to find us culpable."

"Please, for the sake of pity, cut him down." A man

stepped forward, hat in hand in the presence of death. His
thinning blond hair lifted in the wind. His peculiar loose
work clothes seemed too generous for his slight body. "I'm
Gilbert Owen Griffiths," he said, nodding to Rose. "And
this is my compatriot, Earl Weston," he added, indicating
a broad-shouldered, dark-haired young man. "I am privileged to be guiding a little group of folks who are hoping
to rekindle the flame of the great social reformer, Robert
Owen. That poor unfortunate man," he said, with a glance
at the dead man, "was Hugh—Hugh Griffiths—and he was
one of us. We don't mind having the Sheriff come take a
look, but we are all like a family, and it is far too painful
for us to leave poor Hugh hanging."

"It's an outrage, leaving him there like that," Earl said.
"What if Celia should come along?"

"Celia is poor Hugh's wife," Gilbert explained. "I'll have
to break the news to her soon. I beg of you, cut him down
and cover him before she shows up."

Wilhelm assented with a curt nod. "I will inform the
Sheriff," he said as several brethren cut the man down and
lay him on the ground. The morbid fascination had worn
off, and most of the crowd was backing away.

There was nothing to do but wait. Rose gathered up the
sisters and New-Owenite women who had not already made
their escape. Leaving Andrew to watch over the ghastly
scene until the Sheriff arrived, she sent the women on ahead
to breakfast, for which she herself had no appetite. The men
followed behind.

On impulse Rose glanced back to see Andrew's tall figure hunched against a tree near the body. He watched the
crowd's departure with a forlorn expression. As she raised
her arm to send him an encouraging wave, a move dis-
tracted her. She squinted through the tangle of unpruned
branches behind Andrew to locate the source. *Probably just
a squirrel*, she thought, but her eyes kept searching nonetheless. There it was again—a flash of brown almost indis-

tinguishable from tree bark. Several rows of trees back from where Andrew stood, something was moving among the branches of an old pear tree—something much bigger than a squirrel.

Once upon a time Lily and Robert were the pampered offspring of a rich New York family. But the crash of '29 left them virtually penniless until a distant relative offered them a Grace and Favor house on the Hudson.

The catch is they must live at this house for ten years and not return to their beloved Manhattan. In the Still of the Night *Lily and Robert invite paying guests from the city to stay with them for a cultural weekend. But then something goes wildly askew.*

IN THE STILL OF THE NIGHT
by Jill Churchill

"I REALIZED THAT Mrs. Ethridge wasn't at breakfast and she hasn't come to lunch either. I kept an eye out for her so I could nip in and tidy her room while she was out and about and she hasn't been."

"She's not in the dining room?" Lily said. "No, I guess not. There were two empty chairs."

"She might be sick, miss."

"Have you knocked on her door?"

"A couple times, miss."

"I'll go see what's become of her," Lily said.

Robert, who had been ringing up the operator, hung up the phone. "I think it would be better for me to check on her."

"But Robert . . ." Lily saw his serious expression and

paused. "Very well. But I'll come with you."

They went up to the second floor and Robert tapped lightly on the door. "Mrs. Ethridge? Are you all right?" When there was no response, he tapped more firmly and repeated himself loudly.

They stood there, brother and sister, remembering another incident last fall, and staring at each other. "I'll look. You stay out here," Robert said.

He opened the door and almost immediately closed it in Lily's face. She heard the snick of the inside lock. There was complete silence for a long moment, then Robert unlocked and re-opened the door. "Lily, she's dead."

Lily gasped. "Are you sure?"

"Quite sure."

"Oh, why did she have to die *here*?" Lily said, then caught herself. "What a selfish thing to say. I'm sorry."

"No need to be. I thought the same thing. It's not as if she's a good friend, or even someone we willingly invited."

"What do we do now?"

"You go back to the dining room and act like nothing's wrong while I call the police and the coroner."

"The police? Why the police?"

"I think you have to call them for an unexplained death. Besides, if we don't, what do we *do* with her? Somebody has to take her away to be buried."

Patricia Anne is a sedate suburban housewife living in Birmingham, Alabama, but thanks to her outrageous sister, Mary Alice, she's always in the thick of some controversy, often with murderous overtones. In Murder Shoots the Bull, *Anne George's seventh novel in the Southern Sisters series, the sisters are involved in an investment club with next door neighbor Mitzi. But no sooner have they started the club than strange things start happening to the members . . .*

MURDER SHOOTS THE BULL
by Anne George

I FIXED COFFEE, microwaved some oatmeal, and handed Fred a can of Healthy Request chicken noodle soup for his lunch as he went out the door. Wifely duties done, I settled down with my second cup of coffee and the *Birmingham News*.

I usually glance over the front page, read "People are Talking" on the second, and then turn to the Metro section. Which is what I did this morning. I was reading about a local judge who claimed he couldn't help it if he kept dozing off in court because of narcolepsy when Mitzi, my next door neighbor, knocked on the back door.

"Have you seen it?" She pointed to the paper in my hand when I opened the door.

"Seen what?" I was so startled at her appearance, it took me a moment to answer. Mitzi looked rough. She had on a pink chenille bathrobe which had seen better days and she was barefooted. No comb had touched her hair. It was totally un-Mitzi-like. I might run across the yards looking like this, but not Mitzi. She's the neatest person in the world.

"About the death."

"What death?" I don't know why I asked. I knew, of course. I moved aside and she came into the kitchen.

"Sophie Sawyer's poisoning."

Mitzi walked to the kitchen table and sat down as if her legs wouldn't hold her up anymore.

"Sophie Sawyer was poisoned?"

"Arthur said you were there yesterday."

"I was." I sat down across from Mitzi, my heart thumping faster. "She was poisoned?"

"Second page. Crime reports." Mitzi propped her elbows on the table, leaned forward and put a hand over each ear as if she didn't want to hear my reaction.

I turned to the second page. The first crime report, one short paragraph, had the words—SUSPECTED POISONING DEATH—as its heading. Sophie Vaughn Sawyer, 64, had been pronounced dead the day before after being rushed to University Hospital from a nearby restaurant. Preliminary autopsy reports indicated that she was the victim of poisoning. Police were investigating.

Goosebumps skittered up my arms and across my shoulders. Sophie Sawyer murdered? Someone had killed the lovely woman I had seen at lunch the day before? I read the paragraph again. Since it was so brief, the news of the death must have barely made the paper's deadline.

"God, Mitzi, I can't believe this. It's awful. Who was she? One of Arthur's clients?"

Mitzi's head bent to the table. Her hands slid around and clasped behind her neck.

"His first wife."

"His what?" Surely I hadn't heard right. Her voice was muffled against the table.

But she looked up and repeated, "His first wife."

JILL CHURCHILL

Delightful Mysteries Featuring
Suburban Mom Jane Jeffry